COUNTDOWN

For a complete list of books by James Patterson, as well as previews of upcoming books and more information about the author, visit JamesPatterson.com, or find him on Facebook, Twitter, or Instagram.

COUNTDOWN

JAMES PATTERSON
AND BRENDAN DuBOIS

LITTLE, BROWN AND COMPANY

NEW YORK   BOSTON   LONDON

Copyright © 2023 by James Patterson

Hachette Book Group supports the right to free expression and the value of copyright. The purpose of copyright is to encourage writers and artists to produce creative works that enrich our culture.

The scanning, uploading, and distribution of this book without permission is a theft of the author's intellectual property. If you would like permission to use material from the book (other than for review purposes), please contact permissions@hbgusa.com. Thank you for your support of the author's rights.

Little, Brown and Company
Hachette Book Group
1290 Avenue of the Americas, New York, NY 10104
littlebrown.com

First edition: March 2023

Little, Brown and Company is a division of Hachette Book Group, Inc. The Little, Brown name and logo are trademarks of Hachette Book Group, Inc.

The publisher is not responsible for websites (or their content) that are not owned by the publisher.

The Hachette Speakers Bureau provides a wide range of authors for speaking events. To find out more, go to hachettespeakersbureau.com or call (866) 376-6591.

ISBN 9780316457378 (hardcover) / 9780316457385 (large-print paperback)
LCCN 2019937627

10 9 8 7 6 5 4 3 2 1

MRQ-T

Printed in Canada

This is for my parents, Arthur and Mary DuBois.
                                                    —*BD*

COUNTDOWN

CHAPTER 1

I CHECK my watch and if all goes well, the killing will begin in less than two minutes.

I'm hiding with two other members of my sniper team in the barren mountains of northeastern Lebanon, just a few klicks away from the Syrian border. Jordan Langlois is the shooter and Santiago Sanchez is his spotter. Jordan is from the mountains of Kentucky and Santiago is from East LA. From the way they joke and work together, you'd think they were raised in the same orphanage.

No, not really. Just the Marine Corps and eventually the CIA.

I'm originally from Maine, then went into the Army, and now I'm the lead officer for this squad of the CIA's highly classified Special Activities Division—a very bland name for a very dangerous job. We go in way behind enemy lines, kill bad guys, then get the hell out. Along the way, we work very, very hard to ensure that our names and activities never appear in the newspapers.

Considering I'm married to a journalist, that can sometimes be a challenge.

Today we're waiting for a convoy to appear below us on a narrow, rugged dirt road, carrying a number of al-Qaeda fighters and leaders traveling into Syria for a summit meeting. Hypothetically my new place of employment could rain down thunder and fire from any one of half a dozen drone platforms to wipe out the entire convoy and any lizards or buzzards in the vicinity, but the rules of engagement have recently changed.

There's been too much embarrassment and too many scathing news stories (and accompanying editorials) over killing wedding parties and other innocents traveling in convoys in remote parts of the Middle East and Asia during the past few years. Now it's up to a small killing unit like us, sent into the field under secrecy, doing our job directly and quickly, so that mistakes are kept to a minimum and not instantly broadcast around the world.

Plus it's cheaper to kill a terrorist with a 99-cent round through his forehead than with a $115,000 Hellfire missile from a stealth drone—especially if the host country allowing us airstrip access doesn't want to be ID'd as helping out the infidels who are incinerating jihadists.

It's a new rule I'm comfortable with, because I know from sad experience the bone-dead feeling you get when you realize that a squeeze of your finger on a trigger in an air-conditioned room in Kentucky killed half a dozen innocents seconds later.

My spotter, Santiago, thankfully breaks up that dark memory: "Got dust on the westbound approach of the road, Amy."

"Roger that," I reply.

Santiago has a very powerful and highly classified optics system, set on a bipod, that allows him to "see" through the supposedly impenetrable black-tinted windows of SUVs in this part of the world, along with a laser facial-identification system that will ensure our target inside the SUV is indeed our target.

Next to him, Jordan is scanning the road with his weapons system, a high-powered military-issue-only Remington .308 bolt-action rifle whose aiming system is similar to Santiago's. Whereas Jordan is focused on the approaching target, Santiago—as the spotter—keeps a wider view of the target and any emerging threats our sniper can't see.

Me, the superior officer in this group, I'm muddling along with an off-the-shelf German-made pair of Zeiss 10x50 binoculars. Rank sometimes doesn't have its privileges.

I'm spotting the dust cloud now, moving right along in our direction.

According to our latest briefing, there should be four SUVs in the convoy, and we have two targets: hard men from the Abu Sayyaf terrorist group in the Philippines. Once upon a time great men and women thought that with the fall of the Berlin Wall and the rise of Facebook, we'd all live in one harmonious world.

That didn't quite work out, now did it?

A British male voice comes through the earpiece secured to my left ear.

"Zulu Lead, Zulu One here," he says. "We've acquired our target. You?"

Across this narrow canyon is another sniper team, on loan from Britain's famed MI6 intelligence service. The shooter is Jeremy Windsor and his spotter is Oliver Davies, both former SAS troopers. It's Jeremy's cultured British voice I hear in my left ear.

We've worked with them twice before, and despite the usual complaints and competition about the empire versus the colonials, the team has clicked, successfully completing Classified, and later Highly Classified, missions.

Or *successfully killing a number of men who deserved to be killed*. Take your pick.

"Jordan," I ask, turning my head. "How long?"

"About another fifteen seconds, Amy."

I toggle the microphone switch at my lapel; it's connected to the classified Motorola Saber-X radio strapped to my side. "About fifteen seconds, Zulu One."

I hear a *click-click* as Jeremy toggles his microphone in reply.

I keep my chatter to a minimum. I'm dressed like Santiago and Jordan, in a combination of northern Lebanese tribal pants and overcoats, along with sniper veils and ghillie suits that allow us to blend into the rocky background. About the only difference between the two guys and me is the elastic bandage wrapped tight around my torso, to keep my boobs under control.

Nearly a year ago, in training at the CIA's Camp Peary—a.k.a. The Farm—some clown suggested I should stuff a cucumber in my crotch to complete my disguise. That made a lot of folks laugh, including me—right up until that night in the mess hall, when I secured a cucumber from the kitchen and shoved it halfway down his throat.

Also, there's the matter of firearms. Jordan has his sniper rifle, and Santiago and I have 9mm Heckler & Koch MP5 submachine guns with a 40-round magazine, with each of us carrying extra magazines. All three of us are also packing 9mm SIG Sauer P226 pistols, along with a variety of other killing tools. Our rucksacks contain rations, water, extra ammo—nearly every necessity to survive in this hostile part of the world.

The pale blue sky overhead is clear of our drones, so it's just us kids. The CIA recently learned that our supposed allies have been locating our drones and passing along the information to the terrorists, so the fact that the convoy is on the move this early in the morning means they're confident all is safe.

Cue a deadly lesson proving otherwise.

In my binoculars, the four SUVs emerge from the dust about thirty meters below us, clearly heading in our direction. One Abu Sayyaf leader is riding in the second SUV, the other in the rear SUV. The vehicles all seem to be black GMC Suburbans with tinted windows.

"Target acquired," Jordan says.

I toggle a switch on my coat collar. "Zulu One, we're acquired."

"Same here, Zulu Lead," Jeremy replies.

"Go," I say, loud enough for both Jordan and Jeremy to hear.

There's a muffled thump next to me as Jordan fires his suppressor-equipped rifle. "Clear hit," says Santiago. "Driver is covered in blood, bone, and brains."

Jeremy radios to me, "Clear shot, clear results."

I look down at a multiple collision. The second SUV slams into a gray boulder, then another SUV rams it in the rear. Doors pop open and armed men bail out, bees flying out of a tipped-over hive, and Santiago whispers, "Oh, Amy, I would love to stay up here for a few more minutes. Look at all those lovely targets."

Jordan says, "Don't tempt me, Bro."

"No temptation, no nothing," I say, stowing my binoculars in my nearby rucksack. "Time to fly."

I toggle my microphone one more time. "Zulu One, time to break. See you at the rendezvous."

"Absolutely, Zulu Lead," he says. "Zulu Two and I are on the move."

Get the job done, and get the hell out.

I check my watch.

We should be picked up and safely out of here in thirty-five minutes.

But it takes only seven more minutes for disaster to strike.

CHAPTER 2

WE QUICKLY break down our gear and go down a trail we hadn't used before, because any repetition will get you noticed. Santiago is in the lead, Jordan is in the middle, and I'm Tail End Charlie.

I look at my watch once more. Analogue, old-fashioned, reliable. It will never need a battery at the wrong time, doesn't beep to give away your position, and has no electronics to fry in case somebody tosses a nuke into the air someday. It doesn't tell me the date, which is fine, because I know it's May 22.

The path we are on is narrow—broken rock and gravel—and seems too rugged even for goats. Yet we move with confidence and speed toward the safety at the other end of the trail. Like me, Santiago is carrying his MP5 in his arms, head always moving: left, right; left, right. Jordan has his pistol out and is doing the same. As the one bringing up the rear, I have to move and look over my shoulder at the same time.

Jordan says, "This sun is starting to fry me. Where are all the cedar trees? I thought Lebanon was full of 'em."

Ahead Santiago says, "Bro, King Solomon had them cut down, years and years ago."

Then I brake to a halt and loudly whisper, "Hold!"

Santiago and Jordan turn to look at me. I put my left hand to my earpiece.

I press my fingers together on the transmission button clipped to my collar. "Zulu One, go."

Some static, then "...have a bit of a problem, Zulu Lead."

"What is it?"

I turn my head and close my eyes so I can focus on what I'm hearing.

The strained but polite voice of Jeremy quickly comes back.

"It seems we have about two dozen hostiles chasing us."

"Zulu One—"

I hear the rattle of gunfire.

"Chat with you later," he says. "Quite busy now."

I turn and Santiago and Jordan stare at me.

"The Brits are in trouble," I say. "They've made contact with about two dozen bad guys."

"Shit," Jordan says.

Santiago says, "I thought this place was relatively safe. Boss?"

I motion with my left hand, though something dark and heavy has started growing in my chest. "We keep moving."

About ten minutes later, Jeremy comes back on. In a louder voice he says, "I'm afraid the buggers have us pinned down at the moment."

I can hear gunfire in the background.

I swear, trying to remember our location in the mountains and where the Brits might be after leaving their shooting spot. "Hold tight," I say. "We're on our way."

"No, don't do it," says Jeremy. "Trust me...you won't get here in time. Ollie! That bastard over there!"

I hear the loud sound of a three-round burst.

"Good shot," Jeremy yells. Then his radio cuts out again.

*   *   *

Move along, I think, *move along.* My mouth is dry and I'm terribly thirsty, but I know that no amount of water will help. I'm thinking of the MI6 crew and how they're my responsibility, my job to lead, and now they're in the middle of an ambush.

The rocky trail gets wider, and in my mind's eye I know what's about to appear. The CIA does a lot of things wrong but a number of things right, including a detailed briefing of the mission and whatever might be of interest in the area of our operation. The trail is going to curve to the right; then, in a wide portion of a narrow wadi, there will be a stealth helicopter from the Army's 160th Special Operations Air Regiment, ready to pick us all up.

I have full faith in the crew of famed Night Stalkers to get us out safely.

But there's one gigantic rub in all this.

Our rendezvous time is 9:00 a.m.—0900, if you prefer—and if we're not aboard that beautiful, Sikorsky-made escape vehicle by 9:05, it's going to lift off without us.

I check my watch again.

It's 8:53 a.m.

We've got plenty of time.

These three here, I think. As for the Brits...

"Zulu Lead!" comes the loud voice in my left ear.

I skid to a halt, nearly falling over among the sharp rocks and gravel.

"Zulu One, go," I say.

I hear his harsh breathing, hear the gunshots growing louder.

Oh, God.

"It's...ah, the bastards have us surrounded."

"Where are you?" I ask, tugging at a side pouch, trying to retrieve our topo map.

"Doesn't matter," he says. "I don't think we're going to be here very long."

"Zulu One, I need your location. Now."

There's a harsh stutter of gunfire, so loud I have to take my earpiece out. Jordan and Santiago stand closer to me, and even they can hear the desperate battle going on somewhere up there in these harsh mountains.

"Zulu One."

A hiss of static, more gunfire.

"Zulu One!"

A very loud gunshot, a grunt, and a whispered obscenity.

"Jeremy!" I say, raising my voice and breaking radio protocol, as if doing so could magically make him hear.

A harsh cough.

His voice comes back, speaking rapidly.

"Zulu One and Two are signing off, destroying our equipment. A pleasure working with you all."

Before I can say anything else, there's dead silence.

CHAPTER 3

JORDAN AND Santiago stare at me—so bulky and confident in their background, their experience, and the deadliest and most up-to-date weaponry in the world—and I know they're feeling exactly what I'm feeling: utter failure.

We've lost our comrades.

I stick in the earpiece and nod. Like the pros they are, Jordan and Santiago keep moving. Ahead of us, we all hear a low hum that sounds like a leaf blower at work.

There are no leaves here.

And positively no leaf blower.

But that soft noise is our way out of here.

As the wadi comes into view, it's 8:59 a.m.—a minute ahead of schedule. But I can already sense the catastrophe that's going to echo loudly between Langley and London in the next few days. Jeremy and Oliver will shortly be captured, tortured, and probably paraded around or made the topic of a propaganda tape by whatever armed group has found them.

We've all been "sheep-dipped," meaning that whatever paperwork we carry identifies us as contract workers for Global Security Solutions. That means in the event of our capture or death, our respective governments will have plausible deniability for us mercenaries in the field.

A nice cover story, which would no doubt last about as long as it would take an al-Qaeda type to come after one of our feet or hands with a chainsaw.

We're off the trail and at the outskirts of the wadi. Santiago mutters a prayer in Spanish, then says, "There she is. Have you ever seen anything so beautiful?"

Truth is, this latest classified and stealth helicopter is one ugly bird. It has droopy rotor blades and retractable landing skids, and its current color matches the rocky slabs nearby. The fuselage, all sharp angles, has a high-tech liquid-crystal exterior, meaning that when the helicopter finally gets off the ground, its exterior will match the surrounding sky.

Radar can't see it, and bare eyes will detect only flickering shadows, like a distant flock of birds.

Oh, yeah, it's ugly, expensive, and a bitch to fly—and I want to be on it so bad I can taste it. Its engine is humming along nicely, and we move forward and the rotors start to rotate. I look behind me, tail-end Charlie, watching our six, hoping against hope that our British comrades have broken free and are now running down the trail.

No such luck.

The engine is at full power now, the sound a loud hum, the blades spinning into a blur, and I see the frame of the helicopter rise just a bit.

So close.

I check my watch.

It's 9:02.

One after another, I clap Jordan and Santiago on the shoulders.
"Hold!" I yell.

I hunker down and they do the same, all three of us looking back up the empty trail.

Waiting.

Waiting.

The seconds whizzing by.

Jordan leans into me. "Amy! They're not coming."

I check my watch.

It's 9:03.

I yell back, "We wait!"

Santiago swears, but he and Jordan stick with me. Dust is starting to kick up, biting our eyes. I blink hard and look up at the trailhead.

"C'mon, c'mon," I whisper, knowing the odds of their showing up are near zero. But you have to believe sometimes. Believe they can make it. Believe in miracles.

Santiago tugs at my shoulder, points to his watch.

It's 9:05.

"We stay!" I yell back.

Santiago looks at Jordan, Jordan looks to him, and the two of them then look at the chopper, ready to scoop us up and take us out to a Navy vessel in this part of the Mediterranean, on a routine training mission.

Routine.

That's how the deaths of Jeremy and Oliver are going to be reported, if they get killed outright, without the horror of captivity and torture: *Died while on a routine training mission.*

And me?

Lost half my crew in a foul-up.

Almost as one, Jordan and Santiago scream my name, and I look at my watch.

9:06.

The nice crew over there from the Night Stalkers has given us an extra sixty seconds, and maybe I'll live long enough to thank them. But then the helicopter lifts straight up, its landing struts retreating into its belly.

The chopper rises up out of the wadi, soars over a rugged set of rocks, and then it—

Disappears.

Just like that.

Now even its engine sound has gone away.

All I can hear is the heavy breathing of my crew, Jordan Langlois and Santiago Sanchez, who stare at me with murder in their eyes.

I stand up from my crouching position.

"Saddle up, fellas," I say. "We're going back to get our guys."

CHAPTER 4

JEREMY WINDSOR, once with the 22nd Regiment of the Special Air Service and now a member of MI6's Expeditionary Research Branch (code name E Squadron), is squatting in a corner of a dirt-floored farmhouse, wrists handcuffed behind him, rope tied around both ankles, waiting.

He hates waiting.

His head, back, and arms throb from the beatings he and Oliver Davies received after their quickly dug-out foxhole did little to delay their capture. Now he and Ollie are in this stinking room, alone.

Jeremy gives his spotter a reassuring smile. Like him, Ollie has let his hair and beard grow, but Ollie's blue eyes are darting around the interior of the small room. Their clothes are dusty, torn, and soiled. Like him, Ollie came to MI6 via the 22nd Regiment.

"Guess our intelligence boys fouled up," Ollie says. "I never thought we'd get captured."

"Occupational hazard," Jeremy says, wishing he could say more to comfort his mate. "We'll be all right, just you wait and see."

"Too bloody confident, aren't you?"

"Somebody has to be . . ."

From its smell and shape, this room has been a storage area for seed or grains. A couple of rough muslin bags sit in a corner. Two high, small windows—open to the air but barred and covered with chicken wire—allow light in.

When he and Ollie had been sent to work with the CIA paramilitary group, Jeremy initially said no. A bird leading two sniper squads into the field? But he had seen Amy Cornwall's records, saw that she had been one of the few women to pass the U.S. Army's grueling two-month-plus Ranger course—and thought, *Well, she might just work out.*

And she had done exactly that on their two previous missions.

Jeremy was a pro. So he shut his mouth and went along.

But even professionals have a bad day.

"Cheer up, Ollie," he says, once again wishing he could say more to his fellow shooter and friend. "It'll all get sorted soon."

Ollie smiles, but there's a flicker of uncertainty in his face. "Remember the bagging drill?" says Jeremy. "This will be nothing in comparison, I promise."

His spotter's smile widens, and Jeremy recalls all too well the secret and highly illegal bagging drill: being suddenly and quickly stuffed into a large sack by your SAS trainers, then dumped in the barren hills surrounding their base in Hereford, leaving you to find your way back without being noticed or requiring anyone's help.

"If you're right," Ollie says, "I owe you a pint at Berber's."

Jeremy is about to say, "Make it two" when the door is unlocked and flung open.

Five men enter, and Jeremy takes a moment to eye each one. All of them save one are carrying an AK-47, and he has a memory flash of a particularly rugged exercise one rainy day in the Shetlands—and God, the rain could get cold up there—when their trainer, Burke, a scar-tissued and rugged old Scot who had served behind enemy

lines from the Congo to East Germany, had made a pronounce-
ment.

*Some of you wee ones have fantasies 'bout going back in time and
killin' Hitler,* he had said. *If I'd my way, I'd go back an' kill that Russkie
bastard Mikhail Kalashnikov. Every would-be revolutionary and rebel
piece o' shite loves to kill innocents with that bugger's invention.*

The man in front seems to be their leader. He has on dark boots,
gray wool trousers, and a khaki jacket. In his filthy hands he carries an AK-47, and around his thick waist is a weapons belt stuffed
with ammo magazines, a Russian Tokarev pistol, and a long knife.
He has a thick mustache and stubbly cheeks, with a checked kaffiyeh around his head and neck.

Three other men in the group look like they could be his brothers or cousins, for they are similarly dressed and armed. The fifth
man is unarmed, older, and filthy, wearing a black robe, cotton
trousers that may have been white at one time, and a black scarf
around most of his face. He hacks up mucus and spits it on the
floor, then goes to the wall next to the door, squats down, and
starts fingering a string of dark brown *misbaha,* or worry beads.

This bunch had been part of a much larger group that ambushed
and pursued them; the five had then split off to take Ollie and him
to this stinking little farmhouse.

The lead man turns and whispers to the older man, who just
shrugs and spits again on the floor.

Now he's looking at Jeremy.

In Arabic, Jeremy says, *"As-salāmu 'alaykum. I apologize for my
friend and I trespassing on your lands."*

The lead man smiles widely. His teeth are brown. In return he
says, *"Wa 'alaykumu as-salām."* Then the strong voice switches to
English.

"You are British, correct?"

Ollie keeps quiet, and Jeremy says, "Yes, we are British."

He speaks quickly in Arabic—*"Get them both up, now!"*—and two of the men sling their AK-47s over their shoulders, come forward, and gently help Ollie and Jeremy to their feet.

Jeremy allows a moment of relaxation.

It seems to be going well.

The leader smiles again, as do the other men, and he too slings his rifle over his shoulder.

Now it seems to be going very well indeed.

The man taps his chest. "I am Farez."

"Pleased to make your acquaintance," Jeremy says, breathing easier. Ollie seems to sense his relaxation. Jeremy says, "Again, my apologies for trespassing. My uncle George promises he can sort it all out."

"Ah," Farez says, "your wealthy and influential uncle George."

He laughs and the rest of the men—except for the old man sitting against the wall—laugh as well, then Farez comes forward and punches Jeremy squarely in the face. Jeremy gasps more in surprise than pain—*the code word and acknowledgment had been used!*—and staggers back as Farez quickly removes his AK-47 and drives it into Jeremy's abdomen.

He lets out a cough and he's on the ground, and so is Ollie, and the kicks and the blows from the automatic rifles rain down, and he squirms and tries to curl into a ball to protect himself as much as possible, but the handcuffs and ropes make that impossible, and he's drifting into unconsciousness, knowing it's all gone horribly wrong.

CHAPTER 5

ONCE UPON a time I had been a captain in the U.S. Army, serving as an intelligence officer, but a series of unfortunate and bloody events had led me to the precipice of a dishonorable discharge and a life sentence to the Army prison in Leavenworth, until a heavily tanned man working for the Central Intelligence Agency had offered me a way out.

His exit path meant joining the CIA, undergoing their training sessions, then accepting overseas assignments at a moment's notice—missing my husband, Tom, and daughter, Denise, terribly—to do serious work on behalf of an unknowing and mostly uncaring nation.

It was either that or go to prison.

Some days I almost think it was worth it.

But not today.

I'm with my two very skilled and angry killers, about to crawl up to the edge of a ridge, and it's nearing noon on this warm day in the wild mountain areas between Syria and Lebanon. The night before in our little encampment, we and our British friends could see the glow of night raids going on in Syria, not sure if the Russians, Turks, or Americans were doing the bombing—but all of us agreeing it probably didn't make much difference.

It was a damn lonely feeling, but now I feel even lonelier. Jordan and Santiago are professionals, good at following orders—even if it's from someone who uses sanitary products once a month—but I can feel the smoldering anger coming off them after abandoning the exfiltration point back at that wadi.

Now, instead of showering and eating good ol' greasy and fattening American food aboard the *USS Essex* near the Lebanese coastline, we're deep in hostile territory, with few good options facing us.

But there's a hard core of me that knows I'm right.

To hell with our orders.

Classified mission or not, I'm not leaving anyone behind.

We three are strung out in a line and now we're peeking over the ridgetop, using the jagged rocks and boulders for cover. By now Jordan has reassembled his .308 Remington—putting a standard tactical scope on the frame instead of the spooky Star Wars aiming system—and Santiago is using standard binoculars as well.

I say, "There it is."

It being a sad-looking one-story farmhouse and attached small barn, both made of wood and stone, with an orchard of scraggly trees, a fenced-in area where goats are doing whatever goats do, and a small courtyard off to the left, surrounded by a knee-high stone wall.

Looking through his rifle's scope, Jordan says, "Doesn't look like much."

"Langley told us this farmhouse is used as a transit point for smugglers and jihadists. It's the closest building to our ambush site. If our Brits were taken someplace, this is it."

Santiago, his binoculars in his hands, says, "Crappy looking place."

"Yes," I say. "But check out the parking lot."

A dirt lane leads to the farmhouse, and three dark and dented

Toyota pickup trucks, as well as a black SUV, are parked in a semi-circle outside.

"I don't think this is the far outpost of Honest Ahmed, used-car salesman," I say. I gesture to the left. "Spread out. Santiago, that little lump of rock...and Jordan, that chunk that looks like a dog-house. Sound off if you see anything."

They silently pick up their gear and move as ordered.

I look down at the farmhouse.

The only sign of life is the goats.

I hate goats.

In the few minutes it takes for Jordan and Santiago to take up their new positions, only a handful of words are exchanged.

Quietly Jordan says, "She broke orders."

Santiago says, "Yeah."

Jordan pauses, takes off his rucksack. "If my ass ever gets captured, hope someone does the same for me."

"No argument here," Santiago says.

"See you later."

Santiago moves forward. "You bet, Bro."

I check my radio gear.

Still no signal.

Being in the mountains will do that to you.

What now?

I look down through the fine German optics at the Lebanese farmhouse, where I hope my two British comrades are being held. It's a damn UN meeting, it is.

What now?

We can sit here for a while, try to see what's going on. Those parked vehicles mean something of importance must be happening.

But maybe it's not Jeremy and Oliver—those polite, charming, humorous, and utterly stone-cold killers in the service of MI6 and the Queen.

Maybe it's something else.

I could leave Santiago and Jordan here while I find a location that will allow me to reestablish radio communications—and, after getting reamed out, try to pinpoint resources that I could use to find Jeremy and Oliver.

But my gut tells me they're in that building.

How to get them out?

I'm hungry, thirsty, and my feet hurt, and the bandages wrapped around my torso make me feel like I'm going to lose a cup size when this particular op is wrapped up.

What now?

As I start going through the options once more, I think I see a hint of movement off to the left. Then Jordan makes up my mind for me.

"Amy!" he yells, holding his rifle, face to the scope. "We got a situation!"

CHAPTER 6

IN A luxurious yet poorly heated and maintained country estate about thirty miles northwest of London, Horace Evans of MI6 is sitting at his desk, slowly sipping his second cup of coffee—he gave up tea years ago after working for a year at the British Embassy in Ankara—looking over his day's paperwork, neatly set in one pile in the center of his antique desk.

The office is small and suits him. He has been with MI6 for three decades, spanning two centuries, and has enough power and influence to set up his office here, instead of in that ziggurat monstrosity at Vauxhall Cross in London, the butt of many a well-deserved joke and an obscenely explicit target to every sort of enemy overture imaginable, from rocket-propelled grenades to overhead surveillance.

His office here in Lindsay Hall is cold, the radiator rattles, and parts of the roof leak. The entire four-story building with its various rooms and salons is under the control of the National Trust, save one part of the building that's being renovated and is forbidden to tourists or other visitors.

Ever since Horace has been here, the renovations have been ongoing. God willing, they will never stop.

During World War II, Lindsay Hall was used as a training facility for the Special Operations Executive. Here exiled Poles, Norwegians, Frenchmen, and many others were trained in killing and sabotage, and were later parachuted into occupied Europe.

On the wood-paneled walls in his office Horace has a portrait of the Queen right after her coronation in 1953; a photo of Winnie standing among London bomb damage in 1940; and a framed photo of his younger self, standing on a balcony at some long-forgotten reception in Nairobi in the late 1960s. A representation of what was important in his life, and what was important to remember in his line of work.

There is a soft knock on the door. Horace calls out, "Enter!" and his assistant, Declan Ainsworth, comes in, wearing a frown on his plain yet schoolboyish face, even though the lad is approaching forty.

"Sorry to bother you, sir," he says in a soft voice, "but it appears there's been a bit of a muck-up with our Detachment Four."

Declan is dressed in a dull gray Gieves & Hawkes suit with a white cuffed shirt and a striped Magdalen College necktie. His hair is brown, trimmed short, and he wears gold-rimmed spectacles. At an office party last year, one of his section's secretaries said Horace and Declan looked so similar that they could be father and son, which had shocked him, true as it was.

"Oh, damn," he says softly. "And how did this wonderful news reach us?"

"Through a listening station General Communications has on Cyprus."

"I see."

With Declan standing there expectantly, Horace thinks through a variety of questions and decides to start basic.

"What was their mission again?" he asks.

"Jeremy Windsor and another detachment member were paired with a CIA sniper squad. The one led by a woman."

"Ah, yes, that woman. Go on."

"They were sent into the Anti-Lebanon Mountains, northeast, near the Syrian border," Declan says. "Their mission was to terminate two Abu Sayyaf leaders traveling into Syria for a meeting."

"Was the mission a success?"

Declan nods. "Quite. Both men were removed from the board. The problem came later: as the teams were deploying to be retrieved, Jeremy and the other chap"—Declan looks at a sheet of paper— "Oliver Davies, were captured by local militiamen. We don't know the status of our chaps or who the militiamen were."

Horace thinks, *Well done, Jeremy. Well done.*

"I see. The Americans?"

"Well, sir, this is where it gets odd. Their transport out was from their Army's aviation unit, the 160th Air Regiment. But they didn't board the helicopter. They stayed behind."

Damn, he thinks. *That wasn't part of the plan.*

Horace stares at Declan for a moment, puzzling things out. His office is old-fashioned in many ways, with the only concession to modern times being the computer terminal and the keyboard below it. He rarely uses computers—doesn't trust them at all.

He still relies on paper, and on human contact such as this little session with Declan. Among the reasons he distrusts computers is that they never delete anything permanently. But paper can be burned, shredded, altered, and conversations like this one can be forgotten, or misinterpreted, or even denied.

He says, "Well, that *is* an odd little development, isn't it? The Americans chose not to leave?"

Horace goes through his files, finds the one he wants. "This Amy Cornwall, a former Army captain. In military intelligence. Before she started working for our cousins, she was involved in a cross-country quest of sorts, trying to save her husband and daughter.

Along the way she shot and killed at least four, possibly more, gunmen from a Mexican drug cartel."

He closes the folder, looks up at Declan over his reading glasses. "I believe what happened is the American cowboy mentality came up at the right moment. Cavalry riding in to rescue the threatened Old West settlers, that sort of thing."

And he thinks, *That bloody woman—why didn't she go into that helicopter like she was ordered?*

Declan says nothing, and Horace sighs. "Please keep me advised on Jeremy and Oliver—and on the Americans. Remember, at the end of the day, two bad men from the Philippines have been removed. That mean hundreds of innocent Filipino civilians will live to see another day."

Declan nods and Horace adds, "You may see yourself out, Declan. I have a meeting with 'C' in an hour, which means I shortly need to be on the A10."

Declan backs to the door and says, "One more thing, sir?"

"Yes, what is it?"

"Langley," he says. "I'm sure that once the sun rises on their East Coast, you'll be getting a call from your counterpart."

"I imagine I will," Horace says. "When that happens, do tell the nice man from Langley that I'm unavailable."

Declan looks a bit shocked.

"You don't want to talk to the CIA?"

Horace returns to his paperwork. "Dear me, no."

CHAPTER 7

FROM HIS good eye—the one not swollen shut and oozing blood—Jeremy sees it's around noon when he and Ollie are dragged out to a small courtyard next to the building where they are being held. The two of them are kicked, pushed, and slapped, and his muscle memory remembers the previous time he was captured by locals, outside Mogadishu.

He's hoping this capture has a similar outcome, for eventually he was released, though it had gotten quite dicey at times.

The overhead sun is hot and the courtyard is dusty, and Jeremy tries to take everything in, looking at Ollie (bloody but still conscious), the gunmen (still chatting and laughing), and the building wall up ahead.

A light green piece of tarp has been hammered into the stone and wood.

Not good.

He's prodded along with AK-47 stocks. One of the gunmen opens a long, zippered pouch, takes out a tripod and a video camera, and expertly sets them up. He and Oliver are pushed to their knees, side by side.

Ollie whispers, "What's up, Jer?"

"Looks like we're about to star in our own flick," he whispers back. "Lucky us."

But Jeremy knows better. In the standard hostage taping, there's always a flag or a banner in the background, proclaiming the group, militia, or movement that's responsible for the capture.

Yet there's no flag or banner. Just a plain tarp.

What happens next will be the message, not the words on any flag or banner.

"Hey!" he yells out to Farez, the bearded militia leader. "My government will pay a handsome ransom for us! No dickering! No negotiating! Just name your price."

The leader comes over, still laughing, and kicks Jeremy in the side. He groans and grits his teeth, but manages to stay upright. A small victory—perhaps his last.

Farez draws back, spits on the ground. "As if we'd take your British filthy money."

He turns and barks out an order, and the older, heavier man wearing the black robe and black kaffiyeh ambles forward, carrying a small, rolled-up carpet. He bends down, gets on his knees, and unwraps the carpet.

There's more laughter and applause as the object in the rug is revealed.

A curved sword.

The man coughs and tries to get up, and two of the militiamen rush to help him up by his arms. He holds the sword up to the sun, its sharp edge bright indeed, and the yells and chants grow louder. *This is why Britain and America are in the fight of their lives,* Jeremy thinks. *How can one defeat or reason with a movement consumed with such bloodlust? If only those in Westminster and Fleet Street could understand this.*

"Jer..."

"Hold on, Ollie, hold on."

He yells again, in Arabic, *"You proud fighters, you poor men of God, release me and my friend, and you will be rewarded—"*

The swordsman comes forward, a militiaman pushes Ollie farther to the dirt, and in one heavy slice it's over. A heavy *thump* as Oliver's head strikes the ground, spraying the right side of Jeremy's face with his friend's arterial blood.

Now it's hard to see what's going on.

Strong hands are on his back.

He knows it's his turn now.

It was bound to come, here or in any other place Queen and Country sent him. But if Jeremy feels one regret, it's that there's so much left to live, so much left to do, so many who deserve to be killed by his hands.

The swordsman bends down, wipes the blade clean on the back of Ollie's jacket, and Jeremy's anger and fury are cold and steady.

For as long as it will last.

The swordsman comes back, looking down at Jeremy, familiar brown eyes lit bright with pleasure and determination.

Then, a surprise that almost makes Jeremy gasp aloud.

In clear, Oxford-accented English, the swordsman says in a strong voice:

"You should have stayed home, Jeremy."

The sword goes up, up, and up, but Jeremy refuses to lower his eyes. And so he is able to see and hear what happens next.

The sharp *ting* of metal striking metal, and the sword flying out of the man's hands.

CHAPTER 8

I'M RACING as hard as I can, what gear I need bouncing around my waist and back, and Santiago is right next to me as we approach the low courtyard. From behind I hear the sharp, flat *snap* of Jordan taking his first shot. He typically shoots with a sound suppressor, but not now.

I want the knot of gunmen before us to frighten and scatter, and they do. Santiago and I kneel in front of the low, stone wall, and it's over in a manner of seconds, the gunmen holding up their weapons and spraying round after round in our direction, the recoil kicking back and making the bullets whistle over our heads.

But Santiago and I keep low, keep our cool, and in careful, three-round bursts, we kill them all.

"Cover," I say to Santiago. I go through the open wooden gate and run over to Jeremy, who's struggling to get up. His clothes are torn, dusty, bloody. His face is also bloody and one eye is nearly swollen shut. I kneel down, withdraw my Ka-Bar knife, and cut the ropes around his ankles. He kicks free and stands up, sticks his wrists out from the rear.

"I'm cuffed," he says. "That big chap over there missing the back of his head, he was the leader. The handcuff keys might be with him."

I go over to the dead man, work my way through his pockets, find a small key with a long piece of colored rope attached. I return to Jeremy and use the key, and with the sound of the lock unclicking, he bursts his arms free and says, "The swordsman. Where is he?"

I look at the four bodies sprawled in the small courtyard. Santiago is still on the other side of the wall, keeping watch. A shape jogs into view—Jordan carrying his Remington rifle—and I wave at him and he comes through the gate.

I point to the building behind us. "Up you go."

He nods, says to Jeremy, "Sorry I was late."

"Did your best," Jeremy replies, then says to me again: "Where's the swordsman? The man who killed Ollie?"

I say, "Isn't he here?"

Jeremy says, "No. The bastard was dressed in a black robe and scarf. Older and heavier. He's not here."

I give the four sprawled corpses one quick glance and say, "He must have run off when the shooting started. There was lots of movement here. Confusing. You know how it is."

"Damn." He calls up to Jordan, who's taken position on the roof. "Any movement?"

"Just the goats."

"Damn the goats," Jeremy says.

I say, "We need to get moving. Santiago!"

I wave him over and he comes through the gate, and I say, "Santiago, look through the farmhouse, see if there's anything of value."

"I'll go along as well," Jeremy says, staring at the body of his spotter. "I want to see if my kit is in there, along with my weapon."

They go through the near door and I call up to the form on the roof. "Jordan? Still clear?"

"Yes, ma'am," he says.

"Good."

I don't bother telling him to warn us if something approaches. He's a pro, like the rest of us, and knows his job.

As do I.

The killing part of this mission is over. Now it's time for intelligence gathering, and then ass hauling.

Jeremy finds his kit and Ollie's as well, dumped in a corner next to some tables and low beds. Most of their gear is smashed, but at least his CIA-issued H&K MP5 submachine gun and four 40-round magazines are in one piece. He goes through Ollie's rucksack, finds nothing to bring back to his wife and two young boys, which pleases him in a melancholy fashion. He and Ollie had gone into this mission sterile, with no ID, mementos, or reminders of home. Poor Ollie. A brave man to have at your back.

The Hispanic American comes in from another room, holding a computer hard drive and a sheaf of papers. He shoves the items inside his coat and says, "Sorry about Ollie."

"He was a good sort."

"I . . . saw what happened. Did that son of a bitch with the sword say anything to you before he tried to cut you?"

Jeremy gives his H&K a quick check.

"Not a bloody word."

The three filthy pickup trucks and Suburban are empty of anything useful. The documents I get from the four dead men on the ground are pretty thin: prayer cards, newspaper clippings in Arabic, and identification passes from Yemen to Sudan, where restless, angry young men get an AK-47 shoved into their hands and are told they are Warriors of God.

I put these documents in a pocket, knowing that if we get out of here they'd eventually be studied, categorized, and recorded at Langley. These four dead men will then find eternity—probably not in their brand of Heaven, but in computer files among the infidels.

I turn to see Santiago and Jeremy exiting the building. Jeremy strides over to a dead man crumpled near a video camera mounted on a tripod. He picks up the camera and smashes it repeatedly against the stone wall, then picks through the pieces and destroys what I'm sure is the video chip.

Flies are starting to buzz around the dead bodies, including that of a man under my responsibility, Oliver Davies. My throat feels thick and heavy. I see his sprawled-out torso, arms, legs, and the drying pool of blood. Nearby is the lump that is his head—thankfully not looking in my direction—and I say, "Jordan! Come on down!"

He moves fast and gracefully from the rooftop, like a well-trained panther. I take out a folded topo map and say, "A trail about fifty meters down the road. Gets us up in the hills. Once we can find coverage, we'll radio Langley. I'll have to put up with some angry screaming, but hopefully they can get us out of here."

Santiago and Jordan nod. Jeremy looks up at the ragged peaks and rocks, which have an odd name: the Anti-Lebanon Mountains.

"Jeremy?"

"Yes?" he says, still looking into the hills. Looking for what? Safety? Redemption? The swordsman who killed his mate?

I say, "Do you want us to do anything with . . . Ollie?"

Jeremy looks to me now, one eye swollen but both eyes hard and filled with discipline and fury.

"No," he says.

CHAPTER 9

IN HIS small and sterile office at CIA headquarters in Langley, Virginia, Ernest Hollister is drinking a cup of hot water with a slice of lemon in it when a blinking icon appears on his computer screen, sounding a chime and interrupting his morning read of the *Washington Post*.

The icon indicates a FLASH PRIORITY message is coming his way, and he double-clicks the icon, and waits.

And waits.

This may be the most powerful and well-funded intelligence agency in the world, but bureaucrats and the lengthy budget-appropriation process means it has an IT system that was cutting-edge when Bush was president—and Ernest isn't thinking of the man's son.

Still, he loves computers, loves information, loves being tied into a worldwide internet and a surveillance state.

The icon is still blinking at him.

Ernest likes keeping his office clear of plants, books, plaques, and photos. All of those personal items are bits of intelligence, allowing visitors to his remote and obscure office a way to gather information about who he is.

And he will never allow that to happen.

Ernest picks up his teacup. The truth is, he shouldn't be here, over-seeing a section of the Company's Special Activities Division. His only battle experience is one quiet and unremarkable tour as an Army in-fantry officer during the Iraq mess, and his battles since then have all been of the bureaucratic sort. During one of the great upheavals the CIA experiences every few years, his division commander in Iraq was picked to head the Special Operations Group, and in turn plucked Ernest out of an analysis section in the CIA's Asian Bureau.

The gunslingers in his section resent his position, Ernest knows. He had joined the CIA only after a drawdown that essentially kicked Ernest and hundreds of fellow Army officers from active duty. But he knows how to manage, how to operate, how to nav-igate among the bureaucratic shoals that can rip apart someone's career in an instant.

The blinking icon saying FLASH PRIORITY is frozen.

He allows himself to say "Damn," then picks up his telephone—whose buttons indicate inside call, outside call, or encrypted call—and makes a quick inside call to his assistant, Tyler Pope. Ernest knows he could just get up and walk six feet to Tyler's office next door, but why not use available technology to do the job?

Tyler crisply answers the phone on the first ring. "I've got a Flash Priority message indicator," Ernest tells him, "and now my system is frozen. Get me what I need."

"Right away, sir," and there's a race to see who can hang up first. Ernest is sure he's the winner.

Of such little victories a career is made.

There's a knock at his door.

"Come in," he announces, checking the little digital clock on his desk. One minute and five seconds. Not bad.

Tyler is short and pudgy, with brown hair and a rapidly spread-ing bald patch that he's been artfully but unsuccessfully trying to conceal ever since he started working for Ernest. He has on khaki slacks, a blue button-down shirt, and a plain red necktie.

Tyler says, "There's been a foul-up in Operation Stunner."

"Which one is that?"

"The team working with the Brits in the Lebanese mountains, near Syria."

He remembers now. "Right. Two Abu Sayyaf leaders, heading to a summit in Syria. The one led by Captain Cornwall. That . . . difficult woman. Well?"

"The mission was a success," Tyler says. "Both targets eliminated. But it looks like the British team has been captured, possibly by a Hezbollah-related militia."

Ernest doesn't like the sound of that. "I thought our latest intel was that the place had been swept. No hostiles in the area."

"Obviously an error somewhere."

"Obviously," Ernest says. "Our folks?"

"Sir, that's where it gets . . . odd."

"Define *odd*."

"A stealth air platform from the Night Stalkers was at the rendezvous point to exfil both teams. Our crew showed up, but they didn't board the helicopter."

"How do we know our folks were there? Was there radio traffic?"

"No, sir. The Night Stalkers saw them."

"Doing what? Taking fire?"

"No . . . just standing down. Not moving. The Night Stalkers followed their orders. They took off. The last they saw, the three-member squad was returning to the mountains."

Ernest puts his teacup down. "That Cornwall . . ." He pauses, shakes his head. That woman. Talking to her, working with her, planning with her, trying to make her just shut up and understand the Agency's position on intelligence matters . . . some days it's like trying to stop a spinning buzz saw with your fingers.

Still.

An opportunity has just arisen for him, and Ernest is always one for seizing such occasions when he can.

"All right," Ernest says. "It looks like she's run off on a rescue mission. See if we can't get a communications drone overhead. Those mountains can play havoc with receiving and transmitting."

"Yes, sir," he says. "Do you want to talk to Horace Evans, then, to see what he might know on his end?"

Ernest nods. "Do it. Soonest."

Tyler goes to the door and Ernest says, "Tyler, let's set a deadline."

"Sir?"

He carefully thinks through his options. "If we don't hear anything positive in the next twenty-four hours, put out a leak to one of our friendly reporters covering national security. Just a whisper—an indication that a contract force working on their own has lost a team working inside Lebanon."

"Plausible deniability," Tyler says.

"Of course," Ernest says. "If we have to cut them loose to protect the Agency, so be it. As of now, they've gone rogue. I won't stand for it."

Tyler bites his lower lip for a moment. "Don't you think you might be acting...*hastily*? Sir? I mean, twenty-four hours..."

Protect the Agency, Ernest thinks. Both he and Tyler know what's really going on here, not daring for it to be mentioned, but what's really happening is that Ernest is protecting himself and his career, and his boss's career.

Among other things.

The Agency can take a hit.

But Ernest refuses to let that happen to him.

"Tyler?"

"Sir?"

He picks up his teacup. "Make that twelve hours."

CHAPTER 10

AT THE second thirty-minute mark of our slog up the narrow and winding trail, I call for a break.

It's been a long, grueling hike, and I think fondly of growing up in Maine and going with my parents for weekend tramps in our stretch of the White Mountains. Here there's nothing but rock, fissures, boulders, and the occasional winged creature flying overhead, and the distant bare ranges covered with snow and ice.

Jordan has Ollie's weapon and is taking lead, and Santiago is now bringing up the rear. I'm in the middle with Jeremy, and he's been one closed-mouth son of a bitch ever since leaving the farm and his dead comrade.

His clothes are a mess, one eye is swollen, he's limping, there's dried blood on his face—a mixture of his and Oliver's, I'm sure—but I've yet to hear, "Thanks for saving my ass back there."

Which isn't surprising. Special Forces soldiers and sailors operate on a different plane than us regular grunts. They are incredibly competitive and have tremendous endurance—and most have all the conversational skills of a brick.

So Jeremy is typical.

But I know something else is going on.

We're on the edge of a small plateau, with another long climb about fifty meters ahead, and I fiddle with the radio strapped to my waist. The resulting squeal of static in my left ear nearly makes me jump.

"I got a strong signal here, guys," I announce. "Hold on."

I start flipping through the various frequencies I've memorized when Jeremy appears next to me, limping and then slinging his H&K MP5 over his right shoulder.

"Amy, please," he says. "Can I borrow your gear for a moment?"

"For real?" I ask, surprised.

"Please," he says. "Just for a moment."

I pause, but he looks so serious and determined that I undo my earpiece and pass it over to him. Jeremy stands close by, inserting the earpiece in his right ear.

I unclip my lapel microphone and hold it out to him. He works the frequencies on the radio, then nods and calls, "Crown, Crown, Crown, this is Scepter Four, Scepter Four."

Santiago and Jordan see what's going on, step in closer.

"Crown, Crown, Crown, this is Scepter Four, Scepter Four."

I feel closed in with Jeremy standing so near me, smelling his sweat and grime, and I'm about to grab my radio gear back when I hear a voice come through the earpiece.

Jeremy grins. "Crown, Scepter Four." He digs out a folded-over topo map from a coat pocket and says, "Requesting pickup. We're at map coordinates—" He reads off a series of grid numbers, then repeats them and says, "Thanks awfully, Crown. Scepter Four, signing off."

He hands me back the earpiece and microphone and says, "Always have a plan B, am I right? No offense to you and your wonderful Night Stalkers, but I think our airborne asset is just a bit closer."

"How close?" Jordan asks.

"How does twenty minutes sound?"

Santiago grins. "Sounds excellent, Bro."

I give Jordan and Santiago a stern look; getting the message loud and clear, they both walk back to their original positions.

I ask Jeremy, "What the hell do you think you're doing?"

"Arranging a pickup." He gestures to where Jordan is standing. "About twenty meters along this plateau, that's where we need to be."

"I should have known," I say. "This is my operation."

"You know how it is," he says. "The way we do things."

I step closer to him. "I don't like secrets."

His face—bloodied and beaten as it is—remains calm.

"That's my business, Amy," he replies. "Killing people and keeping secrets." He tightens a rucksack strap, takes his weapon off his shoulder. "And that's your business, too."

We stare at each other, and then I start moving along the rocky trail and everyone else joins me.

Jeremy is 100 percent absolutely right. But I'll be damned if I'm going to tell him that.

CHAPTER 11

TOM CORNWALL is walking along Broadway in lower Manhattan with his eleven-year-old daughter, Denise, next to him, keeping pace among the morning crowds. A block away is their destination, Olson Manhattan Preparatory School, and he feels a touch of sorrow walking with her.

Two weeks ago, Denise had said with great solemnness and dignity that she no longer wanted to hold her father's hand as they walked to and from her school. Tom knows this is all part of the growing-up process, but still, it's yet another clear signal that his and Amy's little girl is on her way to leaving little-girl status behind.

It's a beautiful May morning, and Denise looks ahead as they walk, expertly keeping pace with Tom. He is still impressed at how well Denise has adjusted to big-city life: just over a year ago, the three of them had been living in a pleasant little cul-de-sac in Virginia, with lots of open areas to play around in and practice her soccer.

Here, green space is at a minimum. The city is large, loud, and always on the go, but to Amy's surprise and his, Denise had taken right to it.

"I can't believe it," Amy had once told him. "It's like somebody came in the other night and swapped out our little girl with a city slicker."

This particular city slicker has on a school uniform of black shoes, white knee socks, a dark blue skirt and matching jacket, and a plain white blouse. A Vera Bradley knapsack is on her back. When they come to the intersection with Pine Street, the familiar three-story brick building with a wrought-iron fence stands directly across the street. Morning rush-hour traffic roars, rumbles, and honks by as they wait for the light to change.

As he spends these precious moments with his daughter, two things are rattling around in his reporter's mind, one being the story that he's working on. There are just hints and whispers so far from his sources—unexpected movement of military units, meetings of intelligence officials—but Tom believes he has grabbed hold of *something*. If he keeps tugging, he believes it will lead him to a story about a terrorist attack being planned somewhere here or in Europe.

"Dad?" Denise asks, raising her voice to be heard above the traffic.

"Yes, Hon?"

"Where's Mom?"

Ah, the same old question, with the same old disappointing answer. After Amy had taken her new job, the two of them told their inquisitive and smart little girl that her mother was a traveling consultant who helped governments research and purchase military-related hardware. Based on Amy's years of service in the Army, it was the best they could do.

"She's on a business trip. I hope she comes back soon."

"Why doesn't she call? Or email?"

"Well, sometimes Mom's in a place where she can't make a call or use a computer."

Denise sighs. Horns sound up the street. An MTA bus grumbles by, soiling the near air with its diesel exhaust. A distant siren wails from an FDNY fire engine. And among the mass of people waiting for the light to change so they can cross the street, Tom is sure he senses one of his watchers.

That's the other thing on his mind. For the past few days, ever since Amy left for her latest overseas trip, Tom has been convinced he's being tailed. Nothing blatant—no, whoever's doing this is pretty professional—but the sixth sense that has kept him alive while reporting from combat zones has told him folks are out there. A city sanitation worker staring at him for a second too long. A young woman paying undue attention to Tom's reflection in a shop window. An unmarked white van that deliberately runs a red light so it can pull ahead of Tom's place of work and stay there.

"Daddy?" Denise asks, interrupting him.

"Yes, Hon?"

She speaks louder. "Polly's dad is in Brazil working for an oil company. In the middle of a jungle! And he FaceTimes her every night. Why can't Mom do that?"

The light changes, blinking white for the pedestrians to move, and he and Denise join the crowd as it surges across the street. Tom reaches down to take his daughter's hand.

She brushes it away.

"Because she just can't," he says. As the crowd surges past him, *there*—a familiar face passes by: the sanitation worker from two days ago.

Now dressed in a fine suit and a tan London Fog topcoat.

CHAPTER 12

I HEAR the hum of an approaching helicopter and take out my binoculars for a look-see. Even though we're minutes away from the pickup, we haven't let our guard down. Each of us is responsible for a compass quadrant of 90 degrees, so we're lying down, weapons out, making sure nobody comes up and surprises us.

My left ear is still throbbing from the quick and brutal radio exchange I had a few minutes ago with a CIA communications officer overseeing our operations in this part of the world. If one cuts out the code words and phrases and obscenities, it reminds me of the fights I used to have with Dad back in Maine:

You were supposed to be back at eleven! It's almost midnight!

Something came up. It's the truth.

And what was so important that you didn't come back at eleven like you promised?

Dad...

I have an idea that when I get back to the States, I'm going to lose a lot more than just my driving privileges.

The sound of the helicopter grows louder.

So what?

I got Jeremy back. And to my bosses, our primary kill mission was a success. And we got some intelligence along the way.

45

But poor Ollie—poor Oliver Davies. Sometime in the next twenty-four hours, a couple of somber men in dark suits will knock at a young Englishwoman's door to tell her that she is now a widow, and that her love—her husband, the father of her children—is not coming home.

Some success!

And I feel a tinge of guilt, knowing that at some point soon after, I'll be getting home to *my* beloveds—my Tom and our daughter, Denise—safe and sound once again.

"There she is," Jordan calls out.

I squirm and aim my binoculars on the approaching helicopter as it flies close to the mountain peaks and the jagged ridgelines. I focus in and see that it's a Sikorsky S-92 chopper. But it's not military, painted in camouflage or olive drab; it's bright yellow, with blue stripes.

Santiago says, "Where the hell is that thing from—Disney World?"

Jeremy grins. "British Petroleum, friend."

Jordan says, "What? BP?"

I stand up and the others do the same. Jeremy says, "Haven't you ever heard the sun never sets on the British business empire?"

My two Americans laugh and Jeremy laughs with them, but I don't like his attitude. I don't like what's going on with him.

Something just isn't right.

Even though our mission is over and we're seconds away from being exfilled out of here, I sense something else is going on with Jeremy.

It's like he's looking beyond the here and now, to something else down the road.

I don't like it.

The helicopter comes right in to our little rocky landing field, and I can just imagine what the pilot and crew must be thinking:

pulled away from a standard civilian flight in the Mediterranean, then dispatched to this piece of rocky moonscape to pick up a squad of armed and nameless fighters?

I hope they get hazard pay.

I turn and crouch as the helicopter roars in for a landing, landing gear extended down from the large side nacelles, dirt and pebbles striking the back of my neck. When it touches the rocky ground, the near side door slides open, and I don't have to say a word.

Jordan and Santiago race ahead, heads lowered, carrying their gear and weapons.

I join them, and Jeremy is right behind me.

Jordan goes in first, helps Santiago in. A crewman in a blue jumpsuit and wearing a large helmet takes their gear.

I toss in my rucksack and Santiago pulls me in.

I turn.

Jeremy is coming right behind me.

He's coming right to the door.

He smiles.

Salutes.

Turns away.

The helicopter starts to lift up and I make a snap, crazy, and probably deadly decision.

I jump out.

CHAPTER 13

I HIT the ground and muscle memory from my Ranger training takes over, and I duck and roll like I'm landing after a parachute drop. The helicopter dips and increases its speed, and as I get up, Jeremy is standing right next to me, his face red and twisted with anger.

"What the bloody hell are you doing?" he screams.

I check myself and my gear, which isn't much: just my MOLLE harness, radio, pistol, small water bottle, two spare magazines, and my MP5 over my shoulder. I take that off and say, "Pretty obvious, don't you think?"

"You...you get on that radio and you call for someone to pick you up! Now!"

By now the helicopter is gone. "You don't get to order me to do shit, Jeremy. According to both of our respective agencies and paperwork you signed and swore to, I'm still in charge of this operation."

"This operation..." To see a rugged, determined, and armed SAS trooper search for words on other days would be amusing. But my sense of humor isn't up and playing right now.

He grimaces. "Our operation is *over*. Completed. You have no right or purpose to be here. Call your CIA, your military, your goddamn JetBlue or someone to retrieve you, Amy. You don't belong here!"

"Our operation is over when I say it's over. And whatever you've got going on, you're going to tell me, and if I think it's appropriate, I'll assist."

"You . . ."

"You're limping, you've been beaten up, you can barely see out of one eye," I say. "Now, Jeremy Windsor, you have one minute to tell me what the hell is going on, and then we're going to start moving, with me in the lead."

He stares with fury and anger at me, his dirty, torn, and bloodied clothes flapping a bit in the mountain breeze that has come up.

"Pretty soon bad guys with guns in those hills are going to start talking to each other about a BP helicopter that flew in and then flew out," I say. "Those were civilian pilots. You think they know how to do evasive maneuvers or flying? No. Nice job retrieving Santiago and Jordan, but they drew a very long arrow to where we're standing."

Jeremy's still not talking. I say, "Meaning, someone might be hauling ass up here. And when they get here, it's going to be just you and me."

Now he speaks. "You don't know that for sure."

"Perhaps," I say. "But I know something else."

"What's that?"

"You and Oliver, you wanted to get captured. Why?"

It's a pleasant morning and Tom Cornwall decides he'll take the long walk to work, even though he knows there's a spotter or two out there, keeping him in view. He has a new job now, working for a start-up news organization here in Manhattan. About a year ago he was at loose ends, with Amy starting her new position with the CIA—part of him wants to laugh at the absurdity of that, his wife, his Amy, a field agent with the CIA—and after a book deal had fallen through, he was hunting hard for a new job.

And this one had practically fallen into his lap. Dylan Roper, who had once worked with Tom at the *New York Times,* had pitched him on it over lunch one afternoon at the Union Square Cafe. "There's too many amateur voices, too much fake news, too much biased crap out there," Dylan had said. "I've got some financing and I'm getting a crew together to get back to our journalism roots. Hard news, exclusives, fully sourced and backed up, with no agenda except reporting. Criterion News Service. You in?"

He waits at a crosswalk, crowded with other commuters on this beautiful Manhattan morning. After that offer and some long, grueling talks with Amy—"Oh, all right, then," she had said—here he was, working for Criterion, and enjoying nearly every minute of it. It was good to get back to his old reporting days, and despite a harsh temper and a demanding editorial style, Dylan kept his word, providing the technical and monetary support to make the agency a player in the international news-media field.

The light changes.

Tom moves along with the crowd, wondering, as he does most mornings, what his wife is doing right at this moment.

Jeremy says, "You're full of shite."

"No, no I'm not," I say. "The last briefing before we arrived here, we were told the place was clear of any terrorist groups or militia. But no, one group manages to pop up and go after you right after we complete our primary mission."

"It happens."

"Sure," I say, getting cold up here on this exposed plateau, knowing I'll freeze in place if we don't get moving soon. "But why only you? If there had been an intelligence failure, why wasn't another group chasing us Americans?"

"Amy..."

"When you got ambushed, you refused help. You didn't want us coming back, you didn't want us to respond, you didn't even ask me if I could call in a drone or an airstrike. Nothing. And don't take offense, Jeremy, but you surrendered. SAS men fight until they run out of bullets, then they use their knives, and if they don't have knives, they use rocks or their bare hands. Why did you want to give up?"

His eyes are showing me something else—an internal struggle, some kind of debate going on—and finally he says, "Ollie and me...we had another mission. We were to be captured, then brought to a terrorist leader...one we were going to make every effort to kill."

"Who is this guy?"

Jeremy's face twists in anger and despair. "One who's been quietly in the background, financing at arm's length, one who's smarter and more capable than anyone we've ever seen before. He's got something big and deadly planned for May 29—the anniversary of the fall of Constantinople to the forces of Islam nearly six centuries ago."

"And he's here, in these mountains?"

"For a brief moment, that's all. This chap...he makes Osama bin Laden look like a kindergarten teacher, and he's going to hit us hard in seven days, and we don't know how or where. But we have a guess."

"What's the guess?" I ask.

"Paris," he says. "Or New York."

My beloveds, I think, oh, my Tom and Denise.

Tom Cornwall starts across the plaza leading to his place of work, still thinking how fortunate he is to be in Manhattan, to have a well-paying yet demanding job, and to have his daughter at his side, who has done so well in moving to the Big Apple.

But those little questions Denise asked back there still gnaw at him.

Why doesn't Mom call? Or email?

Because, he thinks, she's going up against very bad men who want to do very bad things to young girls and boys like you.

He looks up at the grand and tall building, here because other bad men had gone about their work without being bothered too much by intelligence agencies that acted like independent fiefdoms instead of departments focused on their citizens' safety; that thought cooperating with one another was a bureaucratic betrayal of sorts; that lost sight of what their job was.

One World Trade Center, just a brisk walk from the open-pool tombs of its predecessor.

And he has a thought: *Denise has yet to see where her father works, but Take Your Daughter to Work Day is soon, and that'd be a perfect time.*

On May 29.

CHAPTER 14

"MAY 29 is a week away," I tell Jeremy. "Let's focus on today. Tell me you have a Plan C."

"Of sorts," he says, taking out a topo map, wincing from his cuts and bruises. The wind is starting to come up harder and I don't like being out in the open like this. There are ridges, mountain peaks, and fissures all around us, and I have a thought of armed and angry men looking up at us with their own binoculars.

"Here," he says, pointing to the map. I read the lines and squiggles, and he points to a tiny spot on the map and says, "Small village called Srar. About a four-hour trek if we start now. We should get there before sunset."

"What, you have a cottage there?"

"No," he says, folding up the map and putting it in his coat. "An old man with a taxi cab. Who can take us where we need to go."

"Which is where?"

He looks around at the desolate rock-filled plateau.

"Anyplace but here."

"Agreed," I say.

Ernest Hollister is walking quickly down one of the numbered hallways in the depths of Langley when he stops in front of a small desk that has an armed Marine sitting at it, dressed in blue striped trousers and khaki shirt and necktie. Behind him is a thick, locked metal door with a variety of warning signs posted on it and a long metal handle.

The desk has a telephone, a fingerprint scanner about the size of a tissue box, and an old-fashioned, leather-bound journal with lined pages.

"Sir," the Marine says.

Ernest presents his CIA identification, the Marine carefully writes down his name and service number—there's a piece of cardboard blocking the previous names so even in-house CIA personnel can't read upside down and see who has preceded them—and then the Marine hands back the identification.

"If you will, sir," the Marine says, gesturing to the fingerprint scanner.

Ernest is in a hurry. He doesn't want to put up with this triple-top-secret nonsense, but he also knows he needs to get into that room as soon as possible. Earlier he had read a transcript provided by the Agency's Beirut station of recent communications with Amy Cornwall, before she went dark. The message was short and unsatisfying: *Yes, she knew she had missed the rendezvous. Yes, she knew she was disobeying orders. Yes, but she had done it for a good reason.*

What good reason?

And that's when the communications had ended.

He places his four fingers against the glass scanner. There's a brief flash of green light and the Marine says, "Very good, sir."

He stands up, goes to the door, and unlocks it with a key attached to his belt by a chain. It does look silly and over-the-top, but three years ago a CIA officer had tried to push the process—had tried to get into a room like this without the necessary authorization—and the Marine guard on duty had shot him.

Grasping the handle, the Marine opens the door, and Ernest brushes past him without saying a word.

But the Marine says, "When you need to exit, sir, just toggle the request switch. It's the green square to the right of the keyboard."

The room is small, almost claustrophobic.

The door closes behind him and Ernest sits down at a small table, with a keyboard and a square box with a lit green square in the center. There are three chairs, and Ernest is sitting at the head of the table. At the other end of the table is the wall and a large rectangular video screen.

There are six such rooms that Ernest knows of in Langley. Called "bubble rooms," each is constructed as a room-within-a-room, ensuring that no possible surveillance system could penetrate what is discussed within. Even so, the rooms are swept on an irregular schedule to make sure no recording devices ever get hidden.

Ernest types on the keyboard and the video screen comes alight. A green dot of light means he's being seen at the other end of this encrypted signal, then the screen snaps into focus.

Before him are two sweaty, tired, bearded men: Santiago Sanchez and Jordan Langlois, sitting in a similar bubble room aboard the *USS Wasp,* an amphibious assault ship on station off the northern coast of Lebanon. It contains more than 2,000 Marines, constantly prepared to go somewhere and kick the shit out of folks who either need it or deserve it.

"Langlois," Ernest says. "What the hell happened?"

There's a brief wait as the signal gets scrambled, bounced off a satellite, then unscrambled at the other end on the *Wasp,* and Ernest looks with disapproval at the two men. Greasy hair, dirty skin, beards...when Ernest was in the field during his tour in Iraq, he always made sure his troops were cleaned up and looked sharp, no matter the weather or the fighting.

Langlois says, "We were about one minute away from getting

exfilled by a Night Stalker when Cornwall ordered us away. She wanted to rescue the SAS guys."

"And what did you do?"

Sanchez says, "She was in command. We followed her orders."

"Did you locate the SAS men?"

Langlois says, "We did, in a farmhouse we knew was used by both Hezbollah smugglers and al-Qaeda as a way station." A crackle of static. The video screen flickers, then comes back into focus. "...was dead. Windsor was alive. There was a brief action, we got Windsor and departed. Then Windsor called in...an air asset under contract to MI6."

Ernest pauses, "Then where the hell is Cornwall? And Windsor?"

He wonders if the delay between the two stations is lengthening, because neither Langlois nor Sanchez replies. Langlois looks to Sanchez and says, "Windsor turned back as the helicopter was taking off. Cornwall jumped off to join him."

Ernest says, "Jesus Christ...did either of you know they were going to do that?"

"No," Langlois says.

"No," Sanchez says.

"Did you try to make radio contact as you were leaving the site?"

"We did, but no success," Sanchez says.

"Did...Cornwall or Windsor exhibit any inappropriate activity or communications with each other?"

Again, pauses from the two ex-Marines.

"No," Sanchez says.

"No, not at all," Langlois says.

"Very well, that's all," Ernest says. "When you return stateside, we'll have a more extensive debrief."

He reaches forward and slams the video-disconnect button so hard the plastic case flies into the air.

*   *   *

In the bubble room aboard the *USS Wasp*, Jordan Langlois looks over at Santiago Sanchez. The green dot of light on top of the video screen, indicating a live connection to an identical screen in Langley, is now off.

But both men know better than to say anything in front of the supposedly dead video screen.

They move their chairs so their backs face the screen.

Quietly Langlois says, "What a prick."

"Yeah."

"It's been a few hours. What are you thinking, Sanny?"

"Dunno. Jeremy went rogue—and Amy went rogue with him, at the last minute. Must be something important, something big. What are you thinking, Jordan?"

"I could go for a cheeseburger."

"Christ, yes."

After leaving the bubble room and returning to his floor, Ernest quickly walks to the outside office just next to his own quarters. To Tyler Pope he says, "That news-media leak I was discussing earlier. Remember?"

"Yes, sir," Tyler says. "A news tip that a contract force working on its own has lost a team working in Lebanon. You told me to release it in . . ." He glances up at the clock. "In about nine hours."

Ernest says, "Do it now."

He opens the door, turns, and says, "But before that, try Horace Evans again."

Tyler says, "I've tried three times before, sir."

"Do it again," Ernest says. "I need to know just what the hell they're doing over there in Lebanon. And if we can't get the information from Horace, try any other asset we have in that part of the world."

He goes into his office, closes the door—no slamming the door in public, so that no gossip or rumors ever spread about one's temperament—and goes to his desk, staring at the phone.

Ernest's supervisor is Malcolm Rooney, his division commander from Iraq. Ernest recalls the meetings and briefings he had with General Rooney before taking the job, and how adamant the general was about what Ernest could do for him and the Company once the proper time came.

Still, he waits.

And Ernest doesn't have to wait long.

After ringing for permission, Tyler comes back into his office, looking concerned, and says, "We might have a lead on what that Brit is doing—and perhaps why Amy Cornwall is now with him."

"What's that?"

"Someone we've known for years," Tyler says. "Code name BRO-KER. He was believed to be in that area of northern Lebanon . . . and Beirut tells us they hear MI6 has been after him for quite a while. But there's a complication, sir."

"Always is. What is it?"

"BROKER belongs to us as a confidential asset," says Tyler. "He's on Langley's payroll."

CHAPTER 15

WE KEEP up a steady pace as we descend the trail, heading to the village Jeremy says is our destination. As we move along and at times when we take a break, Jeremy tells me a tale that belongs around a campfire in the deep dark woods of Maine on Halloween night, not out here in the open in these rugged mountains.

At one point I take off my tan-colored boots, wincing, and Jeremy says, "Feet hurting?"

"You know it," I say. "I'm dreaming of getting home and relaxing in some Birkenstocks."

He raises an eyebrow. "What, you take a size fifty or thereabouts?"

I say a naughty word and add, "No, a thirty-eight, you clueless male."

He laughs, and I take a moment to pry open the heel of the boot and remove a small, plastic-covered photo of a man and a young girl, both smiling, wearing swimsuits during a lake vacation in Maine, and both belonging to me. I slip the photo of Tom and Denise back into my boot, knowing I'm breaking regulations by carrying something so personal. But breaking rules is part of my roguish charm—or so I'd like to believe. And seeing that photo of my precious ones improves my mood, so I consider it part of my necessary gear.

Jeremy leans against a boulder, takes a swig of water, and changes the subject as I lace up my boots. "For a while now, we've been looking for Rashad Hussain, a wealthy Arab and committed terrorist who's smart, tough, and very, very patient. He's not part of the Saudi royal family or any of their clans, but he's devout and wealthy—and very much under the radar."

Jeremy hands me his bottle and I take a long sip of the lukewarm water. My feet still ache something fierce. I'm cold and hungry. And that damn elastic bandage around my torso, crushing my breasts, feels like it could go deeper at any moment and slice me in half.

"I've never heard of him," I say.

He glances down the trail and then back up it, his MP5 submachine gun across his lap.

"That's because he's very, very good," Jeremy says. "He works through cutouts and more cutouts. He doesn't care about publicity, about making statements or rambling video denunciations. He's not looking to attract recruits or followers. All he cares about are results. And he also doesn't care about ramming cars into pedestrians, or car bombs, or guys wearing explosive sneakers. He has a grander vision than that."

I'm feeling even more chilled as I return the near-empty water bottle to Jeremy. "Go on."

"Your 9/11," he says, putting the water bottle away in his rucksack. "A lot of time has passed. It's now history, nearly forgotten. But when it happened, it was something so brutal, so out-ofthe-blue, so....*defining* that it shook up the world order. And even though a large portion of your population was thirsting for revenge, to settle accounts, other voices were heard as well. Appeasers. Deniers. Saying we had brought it upon ourselves. They were ready to surrender and give up before the Twin Tower wreck-age had cooled off."

"That's not what I recall," I say.

He scratches at his beard. "Those voices were drowned out, of course. The attack was too raw. But now? Rashad isn't looking for something that's been done before. Through bits and pieces, word of mouth, a few intercepts, we know he's looking to do something spectacular on the twenty-ninth of May, something that will make your 9/11 look like a dustbin fire, something either in Paris or New York. When that happens, those other voices will rise again, taking blame for the West's actions, pushing to disengage from the Muslim world, to allow their caliphate to be reestablished over the blood and bodies of tens of thousands of innocents. And . . ."

Jeremy viciously kicks at a nearby stone with his booted right foot, sending the rock tumbling down a ravine. "And Oliver and I, we had an opportunity to stop it—right here in these bloody mountains. As chance would have it, the little task force that runs our joint hunting trips in the field had two targets from the Philippines traveling in this area at the same time we knew Rashad was nearby with a militia group. Bribes were paid, assurances were made, and as you rightly noted . . . we got captured on purpose. We were to be brought to this group, to Rashad—and we were going to kill him."

I check my watch. "We should get moving if we want to get to that village before the sun sets. Then we can rest up, maybe get something to eat."

Jeremy kicks another rock. "Ollie and I failed. I don't care if the sun sets, rises, or stays up in the sky for twenty-four hours straight. I'm still hunting down Rashad."

"Good," I say. "I'm glad to be part of the hunt."

Jeremy stands up, weaves for a moment, and says, "What's that?"

I check my MP5 out of routine, making sure the safety is off and that the burst indicator is set for three rounds, meaning that with each pull of the trigger only three 9mm rounds will be fired down-range.

"You're not going to do this on our own," I say. "You're tough, smart, and you're SAS, even if you've been detached to MI6. But at some point your reserves will be tapped out. You're going to crash. And I'll be there to pick up the pace."

He shakes his head. "No offense, Amy, but no. I'm doing this on my own."

"No offense taken, Jeremy, but this is still my op. We're still out in the field, and as per our orders, we are definitely responding to an emerging threat. You're working for me."

Boy, does his face darken. "I don't want you—I don't *need* you. This is going to be very dangerous work."

"I can imagine."

"No, you can't imagine. And again no offense, but you're a woman, and you're going to slow me down, and—"

There's movement behind him and I swing and rotate hard, kicking Jeremy behind his right knee.

CHAPTER 16

THE SWORDSMAN has reached his destination, tired but thankful that God has saved him once more. After the gunfire broke out and before he could have beheaded the second arrogant Englishmen, he had raced to the near wall and vaulted over it, landing heavily on the ground. But parked nearby was a black Kawasaki KLR650 dual-sport motorcycle. As the Western fighters headed into the compound, he had pushed the motorcycle away in the other direction, taking cover behind the parked pickup trucks.

Once he was far enough from the farmhouse and courtyard, he had started the motorcycle and followed a rough and bumpy road to a better-quality road. Finally reaching a paved two-lane highway, he had joined other motorcycles, trucks, and cars, passing donkeys and horses pulling carts.

Now he is in the village of Tlayleh—small one- or two-story homes and businesses, crowded narrow streets—and he lowers the motorcycle's speed to a crawl. He turns down one alleyway, then another. There is a locked roll-up corrugated metal door, and with a key retrieved from the motorcycle's rear leather pouch, he unlocks the door and pushes the motorcycle in.

He closes the sliding door behind him, turns, and opens another door leading to the interior of the ground-floor apartment.

It's plain but clean and comfortable, with a living area, well-stocked kitchen, bathroom, and bedroom.

The swordsman goes to the center of the living room and strips off his scarf, robes, and filthy white cotton trousers, and then the padding around his belly and shoulders that had made him look like an older, heavier man. He picks everything up in a ball, goes to the kitchen, and dumps the stinking materials in a trash bin.

From there he goes into the bathroom, uses the toilet, and takes a long, hot, and very pleasing shower, making sure the small bandage on his right wrist remains dry. At first some of the water is rust brown, washing off the dried blood of the British soldier he had killed, but then the wash water gets clearer. When he gets out he trims his beard and combs his dark hair and, once it's dried, goes into the bedroom and its closet. From there he takes down a gray tailored suit from Camps de Luca in Paris and a white cotton shirt from Cairo. The swordsman takes his time getting dressed, at last putting on a pair of Testoni shoes from Milan.

There.

Ready to proceed with the rest of the day.

He goes through the apartment one more time, checking that all is in place, then takes a side door into a concrete garage, its floor smooth and spotless. He gets into his Mercedes-Benz S550, starts the engine, presses a little box attached to the overhead visor, and gently moves out into the traffic of Tlayleh.

And instantly slams on the brakes.

A little girl—barefoot, dirty, wearing a tattered red dress—has run into traffic to retrieve a scraggly gray kitten.

She looks up, fearful.

He pauses, the heavy engine rumbling. This particular S550 had been rebuilt and heavily armored by Russian Spetsnaz troops up the coast in the Syrian post of Latakia, where they had a thriving black-market business retrofitting and armoring vehicles for those making a fortune in the ongoing troubles in Syria and elsewhere.

The little girl gives a hesitant wave.

He smiles and waves back.

She runs back with her precious cargo in her hands, into the streams of people walking, talking, and selling along the street.

He continues on his way, checking the clock in the S550's interior. If all goes well, he'll be in Tripoli in under two hours. From there he will head south to Beirut, then make a flight north.

If all goes well.

It hadn't gone at all well back at the farmhouse. The second British soldier was about to be killed when a rescue team burst out of the hills nearby, killing the holy warriors around him.

That had not been part of the plan.

That had not been anticipated.

Ah, he thinks, *so what?*

Rashad Hussain heads his luxury car west, knowing that one man's death wouldn't make much of a difference—especially since he was going to achieve a hundred thousand times more than that in less than a week.

He continues his drive, pausing only once in the first hour when he finds a herdsman and his goats blocking the Halba-Qoubaiyat Road just outside Halba.

Rashad needs to make his schedule, so he guns his Mercedes and runs through the herd, crushing and crippling at least a dozen screaming animals before his way is clear.

God willing.

CHAPTER 17

ERNEST HOLLISTER is in the large and comfortable office of his immediate boss, retired U.S. Army General Malcolm Rooney, supervisor of the Agency's Special Activities Division. For some reason, Rooney likes to keep the lights in his office dim, almost at twilight, so the only real illumination comes from his computer screen and the old-fashioned green-glass desk lamp that casts a soft glow over his wide and neat desk.

"I spent so much time in the goddamn desert, the sun beating down, I needed a break," was Rooney's explanation to Ernest months ago, and Ernest had left it at that.

Once, back in the desert and flat plains of Iraq, Rooney had cut a slim and taut figure, jogging and working out every morning, which earned him a few positive news articles and a television piece about the older general setting an example for his younger troops. But once the heady days of the Iraq invasion slipped into that damnable long night of insurgency shootings, bombings, and beheadings, the news media lost interest in positive stories—and in General Rooney.

He now has a prominent gut that hangs over his black leather belt. He hardly ever keeps his necktie tight and knotted, leaving his shirt collar unbuttoned and the tie dangling down.

He pauses in his pacing and says, "That's a very disturbing development, Ernest, concerning that Cornwall woman. Thanks for bringing it to me."

"Yes, sir."

The pacing begins again. "I don't like it, I don't like it all. When folks in the field go rogue, exceed their orders, go against their planning, well, I don't like it. And the folks up on the seventh floor, they like it even less."

In the dim shadows of the bookcase-lined office are a pair of couches and coffee tables, plus lots of framed photos of the general in his military career and his subsequent career in the Agency. Lots of grip-and-grin photos with past Secretaries of State and Defense, along with current ones of Senate and House leaders, none of whom Ernest would trust to run a frat-party weekend.

The pacing stops.

"But I trust you, Ernest. I rely on you...the president, when I was selected, he told me of changes he wanted to make within this division. Hard choices and hard decisions have to be made. But I've always counted on your judgment, to protect...the Agency and its interests."

Ernest nods. Perhaps his boss doesn't know it yet, but Ernest knows he's already won.

"Are you sure this must be done?"

"Yes, sir," Ernest says. "She and this British soldier are acting without authorization, going against a restricted target."

One more pace that ends at a midway point, then Rooney is done and sits down at his desk.

"All right, then," his boss says. "To smoke someone...it means a lot, doesn't it?"

Ernest says, "It means the field operative is no longer in our employ. There are no records of her being here. Her telephone and Internet access are removed. All of our stations around the world are ordered not to respond to her, nor to assist her. It's as if she never existed as part of the Agency."

Rooney picks up a pen, scribbles on a notepad. "It will happen before the end of the day, then, Ernest."

"Thank you, sir," Ernest says, rising from his chair. "It will be for the best. Trust me."

"But what you just said . . . you indicated Cornwall and this British soldier, they are going up against a restricted target. Explain."

"We have preliminary intelligence that this British soldier is on his own, going after one of our assets."

"Have you informed your MI6 counterpart?"

Ernest thinks, *I'm trying, but the limey SOB won't answer my calls.*

"That's currently in the process, sir," he says.

Rooney looks tired. "Who is this asset?"

"His code name is BROKER. He's a quiet, behind-the-scenes man who has performed many services for us. It seems like this rogue SAS soldier has a personal vendetta against him, and that he's persuaded Cornwall to go along."

Rooney says, "But wouldn't it make sense *not* to smoke Cornwall, so we can track her movements?"

"That would be too much of a risk, sir," says Ernest. "Cornwall and the Brit may have already killed our asset. Better to remove all trace of her having worked for the Agency."

Rooney nods and asks, "What's the asset's real name?"

"Rashad Hussain," Ernest says.

CHAPTER 18

AFTER I kick Jeremy's tired and injured legs out from underneath him, he falls flat on his back on the jagged and torn rocks. I'm sure he cries out or curses me, but I'm too busy to hear him. Three militants, terrorists, jihadists—whatever, three bad guys with AK-47s—are bolting around a large boulder about two meters up the trail, and with Jeremy on the ground I get a clear shot.

POP POP POP.

My first three-round burst hits the lead gunmen right in the chest. He falls back, almost toppling his near mate, but that second man swivels and with one hand sends a burst of AK-47 fire at me, which misses me but hits a nearby rock berm, chipping off an impressive amount of stone splinters.

I fire off another three-round burst, catching him in the shoulder and head, and he spins and drops.

The third guy is one cool customer. Instead of praying and spraying, holding out the automatic rifle in both hands and emptying the magazine in one long burst, he drops to one knee, brings up his AK-47, and gives himself a second or two to take proper aim at his target, i.e., me.

But I'm faster and squeeze the trigger on my MP5.

Nothing happens.

It jams.

I throw my now-useless weapon at him, hoping to spoil his aim, and fall to the left, using the bodies of his fellow shooters as a quick and dirty barrier. I draw out my SIG Sauer P226 pistol and snap off a quick shot just as the *chatter-chatter* of the AK-47 starts.

My quick shot misses.

So does the second one.

The guy moves his rifle, starts chewing up his former allies to try to get to me, and I fire off one more round.

It takes him down via his scarf-covered forehead.

I get up, moving to the side, going up the trail a couple of meters, looking to see if they have any more friends or shooters following them.

Nothing—not even a goat.

I quickly return, strip them of their AK-47s, and toss the weapons over the side. I find something interesting on the utility belt of the first gunmen, then get to Jeremy.

He's gritting his teeth and is on one side, holding his MP5 in the approved prone position, looking up at the trail.

"Clear?"

"Yeah," I say, "but I'm not too sure for how long. Here."

I toss the item I took from the belt at him, and he grabs it with his left hand. It's a Uniden handheld radio. Jeremy gives it a quick check, then tosses it behind him.

"We're being tracked," he says.

"True."

I look around the rocks and trail, find my H&K MP5, and pick it up. Discovering an expelled 9mm cartridge case jammed in the extractor, I manage to work it free. I then work the action to ensure there's a live round in the chamber.

Jeremy's working to get up, so I sling my MP5 over my shoulder and give him a hand.

"That was quick action," he says.

"Thanks."

"I see what you did," Jeremy says. "No time for a warning, no time to push me away. You give one hell of a kick."

I look up the trail again, glad to see there's no movement.

"You should see how I move in heels."

He smiles and says, "Your shooting was quick, too. How did you know they weren't three lost sheepherders?"

I check my watch, look down the trail, think I spot a road in the flat distance. That would be nice.

"Muscle memory, I guess," I say. "I saw the shapes pop up, saw the AK-47s in their hands...and their stance. They weren't being cautious, and they weren't approaching with their weapons held casually. They were getting ready to open fire."

"Glad you shot first."

"Me, too," I said. "Them, not that much. Let's get going."

"Agreed."

CHAPTER 19

TOM CORNWALL'S office, on the thirtieth floor of One World Trade Center, has a grand view of the Hudson River and the far New Jersey shoreline. Although he will readily admit to anyone—save for his wife, Amy—that he has a number of faults, he does possess discipline when it comes to his work.

So most days the grand view is at his back as he gets busy at his cluttered desk. There's a standard company-issued computer terminal at his elbow, and on his desk are two separate MacBook laptops, each using a different encrypted system to allow him to romp around the wilds of the internet without being easily traced. He also has an office phone, his personal cell phone, and two burner phones he gets from a nearby Duane Reed and uses for a couple of weeks before throwing them away.

At Criterion, Tom's beat is terrorism, defense, and national security, which is pretty ironic, considering that's also his wife's beat, though hers is more up close and personal.

There are bookcases, piles of newspapers and magazines on the floor, and a number of family photos of Tom alone, Tom with Denise and Amy, and one of Amy alone, back when she was in the Army, stationed at an FOB in Afghanistan, wearing battle rattle and smiling for the camera.

The rare visitors to his office always ask the same two questions:
Is your wife still in the Army?

Answer: *No.*

What does she do now?

Answer: *Security consultant.*

And that would always be that, unless someone presses him and asks, "Well, what exactly does she do?" His stock answer to that has always been the same: "Makes enough money so I can be a kept man."

But today's kept man is working hard on his developing story.

He looks up at the clock.

9:00 a.m.

Right on the dot.

He takes out a small notebook he keeps in his leather carrying case, flips through the pages, finds the number he needs. With burner phone one in hand, he dials the number.

Ring.

Ring.

Ring.

"Yeah?" comes the answer, and Tom can hear machinery in the background.

"It's Cornwall. What do you have?"

The man says, "There's some sort of deployment, I know that. Assets are being reassigned."

"Where?"

"Right now it's the Atlantic coast: Boston, New York, New Jersey, Baltimore, Norfolk, and Jacksonville."

"What kind?"

"Recovery and relief," the man says. "Like somebody's expecting the hurricane season to start early. Or maybe it's just a planned drill I know nothing about. Yet."

A couple of horns sound. "Gotta go."

"Thanks," Tom says, clicking off the burner phone.

The man he just talked to is an executive in the Defense Logistics Agency (DLA). Tom had met him years back in Iraq at its main port of Basra, when Tom was desperate to find a battery for his laptop. The man had helped him out, and when the man shyly asked Tom for advice about his teenage son, who wanted to be a journalist, Tom had helped the kid out with article critiques and college recommendations.

The guy had never forgotten—and had been a good source ever since. As Tom learned a long time ago, military amateurs talk strategy but professionals talk logistics, and when it comes to preparing for war or something else, the DLA provides everything from blankets to bullets.

So what's up?

Then there's a *bleep* on one of his open MacBooks, and his iMessage chat logo begins to blink.

Talk about timing.

He double-clicks on the icon, goes into the program, sees who's calling him, and starts typing.

TOM: *Hey, how's it going?*
YURI: *Trying to survive. You?*
TOM: *In NYC, living the dream. Where are you?*

Tom waits with a smile, knowing his correspondent would never, ever tell him where he was.

But Tom does enjoy playing the game.

YURI: *Out in the field again. You should try it sometime.*
TOM: *I like a warm office. Comfortable. Food. Drink. No IEDs on*
    the road.
YURI: *Coward.*
TOM: *Realist. What's going on?*

Tom had met Yuri four years ago, when he was on assignment in northern Syria's grinding, six-sided civil war, embedded with a Kurdish peshmerga fighting force. Yuri—Tom wasn't sure if that was the man's real name—claimed to be a Ukrainian journalist working for the Qatar-based Al Jazeera network, which wasn't a popular group among the Kurds.

But Tom, remembering his childhood of always being picked last in the schoolyard for soccer or touch football, had befriended him, sharing some of his water and rations even though he was pretty sure Yuri was working for the intelligence service of Russia or Ukraine.

YURI: *Something heavy. Interested?*

He quickly types back.

Very. Go on.

Back in Syria, when it came time for the two of them to return to their respective countries, Yuri had pulled him aside and said, "Look. Thanks for your help. I know I'm not working for the *Times,* like you do, but it's the best I can do. I am a good reporter, a good journalist . . . and sometimes, when I find stories my editors won't let me touch, I pass on to you. Okay?"

Tom had said, "Sure," and now here he was. Even now he still isn't sure if Yuri is passing along news tips out of whatever journalist ethics he possesses or because he's using Tom for Yuri's paymasters. But each time Yuri has sent Tom something, it has been of value.

He waits, staring at the iMessage screen.

Has the screen frozen?

Did Yuri change his mind?

Then the message pops up.

YURI: *You know I got sources with FSB. Hate them but we take care of each other.*

Tom thinks, *FSB*. The Federal Security Service of the Russian Federation, the bastard offspring of the KGB, which was begotten from the MVD, which in turn was begotten from the NKVD, and from there Lenin's Cheka, which even had its roots in the czar's Okhrana. A legacy of spying, spreading disinformation and fake news, and sometimes shooting their enemies in the back of their head.

TOM: *I know. Go.*
Pause.
Pause.
YURI: *There is something stirring. Something big. Something aimed at you.*
TOM: *Me?*
YURI: *You, meaning Europe. Or US of A.*
TOM: *What is it?*
YURI: *Don't know. But there's been lots of traffic jams. My sources say one thing, one thing only.*

Tom knows what Yuri is saying when he mentions traffic jams. He's not talking about the Queens-Midtown Tunnel at rush hour. No, he means an increase in intelligence traffic, also known as *chatter*. The easiest explanation he got for *chatter* had come from Amy, back when they were first dating. She had said, "If killer A is communicating with killer B and you can't read what they're saying, but you know they send two emails a week, that's a pattern. If those two emails increase to twenty, or two hundred, or two thousand, even if you still don't know what they're saying, you know they're talking about something important, something big."

That had been the case, Tom recalls, pre-9/11. There had been increases in chatter and message traffic, but nothing that could be deciphered or analyzed to point to a particular target.

All that existed were the indications that something bad was coming, and the usual government idiocy that meant the CIA couldn't talk to the FBI, and both agencies ignoring warnings from their respective agents in the field.

TOM: *Can't you tell me any more? I'm getting the same whispers from this side of the world.*

YURI: *Not now. But my FSB guys are certain: something bad, something bad is coming.*

TOM: *Great.*

YURI: *Piece of advice?*

TOM: *Would love some advice.*

Pause.

Pause.

YURI: *Get out of New York.*

CHAPTER 20

THE PAIN in his side, in his skull, and in his legs grows harsher and more demanding with every step, but Jeremy is determined not to show Amy how hurt he is. He's also determined to keep a distance between them, especially after telling her about Rashad Hussain. That part was true indeed, but as for his offer to let her help him...well, as he knew from experience, sometimes bad things had to happen for the greater good.

Amy is down on one knee in front of him in a narrow trash-filled and urine-smelling alleyway, looking at a two-story concrete building on a street lined with two-story buildings, utility wires crisscrossing overhead, satellite dishes on top of the flat roofs. Dented and beaten-up sedans from half a dozen different automotive brands—old trade-ins from everywhere in Europe, dumped here for one more resale—crowd the street. A dog is barking somewhere. A solitary light on a utility pole at the other end of the street flickers into life as the dusk grows deeper.

She turns to him, H&K MP5 hidden under her coat, SIG Sauer pistol in her hand, and whispers, "Is this it?"

He squats down beside her, gritting his teeth at the pain. "Yes."

"How do you know?"

"The shutters," he explains. "The only one in the street with yellow shutters."

"Okay," she replies. "What now?"

Here goes, he thinks. "Amy...I'm knackered. Can you help?"

"Sure."

Jeremy says, "The house with the yellow shutters. It has the Renault parked in front, missing the rear windscreen. Go across, knock on the door. Ask for Nassim. Tell him Ricky is here. Needs help. He'll know what to do. I'll stay here..."

"*Ricky?*"

"That's how he knows me."

Amy says, "I don't like leaving you behind. We've got a lot to do with Rashad and we can't afford to be split up."

"It's only ten meters or so. I'll be fine. I'll lie doggo here with the trash and wait for the two of you to come back."

She seems to think this through, then whispers, "Very good. Nassim. Don't stray...Ricky."

He makes a point of leaning against the brick wall of the alley. "Wouldn't dare."

Amy doesn't say anything more, just does her job—which is to briskly walk across the street to the parked Renault, dodging a few potholes along the way. When she's out of sight, Jeremy turns and limps as fast as he can to the other end of the alley.

It's near noon and Tom decides to take his lunch outside on this pleasant day in May. The elevator is crowded and makes one more stop as it descends, and a young man in a work uniform steps in, carrying a leather satchel over his shoulder and a wide utility belt around his thin waist, wearing tan work boots and blue chinos. He's dark-skinned, with faint stubble on his face and thick eyebrows, and he has a work ID attached to his dungaree shirt:

MIKE P.

Tom doesn't like how his fellow passengers step away to make room for the utility worker. There's a difference between giving someone enough room to come aboard and another thing to back away because you're afraid you'll smell him or get dirt on your thousand-dollar suit or two-thousand-dollar outfit.

There are knowing smirks among the high-powered passengers, and Tom feels a slow burn start inside him. He grew up in Virginia, and not the pricey and wealthy counties near the District of Columbia that serve as suckerfish around the federal government. No, he had grown up in a small town near the Kentucky border, and he knew from a young age there was no shame in working with one's hands to make a living. Scholarships and writing prizes had gotten Tom out of the rural life, and years of trying to soften his southern accent had worked to eliminate most prejudice, but he still finds that the way blue-collar workers get treated pisses him off.

The young man stares straight at the display, then the elevator stops, the doors sliding open.

The man named Mike walks off. As the doors close, one man murmurs to his friend, "Hey, I didn't know ISIS was hiring here, did you?"

A couple of slight giggles and Tom can't get away fast enough from these people, his supposed peers in upscale Manhattan.

After getting off the elevator, Mike Patel walks with no apparent guilt or fear to the end of the pretty and wealthy corridor, to a plain gray door with a small black sensor lock to one side. He slides his identity pass over the lock and a little green light comes on, then the door clicks open. Mike walks in and carefully closes the door behind him. Somewhere in the security systems that keep watch in this enormous building, some computer somewhere recorded that he, MIKE PATEL, an employee of Chrome HVAC Systems and a lifelong resident of New York State, had entered this equipment bay.

As he goes through another door and into a long corridor filled with circuit boxes, blinking lights, gray cabinets, and conduits, he reflects that the computer recording was two-thirds correct. His name is in fact Mike Patel, and he is an employee of Chrome HVAC Systems. But he is also a British citizen from Manchester, here illegally and serving a second employer.

Who that is doesn't really matter. What does matter is that a young woman had asked him months ago back in Manchester if he was tired of being on the dole, tired of no future, tired of skinheads spitting on him and calling him "dirty Paki."

Mike kneels down, places his workbag on the clean concrete floor, and remembers.

Yes to all three questions.

He opens the workbag, takes out a black box with attached wires and alligator clips, and with practiced ease—in his months working here, Mike has done this at least a hundred times—he secures the box in a hidden area behind an access panel.

What does the black box do?

Nothing, for now.

But he knows what it will do in a very short time, and the thought of those smirking figures on the elevator getting their due justice—well, that is a wonderful thought indeed.

CHAPTER 21

JEREMY MOVES as best and as quickly as he can, knowing the few minutes standing and talking to Amy back there have caused his joints and muscles to stiffen, but he has to get on with it. Eventually Amy will find her way home, being the smart and capable woman she is.

But right now Jeremy is out in the open as night is falling, and he wants to get to Nassim's place as quickly as he can, which—unfortunately for Amy—is not at the house back there, the one near the battered Renault sedan.

His mission is key and he's going to complete it on his own.

He stops at the other end of the alley, looks up and down. There's a small plaza to the right with some shops that are open, and luckily for him, Nassim is on the other end, away from the few lights and the number of villagers milling around.

Jeremy takes a breath, starts out, and—

Something heavy slams into his back, hammering him to the dirty concrete and a puddle, and a sharp blade is stuck to his throat.

Tom gets a thick pulled-pork BBQ sandwich from Hudson Eats on Vesey Street, and is trying to enjoy his early lunch while sitting out in the warm May sun.

The sandwich tastes off, and he knows why. He's warm so he shrugs off his coat and rolls up his sleeves, trying to ignore the old burn scar on his left forearm that brings back dark memories of the time he was in danger, along with Denise, and how Amy put it all on the line to rescue them.

Something is stirring out there, and he knows it. He just knows it. It remains tantalizingly and hauntingly just out of reach, like trying to re-create a previous night's dream.

Another bite of the sandwich. Another squirt of BBQ sauce lands on his napkins, keeping his shirt and necktie clean. A tiny success.

A bit of shade flicks across his view, and he looks up as his boss, Dylan Roper, sits down next to him. At first he thought it might be one of the folks doing surveillance on him, but that would have been too funny.

"Hey," Dylan says. "Am I paying you to have lunch?"

"You are at the moment," Tom says.

Dylan is prickly, abrasive—an acquired taste. He's pudgy and short with thin blond hair, a wide face, and slightly bulging blue eyes that express constant aggravation with the world around him. He's wearing his warm-weather uniform: a blue seersucker suit with a white dress shirt and a tiny red bow tie.

"Tell me you're working on something," Dylan says.

"I am."

"Tell me it's earth-shattering, amazing, and most importantly will give us incredible clicks on our home page."

"How does two out of three sound?" Tom asks.

Dylan turns like a junkyard dog hearing someone climb over a chain-link fence. "That wasn't a goddamn joke, Cornwall," he snaps. "I wasn't asking you to make a joke. I was as serious as a heart attack. I've got my entire savings, stock portfolio, and two mortgages tied up in Criterion. Do you?"

Tom feels a flash of anger, knowing he has confronted worse

men than Dylan—the scar tissue on his forearm is a daily re-
minder—and despite his boss, he does love working for Criterion.

But he doesn't like bullies.

"If you've got a problem, tell me," Tom says. "Otherwise, don't
treat me like a Columbia J-School intern."

Dylan stares and seems to back down a bit, then says, "All right.
Good point. The thing is, Tom, our news stream has been thin this
past week."

Tom says, "The story about the California governor didn't do it?"

Dylan says, "A politician with a sex scandal? That's not really
news. Call that a standing head, a recurring story. Just rearrange the
names, party affiliation, sex, or species, and it's a constant. No, I
need a story with some meat, some strength—something only you
can produce."

Tom considers that and says, "I am working on something."

Dylan smiles. "M'man. What is it?"

"No details right now," Tom slowly says. "But if it goes the way I
think it will, the story will be huge."

"Guaranteed?"

Tom shakes his head. "Can't guarantee, but I'll know better in a
day. Maybe two."

Dylan gets up. "All right. Do what you need, run up any ex-
penses that are necessary, but I'm relying on you to come up with
something that will make the world and my investors sit up and
take notice."

"I'll do my best," Tom says, not liking being forced into a trap
like this.

"Tom," he snaps again. "Get your ass back to work. And show
me your best."

Dylan strides across the plaza, and Tom takes his napkins and
quietly crushes up the rest of his lunch. It seems like his anger is
brightening the burn tissue on his forearm as he stands up and

walks off as well, the twin reflecting pools a couple of blocks away but very much on his mind.

Get out of New York, Yuri had warned him.

No.

He is going to work this story, right here, no matter what.

CHAPTER 22

HITTING SOMEONE from behind isn't as easy as it looks in the movies. Especially if your target is an experienced ex-SAS trooper attuned to his surroundings. But I have the advantage of being in better shape, coming at him by surprise, and being one pissed-off team leader.

I slam into Jeremy and drop him to the smelly wet ground of the alley. Because I want to make my message explicit, I draw my Ka-Bar knife and press it against his right carotid artery.

"Jeremy," I harshly whisper, "you're doing a rotten job improving Anglo-American relations."

He grunts and moves under me, and I push the knife in just a bit harder. I hope I'm drawing blood, because that's the only way I'm going to get his attention.

"You're screwing with me," I go on, "and I only allow one man in my life to do that."

"Amy . . . get off, damn you."

"Only if we reach an understanding," I whisper. "No more keeping me out of the loop, no more trying to leave me behind. We're in this together. I want your vow that the nonsense is over."

"The nonsense is over," he says. "You have my personal word. You will be at my side throughout the duration of this mission."

I almost get up, but quickly say, "And I'm the one who determines when the mission is completed, correct?"

"Christ, you're heavier than you look," Jeremy says. "Yes, you'll make that determination. Now will you get me up? I think my face is in a pile of dog shit."

"All right," I say, keeping my voice low, looking down the trash-filled alley. "Where to now?"

He coughs, and in the dim light he really does look like crap. But I don't feel bad. He tried to dump me and got what was coming to him.

He wipes an arm across his face. "We go see Nassim."

"Oh," I say. "So the mysterious Nassim *exists*. And who lives in the place with the yellow shutters?"

"His cousin Ali," Jeremy says.

He steps out of the alley and I join him in the narrow street, the sounds of radios and televisions coming out from the dark homes, dogs barking, some folks talking loudly or shouting. Across the street, two men huddle in a doorway, smoking; they give us a long, unfriendly look as we quickly stroll by.

Jeremy says, "This part of Lebanon is mostly Maronite Christian. They don't like outsiders. Those types are usually Hezbollah or smugglers."

"Thanks for the commentary," I say, staying close behind him. "Then let's get inside and make them feel better."

We jog down to the right, to an even narrower street, where Jeremy finds a recessed doorway with a little grilled window set near the top of a heavy wooden door. He stands by one side of the door and I stand by the other.

Jeremy hits the door twice with his fist and calls out a quick phrase in Arabic.

Something slides aside from the top grill, letting a little beam of light shine out.

A man's voice replies from inside, the Arabic muffled.

Jeremy replies, louder this time and a bit more frantic.

No answer from inside.

He hits the door again with his fist and—

The door bursts open and at least two men reach out and seize him, then drag him into the house and start closing the door.

I move fast. The door slams shut on my left booted foot.

There's yelling inside and I lean back and slam in with my left shoulder and hip, getting the door wide enough so I can go through it. As I push my way in, I recover my MP5 from underneath my coat and bring it right up, and now I'm in the entryway, taking in the whole mess in one quick glance.

Jeremy, facedown on the floor, a man squatting on his shoulders, a pistol at the base of Jeremy's neck.

Another man, also on the floor, kneeling, pointing a pistol at Jeremy.

And a third man, halfway through another door, AK-47 at his side, but he can't bring it into play because the doorway is too narrow. There are narrow carpets on the stone floor, another closed door, flickering lights, and the scent of incense and something cooking.

Three armed men and me.

Outnumbered, but I'm definitely not outgunned.

But it's a stalemate for sure.

CHAPTER 23

FREDDIE FARRADY is a detective with Scotland Yard's Special Branch, on assignment in Manhattan. He would never admit this to his mates back home, but he's grown to love American street vendors and their hot dogs. He's on Church Street near the World Trade Center memorials, about ten meters from the entrance to the Cortlandt Street subway station.

He's eating another hot dog while waiting for his target to show up. He has on blue jeans, black sneakers, and a plain tan jacket. Topping it off is a New York Yankees baseball cap that's one size too large for his head, allowing him to lower the visor to obscure his face. New York isn't quite up to London standards when it comes to CCTV, but Freddie still wants to minimize the chances of his recorded image being used anytime soon.

He checks his watch. The target is always on schedule, arriving here at the station from his job at One World Trade Center, give or take ten minutes.

Somewhere underneath him in the station is his temporary boss and the other half of his surveillance team, Portia Grayson of MI5. And for all intents and purposes, that's it. Running a two-person surveillance is a bloody strange job—a surveillance like this usually takes six or seven folks—but being with Special Branch means taking on all sorts of strange jobs.

There.

Walking through the early commuters heading home, the target approaches the station.

He is Mike Patel, formerly of Manchester, now a worker with a company doing business at the new One World Trade Center.

The target walks quickly and confidently into the station. Freddie polishes off his hot dog, crumples up the napkin, and drops it into an overflowing waste bin as he races across the street.

He doesn't spare a glance behind him, where the ghost of Tower Two lives in his mind, where his older cousin, Malcolm, worked in American finance—and burned to death back on that dark day.

The station is filthy—no surprise there—but Freddie ignores his surroundings as he follows the target through the turnstiles. Patel goes through and Freddie does the same, two turnstiles down from him, making sure his cap is tugged low.

Patel slowly weaves in and out of the crowd, pausing for a moment behind a steel girder, then stops on the platform and stands still. Freddie pretends to throw something into another overflowing waste bin—really, how hard can it be to empty these bins on a regular basis?—and glances up at the digital readout telling him and a few scores of people that the incoming W line train is only two minutes away.

Freddie waits.

He hears the familiar crackle of a police radio and turns. Coming up the platform are two heavily armed men of the NYPD, wearing helmets, body armor, and cut-down AR-15s slung over their chests. Freddie quickly turns away; he wants to see if Patel has noticed the police—and, if so, is he doing anything.

No, not a thing.

Patel is just staring down at the tracks, waiting, with seemingly not a worry in the world.

Freddie wishes he knew what that was like. Not a worry in the world because among his worries is the fact that not only is he here in Manhattan without an NYPD liaison being aware of his presence, he's also carrying a small Glock 26 9mm pistol strapped to his ankle—quite illegally, of course.

The train's headlight appears at the end of the tunnel. With a *whoosh* and a rattling roar, the train pulls into the station and slows to a stop. Patel gets on with the rest of the pushing commuters, and Freddie joins the fray.

Three stops and twenty-one minutes later, Freddie is back out in the open air on 31st Street near Astoria Boulevard, a working-class area of Queens that has the rattling monstrosity of an elevated highway nearby, with lots of immigrants and poor folks, which means Patel fits right in.

En route to this destination—same as the time before, and the time before that, and so forth and so on—Freddie exchanged his Yankees black-and-white cap for an orange-and-blue Mets cap. He also turned his jacket inside out; it's now a dark blue.

The weather feels better here in this part of Queens, with two- and three-story buildings and the sidewalks bustling with people, and he pauses, reverses course, and continues his tail until Patel goes up the steps of his brick building at the corner of 30th Street and Newtown Avenue. Again, no surprise.

He leans against a utility pole, yawns like he's just gotten off a twelve-hour shift, and waits just a bit more to see if anyone else goes in. Nope—same as before.

There are small stores up and down this crowded stretch of Queens, from shoe shops to bodegas, and a few blocks away is a mosque. Not once has Patel been seen going into the mosque.

Freddie turns and nearly bumps into the MI5 woman, Portia Grayson, who's frowning down at him. Portia is much taller than Freddie and probably weighs about the same. Freddie's farmer granddad would say the woman with the short black hair and skinny face looks like a funny string bean, wearing American gray workout slacks and a dark blue sweatshirt with a faded Epcot seal on the front.

But Portia is not in a funny mood.

"Get walking," she says. Freddie scratches his chin and starts walking, and five minutes later they're at a little luncheonette, taking adjoining booths.

The talk is low and in spurts, so others coming and going can't tell that they know each other.

"You shouldn't hang around like that," says Portia in her disapproving voice. "You'll get spotted."

"Then get us more bodies out here, so we can do a proper job," he says.

"We have what we have," she says. "Stop complaining. Anything out of the ordinary to report?"

"No," Freddie says. "Came off shift, caught the tube, walked to his grotty little apartment. That's it."

"All right," she says. "I'll take the night work. You watch him in the morning when he leaves."

Freddie tries not to sigh, thinking of his squalid little second-story motel room several blocks away on Broadway, with its fights in the parking lot and the yells and come-ons from the local hookers, trying to catch some business.

"Sure, boss," he says. "But I sure would like to know what the little bastard is up to."

"Don't we all," she snaps back.

"He's here illegally, he's Muslim, and he has access to the entire One World Trade Center."

"And?"

Freddie waits for a moment before proceeding.

Oh, what the hell, he thinks. This is a temporary assignment. It's not like she can do too much to his career once this silly job gets wrapped up.

"What if he's placing explosives?" Freddie asks. "He's been there for months. Maybe he's part of a plot to take the building down and—"

Portia interrupts him.

"Don't make jokes like that," she says.

He can sense her anger even though she's not looking at him.

"I'm not joking," Freddie says, his long-dead cousin Malcolm still haunting him.

CHAPTER 24

LONG SECONDS drag by like hours as I stand rock steady, moving my MP5 here, there, and everywhere to keep the three men under watch.

The armed men are staring at me. I decide the guy with the AK-47 will be the first to get it if he attempts to move back and bring the weapon up, because in an enclosed space like this, the inefficient pray-and-spray shooting tactic would actually work.

The guys on the ground are next up: the one with the pistol at the base of Jeremy's neck will be target number two, and—

"Amy."

—because the guy kneeling, aiming at Jeremy, his hand is shaking—

"Amy."

—but if any of the three make a move toward me, they're dead.

"Amy, damn it," Jeremy says, "I'm talking to you!"

I keep moving my MP5, swiveling back and forth, back and forth.

"So you are," I say. "You tell these three assholes to drop their weapons."

Jeremy swears at me. "They're relatives of Nassim. They aren't bad guys."

"They have a funny way of showing it."

"They didn't recognize me, they didn't like the tone of my voice, so they dragged me in," Jeremy says, his voice muffled some because his head's plastered against a carpet.

The man with a gun against Jeremy's neck rattles off a long stream of angry Arabic words. Jeremy replies in Arabic as well, softer, and says, "They wanted to check me out before bringing Nassim out. But then you broke in, and now they're pissed."

"Too bad," I say, still not hesitating in moving my MP5 to keep these three off balance. "I saw you assaulted. Now, tell them to drop it."

"They won't do it," Jeremy says. "You're a woman."

"I don't care," I say. "Tell them to do it."

Jeremy tries another long stream of Arabic. The guy at the doorway seems to relax, still holding his AK-47 — still in a bad position, and not aiming at me — while the guy kneeling says something to the guy on Jeremy's back, followed by some arguing and snapping at each other. Then the fellow with the AK-47 shrugs, puts the rifle down, and steps into the crowded entryway.

I let out a breath. Then, without any more debate, the second guy puts his pistol on the floor and steps back, joining the other standing man.

That leaves just the angry, bearded, armed man on Jeremy's back. The pistol is still pressed against Jeremy's neck, but I feel a lot better with just one target to worry about. I stop waving my MP5 and take two steps forward, aiming the rifle at his forehead.

He nearly spits at me.

"Jeremy..."

"Amy, it's a family honor thing, a macho thing, a—"

I say in my best low and fierce voice, "You tell him if he doesn't drop that pistol in the next three seconds, I'm going to make it a blood-and-brains-on-the-wall thing."

"Ricky?" A man's voice is calling out from deep inside the house. "Ricky? Is that truly you?"

I flash my eyes to the doorway, where a plump, older, smiling man is approaching. His hands are empty. Good. I go back to staring at my target as the new man and his heavy cologne come to join us. He's fifty or so—thick mustache, thick black hair, dark-gray pinstripe suit and vest. A gold pocket-watch chain dangling out front.

Still flat on the carpet, Jeremy says, "Hello, Nassim. We seem to be in a bit of a bother here."

Nassim smiles down at Jeremy and says, "Ah, my boys. They are eager ones, but sometimes so very, very impolite."

He barks out a command, but the man on Jeremy's back doesn't move. He says something back and Jeremy whispers, "Oh, that's not good."

"What's going on?" I ask.

Nassim speaks up. "My apologies, young lady. It seems my nephew Tariq is a bit more...traditional than his cousins. He believes we are buckling under a woman's eye."

I make a quick decision and lower my MP5. "Give Tariq my deepest apologies. Tell him I mean no disrespect, but that I am honor-bound to protect and defend the wounded warrior underneath him. Tell him again I apologize and that I now know my place."

Nassim nods, then speaks to his nephew. Still angry, Tariq looks up at me but then removes the pistol from Jeremy's neck. He slips it into a waistband holster and starts to rise.

I shoulder my MP5 and offer Tariq a hand to help him up, and I think he's surprised by my offer, but he takes my hand and I help him to his feet.

Then I let go, swivel hard, and use my right elbow to punch his nose.

He cries out, stumbles over the form of Jeremy, and slams hard to the ground. I step over Jeremy, disarm Tariq, and stick his pistol in my own waistband.

All the men are staring at me save for Tariq, who has his hands up to his bloody nose.

I shrug.

"Sorry," I say. "I slipped."

CHAPTER 25

IT'S EARLY evening in Paris and Nadia Khadra is heading home after another long day at the Institut Pasteur at 25–28 Rue du Dr Roux. She is a microbiologist by trade and has worked at the institute for three years. The famed facility has spent decades studying infectious diseases from diphtheria to influenza to yellow fever.

She descends into the Metro station and patiently waits for her train on the clean and orderly train platform. For the past year, the institute has been quietly working on another deadly infectious disease—and Nadia considers the day she learned that to be the luckiest day of her life.

And the day she met the wealthy, bearded, and determined older Arab man who financed her was her second-luckiest day.

She pays 1.90 euros for a one-way ticket. The boxy, white-and-green Line 12 train glides in on its rubber tires right on time, and she joins the other commuters entering its sliding doors.

In less than a week, Nadia reflects, she will be riding the subway system in New York City, and she shudders at what she will find there. Friends of hers at the institute have told her that the subways in New York are dirty and loud, with pickpockets and thieves all around. She hopes she will have the bravery to do what must be done.

*   *   *

Half an hour later, Nadia gets off at the Marx Dormoy station and briskly walks up into the open air of the Goutte d'Or section of Paris. It's a relatively poor neighborhood, with more than a third of its residents from North Africa—like her family, originally from Algeria—and she makes enough money at the institute to move to a better neighborhood, but she won't. She has fond memories of growing up here with her *maman,* who was a seamstress in a number of the so-called sweatshops working out of dank buildings and warehouses, and she will never leave what is known in Paris as Little Africa. She never knew her *papa*—never cared to know him; for all Nadia knows, the man is dead.

She stops in at a *boulangerie* to get a fresh baguette for later, then walks the ten minutes home, past little shops and cafés, the traffic honking and burbling along, a number of local women dressed in chadors. Though a few walls bear graffiti from the Front National, France's right-wing anti-immigrant party, Nadia (who is Muslim but hasn't entered a mosque in years) still loves this part of Paris. To those who painted the walls in hate, she wishes she could say, "Why?" These poor people from Algeria, Chad, and parts of North Africa, they were once part of the French Empire. And that empire is responsible for the colonialism and destruction that broke these families and brought them here.

Nadia arrives at her little three-story apartment house at 4 Rue de Torcy, a small yellow building with black shutters and narrow balconies. Before she can enter the door to her first-floor flat, the building's owner—Madame Juliette Therien—bustles out, holding a colored sheet of paper in her plump hands.

"Mademoiselle Khadra, working late again, eh?"

"That I am, that I am," she says, the baguette under her right arm, her large purse over her left.

"Well, I need to show you this," she says, waving the paper in the air. "The electric bill, it came today, eh? But I opened yours by mistake. But look! Look!"

Nadia takes the Électricité de France (EDF) utility bill, thinking, *Oh no, you silly, snoopy old bird, that was no mistake,* and glances at the six-page printout with the familiar blue-and-orange EDF logo in the upper left corner. "Look! Look! You are using three times as much power as me!" says Madame Therien. "And four times as much as the Urbi family!"

Yes, yes, Nadia thinks, *the poor Urbi family, migrants from Benin, shoved into the second floor while Therien resides on the top floor like a queen.* The Urbis are loud—playing music at all hours, their children stomping overhead—but not once has Nadia complained.

Nadia doesn't want to make waves, draw attention.

"I don't see the problem," Nadia says. "I pay the bill every two months. Why should you care?"

Her landlord folds her beefy arms. She's a heavyset woman who wears lots of makeup, exaggerated painted-in eyebrows, and billowing dresses in bright colors, and nearly always, her bare, leathery feet in open-toed sandals.

"I'll tell you the problem," she says. "Whatever you're doing in my cellar, it's putting a strain on my poor building and its wiring and circuits."

"I doubt that."

Madame Therien shakes her head. "I can't take that chance. I must insist that I go into the cellar, see what you're doing down there."

Sweet Allah no, Nadia thinks. She says, "Please...it's delicate work, doing research for my doctorate. You might...ruin something, even by accident."

"It's my building, my cellar."

Nadia smiles as best she can. "I promise...Madame Therien, my work is almost at an end. In a few days...you may inspect the cellar as much as you wish. And in two months I will show you my EDF bill. You will see it drop significantly."

The old woman waits, then reluctantly nods and smiles back. "If you say so, Mademoiselle."

"*Merci,*" Nadia says, brushing past her landlady to undo the three locks on her door. (An additional deadbolt had been installed at Nadia's expense last year.) Madame Therien is just starting to say something more when Nadia closes the door behind her. Her landlady isn't a bad sort, just lonely, and she loves to gossip and advise—from her lengthy life experiences!—on how to find a man.

"And keep him!" she would insist.

Nadia has never had the courage to tell her that she has no time for a man in her life, not at this moment. When her work is done, then she will find the right man for her—a man to love and cherish for the rest of her life.

A few minutes later, Nadia is in the cellar, feeling at ease. The door to the apartment is locked. The door to the cellar is firmly closed. She turns on the overhead fluorescent lights, *click-click*ing into life, as she looks with satisfaction at her homemade laboratory and facility.

Two refrigerators, brought in when her landlady was on vacation in Provence. Four autoclaves. A long metal table with various tools and instruments. Centrifuge. Respirator masks, elbow-length rubber gloves, clear plastic face masks. Piles of round agar dishes for growing spores. A waste cabinet, securely fastened, plus an open biosafety cabinet where she has carefully worked these past months to remove and process what she has been growing.

A stolen gift from the Institut Pasteur.

Anthrax, which she has carefully and methodically processed into a biological weapon.

Nadia steps forward to the table, where a number of metal trays each hold scores of glassine envelopes containing a gray powdery substance.

She gently touches the envelopes.

And hears footsteps overhead.

Oh, no!

Nadia walks quickly across the cellar floor, but no—the door from the kitchen opens, and *thump, thump, thump* Madame Therien comes down into the cellar. "Ah, my girl, I was hoping you could join me later for...my dear, what is this? What are you doing here?"

Nadia swallows hard, tries to keep her voice light. "Like I told you before, Madame, this is part of my—"

Her landlady brusquely pushes by her, starts speaking rapidly: "You said, 'some little pieces of laboratory equipment'...this can't continue...I will call my son and have him start pulling—"

Nadia picks up the small hammer she used to bend pieces of the ventilation equipment, gets right behind Madame Therien, and hits her in the back of her head. The first blow seems to stun her—she turns her head in surprise—then Nadia hits her again, and again, and again.

At some point Nadia stands, breathing hard, her right hand warm and sticky. Madame Therien lies dead on the cellar floor.

Nadia wipes at her face with her other hand, looks to the collection of carefully constructed and placed envelopes in their trays.

One death.

And here, before her, made from her own hands, enough weaponized anthrax to kill tens of thousands, if properly spread and distributed in an urban environment.

Nadia looks down at her sweet dead landlady, blood pooling about her battered head on the concrete floor.

So what will one more death matter?

It won't.

CHAPTER 26

HORACE EVANS of MI6 works late this day and decides to take another long stroll along the grounds of Lindsay Hall before going home.

Ten minutes into his walk he sees his assistant, Declan Ainsworth, coming toward him, and he's pleased the boy isn't running, isn't huffing and puffing in his desire to meet up with Horace. Such things simply are not done.

Horace clasps his hands behind him and turns down another gently paved path. After a few measured paces with Declan at his side, he asks, "Have we received any news about our Jeremy and Oliver?"

"Yes, sir, we have," Declan says. "Davies and Windsor were captured and taken to a farmhouse used by militants in the area. I'm afraid Davies was killed—beheaded, in fact."

Horace sighs. One more death in the field that will never, ever be fully told or revealed, save in red-bordered file folders held and seen only by a fortunate and burdened few.

"Damn," Horace says. "Damn these barbarians."

The path they're on is now under a spreading grove of oak trees, and the suspicious part of Horace is pleased he can't be viewed by overhead assets, either satellites or drones controlled by those damnable Russians.

"Go on," he says. "What about Jeremy?"

He listens as Declan briefs him on the complicated resolution that saw two Americans eventually exfilled by a BP helicopter, with Jeremy and the American woman pressing on alone.

"And where are they now?"

"They hiked to a village, where they met up with an asset of ours who provided them transportation to Beirut."

Jeremy, he thinks with pride and pleasure, *my dear boy.*

"Do we know why he's headed to Beirut?"

"Not officially, no."

"Then tell me unofficially."

"I checked with General Communications for any traffic intercepts in that area. They managed to locate a short cellphone conversation with that Lebanese asset. He briefly mentioned a Brit and an American and how they were looking for someone named Rashad."

Horace halts. "You're sure of that?"

"Quite, sir, and after a records check...it would appear the man is our Rashad Hussain. That is quite the—"

Horace cuts him off. "Enough." He resumes his walk. *Will the American woman contact her superiors and tell them about Rashad?*

Horace resumes his walk. The buildings of Lindsay Hall are coming into view, and this section has buildings open to the public. There are vehicles and tour buses parked to the left, and a long line of tourists ready to go inside.

"I suppose our friend Ernest has been trying to reach me."

"Yes, sir," Declan says.

He takes in the peaceful lines of tourists from here and away, waiting to explore and look at the treasures of a past empire.

"Declan, do you know your history of Lindsay Hall? About the men and women who trained here?"

"Some, sir," Declan says.

"There were times when the trainers here spent long weeks and months training Poles, Free French, Czechs—all in preparation for parachuting them behind Nazi lines."

"Yes, sir," Declan says.

"But there were some unfortunate moments when the higher-ups realized that some of these very brave men and women— they were parachuting to their doom. The resistance cells on the ground, waiting to greet them, had been turned by the Nazis. Yet the parachute drops went on. You know why, of course."

"Ultra," Declan says.

"Quite," Horace says softly. "We had broken the Enigma. We read most of their secret messages, including their successes in breaking up resistance cells. But if scheduled parachute drops had been called off, well, the Germans would be suspicious something was amiss. And that couldn't be risked. So at nighttime, these brave men and women would line up to board their aircraft to be dropped over occupied Europe, and some of the same officers who had trained them smiled at them and wished them luck, knowing that they would be captured within hours, tortured, and killed."

Declan stays silent.

Horace says, "Can you understand being so cold-blooded in your job?"

"Based on our work these past several months, I understand it all too well."

Horace says, "True. Like our predecessors, we have to look at those tour buses and imagine knowing one is packed with C-4 and ball bearings—and *choosing* to do nothing. Because doing so would alert the terrorists that we had penetrated their network...and in saving those civilians, we would allow many,

many more to die down the road, because we would lose our intelligence source. That's the cold heart and hard mind we need to possess in our business."

Then he turns and heads back toward his office. "When Ernest of the CIA reaches out again, wanting to know what's going on..."

"Sir?" Declan asks.

"Keep him away from me."

CHAPTER 27

THERE'S A touch on my leg and I instantly come awake and snap out with my left hand, grabbing someone's ear, then follow it up with my right hand, holding my SIG Sauer pistol, which I shove underneath someone's chin.

I blink my eyes.

It all comes racing back to me. Getting into a BMW sedan, the outside dirty and rusty, the interior clean, with fresh flowers in a glass vase attached to the dashboard. A long drive with Rami, another nephew of Nassim's. Rami practicing his English on Jeremy and me as he goes southbound on Highway 51, which hugs Lebanon's coastline.

Jeremy...

Sitting right next to me in the rear seat, motionless, with my left hand twisting his ear, and my SIG Sauer jammed up into his beard.

"Sorry," I say, dropping my hands. "Habit."

"A good one," he says dryly.

I look around, taking in the lights and buildings of an airport as Rami drives us along the side of a paved runway, with chain-link fencing topped by razor wire nearby. "Beirut airport?" I ask.

"Yes," he says, leaning forward and turning his head to look at the utility lights, the hangars, the parked aircraft. "Although its official name is the Beirut–Rafic Hariri International Airport."

"A mouthful," I say. "Who was Rafic Hariri?"

"Business tycoon. Former prime minister of Lebanon. Helped rebuild Beirut after their civil war made it look like downtown Mogadishu."

"So they named an airport after him—nice," I say, rearranging my pistol in my lap. "I bet he appreciated it."

"Doubtful," Jeremy says. "Like most politicians in this part of the world, he was taken out by a car bomb. Rami, over there—to the left."

"Over there" turns out to be a small hangar with a two-engine jet aircraft nearby, painted white with red and blue markings, the tricolor of France painted on its tail. Rami slows down and stops the BMW. Armed men in tan uniforms wearing red berets stand by the roll-up stairway to the aircraft.

"Here we go," Jeremy says, opening his door. I follow, and both of us sling our MP5s over our respective shoulders. There's not much else to carry, but I put my SIG Sauer in my waistband as Jeremy talks low to Rami, shaking his hand. I go over to Jeremy and Rami extends his hand. When I take it, Rami quickly kisses my own, then steps back, laughing.

I decide not to slug him.

It's warm here, the salt smell of the nearby Mediterranean mixing in with the heady tang of aviation fuel, and I enjoy stretching my legs. Up the way are two Airbus passenger jets bearing the cedar-tree logo of Middle East Airlines.

Jeremy gestures to the two-engine jet. "Our flight out of here."

"Very nice," I say. "A charter?"

"A favor," he says, as we walk toward the ramp. From the open door to the fuselage, a young woman in a black skirt and a white blouse with captain's epaulets quickly descends. Her hair and eyes are black. Her skin is tanned. She doesn't smile as she gives us both the once-over.

"We need to leave," the pilot says, speaking English with a slight French accent. "The control tower is wondering what's taking us so long. So move, please."

"Sorry, dear," Jeremy says, but she's having none of his charm offensive. She points to us and says, "I won't have those machine guns on board. Leave them behind with our guards."

I feel like putting up a fight, but I follow Jeremy's lead as he takes off his MP5 and hands it to the nearest guard. I follow up and say, "We're going to bill MI6 when this is done."

"Stand in queue," Jeremy says. "There are many unpaid bills in front of you."

He trots up the stairs and I follow him.

I enter the cabin and just stand for a moment, taking in the luxury. Padded light-brown leather chairs. A pair of couches with throw pillows. A small dining table. A vase with fresh roses in it. A plasma-screen television hanging from the bulkhead. Luxurious white carpeting beneath our grimy feet. It looks like someone imported a suite from the Waldorf and slapped wings on it.

"You guys must have one hell of an expense account to charter something like this," I say. "This looks like an Embraer Lineage . . . made in Brazil."

"Our expense account is nearly nil," Jeremy says, taking off his dirty and bloodstained coat, wincing as he does so. "But our favor bank is nearly always overflowing. This private jet belongs to a senior official at Total SA in France. Last year an SAS squadron helped the French rescue his son and two other hikers who'd gotten lost in Libya."

"Hell of a place to get lost."

"True," Jeremy says. "Still, it was a good job all around, and the senior official said he was eternally in our debt. Corporations love stability and open borders. They hate terrorists and their supporters as much as we do. When they can, big business passes along information to us, the French, and no doubt Langley."

No doubt, I think, though I wonder what the average Frenchman filling his Renault with petrol costing about $5.50 per gallon would think of his nation's largest oil company springing for a luxurious flight like this.

There's a cheery *bonsoir,* and a male steward comes forth, holding two shopping bags that he places on the floor. He's slim and smiling, but his nose wrinkles for the briefest of moments and I wonder just how foul Jeremy and I must smell to this young man in black shoes, slacks, white shirt, and a necktie featuring the swirling, colorful logo of Total SA.

There's a quick flicker of French between Jeremy and the steward—Jean-Paul—about when we're to take off and other flight details, then Jean-Paul goes forward.

Jeremy picks up the two shopping bags and hands them to me with a grin. "For you, courtesy of Her Majesty's Secret Service."

One bag has a KM logo on its side; the other says Clarks, a shoe company. I'm impressed that Jeremy got someone to go shopping on my behalf during our road trip to Beirut, and now I remember his seemingly innocent comment about my shoe size back up in the mountains.

Good tradecraft.

"For real?" I ask.

He gives a quick point to the rear of the aircraft. "If you head aft, there's a loo available for you. Have a go—change into something clean and comfortable."

I carry the bags with me and walk a couple of feet, then plop my tired butt onto the nearest couch.

I smile up at Jeremy. "Once we're at cruising altitude, I'll do just that. I'd hate to be in the loo while you run out to get some lamb shish kebabs just as the jet decides to take off."

He says, "Still don't trust me?"

"Please, Jeremy. I don't want to hurt your feelings in public."

CHAPTER 28

JEREMY TAKES a seat across from me and sighs, then Jean-Paul comes out and helps us fasten our seatbelts for takeoff. A number of minutes later, there's a *ding* and we both release our seatbelts.

Jeremy leads me to the rear of the aircraft, past another luxurious suite of comfortable chairs, a wet bar, and another couch. He unlocks a door at the rear and says, "All yours."

"Thanks," I say, brushing past him. "Just so you know, if the door locks behind me and I can't get it open, I'll shoot my way out. And to show you how grumpy I am, I'll shoot out a couple of windows, too, just to see what the hell happens next."

Then I close the door on him, turn, and drop the bags on the tiled floor.

Damn.

The bathroom here is larger than the one I have at home with Tom and Denise, and this is the first time I've ever seen a shower in an aircraft. I examine the shower stall, which is padded inside and has plenty of handrails and a corner where you can sit. There's also a marble counter with rounded, padded edges, along with a toilet and a bidet.

I open the two shopping bags, examine what I have, and pull out a two-piece black pantsuit, a plain white cotton blouse, knee socks, beige panties, and a standard-looking white bra with under-wire support. I like the fact that Jeremy didn't lean on his French comrades to get me something frilly, girly, and utterly useless in the field.

The shoe bag has three pairs of black Clarks, in different sizes: 38, 39, and 40.

"Sure are being thorough," I whisper.

Then I start to smell myself, realize there are soaps, shampoos, and hot water within reach. I sit on the toilet, take off my boots and socks, and rub my sore feet. Then I slip out the creased photo of my Tom and Denise.

A minute later I strip out of everything else, leaving the damnable elastic band around my chest for last.

I unsnap that little torture device, then for the next few moments rub, scratch, and move around my soft lady parts in a way that makes me feel like I'm a mama bear, stretching out after a winter's worth of hibernation.

I look at myself in the mirror.

Hair a mess, dirt around my face and arms, scratches on my hands, welts along my chest and side. On one hand and the side of my face, the faint brown of dried-up blood. It comes back to me in a long flash of hard memory: the shooting at the farm, the shooting on the mountain trail. I've killed at least four men, and I bear their blood on my skin.

And now I'm on an unauthorized quest to find and kill one more.

I hug myself and think of my sweet Denise and my brave Tom, wondering how they are, what they're doing. Then, in the private and quiet interior of this beautiful bathroom in this luxurious private aircraft, I start to clean myself up.

The few seconds I've spared for my family are enough for now.

It's time to think about killing again.

CHAPTER 29

WHEN A phone starts ringing, Tom Cornwall looks at the illuminated clock on the nightstand by his too-empty bed, sees it's 3:00 a.m., and switches on a light, fumbling around. Two of his burner phones are on the nightstand, and it takes him long and precious seconds to realize that it's his house phone that's ringing.

He tries to pick up the handheld receiver, knocks it off its base instead, curses, and fumbles on the bedroom floor to pick it up before the ringing wakes Denise. In this day and age, having a landline seems like an anachronism, but Amy has insisted that they keep one in the event the cell-phone networks get overwhelmed or their cell towers get sabotaged.

Tom gets out of bed, steps on the phone, swears again, and picks it up. Thinking *Hey, it just might be Amy,* he quickly answers it.

"Cornwall."

A woman's husky voice comes back at him. "Tom? It's Victoria."

He sits down on the bed, scratches his left side. Victoria, one of the reporters who works for Criterion, and who always insists on working nights. She loves surfing chat rooms and overseas news agencies—"We arrogant folks in this part of the world think things happen only when we're awake," she once told Tom over the phone—and her work often leads to Criterion's getting the jump on the competition during the early-morning hours on the East Coast.

"Victoria, hey, what's up?"

"Sorry to wake you, but I thought you'd like to get a sniff of this before I file my own piece."

Something tingling starts along his feet and hands. Victoria—or Vicky the Vampire, as some call her in the newsroom, since she is never seen during the daytime—jealously guards her sources and her stories, and this phone call is out of place.

"Go on," he says.

"The *Washington Post* moved a little blurb about an hour ago on their website," she says. "Looks like a team of mercenaries got lost in the mountains of northern Lebanon. Three members supposedly out on a rogue mission, hunting terrorists."

"Oh," Tom says, feeling like he's sinking deeper into his bed.

Victoria gives a raspy cough and says, "Sorry about that. Twenty years of Virginia Slims and Seven and Sevens will do that to you. Anyway, a nice little interesting story, so I dug around, and that's why I called you. Tom, two sources confirm to me what the story says: the mercenary team is led by an ex-Army officer—a woman."

Tom closes his eyes, for the briefest moment imagining he can sense Amy's scent next to him on the bed.

He manages to say, "Anything more?"

"Nope, that's it."

"I..."

Victoria says, "Look, I've never met you in person, or your wife, or your kid. But I like you, Tom, and I've poked into your office after hours and I've seen your photos."

"Ah..."

"Hey, not that I'm being weird or anything, but I like to put faces to phone calls, right? So I know your wife was once Army—did some hard things and traveled to bad places—and I know she's working now as a consultant. Right?"

"Right."

"And she's gone now, right?"

Tom's mouth is drying out. "Right."

"So I put two and two together. Maybe I got four, maybe I got twenty-two, but I wanted to give you a heads-up. I'll send you a link to the *Post* story, then mine will be up in about half an hour. Good luck to you and your girl, okay?"

"Okay," he says, and quickly disconnects the call.

Tom is in his home office, careful not to bump or trip over anything that could wake up Denise. The office is smaller than the one he had in Virginia, but he's made do, even with the constant drone of traffic outside their townhouse, the incessant horn blowing and distant sirens, the never-ending symphony of living in Manhattan. Only with Amy's CIA housing allowance could they afford to live here, just north of Greenwich Village. Using another MacBook Pro on the cluttered desk, he goes right to his email and clicks on the link Victoria provided:

A three-person mercenary team believed to be working for a military contractor has been reported missing after coming under attack in the Anti-Lebanon Mountains of northern Lebanon, near the Syrian border, government sources in the intelligence community revealed tonight.

The mercenary team was in the area to kill al-Qaeda operatives believed to be traveling to Syria. It's not known if this mission had been a success.

While identifying details of the mercenaries and military contractor affiliation were not released, sources say the leader of this

*particular team is a woman, a former U.S. Army officer with experi-
ence in the field.*

Tom leans back, then quickly starts working the keyboard, seeing that the *Post* story has been picked up by the Associated Press,
Reuters, Agence France-Presse, and his old employer, the *New York
Times.* But none of them has any more information than the original *Post* squib.

He rubs his forehead, knowing deep down, despite his reporter's
skepticism and cynicism, that this is Amy.

What now?

In a few deep and contentious conversations with his wife after
she joined the CIA, she had warned him there would be times
when she'd be out of contact for several days. She had also cau-
tioned Tom that to help her and preserve her career, he should
never try to contact her or anyone else at the Agency, no matter
what.

Still . . .

One compromise.

She had scribbled down a phone number on the back of one of
his business cards, passed it over.

"If there's a time when either you or Denise are near death or
something equally urgent comes up, you can call this number, and
someone will reach out to me within twenty-four hours," she had
said. "And only then."

Hoping to lighten the mood back then, Tom had said, "What
about a zombie apocalypse?"

She had snapped the business card out of his hand and torn it in
half, saying, "You're not taking me seriously."

Oh, what a mistake that had been! Only after some serious
pleading and apologizing had that been eventually resolved.

Tom opens the center drawer of his desk, starts frantically going through paper clips, scribbled names and phone numbers on cocktail napkins and scraps of paper, expired MetroCards and dead pens, until he finds his business card, creased, stained, and held together by tape.

Seeing Amy's familiar handwriting makes his chest feel as thick as freshly poured concrete. He puts the card down on his desk, picks up a landline handset nearby, dials the number with the District of Columbia's 202 area code.

It rings once, twice, and then goes dead.

CHAPTER 30

IN THE semidarkness of his cluttered office, Tom shakes his head slowly and redials the number, carefully tapping in each numeral written in Amy's clear handwriting.

Rings once, twice, and then goes dead.

No *blew-bleep* from a disconnected line, no frantic busy signal, no bored robotic voice telling you the line is no longer in service.

He wipes at his eyes.

Really stares at Amy's handwriting, so much better than his own. Takes a deep breath, uses nearly thirty seconds to dial in the number again. Knowing Amy so well, he realizes there's no chance the numbers are wrong.

Same result.

"Damn it!" as he punches the cordless phone back into the cradle.

All right, then.

Tom pushes his chair back, reaches to the floor, picks up his soft leather satchel, and digs through the side pockets with shaking hands until he pulls out a small spiral notebook with a red cover. Inside are scribbled addresses, email addresses, phone numbers. It's his first-draft notebook where he records raw info before formalizing it in his online address book.

On the inside cover is a phone number that took him a long time to get, involving lots of lunches and drinks he paid for himself, making sure there was no expense-account trail or any other record that could get him or his sources into trouble. After Amy had given him that earlier number, he wanted a backup. Just in case.

He dials this number, and it rings once before it's answered by a very alert and crisp male voice on the other end.

"Four-two-four-six," the man says, saying the last four digits of the phone number.

Tom hesitates. "Is this . . . is this one of the night desks for the CIA? Is it?"

"Four-two-four-six," the man says again.

"Ah, my name is Tom Cornwall," he says. "I'm trying to get a message to my wife, Amy Cornwall. She . . . she works for you, and I think she's in trouble."

"Four-two-four-six."

"Ah, hold on, hold on," he says, and back into his desk he burrows, coming up with a yellowed piece of cardboard—which he hopes he will never lose—that has Amy's dress size, bra size, shoe size, and Social Security number.

He reads out her birth date and Social Security number, then says, "Look, I know this is the CIA, so don't screw around with me, all right? My wife is Amy Cornwall, and this is her birth date and her Social Security number." He repeats both sets of numbers. "She was previously in the Army, 297th Military Intelligence Battalion at Fort Belvoir, and she's been working with you for the past year. Hell, I was there when she graduated at Langley, so stop screwing around with me!"

There's no reply on the other end.

"Please," Tom says, trying to ease the anger in his voice. "I just want to make sure she's okay. That's all. I don't care where she is, or what she's doing. I just want to know she's fine."

"Hold, please," and the line goes dead.

He waits.

Thinks he hears something out in the hallway.

Waits.

A *click*.

"Sir?"

"Yes?"

"I'm sorry, sir, that individual is not a government employee."

With anger, Tom says, "I know she doesn't work for the god-damn government, she works for the Central Intelligence Agency!"

"No, sir, she does not."

Then the man hangs up.

Tom is about to toss the phone across his office when a voice behind him says, "Daddy, what's wrong?"

He whirls around. Denise, standing in the doorway to his office, wearing light-gray sweats and an oversize NY Giants T-shirt.

"Daddy?"

"Ah, I'm just working, that's all. Something came up. You should go back to bed."

She stares at him, lower lip starting to tremble. "It's Mommy, isn't it? She's in trouble. What's going on?"

Hating himself, he says, "No, it's not Mom. Honest."

Denise stares at him, says, "Daddy . . . you're lying."

CHAPTER 31

AFTER JEAN-PAUL takes away our empty plates following a delicious early-morning breakfast of soft scrambled eggs, crisp bacon, and croissants with strawberry jam—all washed down with cold orange juice and strong French coffee—Jeremy wipes his fingers with a white napkin and says, "I know some of your background, Amy, but tell me: where in the States did you grow up?"

I wipe my fingers as well and say, "A little town called LA," which makes him smile. "Perhaps you've heard of it?"

With that smile I feel sorry—and perhaps a little envious—of any single woman in his vicinity. Jeremy has cleaned up well, and now he's dressed in khaki trousers and a pressed blue cotton shirt. His earlier tangled mess of hair and beard have been washed and closely trimmed by Jean-Paul, the cheerful and talented steward.

"And you?" I ask. "Your folks were pretty tight with information about you..."

I was about to say "you and Ollie," but thankfully I catch myself in time.

Jeremy says, "Rather boring, I'm afraid. Knocked about some boarding schools when I was younger, quite a hellion, and then decided to try the Army. Family business and all that. Found it suited me and I suited it. A few dull years and then I decided to try something more challenging and tried out for the Regiment. Then they lent me to MI6...and what propelled you to work for the Agency from the Army?"

I say, "After a life of crime on the road and facing serious prison time, a heavily tanned man offered me a chance to serve my country and stay out of jail."

Jeremy smiles. "Was this man's name Roger?"

"When I knew him, he called himself Paul."

"How long was your life of crime on the road?"

"About three days," I say, trying hard not to dwell on those bloody memories.

"Was it worth it?"

"Very much worth it," I say. "I ended up saving my husband and daughter from a Mexican drug cartel. But I also pissed off the Army, which is why I'm now a civilian. Still, saving my family seemed a fair trade."

"Ask you another question?" he asks.

"Still happily married, never stray. Does that answer your question?"

He looks embarrassed and I enjoy putting him on the spot.

Then he pulls it together and says, "Please don't take this the wrong way, but you're an outlier. A woman in the field...and a mother as well. Why? What pushes you to do that when you could do something as important and safer, riding a desk?"

I delay my answer by taking another sip of orange juice, then say, "What makes you think I have a choice?"

That seems to confuse him, so I take pity and say, "Ever hear of the expression *tiger mom*?"

"Not that I can say."

"It's a term for a mother who will go the extra mile to make her child a success—and, above all, protect him or her," I explain. "They can be ruthless and pushy, and they spend a lot of money and effort. For me, earlier, I was satisfied being in Army intelligence, thinking my work was protecting my country and my family. And I don't just mean my husband and daughter."

"I think I understand," he says.

"I'm sure you do. Over the years you and I have served with some talented, skilled, and dedicated men and women. We share rations, clean socks, spare ammo, and sometimes...our fears, our hopes. Then they transfer out, or you transfer out. But they're still your family, even if years go by without seeing them."

Jeremy nods. At this moment, American and British, we are definitely speaking a common language. All this talking makes me thirsty, so I take one more sip of the cold juice. "About a year and a half ago...that's when my husband and girl were kidnapped by drug-cartel members from Mexico. I got them free, but only after a lot of bullets and blood were expended."

Jeremy just stares at me, and I stare right back. "That's when I knew I had to be in the field to protect my family. I was no longer the type to sit behind a desk, writing reports that might be ignored or misfiled. If I'm in the field, going up against a bad guy, it's pretty damn clear and simple. Me and him. Or them."

"I see," he says.

"Now that you've mentioned New York as a target...that's where my family lives. And others. So when you told me Rashad Hussain might be aiming for the Big Apple, you put a big target on his back. I'm gunning for him, Jeremy."

Now Jeremy nods, in what looks to be sympathetic understanding. "I see. A tiger mom, that's what you are."

I shrug. "More like a werewolf mom."

A couple of minutes slide by and I ask, "Any chance there's a telephone on this flying palace I can use? I need to check in and get my chubby ass chewed out before explaining what I'm up to."

Jeremy rises from his chair. "Certainly. What do you plan to tell them?"

I get up as well. "I plan to plead for mercy—and tell them this op isn't over."

"That sounds like one challenging phone call."

"Then don't listen in."

He moves forward and in a minute comes back with a bulky phone that looks like it could reach the international space station, if need be. I take it to the rear of the aircraft and duck into a small conference room that has another wet bar and a bowl full of sweets in the center of a polished wood table.

I take a seat in one of the four comfortable chairs and dial a memorized number, and it's picked up on the first ring.

"Identification," comes the recorded voice.

"Cornwall, Amy." I rattle off my twelve-digit service number.

There's a hiss of static, and the recorded voice says again:

"Identification."

Damn it, I think.

I repeat the process, speaking louder and more slowly, and once again the automated electronic gatekeeper refuses me entry.

"Identification."

One more time I go through the identification dance, and then the dance is over: the same mechanized voice says, "Identification process halted. Goodbye."

Disconnected.

I dial the number again, and it goes dead.

Damn it for the third time.

We're airborne somewhere over France, on our way to London, and this bulky phone has a nice display screen and a simple web-browser system, and in a couple of minutes I get the number of the American Embassy in Paris—33 1 43 12 22 22—and even at this early hour it's picked up on the first ring.

Another automated prompt, damn it, but I punch 0 and a young woman comes on the line.

"U.S. Embassy, what is the nature of your call?"

"This is an emergency," I say. "I need to speak to Paul Pruitt."

"Hold, please."

There is no Paul Pruitt at the American Embassy. There will never be a Paul Pruitt. But someone working under that name is a fellow employee.

The phone rings and is answered, "Pruitt."

I take a deep breath. "This is Amy Cornwall," and once again, my service number. "I'll be arriving in London in less than an hour. I need to contact someone in my division for a debrief and update."

The man says, "Repeat your name and service number, please."

I do that and he says, "Identification declined."

The words don't make sense. "Excuse me—say again?"

"Identification declined."

"What?" I nearly shout. "What kind of bullshit is this? I work for Ernest Hollister in the Special Activities Division, and I need to come in and talk to someone from my division or any other directorate. I've found out that—"

The man hangs up.

Fuming, I dial the American Embassy again and punch in 0 once more. This time the woman says, "I'm sorry, Miss, but I've been instructed to decline any phone call made from this number. Goodbye."

Disconnected once again.

Damn it all to hell . . .

A soft rap on the door, and Jeremy comes in.

He sees the look on my face and says, "What's wrong?"

I can't believe the words I'm uttering.

"I've been smoked," I say slowly. "The Agency . . . I'm no longer employed, I've never been employed, I don't exist in their records.

Do you understand? Not only have I been fired, I've been cut loose. Anything I've done in the past, anything I'll do in the future... the CIA will deny any connection with me. When I get to London, I'm on my own. I've got no money, no credit cards, nothing. I could be arrested at any moment, even sent to a black site like Gitmo—disappeared forever."

"I wouldn't worry about anything bad happening to you in London," Jeremy says.

I keep my voice low, level, and threatening. "Why? You know something I don't?"

He says, "We're not going to London. We're going to Paris. Rashad Hussain is there."

CHAPTER 32

ON THIS beautiful and bright morning in May, Rashad Hussain is in the Village Saint Paul section of Paris, a block in the area of Rue de Rivoli and Quai des Célestins. Here are the best antique stores and *magasins de curiosité* in the city, and as Rashad moves along the narrow streets of this district, filled with four-story-high buildings with wrought-iron balconies on the upper floors and plenty of shops and stores, he smiles and nods at the pedestrians passing by, including two women wearing chadors.

Rashad stops at one particular store that has suited him over the years. As he enters, there's the familiar *jingle-jangle* of the overhead bell being triggered by the old wooden door. Inside is the smell of dust, of old things, and the crowded remains of the recent past. There are racks of clothes, glass-enclosed display cases, shelves of knickknacks—everything from old leather cases to ceramic bowls to little figurines. In the corners are poles and staffs bearing tattered French flags and Army banners, and from the rear an old, short man bustles his way out through a beaded curtain, rubbing his hands.

"Ah, Monsieur, it's been a long time, has it not?" asks Hugo Fournier, the shop owner, in smooth, slightly accented English.

"Too long, my friend, much too long." Rashad extends his hand

and Hugo gives it a two-handed shake. Hugo has on dark cotton trousers, a white shirt with rolled-up sleeves, and a black vest. His trimmed beard and hair are marble white.

"Ah, but I have two objects for you," Hugo says, "but knowing your preferences, your pleasure, I have not put them on display. May I bring them out?"

"I would be honored," Rashad says, and the old man disappears into the rear of the tiny shop. He browses for a few seconds, seeing the familiar offerings and displays of centuries of French history, and tries to imagine a Frenchman his own age coming in here. Not so long ago, France ruled lands in Africa and Southeast Asia, controlled resources and millions of people, and was considered a major power in the world.

And now? France is known for its wines, cheeses, and run-down immigrant *banlieux* where young men riot and burn cars in desperation against their Gallic masters.

He reaches over a counter and gently pulls out a long wooden cavalry lance with a sharp metal point, a faded triangular blue-white-red cloth pennant dangling near the top.

Empires. They rise, they rule, they fall.

Always.

He replaces the old French Army lance and Hugo returns with two old pieces of parchment, protected between plastic sheets. He lays them atop the nearest glass counter and says, "See? Something for your collection, am I correct?"

Rashad picks up the larger of the two sheets and Hugo excitedly says, "See? From 1903 . . . a stock certificate for the Baghdad Railway. It is a beautiful thing, is it not? Back then . . . certificates like this, they were works of art."

Rashad whispers, "They certainly were."

The certificate is split into two sections, one in German, the other in Arabic. There are intricately designed Roman columns on each side, two large star-and-crescents, and references to old currencies: francs, reichsmarks, pounds sterling. A banner across the top—in French, no less—reads SOCIÉTÉ IMPÉRIALE OTTOMAN DU CHEMIN DE FER DE BAGDAD. He translates the words in his mind: *Ottoman Imperial Company of the Baghdad Railway.*

"It's beautiful indeed," Rashad says, gently putting the old stock certificate back on the dusty counter. "And the other?"

This piece of protected paper is smaller, and Hugo slides it across. About a third of the page is taken up by a German imperial eagle, along with swirling letters and paragraphs. Rashad doesn't know German, but he thinks he recognizes the scrawl at the bottom of the page.

"The Kaiser?" he asks.

Hugo nods with delight. "Yes. Indeed. The original order from the Kaiser to his ministry to begin the negotiations and process to start the Berlin-to-Baghdad railway project. A rarity . . . and it can be yours."

"How much?"

Hugo quotes a number.

Rashad takes a slim wallet from inside his suit jacket, removes a number of 500-euro notes to match the quoted number, pauses, then adds four more. Hugo lifts an eyebrow.

"That's quite generous," he says.

"In the right circumstances, I can be quite generous. And I know I am assured, with the extra payment, that I still have your utmost discretion."

A deeper nod. "But of course, Monsieur. And now, I shall wrap them up for you." He picks up the plastic-protected bits of history and says, "Monsieur . . . if I may . . . I have many collectors like yourself who shop here. But only you collect memorabilia for a railway that was planned but never completed. May I ask why?"

Rashad replaces his wallet in his jacket pocket. "In some ways the telegraph and the railways, they were the internet of the time, were they not? They erased borders, they passed along information and commerce. And many believed they would usher in prosperity and world peace."

"Ah," says Hugo, shaking his head. "Back then, they were so wrong."

"So very wrong," Rashad agrees. "There are some who say that the diplomatic maneuvers, threats, and actions against this railway helped start the First World War by raising suspicions and fears. A railway causing so much war—so much terror."

"A pity."

Rashad smiles. "A pity indeed, to think a railway ended so many empires back then . . . and may yet do so again."

The store owner looks confused, retreats to the rear of the store.

Rashad patiently waits.

Hugo comes back holding a plain brown paper bag with twine handles, and then Rashad says, "Until later."

"Of course, Monsieur."

Fifteen minutes after Hugo's customer leaves, a slim, well-dressed but intense-looking young man in a simple gray suit, white shirt, and black necktie comes up to the counter and presents a photo.

"Did this man come into your shop earlier, Monsieur?"

Hugo isn't about to say a word—his earlier client has odd tastes but is indeed wealthy and pays much more than required for Hugo's discretion—but the man displays a leather wallet with a photo ID identifying him as an officer with the Direction Générale de la Sécurité Intérieure, and Hugo just nods.

"Yes, he did," Hugo says. "Is something wrong?"

The man with the DGSI—France's internal security and counterterrorism agency—slides the ID back into his coat pocket and gestures to the back room. "Is there someplace private we may talk, m'sieur?"

Hugo leads him into a rear area cluttered with cardboard boxes and overflowing file cabinets, and in the next three minutes explains exactly what his client purchased.

The man nods, seemingly just remembering everything Hugo says without taking notes, which Hugo finds impressive.

Then the agent says, "Is there anything else he said that struck you? Something odd? Unusual?"

Hugo pauses, then nods enthusiastically. "Yes, yes. He said something about railways."

The man seems to come to attention. "What did he say about railways?"

Despite his earlier promise to his customer, Hugo feels pleased that he's helping this brave young man and aiding his France. "Railways...he said something about railways once ending an empire, and how they will once again do the same."

The agent carefully nods. "Are you sure that's what he said? About empires ending because of railways?"

"Yes, yes, I'm positive," Hugo says. "That's what he said. Tell me...is that important information?"

The man nods. "Important, yes. But for you...most unfortunate."

And Hugo stares in disbelief as a small black pistol appears in the man's right hand and the cold muzzle is pressed against Hugo's forehead.

CHAPTER 33

AT LE CINQ restaurant in the Four Seasons Hotel George V at 31 Avenue George in Paris, Rashad is finishing a delightful lunch of grilled pigeon and giblets with his most trusted associate, Marcel Koussa. Young Marcel's skin is so light he could pass for someone who traces his family back to the days when Paris was just a muddy village here, under siege by Vikings from Norway, but he's actually from Libya, the offspring of a female British oil engineer and a Libyan tribal leader who had been schooled in the ways of the AK-47 and international contract negotiations among oil cartels.

Both of his parents died in the violence following the Western overthrow of Gaddafi, and those nations' failure to take responsibility for the chaos they stirred up. His rage and sorrow over that event brought Marcel to Rashad's inner circle.

Marcel has changed from before and is wearing a dark blue blazer and a pressed white shirt with an open collar, and his short brown hair is trimmed flawlessly. As he finishes his lamb semolina, he softly says, "I have heard from our contact in Astana. The flight departed yesterday, and all is on schedule for tonight."

"Very good," Rashad says.

"If I can say, sir, having you there tonight... it's a risky move."

"I know."

"There are too many variables. I would think...hope...that you would remain behind."

Rashad gently wipes his fingers on a perfectly folded white napkin. "All of our great warriors, from Saladin to Sultan Mehmed II, have led from the field. It's only been in the last decades that the cowards have remained hiding in their caves or their cement homes, bravely sending out warriors in their name to do their business. No, I will not let that happen."

"Sir, but earlier today...I..."

Rashad gently nods to his Marcel. He knows quite well that Marcel seethes inside, hating his life and world because of his nature and upbringing, being both North African and British, neither society quite willing to take him in and call him their own. There are tens of thousands of such young men in this part of the world, and Rashad is relying on many of them to help him in his mission.

This particular young man is brave and dedicated, and Rashad feels he owes him an explanation, even though Marcel has disappointed him on occasion.

"Yes," he says. "I asked you to take care of my old friend, Hugo Fournier. And yes, Hugo disappointed me by revealing what he knew about me. I could not let that stand."

"But sir..."

Rashad puts his napkin down. "But I know what you're thinking. Why ask you? Why didn't I do it myself?"

Marcel says, "Yes, that's exactly what I'm thinking."

Rashad takes his wallet from his coat pocket, removes a sheaf of hundred-euro notes, deposits them on the pure white tablecloth.

"I could not do it personally," he says. "Hugo was my friend."

After a brief walk to enjoy the spring air of Paris, he takes a taxi to one of his favorite places in the City of Lights. Within half an hour of his wonderful lunch with Marcel, he is standing on the banks of the Seine, looking across the muddy water at the Île de la Cité and its most famous building, the 800-year-old Notre Dame Cathedral with its twin spires, flying buttresses, and intricate carvings and sculptures. The reconstruction work from the blaze years ago continues, with its completion date continuously being pushed back.

Still, it is a thing of beauty, of history—a monument to a Christian empire.

He shifts the paper bag holding his recently purchased items from one hand to the other, recalling his many visits to Istanbul and its most famous religious building, the Hagia Sophia, which once upon a time was a cathedral like this one, named the Shrine of the Holy Wisdom of God.

Once upon a time.

Then the blessed day of May 29 came, and the shrine was destroyed and converted into a mosque.

Like this beautiful building across the way.

It, too, will eventually be a mosque.

And that other cathedral in New York City, the one called St. Patrick's—that too will be converted.

Once the bodies littering the streets have been removed.

CHAPTER 34

THE LUXURIOUS Total SA jet banks in its final approach, and I'm looking over the rear of the couch through its small windows. Below us is a French Air Force airfield, Orléans-Bricy Air Base, about eighty miles south of Paris. I see the familiar shapes of military jets and four-engine transport planes resting on paved runways, along with hangars and a control tower, and part of me thinks, *Well, one more air base on the visited list.* But I'm seething inside.

Plus a bit scared, which I hate to admit.

Smoked.

And for what reason?

I'll probably never know.

All I do know is that I've been kicked out, abandoned, torn from the flock. In my previous career and missions, no matter how lost I was (like being in a Georgia swamp at night during my Ranger training) or how overwhelmed and frightened I was (like being in a dirt shelter in a remote FOB in Afghanistan while mortar shells thundered into the compound), there was always a deep faith and knowledge that I wasn't alone. That friends and allies were merely a walk away, or a radio call away, or a text away.

Not now.

Having been sheep-dipped earlier, I have no official ID, no credit cards, no cash—not even a Lincoln penny. All I have are the clothes on my back, a 9mm SIG Sauer pistol with two spare magazines, and the photo of my Tom and Denise.

Which means for the foreseeable future, I'll need to rely for my very existence—food, shelter, protection—on the compact man with the trimmed beard sitting across from me, calmly reading a day-old copy of the *Daily Star* newspaper from Beirut.

Me depending on a man for my life?

I won't let that last.

I'm still in charge of this op.

We land and quickly taxi to a far end of the air base, at an apron that has two black sedans waiting for us, along with a set of mobile stairs. When the Total SA jet finally and softly comes to a halt, Jean-Paul bustles forward and expertly unfastens the side door.

He snaps off a quick and happy civilian salute to Jeremy and me, and I descend the stairway next to Jeremy. There's a greeting committee of one man standing at the bottom of the stairs; four others in sunglasses and dark suits stand at a bit of a distance.

"Why here and not Vélizy-Villacoublay?" I ask. "You said you were going to Paris. That's the closest military base to Paris."

Jeremy smiles at the man waiting for us, gives him a quick wave. "Because Vélizy-Villacoublay is where the French Air Force keeps its government aircraft, including their version of Air Force One. We don't need the extra eyes."

We step onto the pavement and it seems to be in the eighties—warm for Paris in May. Once our feet hit the ground, we nearly get struck by the mobile stairway being backed away, and then the engines on the Total SA aircraft whine up in power as it starts to manuever toward the nearest runway.

We get closer to our apparent hosts, and Jeremy calls out, "Hey, Victor! Grand to see you!"

The sound of the jet engines drops off and a thick, heavyset man approaches us, all smiles. He has on a light gray two-piece suit, dark shoes, and a white shirt with some French regimental necktie flapping in the wind. He has a thick neck, a nose that looks like it's been broken and rearranged a couple of times, and jet-black eyebrows. His hair has been shaved down to stubble and he smiles as he comes to Jeremy, then has a flash of concern in his eyes when he spots me.

"Jeremy!" he cries out. "So you've made it." He gives Jeremy a two-handed pumping handshake—I half expect to see the traditional kiss on the cheeks, but maybe Jeremy is too Anglo-Saxon for that. Jeremy pulls away and says, "Amy, may I introduce Victor Martin, with the DGSE. Victor, Amy Cornwall, from our counterparts at Langley, and prior to that a captain in the American Army, in intelligence affairs."

The DGSE is the General Directorate for External Security, or as they say in these parts, *la Direction Générale de la Sécurité Extérieure*. Victor approaches me, I hold out my hand, and he gives it a quick shake.

"Amy," he says. "Charmed."

"I'm sure," I say. "This is my first time in France."

"I trust you'll enjoy it."

Victor then steps back, gestures to the two vehicles—Peugeot sedans—and says, "This way, *s'il vous plaît*. We have a briefing arranged that's only ten minutes away."

We start walking and the muscle up ahead splits into groups of two, each going to one of the Peugeots. As we move along, Victor and Jeremy hang back, and I overhear a brief conversation in French between the two.

"Who is she again?"

"American CIA paramilitary."

"Why is she here?"

"She's helping me hunt Rashad."

"A woman? Jeremy, please—let me handle this."

"No, she stays with me."

"Why?"

"Because I promised. And because I need her."

We get to the Peugeots and Victor gestures to the lead car and says, "Madame Amy, if you wish, you can enter the lead vehicle, and we will be right behind you."

I open the door to the second Peugeot. "I wish to ride with Jeremy."

Victor purses his lips. "It will be crowded."

I wait for Jeremy to enter before me. "We won't mind."

Actually, it is crowded with the three of us—me, Jeremy, and the French intelligence officer—shoved into the rear seat, but I don't care, even if my pistol is digging into my right ribs. But I don't move or shift or do anything to display that I might be uncomfortable, not in front of these two men.

Even though I'm being shoehorned in, the ride is comfortable—much more comfortable than I've been used to in the last few days, bouncing around in up-armored Humvees, the interior all metal and sharp edges. As we race along a wide expanse of runway, passing aprons holding Lockheed C-130 Hercules four-engine transport aircraft, Victor says, "Where is Oliver? Is he on his way to London?"

"No," Jeremy says, the words simple but as hard as iron. "Oliver is dead."

"Oh, Jeremy. My condolences."

"He was beheaded."

Victor shakes his head, says a brief prayer in French.

I keep quiet, and so does Jeremy.

*   *   *

Exactly ten minutes later the two Peugeots pass through the wide-open doors of an aircraft hangar and park near three Puma helicopters, their blades secured to landing struts. We climb out of the cars and the muscle goes ahead of us, to an office at the right side of the building. Everywhere there are large signs saying NE PAS FUMER.

Victor leads us in and there's a desk on one side, a cluster of phones and computer terminals, and nearby, a conference table. Three young men in slacks, white shirts, and neckties are sitting in front of the terminals. The muscle takes up positions near the door and in the corners of the room. On the other side of the room is . . .

What?

Yeah.

A buffet table holding plates of cold meats, at least half a dozen types of cheeses, and assorted fruit. There are juices, wines, and a coffee dispenser.

The French way of counterterrorism, I suppose.

Victor says, "Some refreshments?"

"No," I say, grabbing a chair, pulling it free, sitting my weary butt down. "We're looking for a debrief. Where's Rashad? What's he up to?"

I see Victor look to Jeremy and there's the briefest flicker of an expression on Jeremy's face. That little gesture has just marked an unofficial change-of-command ceremony.

Victor knows I'm in charge.

He says to one of the men, "Michel!"

The youngest man hands over a sheet of paper, and Victor and Jeremy sit down. Victor lets out a long, bone-weary sigh.

"As we were afraid," he says, rubbing the back of his bristly head. "Rashad is here. And tonight . . . if all goes well for him— we hope not—he will be taking possession of an RA-115 from a criminal ring operating out of Kazakhstan. We have heard various whispers here and there that afterward he's arranging transport to New York. Manhattan, I mean."

Through my exhaustion and overwhelmed feeling of being here in France, cut off and alone, part of my intelligence training suddenly roars to life, and I'm not a bit tired anymore.

"Wait," I say. "An RA-115? Are you certain?"

"Quite," Victor says.

Jeremy slowly shakes his head. "That's correct, Amy. A Russian-made suitcase nuclear bomb. And if we don't stop Rashad in the next few hours, it's on its way to New York City."

CHAPTER 35

A FEW dark seconds pass, and I look to Victor and Jeremy. There's birdsong nearby, and the far-off grumble of aircraft engines at work, and I smell the cheeses, and that's when you take a breath and hope that in the next few seconds, the two intelligence men—one from Britain and one from France—will break into grins and say, "Fooled ya!"

Oh, yeah, that's what I'm hoping for: that these two capable and brave men will show their manly heritage and laugh at pulling one over on the naïve American woman. (After all, women will believe anything.) But there's no laughter, no smiles, no knowing glances at each other.

My intelligence mind is really kicking into overdrive now, and I feel sick to my stomach, recalling a certain training module I experienced when I was once an Army captain.

I say to them, "You know what will happen if a nuclear device of just one kiloton—one-fifteenth the size of what we dropped on Hiroshima—were to detonate in Times Square?"

Victor nods and Jeremy says, "I think we all know the scenario."

"The scenario..." I stare at the both of them and say, "Back in the Army, I once took part in a classified training mission, complete with virtual-reality helmets. It was like you were really there, south

142

of Times Square on Broadway, standing on the sidewalk. There was a bright flash of light from the north...and then there were fires. Buildings. Cars. Men in suits walking to work. Sharp young women moving quickly, also on their way to work. Little lines of schoolchildren, heading to school. Instantly...all were turned into flaming lumps of screaming, charred bodies. Some of them moved a few feet before dropping to the sidewalk."

Victor clears his throat and I roll right over him. "Others were cut down by all the flying glass, or crushed by the falling concrete. Paint bubbled up on buses and taxicabs from the thermal flash. That virtual-reality training...I was there. I saw it. Felt it. Heard it. Smelled the burning bodies. The training module said in the very first hours of that one-kiloton burst, seventy-five thousand people would be killed outright in Manhattan, with more than one hundred twenty-eight thousand injured. The radioactive fallout would extend from Manhattan all the way to Stamford, Connecticut."

I pause. "That's what the scenario says."

Another few heavy seconds pass.

I have both men's attention, and even the other French intelligence officers in the room—sensing something has changed in the tone, in the atmosphere, from having mentioned something so deadly and obscene—these professionals have also fallen silent.

I clear my throat, wipe my moist hands on my new black slacks. I look to Victor and then to Jeremy, and back to Victor.

I say, "You say Rashad Hussain is somewhere near here, and is going to receive a portable nuclear device?"

"Yes," Victor says.

To Jeremy I say, "And you want to stop him?"

"Yes," Jeremy says.

I shake my head. "We're not going to stop him."

I pause.

"We're going to cut off his goddamn head and put it on a pike."

CHAPTER 36

IN HIS perfectly clean and ordered office in Langley, Ernest Hollister's assistant comes in and takes a chair, holding two sheets of paper in his hand.

"Update?" Ernest asks.

Tyler Pope says; "The smoke order has been dispatched. Amy Cornwall has attempted to check in via the normal channel and at the embassy in Paris. Neither attempt was successful."

"Good," he says.

"Her husband has also tried to reach out."

"Remind me again who is he, what he does?"

"Tom Cornwall," Tyler says, crossing his legs. "Journalist now working with Criterion News Services out of Manhattan. Covers national security issues. Contacted our night desks twice this morning, looking for information about his wife. The first number he tried had already been disconnected after Amy was smoked. He got through the second time, but no joy, of course."

Ernest nods with satisfaction. "Happy to see a reporter getting stonewalled for a change. Just for safety's sake, I want eyes and ears on Tom Cornwall soonest. I want to know what this poor man is hearing from his wife."

"Poor man?" Tyler asks.

He says, "Any man unfortunate to be married to Amy has to be poor. Tell me, where is she now?"

"Sir, she's still with Jeremy Windsor. The MI6 operative. They were going to London, but now they're heading to Paris."

Now he's not satisfied. "Paris? Why in hell are they going to Paris?"

Tyler pauses. "It seems Windsor is chasing after BROKER. Our asset who's in Paris. And Cornwall is at his side."

Ernest feels a cold, deep anger rise inside him. Damn woman. Damn that woman . . . if she had just followed orders, had done her job, this complication, this horrible complication would not have arisen.

And now it was still on him, even if she had been smoked, had gone rogue.

Amy Cornwall was still his.

Ernest says, "How many snatch teams do we have in Western Europe?"

"Two," Tyler says. "One in Sicily. The other in London."

Snatch teams are civilian contractors working for the Agency and other friendly intelligence services around the world, grabbing terrorist suspects and supporters and transporting them to black sites for interrogation—although, officially and legally, black sites were no longer authorized.

Which is true.

There is not a single memo or slip of paper in all of Langley that indicates that black sites are still open.

Ernest says, "Give them the whole rundown on Amy Cornwall. I want her snatched and dumped into a black site in the next twelve hours."

"Yes, sir," Tyler says.

CHAPTER 37

TOM CORNWALL is in his office at One World Trade Center when his boss comes in without bothering to knock. Tom always keeps his door open, but knows from experience that courtesy is a rarely used word in Dylan Roper's vocabulary.

Dressed in his Upper West Side–style seersucker suit, Roper thrusts a sheet of paper out and says, "You write this?"

Tom fights off a yawn, knowing any sign of fatigue would ratchet up Roper's pissed-off meter a few more degrees, and says, "If it has my name on it, I'm sure I did."

Roper says, "There's not much here beyond the piece that Vicky the Vampire moved overnight."

Tom gathers himself and says, "Vicky's piece was just a news brief. I got a few additional comments from reps in the DoD and unnamed folks I know in the intelligence world, plus some background info on the use of mercenary forces by the government in the past few years."

"Is this the big piece you told me about at lunchtime the other day? If so, it's a piece of shit."

The lack of sleep last night, Denise calling him a liar, and his attempts to find out what's going on with Amy bubble up inside

Tom. "With all due respect, Dylan, it's got my name on it, so it's not a piece of shit. And that's a story that broke overnight. The piece I'm working on is going to be much, much bigger."

Roper crumples up the paper, tosses it in a nearby wastebasket. "How much bigger?"

That message from Yuri:

Get out of New York.

"It might approach 9/11 bigger."

Roper's eyes widen. "You bullshitting me?"

"No."

Roper rubs his chin. "If you're right, that's going to be one hell of a story. Remember post-9/11, when it was revealed that the FBI field office in Phoenix had sent out a warning in July 2001 about Arabic students taking flight-training lessons? Some of them were at the controls on 9/11. Yet that warning was ignored—the intelligence agencies were too busy following procedures and protecting their turf."

Tom says, "Yeah, I remember. Lots of folks have forgotten, but not me."

His boss says, "Imagine if one of those FBI agents back then had gotten angry enough to leak it to the *New York Times* or the AP. The story could have broken back then . . . the plot could have been stopped dead in its tracks. Pulitzers all around, thousands of lives saved, a couple of wars averted."

Tom thinks about that, his hands feeling cool with anticipation. His boss is oh so very right.

Roper says, "How much longer?"

"I'm still working on it."

"Have you reached out to your wife, Amy?"

One of his phones starts to ring. He ignores it.

"My wife and I keep our separate careers separate," Tom says, repeating what he's said before to Roper and others here at Criterion.

"But she works for the CIA, right? Or the NSA? Or something like that?"

His phone keeps on ringing.

"She's a government contractor," Tom says. "You know that."

"So why aren't you using her as a source?"

"She wouldn't be my source," Tom says, "and I'm not going to ask her."

Roper nods with disdain. "All right. Then get the story, one way or another. Nail it—or you can explain to Amy how the two of you are going to support a family living in Manhattan on one salary."

His boss leaves the office and Tom kicks the side of his desk, and notes that his phone has stopped ringing.

Damn.

Which one?

He checks out his office phone and his two burner phones. They turn up empty, but his personal iPhone is winking at him.

Voicemail message.

He checks the number.

UNKNOWN

He slides through the commands on the iPhone and puts it on speaker. The first thing out is a burst of static.

And then another.

Then four words from a familiar voice that rivets him to the chair.

"...Tom, it's me. I'm..."

Then the call cuts off.

Amy.

Amy was trying to reach him, just as he was dealing with his dick boss.

Damn it!

He replays it three times, trying to gather what's going on, how her voice is, her mood.

"...Tom, it's me. I'm..."

Her voice is tired, flat, seems tense.

I'm what?

I'm *okay*?

I'm *wounded*?

I'm *a prisoner somewhere*?

Again he plays the message, gets no further answers.

His reporter's instinct tells him what can be proven, nothing else.

All he knows is that Amy is alive, and that she tried to reach him. But because the number came in as UNKNOWN, he doesn't know where she is.

That's all.

Damn it.

CHAPTER 38

JEREMY WINDSOR'S seatmate hands back his iPhone, disappointed.

He asks, "No success?"

"Some," she says. "Not a total failure, but I was able to leave a message on his voicemail before I lost coverage. At least he knows I'm alive."

"And well," Jeremy says.

"That still remains to be seen," Amy replies.

The two of them are in the same Peugeot, being driven through the French countryside toward the setting sun on the two-lane D4 outside Paris. An identical car in front of them contains Victor and two of his staff; a third one behind them carries three armed men and the driver.

The silence is thick between them in the rear seat, until Jeremy says, "Lot of battles have been fought on this very land we're passing through, during the First and Second World Wars. Hundreds of thousands of Frenchmen perished out here."

"You trying to cheer me up?" Amy asks. "If so, you've got a hell of a way of doing it."

Jeremy says, "Just wanting to make a point. The French get

teased a lot about being 'surrender monkeys,' shite like that. Not true. After what they've been through, they're just a bit more particular in choosing their fights. I've worked with enough of them in the field to know that."

"Is that where you and Victor hooked up?"

The lead Peugeot makes an abrupt left turn without signaling. Jeremy holds on to the seat as their Peugeot follows. The road is narrow, ill-maintained, lots of cracks and potholes, but the ride is still a comfortable one.

"Yes."

"Which field was that?"

"Chad," he says, the memory now coming back to him, associated with burning heat in the day, shivering cold at night, and the smell of camel dung. "Victor and I were on a joint operation, surveilling a Boko Haram group on a march. They were approaching a village...out in the open in daylight." The memory gets stronger and he squeezes his right hand into a fist. "Out in the open! We both were able to contact our respective militaries...we had RAF assets and a helicopter squadron belonging to their Foreign Legion at an airfield in N'Djamena...less than thirty minutes' flying time away."

Amy goes right to the heart of the matter. "Why didn't they answer your calls?"

"Diplomacy," Jeremy says, nearly spitting out the word. "We learned later that high-level negotiations were under way among the EU, the UN, Nigeria, Chad, and Boko Haram. Blasting this column away to atoms was going to upset these negotiations. We were told to stand down...and we watched as the village was burned, the men were lined up and shot, and the women and children were raped and then dragged away in chains."

Jeremy realizes he's let loose information about a highly classified operation, but so what? Poor Amy here is out of a job; she'll probably never even get back to America. So what difference does it make?

He goes on. "That's when Victor and I reached our...arrangement. Going forward, if we ever had a chance to do good and screw diplomacy, we would take it."

Amy says, "I'm with you."

"And glad of it," he says, meaning every word.

"I know."

"Do you?" he asks.

Amy says, "I certainly do. A while ago Victor offered you an opportunity to bundle me up and ship me home. You didn't take it."

Jeremy sits very still for a moment. "You heard us."

"I did."

"You speak French."

Amy says, "I most certainly do. Hard not to, considering where I grew up."

Jeremy quickly thinks things through and says, "You told me you were raised in LA."

"I was," Amy says. "Lewiston-Auburn, in Maine. Two closely knit towns with a huge French-Canadian population. You assumed I meant Los Angeles."

He can't help smiling. "Good job," he says. "You fooled me."

"Let's see if I can keep it up."

The driver in front slips on a set of night-vision goggles.

The Peugeot's headlights switch off.

It feels like he and Amy are rushing through a dark tunnel, alone, unable to see a thing, not quite knowing where they'll end up. But he's still smiling, thinking of her, knowing he can't underestimate her, not ever.

His iPhone vibrates.

Jeremy stops smiling.

He takes it out of his coat pocket, turns the screen so Amy can't see it, notes the incoming phone number. Most calls at this time and place he would ignore, but not this one.

The vibration continues.

From his pocket he takes out an MI6-issued combination earbud and microphone, which he places in his left ear, the one farthest from Amy.

He answers the call.

"Windsor."

Jeremy instantly recognizes the voice at the other end. "Is your mission proceeding?"

"Yes, sir."

"Are we certain Rashad Hussain will be there?"

"Quite certain," he says.

"And is that American woman still with you?"

He waits just a moment too long. The voice returns, louder and more demanding.

"I said is that American woman still with you?"

"Yes, sir."

"Get rid of her," the voice says. "Tonight. No excuses, no exceptions. Understood?"

The rear interior of the car is barely illuminated by the iPhone screen, and Jeremy can just make out her shape. The woman who saved his life twice yesterday—is she looking in his direction, or out the window at the darkness?

"Yes, sir," he says. "Understood."

He disconnects the call and Amy says, "Important?"

"Somewhat," he says. "My boss, wanting to know if everything is proceeding on track."

With a light tone in her voice Amy asks, "And anything else?"

He doesn't bother agonizing over what he says next. "Yes. He wants me to get rid of you. It seems that besides the CIA smoking you, you aren't welcome by my folks to come along."

"Nice to be popular," Amy says. "So when are you dumping me? Tonight? Later?"

He turns to look out at the dark landscape speeding by, recalling all they've experienced over the past few days.

"Never," he says.

CHAPTER 39

IN THE passenger seat of the dark blue Fiat Doblò Cargo van, Rashad Hussain says, "My watch says ten more minutes. How about yours?"

Behind the steering wheel, Marcel Koussa looks at his wrist. "Mine says nine."

"We'll go with ten, then."

"Yes, sir."

The interior of the van is dark. Like Marcel, Rashad has on a set of night-vision goggles—Russian-made gear that was stolen off the secret battlefields of eastern Ukraine. Though he imagines he hears voices behind him, he ignores them and continues to look through the windshield.

They are parked among low brush and saplings at the end of a stretch of cracked pavement belonging to an abandoned runway from after World War II, waiting for a private propeller-driven aircraft to arrive. Earlier Marcel had walked both sides of the bumpy-but-still-usable runway, putting down infrared lights that will be visible only from the sky by their pilot from Kazakhstan.

"Tell me, Marcel, have you ever been to America?"

"Not even once, sir."

"So what will happen in New York in a few days, it has no concern for you?"

Marcel says, "I only wish it were London."

Rashad shifts in his seat. "At one time it would have been London. Another time, Berlin. But like it or not, New York is the capital of the world's leading empire. And that is where I will strike. You see, Marcel, I am this century's Gavrilo Princip."

There is no answer. Rashad is not surprised. He goes on.

"Gavrilo Princip was the assassin who killed the Archduke Ferdinand and his wife in Sarajevo, in June of 1914. Two shots. That's all. And within four years, that one simple man had triggered the collapse of so many empires: Ottoman, Russian, German, Austro-Hungarian. Not bad for a simple Serbian nobody, eh?"

Marcel says, "Impressive, sir."

"And I, in the next few days, will shatter their precious New York City. Which will cause that empire to withdraw, to collapse. And once New York and Washington fall, then London, Paris, and Berlin will fall soon afterward. The Americans are the dangerous glue that holds them together. Even my father's friends and businesses in the Kingdom. They, too, will be swept away."

"Then...then, what sir?"

Rashad says, "I don't know. Which is why I will succeed. I make no demands, issue no proclamations, announce no victories. I just do what must be done. And then a new empire will rise—a new caliphate—and I will die a happy man, knowing I had a hand in its renewal."

"How are you sure, sir? That a caliphate will emerge?"

"Who in Europe and elsewhere has more discipline, energy, devotion to religion and families than our brethren? After the West withdraws and collapses, they will take up the challenge—of that I am sure."

Marcel says, "You will be remembered forever."

"Perhaps," Rashad says, looking at his watch. "But at least I will be known as a much more merciful man than Gavrilo Princip. His actions led to the death of at least seventeen million people. My actions, well, if there are a hundred thousand dead by this time next week, that will be a difference, will it not?"

"That it will, sir—that it will."

Rashad says, "I believe it is time."

Marcel says, "It is, sir." His aide removes a cell phone and dials a preprogrammed number that rings once. Marcel then disconnects the call.

Rashad thinks he hears a *thump* somewhere, but he ignores the sound. He slips on his night-vision goggles, switches them on—

—and flashing lights appear on the runway, welcoming in his fellow warriors, here to get paid, of course, but also to deliver something oh so very blessed and important.

In a week's time his mask will finally slip away, and the whole world will know what one man with funds and vision can do.

Just one week.

CHAPTER 40

WE ROLL in darkness to a small, worn-out building that looks like it was once some sort of storage facility. Our blacked-out Peugeot slides in next to the lead car and dims its interior lights. I step out with Jeremy. The driver—still wearing night-vision goggles— leads us past armed guards to a side door, where we duck through a curtain, and here we are.

There's lots of cigarette smoke and bottles of water on a dirty counter, but no buffet table. Things have certainly gotten serious. Victor, who has quickly changed from civilian to paramilitary clothing, says, "Progress is quickly being made. Let me get you up to date, Jeremy."

I stand next to Jeremy and say, "Just so we're clear, Victor, even though we've only known each other for about thirty minutes, I'm the lead officer here. So yes, I welcome your briefing. As does Jeremy."

Again a flicker of a look between Victor and Jeremy, and I sense I've won once more.

Good for me.

"Very well," Victor says. "We will tell you both. Here, if you please."

"Here" is a concrete wall where a large map is secured. A long table holds communications gear—three CCTV monitors and four computer monitors, with hard young men sitting in front of them. There are about a dozen other armed men in full-battle rattle, with black boots, fatigues, belts with holstered pistols, helmets, and black balaclavas covering their faces. All of them carry my old friend, H&K MP5 submachine guns.

Several of the men have rolled up their balaclavas to smoke.

All of them are ignoring me.

And I'm ignoring them right back.

At the map Victor taps a narrow rectangular symbol and says, "This area south of Lesigny was a dispersal field used by the French Air Force prior to World War II, then by the Luftwaffe, and since 1952, it has been abandoned. We are"—he lowers his hand, taps again—"here, about two kilometers from the airfield. According to our information, Rashad Hussain and an accomplice are located here, at the northern end of the sole runway."

"What information is that?" I ask. "How do you know Rashad and his accomplice are actually there, and not a young man and woman having fun in the back of a van?"

Victor steps away from the map and points to one of the CCTV monitors. There, in ghostly black and white, is an overhead view supplied by a drone. In the middle of the screen is the shape of a van, with the white thermal images of two figures sitting inside.

"We have been watching them, without a break, for more than three hours," Victor says. "Ever since they left Paris."

"Good," I say. "Where's the transfer going to be? What do you know?"

Victor says, "There's a private plane coming into this runway within fifteen minutes. There are three Kazakhstan nationals in that aircraft, escorting the device. One of those nationals is working for us."

"And their plan?"

"Once the aircraft lands and taxis to the end of the runway, there will be a...what you say, a handoff. The device in exchange for five million euros' worth of uncut diamonds. Once we have confirmation that the exchange has taken place, we will strike."

I go back to the map. "Where are your units?"

Victor joins me. "Here...we have a blocking force in place to prevent the van from escaping. We also have a section here...and there...keeping armed surveillance on the van."

"And what happens to the aircraft?"

"Sharpshooters will take out the tires and engine, preventing it from taking off after the transfer has taken place. At the same time, we will be neutralizing the van and keeping it in place while the flanking units move in and seize the two men and the device."

I take in the little symbols, remember all the times I've viewed similar maps before, all the times I've placed similar symbols representing heavily armed and aware men and women, ready to do violence in seconds.

Victor's placement of his forces looks sharp and professional. The armed men standing nearby look like a pack of attack dogs, ready to slip their leashes and go on the hunt. The surveillance view of the van, combined with Victor's information about the one man from Kazakhstan working for the French, makes everything seem like a well-tied, put-together operation.

"Victor?" I ask.

"*Oui?*"

I step back from the map, look to him, then to Jeremy.

"This doesn't make sense," I say. "It's going to be a disaster."

CHAPTER 41

MARCEL'S PHONE chimes. He glances down in the dim light and says, "Aircraft right on schedule, sir."

"Good," Rashad says. "Once they land, make sure the infrared landing lights are switched off. No need to advertise our business tonight, eh?"

"Sir," Marcel says.

Rashad lowers the side window, hearing a few night birds and the low hum of an approaching aircraft. For some reason he thinks of his father, and how for his few Saudi friends at the time, having a father with a private airplane meant comfort and luxury. But for Rashad...a private airplane was a pricey mobile jail, taking him to exclusive schools and clubs where he could be of no trouble to his father. Funny how those memories still burn at him with anger.

The engine sound grows louder, then fades as the aircraft heads to the far end of the runway.

The little landing lights on either side of the runway keep up their rhythmic flashing, like they're saying,

Come to me.

Come to me.

Come to me.

He looks through the windshield and makes out the shape of the aircraft, admiring the skill of the pilot, who lands in a long, gentle swoop. Through the night-vision goggles the engine glows a hot, ghostly white as the aircraft slows down, the propeller still spinning, as it starts taxiing in their direction, then wheels about in a neat 180-degree turn close to this end of the runway, where he and Marcel are parked in a wide dirt area, a narrow road leading off behind them.

The airplane halts.

A door opens on the right side of the fuselage and the ghostly figure steps onto the tarmac.

"Kill the runway lights, send the signal," Rashad says, "and then let's get over there."

Marcel types a command into his phone, then turns on the Fiat Doblò's engine and flashes its headlights twice. Marcel shifts the van into Drive and they move out to the runway, Rashad feeling the wheels of the van get on top of the tarmac.

Just a few minutes more.

CHAPTER 42

WHEN I earlier met Victor, he had the cheerful look of a typical French bureaucrat who slides into work at 10 a.m., takes a two-hour lunch with a bottle of *vin ordinaire,* and heads home around 4:30 p.m.

But right now, in battle gear and heavily armed, he looks like he wants to shoot me dead here in this little building, with the confidence that the men under his command would back him up by saying it was an accident.

"What do you mean 'a disaster'?" He nearly spits out the words.

I've faced men like Victor before: higher-ups who can't believe that someone beneath them has a different view or a different opinion. And, in this case, a different way of using a restroom.

I go back to the map and say, "This is like a bad techno-thriller, don't you think? Abandoned runway. Van waiting for the drop-off. Mystery plane coming in from Kazakhstan, carrying not only a Russian-made suitcase nuke but an informant who secretly works for you and gives you everything in great detail."

It gets so quiet I can hear the gentle whir of the fans coming from the CCTV monitors. I slap at the map. "Here. Runway stuck out in the middle of fields and woods. One road leading in and out. Where's the escape route or alternate exit? And where's the security? This van supposedly has Rashad, an accomplice, and what—five million euros' worth of uncut diamonds? And just two guys in it, sitting on a fortune? Doesn't make sense. It's way too dangerous...for them."

Save for one person—Jeremy—the faces of the French intelligence officers and their boss, Victor, are looking at me with open hostility.

Yeah, I figure.

"The flight is coming in from Kazakhstan, right?" I ask.

Victor's voice, clipped and formal. "Correct."

"All right," I say. "Do you know what kind of aircraft?"

Victor is still staring at me. "Cessna. The 172 model."

I nod. "All right. Based on the distance from here to there, and the average cruising speed of a Cessna 172..." I pause for a moment, then say, "You're looking at a full twenty-five hours of flying time. That doesn't include stops for refueling, rest, refreshments, or anything. That's twenty-five hours, carrying a weapon of mass destruction, betting you won't be rousted by customs officials or local police—not to mention hoping the engine doesn't conk out or bad weather grounds you."

Jeremy looks like he's going to say something, but keeps his mouth shut.

"And then there's TRIPWIRE," I say.

Victor looks like he doesn't want to ask the question, but he does. "What's TRIPWIRE?"

"Three modified WC-135 aircraft," I tell him, "either flown by the Air Force or NATO. Originally they were 'sniffer' aircraft, sampling the atmosphere, looking for isotopes and radioactive materials associated with nuclear-bomb tests. These new aircraft have a next-generation detection system, looking for unexplained airborne gamma-ray sources. Like aircraft smuggling in nuclear devices."

I glance at the map and back at the silent crowd. "If you have an aircraft inbound carrying a nuke, then it's passing through TRIP-WIRE's area of operations, and if it's detected, that aircraft is forced down within minutes. I don't believe these smugglers would use an aircraft. Easier to use a truck or a shipping container. So I don't believe your intelligence. This is either a hoax or a trap."

Victor looks to his crew like he's seeking reassurance.

"Thank you for your input, Madame Amy," he says. "But the operation will proceed."

What a surprise.

"If you say so—but I'm coming along."

He shakes his head. "That's not possible."

I say, "You say you're about to seize a nuclear device to be used against my home country. I'm coming along on this operation."

"No, you're not," Victor says. "Jeremy...yes. He's been with me a long time. But not you, Madame Amy—you will stay behind."

I reach into my rear waistband, pull out my 9mm SIG Sauer, point it at Victor.

"I'm not really a stay-behind kind of gal."

CHAPTER 43

MARCEL PULLS the van up to the left side of the aircraft's fuselage. Rashad removes his night-vision goggles, steps out to join him on this pleasant evening. The Cessna's engine is idling and the spinning propeller kicks up a breeze that feels refreshing.

Marcel goes up to the man from Kazakhstan, who has moved to the tail of the aircraft. They talk for a moment, then Marcel runs back.

"We are ready," he says.

Rashad ducks into the Fiat, pulls out a leather case, hands it to his trusted associate.

"Make the exchange," he says.

A minute later Marcel returns. At the open door of the Cessna, two men are working to remove a heavy, bulky item, rectangular in shape and equipped with carrying straps.

Seeing the package being removed, Rashad takes Marcel to the side of the Fiat Doblò, where Marcel unlocks the sliding side door.

"Do we still have enough time?" Marcel asks.

"Allah is on our side," Rashad says, not bothering to check his watch. "Never doubt, ever again."

Marcel slides open the door, and a familiar scent comes to Rashad, and there are voices as well.

"God is great," is muttered, and Rashad thinks, *God, and his agent here on earth.*

Me.

CHAPTER 44

I SAY, "Be a nice guy, Victor."

One of the men sitting in front of a monitor calls out something in a fast stream of French. I can make out only some of the phrases, since Parisian French and the Québecois French you learn in Maine aren't exactly the same.

But I've heard enough:

The plane has arrived.

The van has moved.

And local detectors are recording gamma-ray emissions from the area of the aircraft.

Shit.

Maybe I'm wrong... but my gut says otherwise.

Victor spits out something and a heavyset armed man with dark skin steps forward. "This is Carlos Paqua. He will be with you and Jeremy, as your armed escort...and now we must depart. And Madame Amy, I'm sorry to say, we have no protective gear for you."

I lower my pistol. "Yeah, I can tell that's really upsetting you. Let's go."

Several minutes later I'm with Jeremy, Victor, and two armed men—one of them our bodyguard, Carlos Paqua—in the crowded rear of a black Land Rover Defender. Another Defender is right on our tail. Carlos keeps his attention on Jeremy. I have a feeling that if something bad goes down, Carlos will defend Jeremy first, then get to me at some point after the shooting stops.

When we climbed into the Land Rover earlier, Victor offered Jeremy a protective bullet-resistant vest, and Jeremy in turn offered it to me, and I took it and dropped it on the floor of the Land Rover.

Not practical, but sometimes my anger overcomes practicality.

Jeremy has a radio receiver in his left hand, with a hearing plug in his left ear, and he gives me a running narration as the Land Rover bounces and races its way to the runway, punching through low brush and saplings.

"An exchange has been made," Jeremy whispers. "Gamma-ray emissions still being monitored. Aircraft is starting to depart. The van is going back down the road. Ah, it looks like—"

We break out and we're on the runway, at the south end, racing down toward the north end. Carlos says something to Jeremy, but I can't make out the muttered words. I can barely see through the armored windshield, but now there's the Cessna just ahead. Suddenly a blur of sharp, heavy gunshots, one after another: *BLAM BLAM BLAM.*

Jeremy says, "The aircraft is being disabled."

The Land Rover picks up speed and Jeremy says, "Van is on the move again . . . van is—what?"

My pistol is in my hand.

"What's going on?" I ask.

"The van . . . it's not going down the road," he says. "It's coming up the runway . . . right at us."

Victor barks a command and the Land Rover brakes to a halt. The rear door flies open and we all tumble out onto the runway. The same happens with the Land Rover behind us. Hidden high-powered floodlights click on from each side of the runway, and I see two things unfolding before me at the same time.

The first is the Cessna single-prop aircraft, shuddering and stumbling as sniper fire shreds its tires and shatters its windows. There's a puff of smoke from the engine, then it coughs off and the propeller flutters to a hard stop.

And there's the van, still roaring up the center of the runway. Victor and his men spread out, their MP5s stuttering out in quick three-round bursts.

I have my pistol in both hands, having brought it up to a shooting position without even thinking about it. The dark blue van skids left, then right as its tires get ripped apart. I almost want to yell out, "Stop shooting at the nuclear device, you morons!" when the van comes to a halt, rocking from side to side.

The airplane isn't moving.

Four armed men burst from the brush and saplings at the far side of the runway, running toward the aircraft as some poor shmuck inside tries to open the pilot's door. The French paramilitary squad obviously thinks he's an emerging threat, because a burst of gunfire tears up the door—and him with it.

The van.

The van holding the suitcase nuke.

Harsh floodlights are on the van, and the paramilitary gunmen rise from their firing positions just as another Land Rover skids to a halt and more armed men bail out. Now a line of paramilitary men—Victor and others—are slowly advancing on the van, weapons up.

I'm behind the line of men with Jeremy and Paqua, the gunman assigned to protect us, and I want to move toward the van as well, to see what's there. But my feet won't move.

My feet stay still.

Jesus Christ.

"Stop!" I scream out. *"Arrêtez!"*

Jeremy says, "Amy..."

"It's too easy!" I yell. "It's too goddamn easy! Victor, tell your men to halt! *Arrêtez!*"

But the brave and well-trained French paramilitary won't listen to an American. They won't listen to someone not in their chain of command, and they definitely won't listen to a woman. So they confidently march a few more steps, right as the van explodes in a mushroom of flame, smoke, and heat.

CHAPTER 45

TOM CORNWALL is outside the Olson Manhattan Preparatory School waiting for his daughter, Denise, his computer bag dangling from his right shoulder. The school has an early release today for an afternoon field trip to the nearby City Hall. A month ago—in a spasm of fatherly guilt for not being the best dad ever—Tom had agreed to be a chaperone for today's trip, and he's been regretting it ever since.

He really doesn't have the time.

Still, all things considered, he's in an okay mood. He's got half a dozen calls and feelers out to various sources to follow up on his initial feeling that something big is stirring—something approaching 9/11 status. Even his mysterious foreign correspondent Yuri had given him a quick iMessage update earlier, saying he had something to share later. Before Tom left work, he briefed Dylan and got an optimistic grunt in return, which was pretty affirming, all things considered.

And yes, there is Amy's phone message.

Just four words, but at least he knows she's alive, and the heavy concrete cast around his heart that had been weighing him down has dissolved and gone away. He has replayed the message repeatedly, and each time he grows more confident. Her voice sounds tired, but not panicky. The fact that he received the message in the first place means she had access to a cell phone or a landline, either with caller ID blocked.

Which means cell-phone service or landline service.

Which means she wasn't in some rocky gorge in Afghanistan or some desert in Syria.

A side door to the Olson Manhattan Preparatory School springs open, and a gaggle of laughing and chatting kids streams out. Broadway's afternoon traffic is still moving and honking along nearby, and other parents are clustered near him—fellow chaperones roped in to do some volunteer work at Olson. They exchange sheepish smiles and nods, and Tom joins them as they walk through an open wrought-iron gate that allows entry into the small, iron-fenced yard.

There she is, and again he is nearly overwhelmed at the conflation of feelings that roll through him at seeing Denise, at seeing this sentient and breathing and oh-so-alive human come toward him, the offspring of him and Amy, and his feelings are a mix of love and affection and hopes and dread for what lies ahead for this eleven-year-old smart and tough little girl.

Denise's colorful Vera Bradley knapsack is firm on her back, and her school ID dangles from a blue lanyard around her neck. She gives him a quiet, "Hey, Dad" and a drive-by hug when she comes up to him, and he squeezes her and says, "Got some good news, kiddo."

My oh my, does that light up her face. Denise says, "Mom?"

He squeezes her shoulder again. "That's right. Mom. She called me this morning."

"Is she okay? Where is she? Is she coming home soon?"

He smiles at her and knows what he's about to do is wrong, but he can't help himself. "You know Mom," he says. "She's good at keeping secrets. But she says 'hi' and says not to worry—she'll be home soon."

Denise looks at him suspiciously. "How soon?"

"Soon enough," he says. "Come along."

There's a bustle of kids laughing and goofing around, and a couple of the other parents try to order them into some sort of line. A sharply dressed, no-nonsense teacher from Olson stands at the head of the mobile line, holding a clipboard with a look that says some magic weapon is failing her.

In the confines of the small, fenced-in schoolyard, there's some pushing and shoving, and then—Tom has to look hard to make sure it's true—Denise slips her hand into his.

He gives her hand a soft squeeze.

How wonderful.

Tom doesn't dare look down at her, thinking he might break the spell. So instead he looks beyond the yard and out to the street, and spots one of his watchers.

CHAPTER 46

TOM CASUALLY turns his head back to the school, but there's no doubt: one of his watchers is over there at the corner of Broadway and Cedar, one block up, this time dressed in sneakers, blue sweatpants, and an oversize T-shirt promoting some rock band. The man's steady gaze tells the whole story.

Denise tugs his hand. "You got your computer bag with you," she says, sounding like a prosecuting attorney. "You gonna work while we're at City Hall?"

He moves his head again, trying to act as casual as possible.

There.

Still standing.

Damn it, this is enough, he thinks. This is way too much, too blatant, keeping watch on him and his daughter.

"Just a little," Tom says. "When there's a bit of talking, I'll sit in the back and check my email."

Denise rolls her eyes. "Working on a big story, right?"

Right, he thinks, but he's also so happy she's holding his hand, which makes it even harder to do what he does next.

Tom leans over, whispers in Denise's ear, "I've got to run across the street, just for a second."

"But you're chaperoning!"

"I know, I know," he says. "But I'll be right back, I promise."

"Dad...you promised."

He slips his hand away, kisses the top of her head. "I'll be right back, okay? There's a man over there I need to talk to. It won't take long. Promise me you'll stay right here, okay? Don't go through the gate—stay behind the fence."

Denise doesn't say anything, and he says, louder, "Denise, promise me you'll stay right here, okay?"

"Okay," she mutters, and he hugs her like any old dad would do. Then, when a line of cars backs up on Broadway, he breaks free and runs.

Tom slides between two yellow taxis, is nearly struck by a battered white van with paste-on black-and-white letters for a plumbing service, and he's up on the sidewalk and racing hard, his computer bag bouncing at his side. Yep, his spotter sees him—and damn, it was worth almost getting hit just to see the look of surprise on the man's face.

The man spins and runs around the corner of Cedar Street.

Christ, Tom thinks, *that guy can move.*

Around the corner now, jogging in and out, avoiding the midafternoon pedestrians, and he spots the guy almost at the end of the other block, running like he just heard a starter's pistol go off. Then the watcher splits left onto Trinity Place and is gone.

Running hard now, the bag constantly thumping him, Tom reaches the corner of Trinity Place and Cedar Street, looks around in every direction.

His spotter is gone.

Shit.

He stands up on tiptoe, craning his neck, but nope, the guy is gone.

Tom gives the area one more glance and thinks that if he was on his own, he'd spend a few minutes ducking into the two nearby high schools to see if the guy was hiding out there.

Or maybe he ducked behind a tombstone at Trinity Church Cemetery.

Or into that pizza shop.

Tom turns and starts walking quickly back to Denise's school, thinking, *Man, you acted too fast. You should have dug out your iPhone, got a couple photos of the watcher…that probably would have spooked him more than being chased.*

But still, it was good to mess things up, to let his watchers know he isn't just a helpless surveillance target.

When he gets back to Broadway, he decides to be a good citizen and wait for the light. Then he joins the other law-abiding people of Manhattan walking across to the Olson school, and there are the chaperones, and the teacher, and another teacher bringing up the rear, and the dozen or so kids eagerly waiting to get to City Hall, where they've been told they might actually meet the mayor.

Tom stops.

Looks up and down the line again.

And again.

Sweet Jesus.

Denise is gone.

CHAPTER 47

LOTS OF things come into focus. Like I seem to be missing a shoe. And the clattering sound of hail has stopped...and I know, uh, *Amy gal, that wasn't hail, but bits and pieces of metal from the destroyed van, landing on the runway around you.*

My ears are ringing.

I sit up.

A man is on the ground next to me, looking right at me, wearing a helmet, a pulled-down balaclava, wide eyes, an open mouth and...

Nothing else.

There's no trunk connected to the severed head.

Where's my pistol?

First things first.

Where's my weapon?

Need to be armed.

There.

Near a crumpled piece of metal I see my pistol, crawl over and pick it up.

There's lots of shouting going on.

Where's Jeremy?

Over there, on his back. His arms and legs are slowly moving, like a turtle that's been pulled from a pond and tossed on its back. I rub my face, turn around, look at what's before me.

The sweeping, curved line of armed, brave, and confident French paramilitary men are gone. There are lumps on the ground, two shapes crawling, and about two meters away is Victor. He's on his back, rolling back and forth. I get up and limp over to him. His helmet is gone and he's looking up at me, face white under the glare of one of the remaining spotlights. The other spotlight, tilted backward from the force of the blast, points up into the sky.

Victor's talking but I can't quite hear him. My ears are still ringing.

But I don't need to hear what he's saying.

His left leg is gone below the knee, a bloody, pulpy, bone-exposed mess.

He's bleeding out.

I tug at Victor's protective vest, pull it off, free two of the straps, and tie off a tourniquet just above the bloody leg wound. Otherwise he'd bleed out and be dead in just a few minutes.

I give the scene another long look.

The van isn't there anymore. There's just strewn wreckage, an engine, and I make out one tire. A flicker of flame comes from part of the shattered chassis. The blast struck even the airplane, crumpling the near wing. The tail assembly is broken and shot through like somebody fired the world's biggest shotgun at it.

A couple of the crumpled shapes on the ground are now stirring. I can make out the sound of an engine, and another Land Rover is racing down from the other end of the runway.

Good.

Reinforcements and initial medical aid are arriving.

I limp back to where Jeremy is sitting up, opening and closing his mouth, examining his body with both hands.

Good once more.

He doesn't look too injured.

Now, where in hell is my other shoe?

The Land Rover we used is parked where we left it, though it has a flat tire and one headlight out. Another empty Land Rover sits a few meters away. A French paramilitary man emerges from around the rear of the first vehicle, coming our way. His helmet and balaclava are off, and I recognize him as Carlos Paqua—our body-guard. It looks like he's limping belatedly to our rescue. I wave at him and he waves back, and I look at the pieces of metal, wiring, and plastic from the exploded van, opening and closing my mouth, trying to ease the ringing in my ears.

I look back.

Carlos is walking straight toward Jeremy.

Right at him.

He has a pistol in his hand, and he's coming right up behind him. Jeremy is still sitting on the runway, examining himself, eval-uating, and Carlos is lifting his pistol and—

I shoot him right in the chest.

Carlos staggers back, his vest protecting him from serious injury, but the force of my gunshot has surprised him, causing him to drop his pistol. Jeremy ducks and rolls and gets out of my line of fire, and I fire three more times, aiming for Carlos's unprotected legs and crotch, and he goes down with a loud scream.

I go over, strip him of a knife and spare magazines, see his weapon on the ground, and give it a good kick. Jeremy is now right next to me, also holding a pistol.

"What the hell was that?" he demands, his voice cutting through the ringing in my ears.

Carlos is moaning in pain and I really don't care. Men from the newly arrived Land Rover are out and desperately working on their injured comrades. I'm in a rotten mood; if anyone comes to help

Carlos, I'll point my pistol at him and tell him to go away and take care of the others first.

"You're not the only one with backup plans," I say. "If the van bomb didn't do the job, Plan B was to have Carlos put a bullet in the back of your head."

Jeremy takes in the wreckage and Carlos, who is lying on the ground, hands buried in his bloody crotch.

I say, "Somewhere along the line, you must have really pissed off Rashad Hussain. Am I right?"

He just nods, face hard and passive under the floodlight.

"Want to be helpful right now?" I ask.

"Of course."

"Help me find my other goddamn shoe."

CHAPTER 48

TOM IS trying so very hard not to panic but he can't help himself, he's gone through the gate and he's looking at the line of students, staring at each and every one of them, wanting to make sure that Denise isn't hiding, hasn't switched jackets or backpacks or is standing behind one of the chaperones or one of the teachers, good sweet Lord, *Where is my girl?*

Bile is filling his throat and mouth, and once again he looks at that calm line of kids ready to depart, and he has to say something—has to go to one of the teachers or chaperones and say, *Excuse me, my little girl isn't here, do you know where she is?*

And he hates himself with a dark fury that nearly knocks him back, thinking, *You had to go be the brave reporter, had to go confront one of your watchers, leaving your daughter vulnerable.*

What were you thinking!

What happened?

One of the crew keeping an eye on him?

A random snatch?

Jesus, someone from a Mexican cartel, looking for revenge for what he and Amy did in Florida and—

How in God's name will he be able to tell Amy?

"Dad?"

He whirls around, nearly shudders from relief—a wave of love and anger flowing right through him as Denise stands there looking bored.

"Denise," he says, wanting to yell at her but trying to keep his voice low. Sweet Mother Mary, he's never once struck his little girl, but the anger in him prompts him to think of giving her a good swat on the butt.

He takes a very deep breath, trying to control his temper. "I told you to stay still! You scared the life out of me!"

Denise shrugs, like he has just told her she forgot to help dry the dishes. "I wasn't gone long."

"You weren't supposed to be gone at all!"

The lead teacher over there—Mrs. Millett—calls out, "Okay, folks, let's get moving now. Don't forget, we travel as one...and Tom, Tom Cornwall, since you're over there, would you mind bringing up the rear with Denise?"

He turns and calls out, "No, not at all." Then he returns to Denise, standing there by the black iron fence, and says, "When we get home, young lady, we're going to have—"

"Dad, I know you told me to stand there, but the police officer said he had to talk to me. In private."

He snaps right to. "What police officer?"

Denise turns and looks down Broadway. "I dunno. I guess he left. We just went around the corner of the building for a sec, that's all."

"Why did he want to talk to you?"

"He said it was important."

"Denise...how many times have we told you, no talking to strangers?"

She rolls her eyes. "He wasn't a stranger. He was a police officer. And you and Mom always said if I ever got lost or got into trouble, find a man or woman police officer. Or somebody else in uniform."

The line of students starts moving through the open gate. He puts his hand on her shoulder just above her backpack and says, "You weren't in trouble."

"But he wanted to talk to me."

He stops as the line ahead keeps moving. "What did he say?"

Denise says, "Dad, the line is moving. We've got to keep up."

"Don't worry about it," he says. "What did the police officer say?"

Denise says, "He told me to give you this. He said it was very important."

His daughter hands over a folded piece of white paper, which Tom unfolds. In clear, hand-printed capital letters—it appears to have been traced with a pen and ruler to mask the handwriting—the note says:

TOM—YOU WERE LUCKY THIS TIME. DON'T EVER LEAVE YOUR GIRL ALONE LIKE THAT, EVER AGAIN.

He crumples the note and Denise says, "Dad, we're gonna be late."

Tom grabs her hand and they catch up to the students, teachers, and chaperones. His unknown watchers are talented indeed, now pretending to be NYPD.

"No, we won't," he says.

CHAPTER 49

THE SUN is starting to come up in this alleged bucolic corner of France, and my mood has improved a bit since I found my missing shoe a few hours earlier. But not by much.

The runway is pretty busy this morning for a place that is an abandoned afterthought, and I'm sticking by Jeremy as the place gets crowded with additional DGSE personnel, medical responders, and red-and-yellow fire trucks from the local *sapeurs-pompiers*. Earlier Jeremy and I had received a severe dressing-down from a well-dressed older woman who I gather was Victor's boss, but her angry Parisian French overwhelmed my translating abilities, so all I got from her was that she was one very angry woman.

Now Jeremy and I are observing a preliminary forensic examination of the destroyed van. We stand in front of what's left of the cab, containing two charred lumps of what were once human beings, but the flesh has turned to dark charcoal and the fused arms have folded back, almost fetus-like, as if in their last few moments of agony in life they were trying to return to the safety of the womb.

Jeremy says, "I doubt any one of those two are Rashad."

"Agreed," I say. "Easy to hire two unemployed migrants or local men to act as passenger and driver." I walk closer and a forensics tech in a white jumpsuit barks at me, but I ignore him. I pick up a charred piece of honeycombed plastic, rotate it in my hand, show it to Jeremy.

"Thermal protective barrier," I say. "You can hide two guys in the van while the drones pick up only the driver and passenger. Simple thing to quickly switch places when the trade was made after the Cessna landed...then you leave the side door open, and when the van heads out to the runway, the original two occupants—Rashad and his friend—roll out and slip into the woods. The drones would be tracking the van, and they would easily miss something like that."

I toss the plastic back into the wreckage. Jeremy says, "I got a quick word with one of the investigators. Two of the Kazakh men are dead. The other was wounded...and all he knew was that he was flying here to drop off a very valuable package and pick up some diamonds."

"There'll be some real diamonds in whatever package they were using," I say. "The rest will be cubic zirconia. Guaranteed."

I walk around to the crumpled rear of the van, where two more forensic types in bright yellow protective radiation gear, respirators, gloves, and face masks are examining some straps; a charred, square-shaped canvas knapsack big enough to hold a refrigerator; wires; and a number of dull-gray tubes.

"Gamma-ray source," I tell Jeremy. "Medical device, small-scale radioactive processing machine—something similar. Shield it so it's covered. At a certain point, pull off the shielding, gamma-ray radiation starts emitting, and if you think a suitcase nuke is coming your way, this will make your detection devices start screaming."

I step back, knowing that whatever's being emitted there is low dose and not too dangerous, but why take chances?

Damn, it feels good having shoes on.

I look at the wreckage at my feet, see a discarded MP5 on the ground with spare magazines taped to it. I squat down, start stripping the magazines of their 9mm rounds.

"What are you doing?" Jeremy asks. His face is blackened and there's a deep gash on his left cheek above his neatly trimmed beard, but otherwise he looks okay. I think of what he said earlier about the bravery of French soldiers, and I shudder, knowing deep inside that the only reason Jeremy and I are walking and breathing is because the line of paramilitary agents in front of us took the blow of the exploding van.

"Reloading," I say, dropping the 9mm rounds into my blazer pockets. "We're still on the hunt, right? And I don't think there's an ammo store around here, do you?"

I stand up, wince at the pain in my side. Probably some good bruising on my right ribs, if and when I get a chance to look at them.

We both turn at the sound of a high-low siren, and three black Peugeots roar down the runway. "It looks like some heavy brass is rolling in," says Jeremy. "Amy, we need to get out of here, and now. We can't afford to stick around and be interrogated."

"Agreed," I say, "but I need to clear something up."

"Make it quick."

"I'll do my best," I say. "Back in Lebanon, Ollie was beheaded, and you were up next for the guy with the sword. That wasn't somebody killing an MI6 team that they captured. No, they would have celebrated your capture, gotten a huge propaganda victory over the infidels, held you for ransom, have the two of you be the lead stories on Al Jazeera day after day, yadda-yadda-yadda. In other words, it was something personal."

Jeremy is watching the three Peugeots brake to a halt. I say, "The swordsman there at the farm, the one who slipped away. Rashad, or one of his men?"

Jeremy says, "Rashad."

"And this whole mess"—I spread my left arm—"had two goals. One was to divert resources from whatever Rashad has planned for May 29. The other was to kill Victor, and kill you. Agreed?"

The Peugeot doors are open. The senior Frenchwoman who had chewed out our asses is now in a huddle with other officious-looking men and women.

"Agreed," Jeremy says. "Look, Amy, we don't have much time—"

I interrupt. "You tell me why he's after you, Jeremy, and why Rashad is making it personal, or I'm going to stay here and reveal all. Hell, I'm not even a government employee anymore. I hear the food for high-value prisoners here in France is pretty damn good."

Jeremy turns to me, his face now haunted. "My father...and Rashad's father. They were once best friends."

A pause that seems as heavy as a barrel filled with lead.

He says, "And Rashad killed them both."

CHAPTER 50

NADIA KHADRA is having an early outdoor breakfast this morning of strong coffee and fresh crossiants at Café Falguière, not far from l'Institut Pasteur. A small part of her is filled with regret that within a very few days she will no longer be working there.

She has made some acquaintances—no true friends, she's never had a true friend in her life—but she will miss the order and discipline of coming here every day and doing good work, then later doing even more vital work at home.

The morning commuters stroll by on Rue Falguière. One well-dressed man with a familiar bearded smile departs from the walking crowds, steps over to the stone patio, and takes a seat with her under the wide red-and-white umbrella.

"*Bonjour,* Nadia," he says, sitting down directly across from her. He's carrying a large shopping bag from Le Bon Marché that he carefully places between his gray-trousered legs.

She just nods in return, trying once again to puzzle out what's behind those cheery brown eyes, that confident smile, the way he carries himself, and how he had seduced her—with his charm and intelligence only—nearly a year ago. He is dressed like other times she has met him: a fine suit of light blue or gray and a white shirt with no necktie, though something bulky is around his left wrist, like he is wearing a bandage under his shirt.

He says, "How is your mood? Are you ready for your travels?"

"I am."

He says, "Very well. I have some items for you. Here."

Her benefactor moves the chair back, brings the bag over so she can look down as he opens the top. Inside is a silver ribbed briefcase with a black handle.

"That will be the container for your items," he says. "Inside is a protected compartment, immune to any scanning device at the airport. To get access, you pull the handle up and twist clockwise at the same time. Understand?"

"Yes, I do," she says.

"Very good," he says. "Your ticket from Charles de Gaulle to JFK is enclosed, along with your American passport—with your own name, which will make it easier for you—and what the Americans call Global Entry."

"What is that?"

With a wide smile, he says, "According to the Americans, you are a 'trusted traveler.'"

Rashad studies the woman sitting before him, a true beauty if she would do something with her rough complexion, trim her heavy eyebrows, and wear something more fashionable—which is why he dips back into the package once more.

He pulls out a thin white cardboard box, far enough so she can view it, and says, "I need the hand-off in Manhattan to go smoothly."

Nadia checks out the box and says, "What is this?"

He puts the box back in. "A simple black dress, that's all. And . . ." Rashad takes out a smaller paper bag and from it removes a thin black belt with a red, jewel-like fastener. "The day of your arrival, you are to wear this dress and this belt."

"It's rather...gaudy."

"I know," Rashad says. "Which is why when you arrive in Manhattan, your contact will be able to see you in the crowd. I will provide you with a cell phone with a preprogrammed number to call him, but with this bright belt there will be no chance of a missed identification. Along with your ticket are the directions to use the New York subway. It has all been arranged."

His woman appears to consider this, then takes the bag and moves it to her side of the table.

"The contact in Manhattan...he is prepared to receive my package?"

"He is."

Nadia looks suspicious. "Are you sure? This...material, it's not effective if you just walk around downtown Manhattan, shaking out the bags. Or drop it off the top of the Empire State Building. You need a delivery system. A sophisticated delivery system."

Rashad is once again impressed by the woman's intelligence. "We have one. One that has been carefully prepared, one that will blend into the background, one that will have the right geographical penetration and get the job done."

She asks, "Passenger aircraft? Trucks? Helicopters?"

"Close," he says. "A transportation system, indeed."

She thinks for a moment and says, "Trains. Subways."

He gives her a pleased nod. He has chosen well.

"Correct."

She glances at the bag he gave her and says, "Very well. If I may...your wrist? Did you injure it?"

Damn, this plain woman is one observant wench!

He makes a point of scratching at the bandage—pulling it free for just a moment—and says, "Ah, nothing significant. Nothing to worry about. But questions...I have just one more for you."

"Go ahead."

Rashad chooses his words carefully. He has gone too far and has done too much to risk it all now, but he needs to make sure this quiet, mouselike, angry woman will do her job.

"What is driving you, Nadia? What has made you do this? How—and please don't be offended—how can I trust you to do what I have asked of you?"

His woman just stares at him, glances down at her coffee cup, and then looks back to Rashad. Her expression is a haunted one.

"My grandparents...they were from Oran, in Algeria. They came to Paris after the war. Then the Algerian War began...in 1954. My grandparents worked for the independence. In October 1961, they took part in a large demonstration, seeking peace and an end to the war." The woman pauses, and Rashad watches her closely. He senses that he has passed her defenses and is now about to learn all.

"Do go on," he says.

"My peaceful grandparents, my dear grandparents, they were gunned down here, in Paris. At first the police lied, as all police lie, especially from a ruling empire. Only two demonstrators were reported to have been shot. Two! It took years for the truth to come out: that more than two hundred men, women, and children had been massacred by the police, with some of their bodies tossed into the Seine."

The fire in her eyes impresses Rashad. "Then you are not doing this as a jihad, for God?"

She nearly spits back at him. "What do I care for jihad? And I don't believe in God. I believe in vengeance, that's all."

Rashad reaches over, gently caresses her wrist. She nearly blushes. He says, "Again, please forgive me, but this...this all happened to your grandparents more than half a century ago, well before you were born. How can I be sure you will travel to Manhattan and make the delivery, knowing what will happen to all the innocents later—all because of something from history?"

Nadia is quick to reply. "My landlady is a dear old woman, Madame Juliette Therien. She is in her sixties, a widow, a grandmother with two sons and lots of grandchildren. She remembers my birthday, and Christmas, and charges me much less in rent than others in the neighborhood, all because she secretly thinks of me as her own daughter."

"I see." Impressive—very impressive indeed.

Nadia says, "If you wish, we can take a Metro train and be at my flat in thirty minutes. I will lead you to the basement, where Madame Therien lies dead on the cellar floor because she learned what I was doing. Instead of telling her a lie, or begging her to keep my work secret, I bashed in her brains with a hammer."

For once Rashad does not know what to say.

Nadia asks, "Does that answer your concern?"

He smiles. A warm feeling of success swells within him. This will happen. This mad young girl is about to fulfill her destiny, and his.

Rashad touches her wrist once more. "It certainly does."

CHAPTER 51

IN HIS sterile and tidy office, Ernest Hollister just sits there, contemplating what Tyler Pope has just told him.

Ernest says, "That was a fine briefing. Are you sure it's good?"

Tyler says, "Ah, it's the best I could put together based on—"

"Is it good?" he repeats. "Don't fence with me, don't parse words, for Christ's sake, speak in plain English. I'm about to take this Cornwall matter to an entirely new level. So I need to know before I go ahead, Tyler, that your information is good. That it is reliable enough that I'm about to put myself into great exposure. Do you understand?"

"Yes, sir."

"Is the information good?"

"It's good, sir," Tyler says.

"Glad to hear it." Ernest points to a chair across from his desk. "Have a seat. You're going to have a busy afternoon."

His assistant sits down. "And the first thing you're going to do is get me on a Company jet, heading to the UK, as soon as possible."

With Amy keeping pace with him, Jeremy Windsor walks with assurance and coolness to the closest Land Rover Defender not damaged by the earlier blast. Amy says, "What's the plan?"

This woman, he thinks. She has saved his life three times in the past few days, and if she's been shocked or rattled by what's happened—by the travel, the shooting, the desperate moments of being under fire—well, she's very good at hiding it.

"Getting out of here is the plan so far," he says. "Not much beyond that."

He goes to the Defender. All four tires are inflated and in good shape. At the rear, on the pavement, are a used fire extinguisher, some clumps of bloody bandages and a crumpled-up balaclava, and a scattering of empty brass cartridges.

Perfect.

"Amy, I—"

"Hey!"

He turns, and a red-faced, sweaty French paramilitary officer is standing there, MP5 in his hands.

In rapid French the man says, *"What the hell do you think you're doing?"*

"Just looking things over," Jeremy replies.

The officer moves his head, his face angry. *"Then come with me. My superior wants to talk to you and the bitch."*

Jeremy says, *"Please, can you just give me a minute—"*

"No!"

"I really don't—"

"Move!"

Then, in English, Amy—quietly standing half a meter away—says, "Jeremy, are we being serious now? Are we?"

The Frenchman is still staring at Jeremy with rage.

Jeremy nods. "Quite serious."

Amy moves quickly: she grabs the red metal fire extinguisher and with one hard swing she hits the French officer right in the back of his head.

He drops like a sack of cement. Amy strips him of his weapons, tosses them in the rear of the Land Rover, then rolls the groaning man over. She binds his arms behind his back and shoves the discarded balaclava in his mouth.

Amy slams the rear door shut.

"I'm serious, too," she says, moving around to the front. "And I'm driving."

CHAPTER 52

FORTUNATELY FOR all concerned, this Land Rover Defender starts up with just the shove of a button. In ops like this one, you don't want to fumble around in an emergency, asking, "Who's got the keys?"

The Defender's transmission is manual, and I get savage satisfaction from hammering the clutch and accelerator and making a quick U-turn. Hard to believe, I know, but when I went through my CIA training at The Farm, some of the recruits had to be taught to drive a standard.

Jeremy doesn't even buckle in as we roar off to the end of the runway, heading for the access road Rashad had used. We travel off the pavement onto a dirt area, then get on a narrow, rough road. Tree branches whip the vehicle's sides as I drive as fast as I dare. The interior smells of gun oil and stale cigarette smoke.

I say, "Hopefully that guy's friends will see him on the ground and think he was one of the KIAs. We should have about ten minutes or so of grace time before they figure out we're gone."

"Maybe not," Jeremy says. "Look what's ahead."

Up ahead are two blue-and-white French police cars, parked at an angle and partially obstructing the road. Two officers in standard uniform stand between the cars, blocking the way to the country road that leads to the D5 highway, based on what I had seen earlier on that large map.

I say, "They'll recognize this Land Rover as belonging to the DGSE, right?"

"They should," he says.

"Well, we're about to find out," I say. "Hold up an identification card, wave it at them."

"What? I don't have an ID card like that!"

"Then use your National Health ID or anything...Now, Jeremy."

I hold on tight and keep our speed up, and Jeremy is waving something back and forth. I join the action, gesturing brusquely with one arm, and when we're a few meters away, the two policemen step back.

We blast through without hesitation. A few minutes later I make a turn and we're heading toward the D5.

I say, "Tell me again about the bravery of the French?"

"Not a good example," he says sharply. "Some are, some aren't."

"I know," I say, speeding up the Land Rover. "I was just busting your chops. And some brave men back there are dead because they protected us."

Jeremy says, "Go faster, Amy"

"Okay."

An hour later we're at a rural cottage south of Lognes—to the east of Paris—in a dark green Saab sedan Jeremy had quickly and expertly stolen from a Super U supermarket parking lot about twenty kilometers away. He directs me down the dirt driveway to the overgrown rear yard, and I switch off the engine.

"You drive well," he says. "Glad you knew how to use a standard."

"Always full of surprises," I say, and we get out. The tiny rear yard is nearly overgrown with brushes and small saplings, and there's an uneven brick patio covered with moss next to the Saab's front wheels. Jeremy goes to a specific brick, pops it up, and removes a key. We go to the rear door of the cottage and Jeremy keys open the heavy-duty lock, and we go in.

Very unimpressive.

Dusty old furniture, a kitchenette that's filthy, and piles of French books and magazines on the carpeted floor. I pick up a copy of *Paris-Match*; it's three years old. The Oriental carpet in the center of the living area looks like it last got vacuumed when de Gaulle was running the place.

"Charming," I say. "But safe houses don't need to be charming."

"That's right," Jeremy says.

"And why do we need to be in a safe house? I thought you were best buds with Victor and the DGSE."

"Victor's section of the DGSE, not the whole agency," Jeremy says. "And there's France's General Directorate for Internal Security, and their military intelligence. We could be scooped up to embarrass the DGSE or MI6, or for any other reason. I don't want to present anyone that opportunity."

I go in farther as he switches on some lights. The illumination doesn't make the place look any finer. I find a toilet with a brown bowl and a shower stall that has mold growing up the walls. A tiny bedroom with a single bed, absent covers or blankets.

Nothing else.

He looks to me, smiling slightly. The abrasion on his left cheek looks better.

"Move, will you?" I ask.

He takes one step to the left.

"Further," I say.

One more step.

"Get to the rear door, will you?"

He smiles once more and heads for the rear door.

I go and move the heavy couch and two chairs off the dull brown Oriental rug. I pick up a corner of the rug and dust flies off, and then I roll it up.

The floor is cement.

Save for a smooth rectangular metal hatch in the center. It has a recessed ring and a keypad.

Jeremy says, "Nicely done."

"Mind telling me the combination, or do you want to open it yourself?"

He strolls over. "I need to keep a few secrets, otherwise my boss will give me quite the dressing-down when this op is finished."

Jeremy squats down, his fingers fly, there's a muffled *click,* and he stands up and pulls on the recessed ring. The heavy-looking hatch—counterweighted somehow—easily comes up, revealing metal stairs descending into a well-lit basement.

"After you," he says.

"Oh, no," I say. "I insist—after *you.*"

His smile remains the same, and he goes down with me following him. The hatch slowly descends behind us, and just because, I have my SIG Sauer out and behind my back.

CHAPTER 53

THE BASEMENT is clean and well-ordered, and after we both take turns visiting a bathroom that's not slippery with filth, Jeremy goes to a metal cabinet in a small kitchenette that also contains a small table and two chairs and removes a light-green cardboard box with French lettering. Across the top in large type is RATION DE COMBAT INDIVIDUELLE RECHAUFFABLE. In smaller type below that is the translation: *Reheatable Individual Combat Ration.*

I ask, "What? Not supporting Queen and country with your own rations?"

He starts opening the cardboard. "I will sacrifice almost anything for Queen and country, save for my digestion. Especially when the host country makes the best combat rations in the world."

A while later we're eating at a small kitchen table. My meal today is a duck mousse appetizer, followed by Alsatian pork stew. Across from me Jeremy is dining on an appetizer of venison terrine and a meal of white bean, sausage, and duck casserole. We're both drinking warm flat water with our meals.

There are black locked cabinets against two of the walls, shelving, and two single beds. The lighting is recessed and comfortable, and the air is dry and cool.

Jeremy says, "While you were using the WC, I checked in with the home office. Rashad is in the UK. Possibly going to London."

"Then let's get moving," I say.

He nods. "Over in that corner there, we have photo equipment to give us both new passports. You feel like being Canadian?"

"Why not, 'ey?" I ask. "But I need a bit more information before we head out. That runway attack. Nice way to spoof you and the French, and come close to killing you and maybe Victor. But was that a one-off? Was it just Rashad looking for revenge? Are you still certain he's planning a mass attack?"

"I am," he says.

"Then share," I say. "If this op is going to nail Rashad Hussain before he attacks New York City, I'm in one hundred percent. I don't care if I'm smoked and depending on you for food, shelter, and travel. The stakes are that high. But if this is just a deal to settle a grudge because he killed your dad, then I'm out."

Jeremy says, "Fair enough." He takes another bite of his casserole. "We've been following him for years. Rashad was always one to be in the shadows, staying aside, not even pulling the strings...but pulling the strings of someone else who was pulling the strings. A suicide attack on a hotel in Mumbai. A bomb at a cruise-ship terminal in Marseilles. A sarin-gas attack in the Tokyo subway. The perpetrators would be captured, and their paymasters and organizers would be identified, and then...the trail would stop. But always, always, Rashad Hussain was there in the far background. One of his corporations or companies or business interests would be nearby, serving as a paymaster. A place for research. Or a gathering point. But nothing that would stand up in the usual court of law."

"What kind of businesses is he involved in?"

Jeremy smiles. "Not oil or anything petrochemical. Amusing, isn't it? Plastics, software development, transportation, computer hardware...even construction equipment and machinery, like the bin Laden family. And for the past year the chatter has increased, saying those working with Rashad were going after something big, something to happen on May 29. And this time he won't be in the shadows. He'll be right in the middle of it. Almost like all of his earlier activities were just practice drills, until this, the main event."

"And your father? And his father?"

"They both attended Sandhurst. He was from Saudi Arabia, my father from...well, what passes for the nobility in dear old England. They both went into their respective militaries, and then into government service. They kept in touch over the years—both of them using each other, I suppose, in the service of their nations."

"Were you and Rashad friends?"

Jeremy grimaces. "That would have been a storybook tale, correct? Two lads from different worlds, finding a common bond from their fathers. But we never got along, because Rashad hated his father and couldn't understand why I didn't have the same attitude toward my own. You see...Rashad is illegitimate. He couldn't get over the shame. He has three half-sisters, but they've always ignored him. I think he hated me for having a relatively normal family life, and he hated my father because he was friends with his own pater."

I finish off my stew, wondering if I can order these French rations for my future overseas ops—that is, if I ever get my smoke order reversed. "And he killed both of them?"

A slow nod. "Yes. Rashad's father was a pilot. One day during a visit, he took my father up for a flight from Jeddah, over the Red Sea, flying his private Learjet 40. A nice, safe, routine flight, but they never came back. A wing was found, nothing else. And later...when I met with Rashad following the air-and-sea search, he smiled and shrugged and said, 'Engine failure. Poor repairs, no doubt.'"

I think about that and say, "He was taunting you. The aircraft they were on . . . it was sabotaged. By recent maintenance work."

Jeremy says, "By an aircraft-maintenance company owned by Rashad."

"No real proof."

"Real enough," he says.

I take in our comfortable little safe house, eager to get the hell out, and look to the stairway leading up to the first floor. Just one way in and one way out. I don't like it.

"And what of New York?"

Jeremy now looks troubled—a look I'm not used to. "I know he's after it."

"How?"

"Because he told me," Jeremy says.

CHAPTER 54

RASHAD HUSSAIN is sipping from a small cup of tea in the foyer at the Claridge Hotel in London's Mayfair section when Marcel Koussa sits down across from him. The ivory-colored room has high windows, sculpted arches, and Roman-style columns in the corners.

"Are they ready?" he asks, gently setting the teacup down in a fine China saucer.

"Yes," Marcel says, looking uncomfortable. "But sir... it's such a risk. Again, I don't think it's wise. After the events of last night, wouldn't it make sense just to... avoid entanglements?"

Rashad says, "It's not up to you, or to me. But it is up to God."

Marcel nods. "As you wish."

"Very well," he says. "And all is ready for tonight's festivities?"

"It is."

"Good."

In a three-room suite upstairs, Heather Morrissey is patiently sitting with her coworker Nancy Pullman as they both wait for their client. Like her, Nancy is dressed like a typical American tourist: mom jeans, loose plain blue sweatshirt, minimal makeup and jewelry. But even with the sweatshirt, Heather can tell her redheaded companion is curvy and bosomy.

Nancy says, "He should be here in a few minutes."

"He should," she says, flipping through the fashion magazine *Grazia*. "But you know the drill...the client is never, ever wrong."

Aside from the few years in Los Angeles when she tried and failed to get an acting career going, Heather has spent her entire life in Montana, except for work travel like this. She has a horse ranch with a detached house that allows her elderly parents to live safely and comfortably, and this job—and its high pay—has allowed a good life for the three of them.

Nancy says, "My gig is cheerleader. What's yours?"

"Soccer mom."

"You got kids? You know he's gonna check."

"No," Heather says. "But I've got photos of me with my two nephews. So relax already."

Nancy looks at the large bed nearby, and the black rubber mats placed around it.

"I am relaxed," she says. "But that rubber...and the rubber sheet under the covers. Makes you wonder how weird he is."

Heather was going to say, *Girlfriend, if you're still concerned about weird clients, you sure are in the wrong business,* but the room door opens and a handsome man strides in, with a relaxed, open, and inviting smile.

"Good day, ladies," he says, nodding. "I trust you're both doing well."

Heather quickly scopes him out. He stands a good six feet tall, trim and well-built, in his mid- to late thirties. Fine tailored gray suit with white shirt, no necktie. Gold cufflinks and Italian shoes. The suit-jacket pocket on his right sags just a bit, like he's got an iPhone secured there. Trimmed beard, closely cropped black hair.

Middle Eastern type, which is fine by Heather. She isn't prejudiced in the least, but she wants to give those brown eyes a steady gaze.

He returns her stare, still smiling.

Heather relaxes. Some clients, they have cold lizard eyes. That's when you know there is going to be trouble, and that's when you walk, no matter the penalty fee.

She says, "Doing fine, thank you, sir."

"Same here." Nancy chimes in, arching her back just the slightest, which Heather thinks is a tad crass. Too soon, she thinks, let's wait awhile.

"Very nice, my ladies," he says, and he walks over, still smiling. "I trust . . . well, I had requested two very specific American women. I hope you're not offended."

"Nope, not at all," Heather says, although a deep part of her that remains a stubborn teen girl from Montana wants to say, *Screw you, what are you looking for, a couple of breed sows?*

"Same here," Nancy says. "I don't mind reliving my cheerleading days."

From a small black leather clasp purse, Nancy removes three photos and the man examines them, pursing his lips, nodding. From her vantage point, Heather can make out a teenage Nancy in a skimpy high-school cheerleader's uniform, the kind that exposes a flat and tanned stomach.

"How sweet," the man says, handing the photos back. "I bet you got a lot of attention from the school boys back then."

Nancy accepts the photos, smiling. "And some of the teachers, too."

The man laughs and moves next to Heather. She offers up photos of her standing with her twin nephews, Justin and Paul, at a soccer field, both young boys grinning with satisfaction into the camera. "Ah," the man says. "The proverbial . . . what do you say, *soccer mom*?"

"One hundred percent," Heather lies, putting the photos away in her own small handbag. The man goes to the other side of the room, retrieves a chair, and puts it near the end of the king-sized bed. He makes a polite gesture.

"Ladies, if you please?"

Heather steps up, slipping into performance mode, and says, "C'mon, Nancy, I've been waiting for you since we got here."

Nancy giggles, comes over and grasps her hand, and the two of them get onto the bed. When Heather starts kissing Nancy, she's happy her companion has recently brushed her teeth.

She glances over at their client. Sitting in his chair, stolidly watching them both. Heather still has her eye on his suit coat that's heavy on one side. She hopes he'll take off the jacket at some point and join them.

And that's when she plans to earn a nice bonus by stealing the man's phone.

Heather's not sure who's paying her extra to steal the iPhone—the CIA, the FBI, the Israelis, the Brits, the French—and she doesn't care. She's done odd jobs like this in the past, sometimes just later repeating pillow conversations from rich and prominent men to intense young men or women who take extensive notes. The extra under-the-table bonuses help provide for her elderly and ailing parents.

This job, though—there's an edge to it. The man who set it up had said, "It's vital that you get his iPhone. I can't emphasize how important it is."

How important? Twice-her-usual-fee important.

Wonderful.

And when the man joins the two of them, frenzied with lust, stealing his phone will be a breeze.

*   *   *

Rashad checks his watch.

An hour has passed.

The two women are nude, their skin is flushed, their bodies are glowing with what appears to be satisfaction, and Rashad is satisfied as well.

Not once during their performance has he stirred.

Not once has he gotten aroused.

As the two paid women performed for him, he sat quietly in his chair, repeating *ayats* from the Koran as they giggled, laughed, sighed, and moaned. Allah had surely been with him this past hour.

Rashad gets to his feet and the two women look up at him with open expressions of lust and submission. An intoxicating mixture to be sure, but Rashad pays them no attention.

Instead he says, "You have both done so well, have pleased me so much, that I will give you both a bonus."

The one on the left—Heather—looks on with keen interest as he puts his hand into his right suit-coat pocket, and the other one, Nancy, covers her mouth as she yawns.

He quickly takes out an Emerson Bulldog combat-grade folding knife, snaps it open, comes forward. Heather yells, "Girl, run!" as he plunges the knife between the soccer mom's right ribs, causing her to cry out in pain and fall back. As the former cheerleader tries to run, Rashad grabs her long red hair, yanks her back, and slits her throat, blood spurting up into the air, over the sheets, and onto the rubber mats.

He moves and the other girl, growing pale, both hands trying and failing to stop the blood flowing from her side, looks at him. He's surprised to see no begging in those soccer-mom eyes.

Rashad reaches into the left pocket of his trousers and removes his iPhone, which he takes special delight in displaying before her rapidly graying face.

"Looking for this?" he says, moving it back and forth in his hands. "How do you feel, having failed to succeed at what you were paid to do? Do you think I have lived these long years among killers, thieves, and betrayers in a desert kingdom to be fooled by a woman?"

The dying American woman spits, and whispers, "You bastard."

Rashad nods. "My father was a Saudi prince and my mother a Yemeni maid, so what you say is a matter of record. No offense taken, whore."

Then he slits Heather's throat as well.

CHAPTER 55

WE DUMP the stolen Saab about a five-minute walk away from the Lognes train station, a two-story concrete-and-glass building. After each paying our fare of two euros, we're soon heading west on a train from the RER A line, the cars colored white with a gray stripe bisecting each one.

Jeremy and I locate an empty corner of the near car, sit down, and Jeremy says, "In about a half hour, we'll get to the Châtelet–Les Halles station. From there, a quick transfer and five minutes later we'll be at Gare du Nord, catching a Eurostar to London."

"Got everything planned out," I say.

He shakes his head. "I wish."

A number of Vietnamese women and their children huddled at the other end of the car. Outside the windows, the passing French countryside is a depressing mix of factories and government housing, the buildings all covered with graffiti. Even in French, the painted scrawls and marks look barbaric.

One after another, we quickly stop and restart at a number of stations: Noisiel, Noisy-Champs, Noisy-le-Grand–Mont d'Est.

"Tell me what Rashad said to you, when, and why you believe him," I say.

"When?" he says. "At first I thought it was an accidental en-counter...but later I realized Rashad is not one for accidents."

"Where was this?" I ask. "In some slum outside Damascus? A mosque in Riyadh? Dinner in Soho?"

"No," he says. "At the British Consulate on Second Avenue, in Manhattan. The United Nations were in town and the consulate was having a reception for the ambassador and about a hundred of his closest and dearest friends."

"Including you?" Amy asks.

"No, not me," Jeremy says. "At the time I was seeing a woman at the consulate, an agricultural attaché. Amanda Trevor."

"Not much agriculture in Manhattan."

"Please," he says. "Let me go on." He pauses, takes a breath. "As you can imagine, the reception was crowded. Very posh. I found a quiet spot near the windows, looking over Manhattan. And then there was a hand on my shoulder."

"Rashad."

"Quite," Jeremy says. "I turn and I'm...shocked. I hadn't seen him since that day in Saudi Arabia when both of our fathers were killed. And he just smiled and nodded to the lights out there, and said, 'Someday soon, my friend, someday soon, the lights down there will be snuffed out. And I will be the one doing it.'"

"Quick question?"

"Sure."

"Why didn't you take the bastard down to the consulate's cellar and waterboard him right there, find out what he had planned?"

"I was sorely tempted to, but then he went back into the recep-tion, and after a few inquiries I learned that Rashad was there as a guest of BAE Systems," Jeremy says. "Couldn't quite cause a diplo-matic row over someone there as a guest, now could I?"

Our train briefly stops at Val de Fontenay, then resumes. More residents of Asian descent board the car. I say, "If I had to, I would have followed the son of a bitch back to his hotel room and then have the proverbial *frank and open exchange of views.*"

"That was a thought," Jeremy says. "Still, later, after the reception was really under way, I tried to locate him...but he was gone."

"And you've been looking for him ever since."

Jeremy doesn't reply, which makes sense, since I already know the answer.

We make a quick transfer at Châtelet–Les Halles. As Jeremy predicted, five minutes later we're at Gare du Nord, the huge transportation hub of Paris. It's one of the largest train stations in the world and certainly fits the bill. We emerge into a mass of shops, wide hallways, and overhanging video displays. I stick close to Jeremy as he purposefully strolls through the chaos of all these people leaving trains and getting onto them.

It's noisy from the PA systems, music, people talking loudly. Jeremy leans in and says, "Watch out for pickpockets—this is one of their favorite playgrounds."

I reply by saying, "They should be watching out for *me*," but then something catches my eye: two French gendarmes in body armor and black paratrooper boots, carrying FAMAS G2 automatic rifles. Seeing these officers slowly walking through the crowd reminds me that I'm currently violating probably half a dozen French gun-control laws with the SIG Sauer in my rear waistband, along with the handful of spare 9mm cartridges rattling around in my left jacket pocket next to a spare magazine.

"This way," Jeremy says, and we step onto a crowded escalator beneath a large video display of a British flag, with signs pointing the way to the Eurostar. A sign to the right says BIENVENUE DANS LE HALL LONDRES and its English translation: *Welcome to the London Hall.*

When we get off the escalator, a number of Eurostar automatic-ticket kiosks are set in a line, and as we stroll past them, I say, "I get the feeling we're not getting on the Eurostar via the traditional method."

He smiles. "Has anything these past few days been traditional?"

I understand Jeremy's pleased look—he's acting as my escort through Paris and then on to London—but I confess I'm also irritated by his cocky attitude, shepherding this seemingly helpless woman at his side. Okay, this woman is a former Army captain and currently a former field officer with the CIA, but it still ticks me off.

I wish for a moment that I could take him down a peg or two.

We go past the kiosks to a gunmetal gray door with a large sign warning DÉFENSE D'ENTRER and a doorknob with a key-card entry system below it.

Jeremy once again shows the rules don't apply to him: blocking the keypad from my view, he taps in the correct code and opens the door.

"This way, Amy," he says.

We enter a narrow corridor with overhead fluorescent lights, and the door slams shut behind us. The floor is scuffed tile and there are three doors before us: one at the end of the short hallway, the others to our left and right.

Jeremy starts to say something when the two nearest doors fly open and the corridor quickly fills with nice-looking young men in fine suits, all of them pointing pistols at us.

I remember my earlier desire to take Jeremy down a peg, and with it that old, wise saying.

Be careful what you wish for.

CHAPTER 56

AFTER A long, refreshing shower, Rashad Hussain is enjoying a traditional afternoon tea with his trusted associate Marcel Koussa at the Millennium Hotel London Mayfair, directly across the street from Grosvenor Square.

When he was at boarding school in Scotland, the afternoon tradition was lukewarm tea, stale scones, and sour jam. Here, costing more than thirty pounds, the service includes homemade sandwiches; warm, home-baked fruit; and plain scones served with Devonshire clotted cream, lemon curd, and preserves.

"Here," Rashad says, pouring Marcel a cup of tea. "My turn to be mother. How did the cleanup go?"

"It went well," Marcel says, drinking the tea with just a touch of cream. "A dedicated forensics team, with the latest equipment and lots of time, may find trace evidence, but I doubt it. My cleanup crew is from Chechnya. They know how to do a good job and keep their mouths shut."

Rashad nods in satisfaction, but there's an edge to Marcel's voice that he doesn't like. Marcel is a good boy and for the most part can be entirely trusted, but Rashad wants to know what he's thinking.

"You don't approve," Rashad says quietly.

Marcel replaces the teacup on the table. "It's not my place to either approve or disapprove, sir."

"But I sense you seek an understanding. True?"

"If you wish to give me one, sir, I will not object."

Rashad lowers his voice. "For years I have been a warrior, and a warrior—above all—must be dedicated to his service, to his God, and not allow any distractions or obstacles to get in the way of completing his mission. I've had success upon success these past years, with your assistance and that of others, but as always, there can be doubts. Am I doing the right thing? Am I understanding God's word? And...above all, do I still have the drive to remain focused?"

Marcel seems to consider this, and Rashad continues.

"My encounter with those two whores was a test. A test to see if I could resist their wiles, their flesh, their sexual temptation. Through God's power, I was able to resist on all fronts. And then... well, there must be no witnesses, at such a delicate stage. Correct?"

"Absolutely."

Rashad picks up another small sandwich, the crusts cut away. "Are you ready for your trip? And the meet-up?"

"All is in place."

He starts to talk and spots a quiet bustle at the other end of the hotel dining room, past the curtained windows and paintings hanging on the pale blue walls. Rashad has a shock of recognition as he spots an older man talking to a hostess, with two younger men behind him. Rashad turns his head, but it's too late.

He's been spotted.

Marcel says, "Sir?"

"A man is coming over here who thinks he's my friend. Act accordingly."

Marcel nods and the approaching man says, "Rashad! What an unexpected surprise!"

Rashad stands up, extends a hand, receives a quick shake in return. The man is stout, dressed in a fine dark-gray suit half a size
too tight, with a white shirt and regimental tie. His thick white hair
is combed to one side, and there are fine webs of broken capillaries
on his nose.

"Sir Mark," Rashad replies. "A pleasure. Care to join us?"

"Oh, no, no, no, can't do that," he says, eyes flicking around the
room. "Here for a brief meet with a writer from *Jane's*. Really hate
to waste the time but one does what one has to do."

Marcel is now standing, and Rashad says, "Sir, if I may, my associate, Marcel Koussa. Marcel, this is Sir Mark Robathan, Minister of
State for the Armed Forces."

Marcel's face grows pale as he shakes the man's hand, and Robathan gestures for the two of them to sit down. "Well, I need to
depart and wait for my guest. A delight meeting you like this, old
boy, and you know, I still miss your father. What a grand fellow."

Rashad says to Marcel, "They both attended Sandhurst."

"Yes, yes," Robathan says, now turning around. "Quite the time
back then, quite the time. Well, must be off. Enjoy your tea. Will
we see you later, at the society's get-together?"

"Wouldn't miss it," Rashad says.

"Ah, wonderful," Robathan says, and he adds, "A pleasure meeting you, Marshall."

Rashad doesn't correct him, and neither does Marcel. The old
man turns and nearly bumps into a chair, and Rashad feels the gaze
of the other two men upon him. They are tough-looking men with
short haircuts, with earpieces and bulges under their jackets signi-
fying weapons, and Rashad returns their hard stares.

They are the guard force for the minister, perhaps MI5 or officers
from the Ministry of Defence Police. Like well-trained guard
dogs—Dobermans or Belgian Malinois—they are taught to respond to emerging threats or danger, and Rashad knows that deep

down these two men recognize him as a threat, as a danger, something to be immediately dispatched.

But all they can do is stare.

They have no proof, no evidence.

Smiling, Rashad stares right back, daring them to do something.

"Later," Robathan says.

"Oh, yes," Rashad says. "Later."

CHAPTER 57

NOW HE and Amy Cornwall are in a small, cramped office at the end of the hallway. There's a metal desk, phone, four metal chairs, and another closed door. A photo of the current president of France is on the cracked plaster wall. A slim woman in black slacks and a white blouse is sitting at the right side of the desk, a thick black leather briefcase at her black high-heeled feet. Behind the desk is a short, plump man in a dark blue suit, with thin black hair and mournful eyes behind black-rimmed eyeglasses.

The moment Jeremy was escorted into this room by the four armed men and quickly and expertly disarmed—his weapons going into one paper sack, Amy's 9mm pistol going into another—Jeremy recognized the man behind the desk. The man motions to the two empty chairs, and he and Amy sit down.

For all that's going on, he's thankful Amy is allowing him—at least for now—to take the lead.

"Sir," he says. "This is unexpected."

The man sighs, places his hands across his belly. In only slightly accented English, he says, "Jeremy, I have been talking to your boss. He is not a happy man."

"Not many happy men in his line of work."

The man turns his attention to Amy. "And you are Amy Cornwall, late of the American Army, and recently of the Central Intelligence Agency."

Amy says, "Charmed, I'm sure... more if I knew who you were."

Jeremy says, "Amy, this is Maurice Richard. Head of the DGSE."

Amy says, "Based on what happened a few hours ago, I bet you're not a very happy man either."

He smiles. "Quite an observation." Then his smile disappears. "Now. Jeremy, this morning's matter at the runway... a very bad business, very bad all around."

"How many did you lose?"

"Officially, four brave men of the DGSE died in a training accident today, with several others injured. No nuclear device, no Rashad Hussain. Quite the muck-up, was it not?"

"A shared muck-up," Jeremy says, "between Victor and me. And Rashad was there. He just managed to get away."

"Yes," Maurice says, rubbing at his nose. "And now your great white whale has swum off to parts currently unknown, although there is a report of a private jet departing the area soon after the shooting began."

"That must have been him, because he's in the UK," Jeremy says.

"Really? Quite fortunate for us all, eh, that he has left France? And that I can rely on you and Horace to resolve this situation to everyone's satisfaction?"

"Fortunate for you indeed," Jeremy says, knowing that while Maurice Richard is an ally, he's also a wily old bureaucrat who is keen on defending his turf, both literal and in the halls of government.

Richard says, "But before you leave, in the interest of French-Anglo relations, I wish to share something with you." In rapid French he speaks to the woman next to him, who nods, dips down to her black leather case, and removes two glossy color photos.

Maurice passes over a photo to Jeremy, who looks at it and then hands it to Amy. "That's Rashad," Jeremy says. "Where was he?"

Maurice says, "At the time of the photo, yesterday, he was in the Village Saint Paul section of Paris. We got this photo from a CCTV system in the area, set up to track . . . well, never you mind. Facial-recognition software on a routine matter popped him up in our system."

Amy says, "What was he doing there?"

"Your wealthy killer and potential mass murderer was about to enter a curio shop. One he has apparently been to a number of times . . . which raises this mystery."

The second photo is slid over. Jeremy looks at this one more closely. A different angle, some distance away, a slim man hurrying out of a storefront, his face obscured.

Maurice says, "Not sure who that fellow is, but shortly after he left, the owner of the store, one . . . " A quick sentence in French, the woman replies, and Maurice says, "Yes, Hugo Fournier. An older shopkeeper, has been in that same location for nearly two decades. Shot twice in the forehead."

Jeremy says, "Nothing taken, I imagine."

A slow nod. "Accurate. Several thousand euros were left behind. As well as some valuable antiques. And the time of his death following Rashad's arrival there . . . a connection."

Amy says, "Sending a message, or tying up loose ends."

Maurice ignores her and says, "But another thing, Jeremy. Our forensics crew dug deeper, and we found something of interest, which we will share with you."

Jeremy says, "Again, in the spirit of French-Anglo cooperation."

"Such things are done, and I hope you will tell my friend Horace this when you see him again. It seems we learned that your Rashad has been a longtime customer of Monsieur Fournier, always looking for the same thing: railroad memorabilia. It appears that—"

Amy interrupts him. "Railroad? Like model railroads?"

A half-second pause from Maurice that indicates severe irritation, Jeremy knows. "No, not model trains," he eventually says. "Real trains. Especially memorabilia from the Berlin-Baghdad railway of the early twentieth century."

"Interesting," Jeremy says.

A nod. "Trains. Who knew? Well, even Hitler loved dogs, so there is that. And here it ends. Arrangements can be made for you, Jeremy, to return to England, to resume your quest. Alas, Amy Cornwall is going to stay with us."

"No," Jeremy instinctively says.

Maurice opens his hands. "Again, my apologies, but that is not up for negotiation. Horace demands that I separate you two, and I am afraid I owe him one. You may go. She must stay."

Jeremy was once in the empty wastes of western Kuwait when an approaching thunderstorm unexpectedly collapsed, the rush of cold air causing a *haboob*—a blinding, deadly sandstorm—to suddenly hit hard.

That memory comes to him now as there's a quick movement to his side, then a grunt and the sound of a chair falling. He turns his head and Amy is standing there, her foot on the neck of one of the armed men, his pistol in her hands.

Her voice is steady and calm.

"Let's reopen negotiations, all right?"

CHAPTER 58

I DON'T think I'm ever coming back to Paris, so I feel pretty good about hammering the DGSE guy behind me and disarming him. That leaves only two threats in this little room—I don't count Jeremy as one, which may later prove to be a mistake—but I'm keeping an eye on the other armed guy, Maurice, and his female assistant. She's young, slim, and attractive, but I wouldn't put it past her to dip into that open leather briefcase and come out with a sawed-off Verney-Carron 12-gauge shotgun and blow me in half.

I say, "Here's my opening statement. I'm leaving with Jeremy, we're not to be obstructed, and we're going to catch the next Eurostar to London."

Maurice stays quiet.

Jeremy says, "Amy . . ."

"Jeremy, with all due respect and affection, shut your trap." I take a smooth breath and help the DGSE guy to his feet. "We're on the trail of a man who has sworn to kill thousands of innocents in my nation's largest city, and I'm not going to sit on my ass while you match favors with British intelligence. Do you understand?"

"A bit," Maurice says. "But it is still not a compelling argument."

"Maybe not," I say, "but try this. You owe me."

He nearly sputters at that. "Owe you! Are you mad? One of my men is in the hospital with a concussion, due to you striking him back at that runway. How can I *owe* you?"

"Because there's another man of yours in the hospital, Victor Martin. Still alive, I hope?"

The Frenchman just nods. "How do you know of Victor?"

"Because I'm the one who saved him," I say. "Tied off his left leg with a couple of straps after a good chunk of it was blown off this morning."

He turns to the woman and says, *"C'est vrai, ça?"*

A one-word answer. *"Oui."*

He turns back to me, nods once more. "I was not aware of those circumstances. You have my thanks. But still…"

Sensing that I'm making progress, I say, "And if we're keeping score, I also prevented one of your men from assassinating an MI6 officer invited on your soil. How would you like explaining *that* to your British friend? This would-be assassin, Carlos—a jihadist?"

Maurice purses his lips. "Only because he was so heavily in debt, as we've recently learned. His…actions were mercenary in nature, not religious."

"Well, my actions aren't mercenary, nor religious."

I thumb the side button on the semiautomatic pistol and the magazine drops out. I work the slide and the 9mm round in the chamber flies out and tinkles to the floor.

I toss the pistol on the metal desk with a loud *thump.* It seems everyone in the small room is shocked.

Including me.

"I've got a mission ahead of me, and I need to work with Jeremy to get it done. My nation's largest city is at risk. If Paris was facing a similar risk, I think you'd do the same thing I'm doing."

The slightest of smiles. "Which is?"

"Which is raising hell and not listening to supervisors when there's no time to argue or debate."

It gets quiet in the room, even though the disarmed DGSE man is staring at me with such hate that I'm sure sound frequencies somewhere are being disturbed.

"*Bon,*" Maurice says. He reaches over and picks up the two paper sacks with our respective weapons, putting them on the edge of the table. "You are correct, Amy. I *do* owe you: for saving Victor, and for preventing the assassination of our mutual friend Jeremy. Get going, and get your job done. For you and for us."

I reflexively glance at my watch. "I think we're going to miss the next Eurostar."

Now Maurice is smiling wider, a hand going to the telephone at his elbow. "No, you won't. *Bonne chance.*"

I step forward to get our weapons. "*Merci,*" I say. "*Nous allons en avoir besoin.*"

Yeah, I think, we are certainly going to need it.

More than two hours later, we're less than thirty minutes from arriving at St Pancras Station in London. I've scored both a good nap and a fine meal, and now I regard Jeremy from our facing seats in Business Premier. On occasion wealthy and well-dressed businessmen and women have strolled past us, sniffing their noses, looking at our wrinkled clothes and unwashed hands and faces. The playground-age Amy inside me wants to snap out, *Give us a break, we're trying to save thousands of innocents like you.* But I keep my mouth shut.

Instead I say to Jeremy, "What do we do when we arrive at St Pancras?"

Outside, the rural landscape of this part of England starts to appear more crowded with buildings, paved roads, and highways.

"We meet up with two of my associates," he says, "and continue the hunt."

I give the buildings outside a nice glance, and suddenly we're back to farmland, rock walls, brush, and small trees. A bit of Shakespeare pops into my exhausted mind:

"This blessed plot, this earth, this realm, this England."

Damn, that Will could write.

I turn back to Jeremy and say, "Why only two?"

"That's what we have."

I shake my head. "No, wrong answer. There's you, who's exhausted and worn out. There's me, who's been smoked. And you have two under your command. All chasing down a cold-blooded terrorist killer who beheaded your comrade in the field, worked up an elaborate scam involving a fake nuclear device just to kill you, and now . . . we're nipping at his heels and trying to nail him before he attacks Manhattan. Killing thousands. Maybe tens of thousands."

Jeremy's lips and eyes tighten.

I press him. "Only four? For real?"

"I've got both field and technical support," he says.

"But just four," I say, once again remembering my Shakespeare. "Not really what you'd call a 'band of brothers.' So what's going on? This isn't a sanctioned op, is it?"

Jeremy, bless him, comes right out and tells me the truth. "Officially, no. My boss, Horace Evans, couldn't get the sign-offs, the necessary approvals. Hard, actionable intelligence isn't there. Plus . . . Rashad has prominent friends in some circles in Britain, and elsewhere, due to his business dealings. He feels confident enough to be seen in public on occasion. But Horace knows . . . and I know, what Rashad wants to do, what he's capable of."

"Like 9/11 once again," I say. "Information that doesn't fit the narrative doesn't get acted upon. Nineteen guys with box cutters able to kill thousands and cause billions of dollars of damage in the space of a few hours? Could never happen."

He nods. "And without the knowledge the higher-ups say they need, nothing ever happens."

I say, "Known knowns."

"What?"

"Poor Donald Rumsfeld, SecDef back in the day. For a while he was a military genius, until he stuck his foot in Iraq and couldn't get it out. Now he's forgotten, hated, ignored. But he said one thing that we in intelligence know so well."

I remember being straight out of one of my early intelligence schools, receiving a speech from Rummy himself. "There are known knowns," I say, "when you know what an adversary is up to. Then there's the unknown knowns . . . where you don't have a clear idea of what your opponent is up to, but you know his desires and capabilities."

Jeremy says, "Yes, absolutely. And then there's the unknown unknowns. Sounds gibberish, doesn't it? But that's the worst: the things out there you don't even suspect, have no intelligence on, no information. Pure unknowns."

I say, "True. Now, tell me something you know that I don't: How in hell are you tracking Rashad?"

That seems to knock him back and I take advantage of his surprise. "There's been a few times you've slipped away to make a call, or receive a call, and each time you've come back like you're Father Christmas dispensing a gift: 'Rashad is on the move. Rashad is in Paris. Rashad is in the UK.' How are you doing it? It can't be his clothes, or shoes. Smart fella like this bastard would change into fresh stuff every day. Maybe an associate, but if that's the case, I'd figured you'd have him rolled up by now. Has to be something internal to him. An implant? Tracking device?"

"Jesus, Amy," he says, leaning forward to me. "Keep your voice down." He lets a second pass, then with a lowered voice says, "Two years ago, Rashad fell while playing tennis near one of his estates here. Broke his wrist."

"Too bad he didn't break his neck."

Jeremy ignores my humor. "There had to be an operation. We found out about it. Highly illegal, very highly unorthodox, but while they were resetting his radius bone and inserting two pins, a tracking chip was installed."

"How good is it?"

Jeremy leans back into his comfortable seat. "Not good enough. Powered by a radioactive source that's fading. When it started, we could practically come up with his exact address. Now, it's hit or miss. It appears for a few seconds, then fades out. And the past few weeks have been the worst."

"So we're running out of time."

"Always, always," he says, looking at his watch. "We're running out of time."

Now the landscape has returned to a more urban environment. There are train tracks running parallel to us, and other trains as well, both freight trains and local passenger lines.

"In the meantime . . . why is he so focused on trains?"

No answer from Jeremy, and no answer from me either.

We plunge into a tunnel for a moment, into darkness.

CHAPTER 59

FREDDIE FARRADY of Scotland Yard's Special Branch is having a troubling and confusing day, and it shouldn't be happening.

Yet here it is.

And here he is.

In New Jersey.

Trailing Mike Patel.

This morning he's traded off surveillance duties with Portia Grayson of MI5, and surprise number one is seeing his target— and suspected terrorist—standing on the subway platform in Astoria carrying a heavy-looking knapsack on his back and a black satchel in either hand.

Surprise number two is shadowing Mike as he takes the W train, passes his Cortlandt stop, then gets off at 34th Street and Herald Square. That's the first time Mike has *ever* changed his regular routine, and Freddie doesn't like it. He likes it even less when surprise number three pops up and slaps him across the face.

Mike takes a PATH train, which goes underneath the Hudson River and deposits him and a few hundred other folks at the bustling Hoboken Terminal in New Jersey.

Now seeing Patel with the large backpack and the two satchels in the middle of all these busy and moving commuters, Freddie grows nearly sick with concern. What is Patel up to? Why is he in the middle of this crowd?

Although he's armed with his illegal Glock 26 9mm in an ankle holster, he also feels desperately alone, with no backup or resources. He can call Portia Grayson, his MI5 boss, if necessary, but what would he say? *Patel is in New Jersey, with luggage?* For all he knows, Mike Patel is running away from his new home.

Luckily the crowds have been heavy this morning, all the way from Queens to here, and keeping track of Patel has been pretty straightforward. Either Patel is one very cool customer, or is innocent, which is—

Damn it!

In the well-lit and high-ceilinged central part of the terminal—looking like a distant cousin of Grand Central—Patel is putting the satchels down and taking off the backpack right near one of the main doors, where hundreds of people are funneling out.

Freddie drops to one knee hard, pretending to tie his shoe, ready to grab his pistol and start shooting if he sees Patel reach for wires or some triggering device. Maybe he'll cause a diplomatic crisis by shooting him, but better that than—

Wait.

Patel readjusts the straps of the backpack and shoulders it again, then grabs the satchels and goes outside.

Freddie gets up and follows him out into the sun. Patel moves quickly, walking south, going one block, then two, and then turning right onto 14th Street, approaching a gated entrance. There are high fences going up and down the block, and there are freight trains and locomotives lined up, some of them slowly moving out. The fences look shiny new.

Patel approaches a small gatehouse and talks to a uniformed security guard. A door within the wide gate is opened and Patel walks in, then disappears from view.

What the hell?

Freddie crosses the road, looks at the large signage near the gate-house.

HUDSON VALLEY RAILROAD — SOUTH TERMINAL

He digs into his back pocket, takes out a folded street map of Manhattan and the surrounding boroughs and cities, flips it open. Computer maps on cell phones are fine, but sometimes it pays to look like the stereotypical tourist.

He passes a billboard attached to the fence, where there's a graphic cartoon of New York's Hudson Valley all the way up to Albany, with train tracks and trains displayed.

At the gatehouse a young African American man in a security-guard uniform—crisp dark blue trousers and light blue shirt—comes out as Freddie walks up to the open door.

"Help you?"

Freddie decides to play it up some. Broadening his British accent, he says, "Sorry to bother you, old man, but I'm curious about this place. Is it new?"

The security guard smiles on hearing his British accent. "Couple of years, I guess. It's a rail line that hauls shit from here and up to Albany and then back again."

"Do you know who owns it?"

He shrugs. "Don't know, don't care. All I know is, the pay is good and so are the bennies."

Freddie summons his best friendly cheerio and pip-pip smile. "Mind if I go in and take a poke around?"

The guard smiles wider. "You're one of those train fans, right? From England? Train spotters, am I right?"

Freddie sees his opening. "That's right, good sir. A train enthusiast. I would dearly love to go in and see what's what."

Now the smile is gone and the guard shakes his head. "Sorry, man—no can do. Only folks in there are ones with a job to do. No tourists. Sorry."

He goes back into the guardhouse and Freddie steps out onto the road, in front of the gate.

So Patel—an HVAC worker at One World Trade Center—is in this rail yard, "with a job to do."

Damn it, what kind of job?

CHAPTER 60

IN LONDON, Rashad Hussain relaxes at the head table of the function room at Quayle Hall on Uxbridge Road in the west of London. The air is thick with smoke and conversation among old friends dressed in formal evening wear, and the Union Jack bunting along the walls frames photos of some of these old friends when they were younger and tougher, as well as a large photo of the Queen under a banner noting the QUEEN ELIZABETH II RAILROAD SOCIETY. A table covered with a white cloth displays models of 1940s locomotives and rolling stock, and there are several framed photos of the Queen taken in World War II, when she was Princess Elizabeth Windsor and a second subaltern in the Women's Auxiliary Territorial Service.

A tap on his shoulder. He turns and Marcel Koussa is there, also dressed in black-and-white attire, and Marcel whispers in his ear, "Sir, your ride is waiting."

"Very well."

He pushes back his chair and the oldest man he knows—sitting slumped next to Rashad—clasps his arm and croaks out, "A delight, my dear friend, a true delight." The man is shrunken, loose leathery skin wrinkled on his face, his dentures very white and his black-rimmed glasses very thick.

Rashad smiles at the old man with true affection. "I will see you next time, my dear friend."

The old man hacks and coughs in what may pass for a laugh and says, "Don't bet on it—God, don't bet on it."

He pats the thin shoulder, which feels like old sticks under parchment. Along the man's left breast pocket is a line of miniature medals from his service in World War II.

"The two of us, we will beat the odds, as we always have," Rashad says. "Always."

One more loving smile, then Rashad Hussain strolls with confidence out of the hall, giving a cheery wave as well to Sir Mark Robathan, second-in-command of this old nation's utterly useless armed forces.

Mike Patel is done, pleased with his work, pleased that he'll be heading back to his flat in Queens in a little while. The day is hot, his water bottle is empty, and he's sick of the smells of oil, diesel exhaust, and old trash and debris. Walking and stumbling among the freight cars and the tankers, checking their serial numbers, making sure the equipment is installed correctly and in the right position . . . grueling but necessary work.

The two satchels are folded into his knapsack, which feels light on his back, and—

"Hey! You! Stop right there!"

Mike freezes, then lets his hands rise a bit—not too much, not too far, you don't want the man back there to know that you have experience in being arrested—and he calls out, "May I turn around? Please?"

"Slow," says another voice, and Mike thinks, *Damn, there are two of them.*

He turns and two security guards, both white, are staring at him with flushed faces. Without their saying another word, Mike knows they must be ex-cops or ex-military, looking to bank another salary following their retirement. They have the same uniform as the man in the guardhouse, except these two are also wearing billed caps.

The one on the left is fat and sweating heavily, with crescents of moisture under the armpits of his light-blue uniform shirt. His pistol is out, held at his side.

"The hell you think you're doing here, hunh?" he demands.

"What's wrong?" Mike asks, trying to keep his voice gentle and nonthreatening.

The guard on the right is taller and skinnier, with thin brown hair. "What's wrong is we've been getting a lot of junkies and homeless in here," he says, "trying to steal anything that can be hocked for a buck."

Mike shakes his head, "No, I've been working. That's what I've been doing."

"What kind of work?" the heavier one demands.

Mike says, "I've been installing instrumentation on some of the tankers and freight cars."

"Instrumentation?" the fat one asks. "That's some fancy shit you're slinging, buddy."

"You got a funny accent," says the skinny one. "Where you from?"

"Manchester," he says.

"What, the place in New Hampshire?" the fat one says. "That's bullshit."

"No, no," Mike says. "Manchester, in England."

"Give us some ID," the other one says. Mike quickly complies, sourly thinking of how many times he had to do this back in Manchester. Sharp demands of *Paki! Papers—now.*

The two guards look at his papers and the skinny one says, "Well, it looks—"

His partner is having none of it. "I don't like it, Carl," he says. "Let's bring him back to the office, get him checked out."

Mike is still smiling but this won't work. He can't afford to be rousted by these two, and part of him starts planning how to handle them—a blitz punch to the guy on the right, then grab his pistol and shoot the slower one in the face—when he remembers something else.

"Please," he says. "I have paperwork. Please."

He goes back to his jacket, hands over a folded sheet of light-blue paper. The guard on the left tries to grab it but his companion is quicker, snatching it out of Mike's fingers. He unfolds it, starts reading—silently mouthing the words—and says, "Ralph, I don't know. Looks legit. It's a work order from Albany about installing some...Christ, lots of numbers and abbreviations. Even identifies this guy: 'M. Patel.'"

Ralph's mood seems to lighten, and Mike—remembering all the awful American political talk shows he watches at night—thinks of something more.

"It's busywork," Mike says. "A waste of time. It's instruments from...the environmental agency."

"The EPA?" Ralph asks.

Mike nods with gratitude. "That's right. Some sort of instruments to measure the air around the trains, check out global warming. That's what they're doing. Me? I just do my job, get paid shit, that's all."

Carl hands him back the phony work order. "Nutty tree huggers," he says. "Always trying to save the world."

Mike puts the paper back in his work jacket, picks up his near-empty backpack. "What fools, eh?"

"You said it, pal," Ralph says, and then Mike just walks away, smiling with relief and delight, knowing that if they are still working in this very spot in just a few more days, they will both be dead men.

CHAPTER 61

THEIR EUROSTAR train is pulling into St Pancras Station in London when Jeremy gets out of his comfortable seat and starts to walk rapidly toward the nearest door, Amy Cornwall right on his heels, pushing through the high-priced passengers who think they're the ones with important missions. He turns to Amy and says, "When we get to our transport, you should be able to make your call then."

Amy looks tired and driven, but in her eyes Jeremy sees the need of a wife and mother to check in with her family. Earlier Jeremy had offered his own iPhone to make a call, but Amy had refused it. "It's not like before back in the airfield when I made my last call," she had explained. "Too much is now going on with my folks, your folks, and the French. I don't want to get Tom entangled in this shit show. If you've got an encrypted system inside your magic bus that works better than what's on your iPhone, I'll wait."

Now he has pushed his way to the closest door as the train sighs and finally slows to a stop. There's a bell and a thump and the door opens up, and he joins the mass of passengers stepping out onto British soil.

Amy is at his side and she spares a glance at the steel arches and girders high overhead, sunlight streaming through the hundreds of windows up there, and says, "You guys sure knew how to build empires and train stations back in the day."

"That's what binds empires," Jeremy says. "Trains. And we built the first ones. Come along, now."

He strides forcefully through the crowds ebbing and flowing around him, thinking of what's ahead, feeling like one of those fox hunters—"the unspeakable in pursuit of the inedible," Oscar Wilde called them—and he knows that in certain polite circles his work and background *do* make him an unspeakable. But the fox he and Amy are chasing is one part sly and two parts evil.

But has the trail gone cold?

Where is Rashad?

And will they get to him in time?

Outside there's a blast of noise—horns, car traffic, the rumble and roar of trucks and black taxis, white vans and buses. Parked near a brick building is a red van with yellow lettering that reads EXPRESS LONDON DISPATCH. Jeremy opens the passenger door and feels relieved to see who's waiting for him behind the steering wheel.

It's Winston Blake, squat and muscular, smooth fleshy face and bright yet hard blue eyes, wearing dark blue overalls with the fake Express London Dispatch logo over the left breast.

"Jer, let's get a move on," he calls out. "I've already been rousted by coppers a couple of times, wanting me to get going."

Jeremy steps aside, says, "Winnie, Amy Cornwall, former American Army, late of Langley, Virginia. She's with me."

A woman's voice from inside the rear of the van calls out: "Hurry up, will you? Winnie's been singing to pass the time, and I'm about to crown him."

Amy passes him by, crawls over the passenger seat, and goes to the rear of the van. Jeremy gets in and Winnie moves the van out into traffic.

"Update?" Jeremy asks.

"Our little bastard is here, in West London," the woman says. Jeremy turns in his seat, peers into the van's crowded rear interior. In the far right is a sealed chemical WC for those long surveillance ops, a hot plate and a small fridge. The rest of the van is choked with communications and surveillance equipment: computer terminals, encrypted radio transmitters and receivers, CCTV screens, and a mass of cables, wires, and two keyboards.

At one keyboard, her swivel chair right up against a counter, is Felicity Cooper, who in another time and place would have been one of the Bletchley Park girls. She's wearing a black pantsuit and a mic-and-earphone combination over her short-styled blond hair.

"Where in West London?" Jeremy asks.

Felicity's soft, pudgy fingers slap the keys as she gazes up at a CCTV screen displaying a real-time map of London. "Along the 600 stretch of Uxbridge Road, in Shepherd's Bush."

Jeremy feels his skin tighten and his breathing quicken—signs of being on the hunt, of knowing your prey is coming into view. "Felicity, could you set up a secure and encrypted phone line for Amy? She needs to make a phone call straightaway."

"On it, Jer," she says, as Winnie mutters something, a horn blares, and Jeremy wonders if it's time to reach out to Horace. Felicity says, "All right, dear, here you go."

Amy takes a small phone keyboard with mic and earplug. She shoves the plug into her right ear and asks, "Do I need to use the international code for the States?"

Felicity says, "No, just dial as if you were in the States, making a long-distance call."

Jeremy turns in his chair, rubs his hands. What to do? Contact the locals, turn them out, make a show of it? Or just use himself, Winnie, and Amy to make a targeted attempt to grab Rashad?

He's looking through the windshield as Winnie—a former taxi

driver who spent years being schooled in "the knowledge," learning every street and alley in London—expertly guides them onto the A40 highway, heading west.

About twenty minutes out.

And even though he's rapidly sifting through options, plans, and possibilities, Jeremy can't avoid listening in as Amy makes her call.

"Tom!" she says, her voice filled with relief and a tone Jeremy has never heard from her—that of a loving woman talking to her partner. "I'm fine…things are all right…I don't have time for a lengthy talk, all right? All right, hon? Okay…Denise…how's she doing? Oh…she met the mayor? Did she wash her hands afterward?"

For the first time since the mountains of Lebanon, Jeremy hears Amy laugh. It's a sweet, delightful sound.

Then her voice switches instantly, like turning a channel on the telly.

"Tom…listen to me, okay? Our vacation trip's been moved up, the one to Ticonderoga. You know what I'm saying. That's right. Ticonderoga."

A slight pause. "Yes, I know. But that's what it's going to be. Love you…give my love to Denise. I'll talk to you as soon as I can. Bye now."

Jeremy gives her a moment, then turns to see Amy staring blankly ahead.

"Bugger all!" Felicity yells, tearing off her headset. "He's moved, the bastard's moved, but my God, what a strong signal! He's at Heathrow…"

"Winnie?"

"Thirty minutes, Jer!"

Jeremy goes to his jacket, takes out his pistol.

"Make it twenty, Winnie."

"Got it."

It looks like her call home shook up Amy, so Jeremy briefly wonders if she'll be up to the job. That's one thing he learned the hard way, serving in the regiment and then going over to the intelligence services: a married life was well nigh impossible, because you can never focus 100 percent on the mission when you have family responsibilities at home.

After that call to her husband, talking about their daughter, looking distracted, will Amy be a help or a burden if and when things go pear-shaped?

There's the sound behind of metal hitting metal, and Jeremy swivels his head for a moment, sees Amy is checking over her own pistol.

He turns back, wondering why he ever had any doubts.

CHAPTER 62

IN HER room at the Hôtel Best Western Paris CDG Airport, Nadia Khadra is examining her luggage one last time before her flight tomorrow, from De Gaulle to JFK in America. Her silver case with the weaponized anthrax is on the blue-carpeted floor, which has several stains on it. Holding the simple black dress provided by her benefactor, Nadia takes out the leather belt with the ugly red-jeweled fastener.

She steps over to the poorly cleaned bathroom and holds the dress and belt up, looking in the mirror.

Ugly indeed—but if it gets the job done, so what? There is also a cell phone programmed with the number of her contact in Manhattan, and she appreciates the steps her sponsor has taken to make sure everything works.

She hears the roar of a jet taking off from the airport nearby. This hotel isn't luxurious, but it's reasonably priced and full of travelers, so there's little chance she'll run into anyone she knows. It also has the benefit of a free—and anonymous—shuttle service that will take her to Charles de Gaulle.

Nadia goes back and tosses the dress and belt on the bed, sits on its edge and reinspects her passport, her boarding pass, everything she needs to leave early tomorrow and fly to America.

America.

Something cool is at the back of her throat, and she imagines all of the agencies out there in America—all looking for her, perhaps: Homeland Security. FBI. CIA. New York Police Department. Can she do it? Can she?

Her hands start to tremble.

Does she have the strength?

Nadia reaches across the bed to her small brown purse, opens it, and takes out her wallet. From deep in its recesses she removes two black-and-white photos. One is of her *papy* and *mémère* back in Oran, smiling happily at the camera. She brushes the photo with her fingers, feeling a bond with them even though they were long gone before her birth.

And then there's the other black-and-white photo, which she had gotten after years of research, nagging, and bribes. It's been folded and refolded many times, and stamped on the border at the bottom edge of the photo is the word *CLASSIFIÉ*.

Nadia bites her lip as she looks at the photo, which shows two dead and bloated bodies being dragged out of the Seine like so much trash by French Army personnel.

Her *papy* and *mémère*.

She puts the photos back in her wallet and smiles as she realizes her hands aren't shaking anymore.

In the departure lounge, waiting to be called, Rashad Hussain crosses his legs and sips his tonic water with lime, and lime only. The room is comfortable and quiet, with no blaring TVs dangling from the ceiling, broadcasting CNN International or some other nonsense.

He feels relaxed, fine, and filled with the sharp pleasure of knowing that his mission is succeeding, and that he's ready for the next step: to go to the heart of the empire he despises most and oversee its collapse.

Another sip of the sharp, biting drink. His right arm feels stiff. Like his dear Nadia from l'Institut Pasteur, he, too, is a trusted traveler, heading out under another name.

Rashad looks around at the other first-class passengers waiting here—the "one percent of the one percent," as some rabble-rousing newspaper writers and commentators have bitterly called them. It's not their money or influence that should be critiqued, Rashad thinks, but their utter insulation from how the rest of the world lives.

The comfortable men and women reclining here—the bounties of the world instantly available with just the wave of a finger—have no idea that their lives are based upon a system of cruelty and oppression, with New York City its center.

A woman employee in a finely tailored suit approaches him quietly and says, "Monsieur Mohammed, it's time."

"It certainly is," he says, responding quickly to his fake name. Rashad puts down his drink and rises from his chair.

CHAPTER 63

THIS LITTLE band of not-so-merry warriors is hurtling down the M4, and I'm seeing the signs for Heathrow flash by as my stomach clenches with both fear and anticipation.

"Jer!" Felicity calls out, not moving her head. "We need to let Mini-Spit out if we want better tracking."

Jeremy turns to me from the left front seat while from his right Winnie brings us back into traffic. Hearing a *thump* and a *buzz* from the van's roof, I tilt my head back.

"Not a flying car seat like 007, but our mini-Spitfire drone can give us close-in tracking and video surveillance when we close in on a target. Felicity?"

"Hah!" she cries out, clapping her hands in triumph. "The bastard's in the Club Aspire lounge...Terminal Three. Thank you, Mini-Spit!"

I call out, "Heathrow? A lounge? Pretty goddamn public, don't you think?"

Traffic starts to clog up and Jeremy says, "Arrogance is one of Rashad's many faults. Felicity, call SO18 at Heathrow. Tell them we're rolling in hot and to meet us at the first-floor departure area for Terminal Three."

I unsnap the seat belt and harness and lean toward Jeremy's seat. "Do you have a plan, or are we going in guns blazing?"

"We're going in with guns," he says, "but no blazing—not at the start." Behind me I hear Felicity talking calmly and strongly to someone at Heathrow, using a lot of code phrases and number sequences. "We're meeting up with the specialist aviation unit for the Metropolitan Police."

Winnie moves a couple of switches and the familiar high-low of a British police siren erupts. From the reflection off nearby cars and trucks, I can see the van has hidden flashing blue lights in the front grille and above the windshield. Jeremy reaches under the dashboard and retrieves a communications device with an earpiece and a lapel mic; he clips the latter to his jacket.

Felicity calls out, "A squad is waiting for you, Jer, right at the first-floor entrance. Inspector Collins is lead."

"Great."

Winnie says, "Here we go," and he squeezes between a large lumbering bus and a white delivery truck, their horns blaring, and pulls right to the curb.

Jeremy says, "Amy, you—"

"I'm coming along," I say. "No way I'm staying here."

He and Winnie get out, and as I'm climbing over the seats Felicity turns and says, "Get the bastard."

I just nod, because there's not much else to say—and because I now see that Felicity has no legs; her black trousers are pinned back just above the place where her knees would be.

Outside the air is thick with diesel and the sounds of near traffic and the heavy roar of jet engines. We go through sliding-glass doors and meet up with four heavily armed men dressed in black fatigues and combat boots. Each carries my old friend, the Heckler & Koch MP5, and wears a ball cap with black-and-white checks. One steps forward and says, "Collins."

And Jeremy says, "Windsor."

"What do you have?" he asks.

"A terr holed up in the Club Aspire lounge."

He nods, face set and hard. "Right. That's near Gate Nine. Off we go."

My pistol is in both hands. Jeremy and Collins are leading the way, Winnie is beside me; from under his jacket he pulls out a cut-down Israeli-made Uzi 9mm submachine gun.

Then Jeremy holds up a clenched fist, whispers, "Halt," and we all stop. There are flashes of light as some brave tourists take photos of us.

I turn my head.

I don't need the attention.

Jeremy drops his hand. "He's moved! We have a bearded Saudi national, about six feet tall, in the loo right next to Burberry's."

A young man in jeans and a black jacket emerges from the bathroom, dragging a suitcase. Collins and another armed Met officer grab him.

"You!" Collins says. "How many more are in there?"

The man's eyes widen right up. "Shit, mate, I just went in there to piss. I wasn't keeping count."

He gets pushed away. Two more male passengers come out.

Neither of them is Saudi or bearded.

We wait.

I hate waiting.

Jeremy says, "We need a dynamic entry, and now."

Collins shakes his head. "My airport, my rules."

"This is a security matter."

"No," Collins says, "this is an airport matter, which means it belongs to me. We're getting additional forces here, and soon."

"We can't wait!" Jeremy says.

Collins says, "Sorry, mate—that's the rules."

I take a breath and push past them, going straight into the men's room.

"Not mine," I say.

CHAPTER 64

THERE'S LOTS of cursing behind me, and someone's hand—I'm sure it's not Jeremy's—brushes my right shoulder like he's trying to pull me back. Lucky for the both of us, he misses grabbing onto me.

I lower myself and glance around the corner. Two dark-skinned Asian men in suits, white shirts, no neckties are at separate sinks, one brushing his teeth, the other washing his hands. The one maintaining good dental hygiene spots me—halts with the toothbrush in his mouth—and nudges the man next to him.

I put a finger up to my mouth—the international sign for *Keep your damn mouth shut!*—and with my other hand, holding my 9mm, I gesture them to move outside.

"Slowly," comes a whisper, and I don't turn.

It's Jeremy.

There are sinks and mirrors to my right; to my left, a row of stalls.

Every one of them is open save for the one at the end.

Door closed.

I turn and point to the stall with the closed door. Jeremy nods. He points to himself, then to the far end of the bathroom. He gestures at me to stay behind.

I give him that.

He slowly walks down the bathroom like he's waiting to do his familiar business, but his eyes and pistol are on the last stall. In a few seconds I move as well, following him, then I duck down and peer under the door.

Empty.

I wave and catch Jeremy's attention, point to the bottom of the stall, then shake my head.

He gets the message.

He goes to the end and swiftly turns, then hammers the door open with one well-placed kick.

"Hey!" comes a shout, and the next few seconds are a confusing mess of Jeremy reaching in to grab a man squatting on the toilet seat with his feet. As he starts to drag him out, I reach in, grab a shirtsleeve, and tug him out as well. The man flips and falls to the floor, hands held up in terror.

It's not Rashad.

He's in his twenties, dressed well, and from the corner of my eye I spot a gray suit jacket hanging from a hook. The man's right shirtsleeve is pulled up above his elbow, and a length of rubber hose is tied around the upper bicep.

"Hey...hey...hey..." he protests. "Come on...please..."

I look inside the stall, spot a hypodermic and small plastic cap, and a cotton ball.

"Just a junkie," I say. "Just a goddamn junkie."

The bathroom is then crowded with armed men, and Jeremy repeats again and again, "He was here, our guy was here, damn it... we had good intel!"

Before Inspector Collins can object, I go to the end of the sinks, where's there a paper-towel dispenser and an open trash can.

I peer into the bin.

Spot something.

Gingerly pull it out.

"Hey," I say.

I pick up the bloodstained gauze. The small metal object inside it is about the size of a fat rice kernel, with a millimeter or two of wire sticking out.

"Rashad was here," I say. "And he left his calling card."

"He's gone," Jeremy whispers, looking at my hand.

I say, "Gone—and with no way of tracking him."

CHAPTER 65

TOM CORNWALL is in his home office, digging through the top drawer of his desk once again, automatically looking for a particular business card, but also recalling the oh-so-brief conversation he had earlier with Amy.

Ticonderoga.

Time to pack for the trip to Ticonderoga.

Years back, when Denise was just a toddler and Amy's career in intelligence was beginning, over glasses of a fine Australian merlot one night in front of the fireplace at their old home in Virginia, Amy had said, "Just to be clear, you're not to ask me anything for any story you're working on. Not a damn thing."

"Agreed," Tom had said, but Amy had taken it one step further.

"But..." She had hesitated briefly, then plunged ahead: "But if I ever come across something that I think will mean immediate danger to you and Denise, I'll warn you somehow. A word, a phrase."

"Like 'Alas, Babylon,' from that old World War Three novel?" he had asked.

"No," Amy had said. "Too many people know that one. No... if the time comes that I think you and Denise need to head for the hills, I'll tell you to plan for a trip to Fort Ticonderoga. How does that sound?"

The wine had made him feel fuzzy and agreeable, so Tom had said, "Sure."

But Amy wasn't going for a snap answer. "Tom, this is what you're agreeing to, all right? If you hear me saying 'Ticonderoga,' then there's no arguing, no debate—just agreement."

"Sure," he had said, and later that night they had sealed the deal with a wonderful bout of lovemaking that their infant Denise had slept through.

Now Tom finds what he's looking for: a ConEd business card with the name JOHN CORNWALL on the front and, on the back, a local number. His Uncle John, a ConEd retiree, now living at the southern end of Staten Island—a place Denise loved to visit because of Uncle John's boating and fishing expertise.

A slight electronic *ding* disturbs him, and his iMessage chat icon is flashing on his MacBook screen.

He puts the card down, double-clicks, and sees it's his Russian associate, Yuri.

TOM: *Working late, are we?*
YURI: *Or early, depending on my time zone.*
TOM: *Oh, and where's that?*
YURI: *Hah. Good try tovarisch. How are u?*
TOM: *Fine. Working on a story, ready to head out.*
YURI: *Head out why?*

Tom pauses, wondering why he let that bit of information slip. He resumes his typing.

TOM: *The story I've been working on . . . the possible attack on NYC. It's getting too real. I'm taking my daughter and getting out of town for a bit.*

There's now a pause on the other end, the icon blinking.

YURI: *Losing your nerve?*

Ouch, that stung.

TOM: *Doing my job as a dad. Taking my daughter to safety.*

Another pause.
Longer.

YURI: *Is this the same Tom Cornwall who shared rations with me in Syria? Who stood up for me against the Kurds? Who refused an evac because the story wasn't done yet?*
TOM: *Same Tom. Different responsibilities.*
YURI: *You head out, you'll miss the story.*

Screw you, Tom thinks.

TOM: *I stay, my daughter might miss her father. Forever.*

Yuri quickly replies.

YURI: *Sorry to see you lose your nerve. Reporters like us stayed in Leningrad, landed in Normandy, ran to the Towers, rode into Baghdad.*

Tom is slowly getting more and more irritated. He quickly dips into a file folder marked KURD PIX, finds the photo he's looking for, and sends it along to Yuri.

TOM: *Reporters like this? Believe me, I've not changed. Not at all.*

A silence. To reacquaint himself with what he just sent Yuri, Tom opens up the photo. It shows a squad of Kurdish peshmerga fighters resting against a dirt berm, smiling for the camera. At the right side of the squad is Tom, also smiling, and Yuri, seemingly distracted, digging into a green knapsack.

The pause grows longer.

YURI: *Didn't know you had this photo. Who took it?*

TOM: *Correspondent from CNN, a souvenir. That's who I am. Even if I'm here in New York. But this time the story's on my front doorstep, with my daughter right next to me. That's the big difference, friend.*

Then comes the abrupt and final message:

YURI Has Signed Out.

Tom stares at the blank screen, then looks around his office, with its books, newspapers, and notebooks. Plaques and awards clutter the far wall.

Damn that Yuri.

He sure knows how to needle a guy.

He picks up the phone and makes a call. When a gruff voice answers, he says, "Uncle John? It's Tom. Hey, I was wondering... something's come up at work. Would you mind keeping Denise for a few days?"

His old uncle coughs and clears his throat. "Sure. She's a handful, but she keeps me moving. You coming with her?"

"No," Tom says.

CHAPTER 66

I SLIDE away from Terminal Three at Heathrow and climb into the red van lettered EXPRESS LONDON DISPATCH.

Felicity is sitting in her chair, pointing a pistol in my direction.

She shrugs, lowers it. "Suspicious sort," she says. "Sorry. When you can't move around well, you tend to get paranoid about being stuck in one place."

I settle down in the second chair in the rear and get a better view of her lower legs. She notes my gaze and I say, "Iraq? Or Afghanistan?"

"Neither," Felicity says. "Tavistock Square, about 25 kilometers from here."

It comes to me almost like a slap to the face.

"The July 7 London bombings," I say. "You were in the double-decker bus?"

Felicity looks pleased that I know the reference. "That's right. The blast took off both of my legs, sent shrapnel through the rest of my body. More than fifty were killed, about 700 injured . . . and it's discussed in historic terms, like the Coventry bombing in 1941. It's all forgotten . . . but I don't forget. Can't, actually. I had been planning a boring career in the civil service. But plans change."

I say, "Rashad's not in there."

"I figured as much, with the tracking chip staying in one place after you lot raced in. Did he dig it out of his wrist himself?"

"Yes," I say. "Tricky son of a bitch, isn't he?"

Felicity says, "Oh, but he has a weakness. And it's the same as what he regards as his strength—his determination and focus—such that he'll plan the deaths of thousands while taking a knife to his own skin to dig out that tracker. That sense of superiority can lead to overconfidence."

More horns and honks, the high-low sirens of additional police vehicles roaring in. "You said earlier that you had spotted him in Paris, then on a section of..."

"Uxbridge Road," she says, returning to the video screen. "I managed to narrow it down to either a fish-and-chips takeaway or a function hall owned by a local charity, the White City Relief Association."

"Wait," I say, something coming to me. "That function hall. What was there tonight?"

Back to her keyboard and screen, and in just a few moments Felicity says, "A historical society."

"What group?"

"The... Queen Elizabeth II Railroad Society."

Railroad.

Yes!

"Felicity, can you locate Jeremy and Winnie? We need to get going. Now!"

And then I look and—

No keys in the ignition.

Damn it!

A soft tinkle. I turn. Felicity is dangling a set of keys in her hand.

CHAPTER 67

RACING EAST along the M4, heading back to London, I recall the power of my first driving lessons back in Maine. The worst part of driving this van is its gearshift, and using it with my left hand; but I wasn't intending on going into reverse anytime soon.

"Hey," I say to Felicity, "can you print out a photo of Rashad before we get there?"

"Of course," Felicity says, "but first can I give you a bit of advice?"

"Please," I say, as a white tractor trailer cuts me off and my right foot flails for a second, seeking out the brake pedal.

"In the States, where you drive on the wrong side of the road, it's easy to visualize your left tire being aligned with the center line because the steering wheel is on the left," she explains. "Here, just flip it: visualize your right tire hugging the center line, and—Jesus Christ, look out for the lorry!"

More horns, another tap of the brakes from me, and then Felicity shouts, "We're coming up to the roundabout! Take the second exit, to Great West Road!"

In addition to the horns, there's an awful screech of metal as a black taxicab sideswipes us, but I don't brake.

*   *   *

This section of Uxbridge Road has two- and three-story brick buildings.

"Here, here," Felicity says. "Right there, the place with the sign hanging down over that picture window."

I slam on the brakes but don't see any parking spots, so I make do by driving up on the sidewalk. And then I'm out and running.

I burst through the swinging glass doors, into a foyer with a coat-room, and beyond is a short hallway that takes me to a large banquet hall. There's the smell of stale beer and tobacco smoke, and two young women are on stepladders, taking down UK flag bunting. Even as waiters fold up tables and chairs, four older men in formal evening wear with miniature medals over their left breasts linger in the far corner with their drinks.

I thrust the freshly printed-out photo of Rashad toward them. "This man," I say. "He was here tonight."

The tallest man among them takes the photo and says, "Oh, yes, of course, that's Randy."

"Randy?"

He nods, hands the photo back to me. "Yes. Randy Hussain. A great train enthusiast, supporter of the Society, and friend to Perkins."

"Who is Perkins?" I ask.

"Perky was in the war, a true hero," he says. "He was in the SOE."

It comes to me then.

"Special Operations Executive," I say. "Behind-the-lines spies and commandos."

A man with a white, walrus-style mustache speaks up. "Perky was probably the best saboteur Churchill ever had. Killed hundreds of Krauts."

The taller one corrects him. "Not hundreds," he says. "Thousands."

CHAPTER 68

WINNIE HALTS the police cruiser just beside their van, turning on the blue flashers, and he gets out and Jeremy is right next to him just as Amy Cornwall runs out of the building.

"Hey!" she says. "Good to see you've caught up with us. I've got a good lead on Rashad."

Jeremy says, "Good God, woman, do you have any idea what—"

"Perkins Gloucester," she says, breathing hard. "Lives in a nursing home about five klicks away. Best friend of Rashad's while he's been in London. Now. We can get a good lead on what the hell that bastard's up to."

While Winnie is speeding their van along, Amy says, "Hey, Felicity, if you can, dig further into those tracking sightings of Rashad in Paris. See if he was anywhere near something of interest. I'm sure you'll know it when you see it."

Jeremy waits for Felicity to seek permission from him to proceed, but the clicking of keyboard keys tells him she's following Amy's orders.

Winnie calls out, "Got it!" and halts the van outside a one-story brick building with white pillars, a wide entrance, and a sign reading NORTH ACTON CARE HOME.

Jeremy flashes a Metropolitan Police warrant card to the chubby receptionist, and within a few minutes he and Amy are led into the room of Perkins Gloucester, former Second Lieutenant of the Royal Engineers, detached to the SOE from 1942 to 1945.

There are two chairs and Perkins is sitting in one of them, a checked blanket over his lap. With his wrinkled face, pale eyes, and thin brown hair barely covering a freckled scalp, he looks like a shrunken gnome.

"Mister Gloucester," Jeremy says. "So pleased to meet you. My name is Jeremy Windsor, and I need to ask you a few questions."

Perkins nods and his smile widens at seeing Amy standing there. "How pleasant, how pleasant—and is this gorgeous creature your wife? Your secretary?"

Jeremy shakes his head. "No, sir, I'm with the SIS and Amy, she is with the CIA."

"But on a day like this, sometimes I wish I *was* a secretary," she says.

The old man looks at both of them and says, "Ah, I should have known—that American accent."

Jeremy displays the photo of Rashad. "This man," Jeremy says. "Randy. What do you know of him?"

"Ah, yes, Randy," he says, settling back in his chair and smoothing the blanket. "Oh, he was an inquisitive sort, he was. He wanted to know all about blowing up trains. Managed to fatten up our society's bank account, he did."

Amy interrupts him. "Mister Gloucester...you have special knowledge, then, on how to blow up trains?"

An eager and satisfied nod. "We learned that quite early in the war. A small bomb or removing a piece of track, it's only a small derailment. That's all. Hunh. They get it fixed the next day. No, my real job was to sabotage different railcars and other stock so that you can destroy the whole train in minutes, tie up the entire rail line for days. And that's what Randy was so eager to learn about, even though it's still highly secret."

Jeremy tries to get the conversation back to the present. "But why are your activities still classified?"

"Why?" Perkins asks, still smiling. "My dear boy, it wouldn't do for any Tom, Dick, or Harry to know the best way to easily blow up a train line, now would it?"

CHAPTER 69

JEREMY AND Amy leave Perkins's room and the care home to find Winnie coming at them from the open passenger door of their damaged van.

"Felicity dug deeper into the tracking hits we got from Paris. All but one turned up empty...nothing of any real interest. But that one hit, the one that lasted the longest—about five seconds of a strong signal—came from a little restaurant in Paris, the Café Falguière. Right next door to the Pasteur Institute. Where they do research on various infectious diseases."

Jeremy sees Amy's face pale. "Go on."

Winnie says, "Felicity got deeper into the French internal-security computer servers, looking for anything odd or untoward concerning the Pasteur Institute," he says, motioning them to a park bench near the entrance. "Like missing vials, a break-in—anything like that."

Amy says, "And?"

Winnie shakes his head. "Nothing to do with the institute proper, but one of their microbiology techs, a woman named...yeah, here it is. Nadia. Nadia Khadra. She's been missing for two days. And her credit-card statement shows she was having breakfast at that same restaurant, the same time Rashad's tracking device pinged its location."

"Winnie," Jeremy says, "that's all well and good, but—"

"Damn it, Jer, let me finish," Winnie snaps. He takes a breath and goes on. "Like I said, Nadia's been missing for two days. The local gendarmes went to her ground-floor flat, and when they checked the basement they found her landlady dead."

Amy says, "How?"

"Multiple blows to the rear of the head," Winnie says. "And it gets worse, much worse: They found she had converted the basement into a laboratory—petri dishes, refrigerators, autoclaves. And when they tested the area, they found traces of anthrax."

Jeremy can't say a word. He's been in desperate firefights in hellholes across the world, has jumped from aircraft of all types into the freezing night, and right now, seeing the innocent and thankfully ignorant civilians strolling by him on this warm spring evening, he thinks of them crowding into hospital wards, coughing out their lungs and lives, and those thoughts scare him more than anything else ever has.

Amy says, "What now?"

Jeremy gets off the bench. "That bastard Rashad was saying *so long* to Nadia before she left to go to New York. Come along, we've got to get the word out."

Amy and Winnie stand with him, and they start heading to the van. Amy says, "Trains? Blowing up trains?"

Jeremy says, "Could be a way to disguise the anthrax disbursement. Blow up a few trains in a crowded civilian environment, mix the anthrax into a cloud, and soon enough, chaos and death."

They are about three meters from the van when it happens, and later, Jeremy has to admire how quickly and professionally it all went down.

On the sidewalk, a plump, older woman wearing comfortable

clothes and pushing a pram takes something from her coat pocket and sprays Jeremy with a liquid. His eyes burn and his breathing freezes, and though he fights against the chemical he is forced to his knees, unable to catch his breath.

Winnie calls out as he falls as well, taken down by a slim woman jogging by, likewise holding a spray dispenser in her hand.

Jeremy tries to shout something but a white van screeches to a halt, the side door slides open, and three men in black clothing and masks pile out, grab Amy Cornwall, and put a sack over her head, and in seconds she's gone.

Amy Cornwall is gone.

CHAPTER 70

ERNEST HOLLISTER watches in satisfaction as Horace Evans puts his phone down in its cradle and with a tired voice says, "It's done. Amy Cornwall has been seized by your contract force."

"Good," Ernest says, feeling satisfied indeed, but not wanting to stay here much longer and revel in his win. This room is old, creaky, and damp, and he's sure the air is filled with mold spores and dust. How in hell could anyone of worth stand working in this dump?

Horace says, "I trust you and your force will be discreet."

"Absolutely."

"And I imagine you will shortly return her to the States?"

"Perhaps," Ernest says. "Then again, it may be worthwhile to keep her in place for a few days, to conduct an interrogation."

Horace purses his lips. "That's not discreet."

"It's discreet enough if no one knows about it, am I right?"

When Horace doesn't reply, Ernest says, "Just to ensure that we have a clear understanding, you are to halt all operations—sanctioned or unsanctioned, official or unofficial—against Rashad Hussain and his associates. Is that clear?"

His MI6 counterpart seems to struggle with his temper. In a

weak voice he says, "That is incredibly shortsighted. We have intelligence that Rashad is—"

"...that Rashad Hussain is a completely vetted and supported confidential source for our operations in Langley," Ernest says. "He has been responsible for us disrupting three terrorist plots against civilian targets in the United States. What you have, in comparison, is idle chatter, suspicions, and what is most likely a personal grudge harbored by your Jeremy Windsor."

"That still doesn't mean—"

"Look, we're done here," Ernest says. "I told you politely to cease your ops against Rashad. Now I'll be impolite: *back the fuck off*. All right?"

Horace gives the slightest nod, indicating a great surrender. Despite the dust and mold in the air, Ernest is looking forward to what he's going to say next.

"Now, let's get to Jeremy. I want him taken care of, just like Amy."

Horace says, "I assure you, there will be disciplinary actions."

"Tell me, Horace, is it my American accent that's screwing you up, or are you that dense? We have a phrase on our side of the pond to smoke an officer, or *Gitmo* him. I know you have something similar—to be *Faroe'd*. Correct? I want Jeremy Faroe'd."

"No," Horace says.

Ernest says, "My boss is Malcolm Rooney, head of our Special Activities Division. Former Army general. I served with him in Iraq. He trusts me fully and explicitly. One of his duties is serving on a committee responsible for allocating funds to our fellow intelligence agencies, especially those who have fallen on hard times ever since their great and mighty empire collapsed. And if I give him a recommendation to cut your funding allocations in half, Horace, he'll do it without hesitation."

Silence in the dusty room. Then, in a low and nearly trembling voice, Horace says, "It might take some time. There are…procedures to follow."

Ernest says, "I'm a reasonable fella. Take the time you need…as long is it's quick, and it's done."

"But there's the matter of the Parisian woman, the one—"

"Yes, the amateur biochemist," Ernest says. "She's French, her crimes took place in France—let France pull its weight for once. There's no evidence she's left the country."

After spending so many days being ignored by this sad little man before him, Ernest takes pleasure in one last dig. "And in this mess you call an office, I'm sure a few things can be overlooked, Horace. So don't overlook this: we have the deep means and resources to ensure that you keep your word. Uncle Sam will be watching and listening. So don't screw this up. Stop hunting and harassing Rashad, let the French take care of their problem, and handle Jeremy Windsor. He aided and abetted one of our officers in going rogue. That can't stand."

Horace's hands move across his paper-strewn desk as though he's trying to hold on to something for reassurance. "This isn't a good day for Anglo-American cooperation, now is it? Our special relationship."

Ernest gets up, his skin nearly crawling from the dirt in this office. "Haven't you heard? Since the last election, it's a new world out there. We're America, bitch. That's all you need to know."

CHAPTER 71

IT'S VERY late at night and Rashad Hussain is finishing a delightful meal in his first-class cabin aboard the RMS *Queen Victoria,* a cruise ship on its maiden voyage, speeding toward New York City.

His luxury cabin on Deck Six has twenty-four-hour personal concierge service and a king-size suite with floor-to-ceiling windows and a private balcony. In the private dining room Rashad is hosting Abdullah al-Fahd, a prominent Saudi imam who is an old family friend. At the far end of the cabin stand the imam's two Russian bodyguards, their cheap and ill-fitting black suits not quite hiding the bulges of concealed weapons. Each has a fleshy face, short-trimmed blond hair, and dead blue eyes.

The imam is dressed in plain brown robes and an equally plain white kaffiyeh. His beard is dark brown, thick, reaching almost mid-chest, and his brown eyes are bright and full of warmth.

"A fine meal, my son," he says, wiping his fingers again on a white napkin. "Hard to believe that a ship like this can produce such a delicious *haneeth.*"

Rashad nods in pleasure at the compliment for the traditional Saudi dish of spiced lamb and basmati rice. "I chose the chef myself—stole him from the Al Orjouan at the Riyadh Ritz-Carlton. After all, I own a good portion of this ship."

He pours the imam another cup of sweet Saudi coffee, and the older man smiles. "Allah has graced you."

"And you as well, *ya sheikh,*" he says, raising his porcelain cup in salute. The old family friend earned his knowledge at the Imam Muhammad ibn Saud Islamic University in Riyadh and is now a noted scholar and teacher at the Umm Al-Qura University in Mecca.

For years Abdullah al-Fahd has been ignored, shunted aside, persecuted because his view of Islam does not fit into the conservative Saudi tradition. But now, with a new prince leading the kingdom and a new openness to the West, the imam has gained power and influence.

The imam gently replaces his coffee cup on a saucer and says with wonder, "Look here: we are speeding across the Atlantic, yet the cup barely vibrates."

Rashad says, "On our maiden voyage, I gave orders that we try to win the Blue Riband for the speediest crossing. The current record is just under three and a half days. I mean for us to smash it."

The imam smiles, but it's not one of pleasure or accomplishment; it's the sad smile of a man about to disappoint his host.

"*Ya akhi,* I am so proud of you and your accomplishments, and your commitment to jihad, but I beg of you to please reconsider the life you have chosen," he says in a soft and cultured voice.

"And what life is that, *ya sheikh?*" Rashad asks.

The sparkling and open brown eyes of his beloved guest harden. "Please, let's not play games here, Rashad. I know of your commitment to Islam, your donations, your public acts. But your other acts...your other jihad. There is no true evidence, but you and I know the truth. There is the blood of many innocents on your hands, and I know that you have plans to spill much, much more."

Rashad speaks carefully. "From whom do you receive such news?"

The imam speaks just as carefully in reply. "From brethren who have worked with you, and continue to work with you, and who are starting to have doubts."

There is silence for a few seconds. After another sip of coffee, the imam says, "These are new days, new times. After decades of bloodshed, the car bombs, the hijackings, the civil wars...we are taking the first gentle, tottering steps toward peace with the West, toward an accommodation."

"A surrender," Rashad says.

The imam shakes his head. "Oh, no, no, my son. An *understanding*. A realization that compassion, friendship, and openness will serve us much more in our House of Peace—*Dar-es-Salaam*—than violence and bloodshed."

"But jihad demands—"

The imam gently interrupts. "Jihad has meant many things over the centuries, my son. It does mean struggle, of course, but there is a realization now that it means striving or struggling on a personal mission, especially one with a praiseworthy aim."

Rashad says, "And setting the stage for a new caliphate, that is not a praiseworthy aim?"

"Over the bodies of hundreds of thousands of innocents?"

Rashad wants to yell, *What innocents? Who are indeed innocent in this world?*

But he keeps his composure, steps up and away from the dining-room table, extends a hand. "*Ya sheikh,* will you join me for a breath of fresh ocean air?"

Imam Abdullah al-Fahd smiles. "That would be a delight."

Rashad crosses the dining room and opens the doors onto the suite's private balcony. Outside the North Atlantic air is brisk, and even with the running lights from the RMS *Queen Victoria* the stars overhead shine bright and crisp, as if from the depths of the Empty Quarter.

The imam slides his arm into Rashad's. "Look at Allah's glory and creation all above us. Do you think Allah wants us to live with hate, fire, deaths, explosions?"

Before Rashad can answer, the imam says, "Please, my son. Please tell me you will reconsider your actions. Choose the jihad of a commitment to understanding, to peace."

Rashad pats the man's hand. "I will consider it. Honestly, I will consider it, *ya sheikh*."

The imam doesn't reply, but Rashad can sense the man's pleasure at his words.

A few moments pass and the imam says, "That prize you hope to win . . ."

"The Blue Riband."

"Who holds the record now?"

Rashad says, "The record is nearly seventy years old, and was set by the ship the SS *United States*. Named after a place I still hate, old friend, even after my reconsideration."

The imam breaks away from Rashad's grasp, motions his hand and the two Russian bodyguards are now on the balcony. As they crowd him away from Rashad, the imam's voice is sharp: "I have survived many years, with many enemies. It saddens me that I need protection from a longtime friend such as you."

"It saddens me as well," Rashad says. The two bodyguards advance on Abdullah, and in one smooth motion they toss the man of peace and love over the side into the unforgiving ocean.

CHAPTER 72

IT'S EARLY morning at Gatwick Airport near London, and Marcel Koussa is in the South Terminal at Gate 14, waiting for his British Airways flight to take him to America. He's pacing back and forth in both anticipation and fear.

For the past three years Marcel has been at Rashad Hussain's side, performing the oddest tasks—like traveling to Istanbul to purchase a mock-up of a steward uniform for the never-completed Berlin-to-Baghdad railway—up to and including the bloodiest of tasks, like disposing of that antiques dealer in Paris the other day.

Grim work, but all part of the job, all part of the actions that have led to a reasonably comfortable life and fat bank accounts secretly stored in the Cayman Islands, the Seychelles, and Bali. He has traveled far, has met with a number of desperate and determined characters, all in exchange for the comfortable life he is planning once Rashad's latest—and deadliest—attack takes place.

But now that job and comfort—and his future—are threatened.

Marcel looks up at the display board.

His flight will begin boarding in about ten minutes.

He pulls from his carry-on the burner phone he had purchased yesterday at a Tesco store, and dials the memorized number once again.

It rings, rings, and continues ringing, until Marcel disconnects the call in frustration.

A woman's voice breaks into his foul mood with the first boarding announcement.

A brief flurry of movement as families and the disabled start heading to the open gate door.

Damn.

He hits Redial.

He has a lot to report, but there is still no answer.

"Ladies and gentlemen, again, good morning," comes the voice from the attractive blond British Airways woman at the counter. "We will now board First Class, Club World, Club Europe, and World Traveller Plus passengers."

One of the perks of working for a man like Rashad is first-class travel, but Marcel stays behind for the moment. Once he boards, he won't be able to use his cell phone, followed by an eight-hour flight without any type of secure communication.

Unacceptable, he thinks, nearly bumping into a yawning American businessman who steps by him, carrying a copy of that day's *Financial Times* and a Starbucks coffee container.

Barbarian. He thinks again of what Rashad has planned in four days. *I've got to make that call, have got to get things confirmed.*

"And, ladies and gentlemen, we will start boarding..."

Another phone call placed.

Another phone call unanswered.

Marcel pauses, thinking furiously.

He has to keep to the plan.

Has to.

Because if he doesn't arrive in JFK in eight hours, Rashad will accept no pleading, no excuse.

"Ladies and gentlemen, this is the final boarding call for British Airways Flight 203..."

The decision is made for him.

He will leave.

He grabs his carry-on, picks it up, and with his boarding pass in hand he approaches the smiling blond woman at the gate. His thumb hits Redial one last time.

And by the time he reaches the gate and displays his boarding pass, Marcel disconnects the call again, bitterly disappointed.

For God's sake, why won't MI6 answer their damn phone?

CHAPTER 73

I'M SITTING on a bolted metal chair in front of a bolted table in an empty square sterile concrete room, my arms and lower legs fastened to the chair by chains. There's a sore spot on my neck where I was injected with a sedative, my left eye is throbbing, and I'll probably end up with a black eye by the end of this dark day. My ribs also ache from a good pounding I got from my two captors when I tried to make a break for it as they were chaining me to this chair.

Up in a corner of the ceiling, a little black plastic dome tells me I'm being recorded. There's a chair on the other side of this dull-gray metal table, and a door in the wall; the door opens and my old boss Ernest Hollister comes in and sits down, an iPad in his hand.

He looks tired and angry, and I'm sure I'm responsible for both of those moods, and I'm fine with that.

He opens the iPad and says, "You've been a very bad girl, Amy."

I say, "Sorry, Ernest, I haven't let anyone call me a *girl* since I raised my right hand and swore an oath to support and defend the Constitution of the United States against all enemies, foreign and domestic."

He shrugs his thin shoulders. "Semantics, Amy. Just semantics."

"Then semantic this," I say. "Why in hell did you smoke me?"

"You went rogue and disobeyed orders."

"I was responding to an emerging threat."

"What threat was that, Amy?"

I know he's trying to get under my skin and I'm pissed he's succeeding.

"Rashad Hussain," I say. "Saudi national and businessman, terrorist financier. He's planning a massive attack on New York City on May 29."

"Oh," Ernest replies. "Says who?"

"Says MI6."

"I see," he replies, voice still bloodless, like that of a bureaucrat kept alive over decades, designed only to implement long-dead policies and throttle any risk-taking or important decisions. "And was that all of MI6? Was it one of their intelligence-assessment committees? Or was it just a single individual?"

I'm getting angrier as I see the cold logic in his voice. "One MI6 officer that I've deployed with three times in the field, and whom I trust. Which is more than I can say of you."

"So you trust this Jeremy Windsor that Rashad Hussain is on a mission to attack New York City, kill tens of thousands of people? Correct? The same Jeremy Windsor—who with an equally deranged friend from the French foreign-intelligence service—thought that Rashad Hussain was delivering a Russian-made nuclear device to a runway in France? When it turned out to be a container of medical waste and smoke detectors from Romania?"

I pull against the chains on my legs and arms. That's all I seem able to do.

"There's more to it than that," I say. "There's a French microbiologist missing from the Pasteur Institute. She's been weaponizing anthrax."

Ernest says, "That's the allegation, isn't it? So far the French have told us that they have the matter under control, and there's no firm evidence connecting her to this hidden terrorist of yours."

My former boss opens up his iPad, rotates the screen so I can see it, and starts toggling through a variety of photos.

"So you believe this Saudi businessman and philanthropist, Rashad Hussain, has designs on the United States." He slides a finger. "Rashad, here with the vice president last November."

Another swipe of the finger.

"Rashad, here with the Secretary-General of the United Nations." One more swipe.

"And here, with the head of the International Red Cross."

"I don't trust the photos," I say. "I trust Jeremy."

"Oh," he says, smirking, and then turns back to the iPad. "I trust that you do. And I also trust that Jeremy has vengeance on his mind: to kill the man who he believed killed his own father. That may be honorable and right, but it's not the problem of the United States."

I say, "For Christ's sake, Ernest, you're giving up? Just like that?"

"No, I never give up," he says. "I look at the facts, beyond the photos I've just showed you. For example, this same Rashad Hussain has been a confidential field asset for us, providing information that led us to prevent three terrorist attacks on American soil."

I say, "You moron, he's been fooling you—sending out sacrificial goats so you won't respond to this latest intelligence."

He slaps the iPad shut. "Some years ago, I had the honor of serving in Iraq with one of the finest men I've ever known, General Malcolm Rooney. Innovative tactician and expert in logistics. He was able to achieve his military goals during the 2003 invasion with a minimum of casualties—on both sides. And when the Iraqi army collapsed in his area, General Rooney worked very hard with the local tribal leaders to achieve some sort of peace and political autonomy."

Ernest suddenly gets up. "And it was for nothing. Nothing! This general and his troops, they were wasted, they were stuck in a quagmire, good boys and girls getting blown up by IEDs and crippled by snipers because the intelligence agencies failed them—failed us. Every one of them. No weapons of mass destruction, we weren't greeted as liberators, and deep down those people weren't craving a Jeffersonian democracy."

He heads to the door. "And when I went to work for the general at the Agency, I vowed that never again—never!—would hunches, guesses, and lousy intelligence have a hand in anything I do. Just facts."

I say, "So what now?" I strain again at the chains. "When do you haul me onto a black flight and take me back?"

A thin-lipped smile. "How about never? How does *never* sound?"

"You can't get away with that."

"Why not?" he says. "You've been smoked. You don't exist. You've caused me lots of heartburn and stressful days, girl, and you'll stay here until I get tired of punishing you."

One more step from him and I say, "Ernest? Ask you a question?"

He's at the door. "Why not?"

"The men and women who captured me, the ones holding me here, the ones who assaulted me while putting me in this chair." I rattle the chains for emphasis. "Are they Agency or contract?"

"Contract," he says. "What difference does it make?"

I say, "I guess I still have some loyalty to the Agency, despite what you've done to me."

"And?"

"And when the time comes, I'm going to kill each and every one of them."

Ernest looks at me with pity. "Aren't you the considerate one?"

I say, "I'm not that considerate, Ernest. Because when the time comes for you, I won't care who you're working for."

CHAPTER 74

TODAY IS the day, and Nadia Khadra is surprised at how calm she feels. She has spent her first two days in America staying at a Howard Johnson's near the JFK airport, and despite eating at a local Burger King and McDonald's, she still feels refreshed and ready.

She's standing on a crowded platform at the Rockaway Park–Beach 116th Street New York subway station. In her right hand is her special metal carrying case, in her left the handle of her roll-on luggage.

Nadia glances down at the black dress she is wearing, with its leather belt and gaudy red clasp. Around her are working-class members of the American *petite bourgeoisie,* smelly and ill-dressed, and she feels out of place wearing such a formal dress. Before leaving that dingy hotel an hour ago, she had considered wearing something else—until she thought of the mentor who had changed her life, had set her on this noble path.

So here she is, wearing the party dress her mentor had specified, waiting for the A Train to take her to Manhattan. The trip should take an hour.

Should.

But this is America and the trains, and the trash, and the jostling, noisy, dirty, and filthy people . . . all part of a greedy, grasping empire. When the taxi had dropped her at the station, a small part of her wondered if she could go through with her task, knowing there was a very good chance the people she would ride in with this morning would shortly be dead—all because of her.

From a small compartment at the top of her carry-on luggage, she takes out the programmed cell phone Rashad gave her in Paris, pushes Dial, and raises it to her ear.

It rings once.

"Mike," comes the strong male voice.

"It's Nadia," she says. "I'm at the subway station in Queens."

"Excellent," Mike says. "I will be waiting for you at the southern end of the park."

His voice is confident, and she blurts out, "These trains . . . they may be late. Just so you are aware."

Mike laughs. "I know American trains. No worries. You are worth waiting for. I will see you soon."

He disconnects the call and Nadia stows the phone, knowing she will use it only once more.

That voice, that man.

Even from this short conversation, she feels the same shared sense of justice and mission.

Nadia stands a bit straighter among these workers, crabby children, and homeless, and she feels no guilt at all.

When Mike Patel started work at One World Trade Center nearly a year ago, he had been concerned that his skin color, his accent, would cause him increased surveillance attention from the NYPD and the American intelligence services. But save for a few awkward glances and half-heard insults and jokes here and there, the people he has met have generally left him alone. He performs his work quietly, efficiently, and ahead of schedule, which means his supervision is practically nonexistent.

He is in a men's restroom on the sixth floor of One World Trade Center, changing out of his work clothes into a simple pair of Levi's blue jeans and a white T-shirt, preparing to absent himself from his day's work to ensure that most of the people he has met here over the months will soon die an agonizing death, choking on their own fluids.

He fastens the jeans.

They should have paid closer attention to him.

Freddie Farrady is strolling the streets around the base of One World Trade Center, remembering the conversation he had last night with his MI5 supervisor.

Patel is up to something, he had said. *He left work and went to a railway yard in New Jersey.*

And?

And that's out of character, he had said. *He's never skipped work like that—not ever.*

Did you see if he met anyone?

No, he had said.

Did he do anything illegal in New Jersey?

I bloody well couldn't tell, now could I? he had said. *He was behind a tall fence in a secure railway yard.*

Then maybe he has a part-time job over there. Just keep watching.

Yeah, Freddie thinks, stretching his legs once more, conducting a roving surveillance of the four entrances and exits at One World Trade Center. He walks west along Fulton Street, goes up the busy corridor of West Street, east along the relative quiet of Vesey Street, then takes Greenwich Street back to Fulton.

Wash, rinse, repeat, he thinks. On what passes for a normal day—except for that jaunt into New Jersey—Patel goes to work in the morning and leaves in the late afternoon.

Staying outside all day is a waste of time. What he should do is talk to Patel's coworkers, to his fellow tenants at his apartment building in Queens. But Portia Grayson of MI5 will have none of it.

"Observation," she keeps on saying. "That's all you're going to do. Observe and report. See if he meets with anyone."

So a-roamin' he keeps goin', sometimes resting on a bench, conscious that the World Trade Center Memorial is within a stone's throw—and that somewhere in this vicinity, so many years ago that an entire generation has grown up without knowing about it, his terrified cousin Malcolm had leaped hundreds of feet to his death, his clothes and hair on fire.

He crosses his arms.

Lunch, soon.

Time to try the sidewalk vendor he had sampled three days ago—the Egyptian selling a kind of Middle Eastern gyro-meat sandwich on folded bread. It had been a nice change of pace from his usual hot dogs.

Freddie uncrosses his arms.

What the hell?

Mike Patel emerges from the Vesey Street entrance, turns right, and starts briskly walking east. He's not wearing his typical work uniform, and his hands are empty. He's moving at a good pace, like he's about to meet someone.

Freddie waits a few seconds, then stands up and starts walking as well.

What the hell one more time.

The trip to New Jersey—and now this?

Mike Patel is definitely up to something, and Freddie is determined to find out what.

As he walks, there is the comforting weight of his illegal Glock 26 9mm pistol on his ankle, and that is a good feeling indeed.

CHAPTER 75

WALTER WILCOX is sitting in a dusty living room with dreadful pink wallpaper in this old English farmhouse, yawning and watching the two television monitors set before him on a low counter. There are actually four, but only two are live: one shows the basement cell containing a Nigerian man who spends most of the day sitting on the floor, moving back and forth and praying to himself, and the other an American woman, a traitor who appears to be going nuts.

Walter sips from a cup of coffee. Blah. He has been in this cold rainy country for nearly a year and has yet to get a decent cup of coffee. Before this he worked in the Pentagon Force Protection Agency—guarding VIPs within the Department of Defense—until a shooting incident in Karachi kicked him loose, to be scooped up by Triangle Executive Solutions, a private security force that overlooked his drinking and other illegal activities to give him this job.

He's dressed casually: dark-blue polo shirt, khaki slacks, and a holstered 9mm Beretta 92FS at his side. Before Walter on the counter sit a handheld Motorola radio, a phone system, and a computer terminal. The radio is hooked up to the three other security guards stationed here: Frank Quinn, in the small kitchen preparing dinner; Henrietta Diaz, out on sick leave; and Desmond Hope, upstairs deep in sleep.

All of them are heavily armed and well-paid, and all of them are here from the Island of Misfit Military Screwups.

On one screen the Nigerian is still praying. On the other the American traitor lies curled up on her simple bed. Walter has enjoyed watching her the past four days. The woman has paced her small cell, cursed, torn at her hair, and shouted up at the hidden camera and microphone she knows are in the room.

She's been stripped of her shoes and jacket, is wearing only a white blouse and black slacks, and her undies. Somewhere in an encrypted folder on his personal PC, Walter has some hot videos of dark-site prisoners better looking than this bitch who had desperately stripped and performed sex acts on themselves in the hope of being set free.

But not this woman.

Not yet.

Eventually she will break, like the rest. She's on Confinement Regimen Four, meaning that a thermostat program will randomly vary the temperature from 50 to 95 degrees F. and that the lights will randomly dim to dark for periods ranging from two hours to twelve. The food slid into her cell will be two breakfasts in a row, then a heavy stew, a sandwich, and three breakfasts in a row. All designed to screw up one's internal clock, making the prisoner susceptible to future interrogations or punishments.

Another sip of this damnable coffee. He surveys the woman's simple cell: door, bed, combination stainless-steel sink and toilet. One of the other security personnel here—Quinn, the chef—likes to keep videos of the women prisoners squatting on the throne. Walter is pretty openminded, but that's a weirdness too far.

The woman is wailing. She's pulling her blouse over her head and chanting something that sounds like the Lord's Prayer—only she's repeating "Our Father" over and over again, and nothing else.

Walter is not impressed. This one is a former Army captain and CIA field officer, and the way she's collapsed and has been wailing the past couple of days only reconfirms Walter's belief that women deserve but two jobs: in the kitchen and in the bedroom.

The woman suddenly springs to her knees, facing the camera. She's holding up her wrists.

Dripping blood.

"I'm dying!" she screams.

Holy shit, Walter thinks, and he grabs his Motorola radio.

"Quinn, Hope, we've got a medical emergency in Cell Two!"

Walter grabs a first-aid kit and heads for the stairwell leading downstairs as he flicks on the light. The rules and regulations for being bad babysitters here in this hidden CIA safe house are few and far between, but the big one is to protect the prisoner. Mistreatment and torture and waterboarding and starvation are all fine, but by the end of the day, the prisoner still has to be alive.

And this one—on his watch!—has just slit her wrists.

Damn her!

Walter skids to a halt before one of the four solid and keypad-locked doors in the basement. He drops the first-aid kit and punches in the access code, and the door swings open.

The air inside the cell is cold as it washes over him. Must be at the low point of the thermostat control.

The woman is on her knees, sobbing. Blood has pooled on the floor in two puddles near her bloody wrists.

"Hey, get up!" he yells.

The woman doesn't move.

"Get up, damn it!" he yells again, wondering why in hell Quinn is taking so damn long to get here. He needs to bandage those wrists up, *now;* Walter knows from experience just how quickly someone can bleed out from severed wrist arteries.

She's gibbering now, making no sense, and he steps forward, ready to grab her hair if need be, when the woman springs up and, with the heel of her right hand, breaks his nose.

CHAPTER 76

IN THE movies and TV shows, nailing a guy's nose with the heel of your hand will drive bone fragments into his brain and instantly kill him. But real life is always messier than the movies: I've hurt the heel of my right hand and only stunned one of my captors. Still, I use those key few seconds to punch him in the throat and kick out his legs.

He thumps to the concrete floor. I grab his radio and strip him of his pistol, then stomp on his throat with my bare foot.

There's the crack and crunch of bone and cartilage shattering; obscene gurglings strain out of his mouth, and I drag him into my former cell, then return to the hallway and slam the door shut.

There.

Short hallway and a stairwell, heading *up up up* and the hell out of here.

So far, no shooting.

I'm pleased.

I start moving on bare feet, the rear of my head hurting something awful. As I get to the stairs, a heavyset guy in jeans and a black turtleneck sweater rolls out, holding a pistol in one hand and a white case with a red cross in the other.

He looks surprised.

I'm not.

I expected it.

But he moves fast, throwing the case at me and swinging around to grab his pistol with both hands to assume the proper shooting position. Me, I'm not in the mood to be proper, so I start shooting with my right hand extended. At least two shots nail him in the chest and drop him in a jumble of arms and legs.

I keep on running.

Right up the stairs.

Out into a small room. To the right, a kitchen. To the rear, another narrow set of stairs, going up. To the left, a living room transformed into a control center for this little slice of black sites.

To the front, a blessed door.

I make it to the door, open it up, and run outside, dropping the radio, just in case it has a tracer device on it.

So there has been shooting after all—and that's fine by me.

The innocent-looking cottage with an old-fashioned thatched roof looks like something out of a Jane Austen novel, but I take only two seconds to admire it before running into the woods. A dirt road leads out, but I don't take it; that stretch of lane must be surveilled and bugged from one end to the other.

The same thing for the parked dark-green Land Rover near the front door. I could waste a few moments trying to jump-start the darn thing and get it going, only to have it blow up because I didn't know the phone number to call to disable the plastic explosives hidden under the front seat.

So into the woods I go.

After I've run a few minutes, the adrenaline and endorphins begin to fade, and various aches and pains make themselves screamingly known. The back of my head hurts something fierce—a burning sensation that has left blood pooling in my hair. Earlier in my cell I had tugged my smelly blouse over my head, the better to gain access to my bra and its underwires, and trust me, you haven't lived until an underwire has unexpectedly snapped free and poked into your ribs during an office briefing.

I had then used the sharp end of the underwire to cut into the back of my skull, causing a head wound that bled like a torrent. With that blood smeared on my wrists—well, it had worked.

So now my head is burning and my feet are raw and bleeding as well, but I don't care.

I'm free.

I run away from the cottage, but I run with a purpose. Most people in an escape situation blunder and propel themselves into being captured again: human nature is to run in a circle, and you end up right where you started.

But I pick out landmarks—a birch tree, a rock outcropping, a trio of pines—and run in a straight line. Then I do the same, but at a different angle. And again.

So I'm escaping, but not in a straight line and not in a circle—but instead in chance bursts of direction that will get me away in an escape mode that's random and can't be predicted.

My attention is fragmented—being all alone, Rashad Hussain, Tom taking my *Ticonderoga* warning seriously—but I'm trying to stay focused on putting as much distance as possible between me and the CIA black site before daylight ends.

And what day is it?

No idea.

I know they were screwing with my food, temperature, light and dark, and—

The woods and brush end.

I'm on a narrow country road.

There's a stone wall nearby.

I go over to it and sit down, examine my feet, wince, and put them back on the dirt.

Somewhere out there, it sounds like someone is mowing a lawn.

I catch my breath.

Pistol in my lap.

I touch the back of my head.

My hair is a bloody, thatched mess.

My wrists and hands are stained with my blood as well.

The lawnmower sound gets louder.

I just sit.

And wait.

A truck ambles by, its horn honking.

I wave.

Not *a truck,* I chastise myself.

It's *a lorry.*

I wait.

A black Lexus comes down the road, slows, and stops.

The driver's window—still on the wrong side, my American mind complains—slides down, and a smiling Jeremy Windsor calls out to me.

"Looking for a ride, Luv?"

I stand up, grimace, and hobble across the road to the car.

"You know it," I say.

Then I hold up my pistol.

"Just don't try anything funny."

CHAPTER 77

THE INTERIOR of the Lexus is soft, warm, and oh so comfortable, and I know I'm going to collapse and maybe even doze off, but I manage to squeeze out a few questions before I do. Out to the west, the sun is setting.

"Good to see you," Jeremy says, looking at my bloody wrists and hands. "Your blood, or someone else's?"

"Mine," I say. "Bit of a sacrifice to get me out."

"Want to tell me about it?" he asks.

"No," I say.

Several seconds pass and I ask, "How long has your little drone been looking for me?"

"Since you were snatched outside of Perky's care home," he says, passing over a soft white towel and a plastic bottle of water. I unscrew the cap, take a long drag of the water, splash some on the towel, and do my best to clean up my bloodstained flesh.

"You guys know where the CIA has its secret black sites?"

Jeremy says, "What kind of intelligence service would we be if we didn't?"

"Are Winnie and Felicity around?"

"No," he says, speeding up as we get onto a highway called the

M1. "There's been a big blowup at home. Winnie and Felicity have been called off . . . and if I answer my phone, I'm sure the same's going to happen to me. Still, this is where I knew you were."

He taps on a screen about twice the size of an iPhone that's attached to the dashboard. There's an overhead view in black and white of where I had just been. Nice view, especially since I'm not there.

I take another drag of the water. Cold and so very refreshing. "Why?"

"Your boss and my boss had a fight over Rashad," he says. "My boss lost."

"Here? On your home turf? Why didn't your boss tell my boss to go to hell?"

Having been in solitary for a few disturbing days and nights, it's great to be out in the open, among the happy, innocent, and ignorant civilians speeding by in their vans, buses, and cars.

"Your boss controls the purse strings for a lot of our operations," Jeremy says. "Losing that funding over a possible terror attack, not based on actionable intelligence . . . a nonstarter."

I give out a big yawn. "Okay," I say. "You're alone. No Winnie, no Felicity. What, you were just going to keep an eye on the black site until you saw my remains hauled out in a body bag?"

"No," Jeremy says, speeding up the Lexus. "I had contacted some of my mates in the regiment."

"You were going to bust me out?"

"Yes," he says. "You know how it is in the military: steel-hard friendships, always ready to do a favor for a mate."

Another yawn, and my eyes get heavy. "Jeremy . . . what's the date?"

"May twenty-eighth."

"Then we have one day left before the attack."

"We do," he says.

Then, just as I predicted, I doze right off.

What else could I do?

Later that early evening, we're in a small house on the outskirts of one of those perfect little English villages you think exist only in a Julian Fellowes screenplay, and I'm happy to be at Jeremy's place. It's one story—white exterior with gray shingles—and surrounded on three sides by gardens. Inside there's a big kitchen, an even bigger living room with wide plank floors, a stone fireplace, and lots of books packed into bookshelves. The old-style windows are made of small glass triangles.

And no television.

He points me to a bathroom and I say, "Great place. Must have cost you a bit."

"Some," he says. "But I've never regretted it."

I yawn once again, feeling my legs quiver. "Bet you have lots of good parties here."

"No," he says, heading to the kitchen. "No one ever comes here."

"Not even female friends?"

"Especially female friends," he says, opening up a stainless-steel refrigerator. "Amy, nobody knows about this place. Even my coworkers, even my boss. I bought this through a variety of cutouts and offshore real estate companies. It's my little nest."

I head to the bathroom.

"Thanks for inviting me in," I say.

He doesn't say a word, and then, neither do I.

After a shower—and after Jeremy trims some of my wet hair to bandage the deep scratch I'd given myself—I'm surprised to see my clothing laid out on his bed, freshly washed and dried.

He offers me a pair of soft leather moccasins. "Best I can do at the moment."

"One of these days you'll make someone a perfect husband," I say, sliding them on. A bit too large, but they'll work. "Or wife. Depending on your mood and the current language of gender."

"One of these days," he says. "Come along, before our meal gets cold."

The meal is a hot omelet with cheese, veggies, and bits of sausage. There's also hand-sliced toast made from a white-bread loaf. We're drinking cold orange juice; at Jeremy's elbow is an open laptop computer.

As we eat on his butcher-block dining table, I say, "We've got to get across the pond. More resources available to us over there."

"Even with you smoked?"

"Not a problem," I say, trying to slow my chewing, because with the smell of the freshly cooked meal, my appetite's dial is pegged at 11. "I've got a source I'm sure will help us at the right time."

He says, "I might be able to get us both over there, using some of my friends to grab us tickets on a transatlantic flight without getting too particular about passport control. Tricky, but we could probably get there before midnight tonight, New York time. But then what?"

"Rashad wants to be there, don't you think?" I ask. "He wanted to kill you and Ollie, up close and personal. It's certain he was at the airport runway with that fake nuke. And he was on the scene with you when you flew to Saudi Arabia after your father was killed."

He nods, dabs a napkin on his bearded chin. "Good call. Hold on. Let's see if I can get some transport lined up."

Jeremy grabs the laptop, swivels it around, and starts working the keyboard. I say, "If you think no one from your agency knows about you and this place, you have a funny way of showing it, going online like that."

He stays focused on the screen. "I use two encrypted systems that rotate among servers in the Baltics and the Caribbean. Sometimes it's slow, but I'm confident that...hold on."

I hold on.

I keep on eating.

His brow furrows.

Something is wrong.

He works the keyboard again.

Shakes his head, looks up at me.

"Hurry up and finish your meal," he says, powering down the laptop.

Shoveling the delicious omelet into my eager mouth without really tasting it, I ask, "What's going on?"

He gets up from the table and walks his plate to the sink. He doesn't even bother scraping off the half-eaten meal.

Jeremy quickly washes his hands. "You have a saying over there about *being Gitmo'ed.* A verb meaning that you've been sent to your Guantanamo Bay, with no hopes of ever coming out again."

"Yes," I say, eating faster, growing concerned about where this conversation is going.

Jeremy heads out of the kitchen, going to his bedroom. He calls out, "We got something similar: *getting Faroe'd*—being sent to our black site up in the Faroe Islands, at the northern tip of Britain."

I get up and take my plate and glass to the sink. "Never heard of it."

"Other times I'd say that was a good thing, Amy, but not today," Jeremy tells me, opening a closet in his bedroom. "All of my computer access has just been removed, and a tracking program I have on my PC says somebody has cracked my online program and is tracing it back here."

I go into his bedroom and suddenly wonder where my stolen Beretta is.

"They're coming after you," I say.

"Yes," he says, "and we've got to leave, right now."

Spotting my Beretta on the other side of the bed, I go over to pick it up and stick it in my waistband. "Any idea where we're going?"

"Eventually to the States," he says. "But for right now I'm happy the two of us aren't in the back of an unmarked lorry, heading north."

I turn out of the bedroom. "I'll get the car started."

"But I'm driving," he says.

"Oh, you know it," I say.

CHAPTER 78

NADIA KHADRA takes a moment to look around her in awe at the tall and forbidding buildings of southern Manhattan. What a city! Paris is a jewel—the City of Light, a center of civilization—but never has she seen such buildings, standing proud and conceited around her.

She is on the corner of Fulton Street and famed Broadway, having spent a long and uncomfortable hour on the disgusting, clattering subway system that has finally brought her here to fulfill her destiny and achieve her long-sought-after revenge for her *papy* and *mémère*.

Horns are blaring from the crowded traffic on Broadway, the sound snapping her back to her task. With the precious metal briefcase in her hand and her carry-on luggage at her feet, Nadia makes the call.

It's answered on the first ring.

"Mike," the confident man says.

"I'm here," she says. "Just got off the train."

"Well done," he says, and the tone of pride in his voice nearly makes her shiver. "Walk north now, two blocks, and you'll come to a park. At the south end of the park there is an outdoor fountain. I'll be waiting there for you."

"I . . . I so look forward to meeting you," she says.

"As do I," he says. "But you're wearing the black dress and belt, correct?"

"Yes, yes, I am," she says.

"Wonderful," he says. "I'll know you when I see you. But if for some reason I don't show up in two minutes, call me again. Just to be sure."

"I understand," Nadia says. "We must be sure."

"Goodbye," he says.

Nadia slips the phone back into a pocket in her luggage and starts walking, allowing herself a moment to fantasize, to dream. This man . . . he sounds so strong, so confident, so fearless. After she delivers him the valuable case that represents nearly a year of fine and deadly work, well, what then?

It will be too dangerous to stay here, in the United States.

Go north, she thinks. To Quebec. Yes, there, in that French-speaking province, she will be able to fit in.

And . . .

A tingle of excitement nearly makes her shiver.

Perhaps this strong man will accompany her?

After all, he, too, will need a place of shelter.

She pauses at a street corner, and for some reason she turns her head. At the sight of One World Trade Center rising arrogantly into the sky, she smiles.

Freddie Farrady watches Mike take a phone call, then walk across Broadway to the southern end of City Hall Park. For more than an hour he has followed Mike all around this part of Manhattan, a boring stretch of time. But now he's no longer bored.

Someone has called Mike Patel.

But who?

Freddie joins the frantic stream of people going across Broadway and keeps eyes on Mike, who doesn't seem to care that he's being followed.

But the phone call.

It's the first time Freddie has ever seen the man take a call.

So who could it be?

A feeling comes to him so fast and so strong that he can almost taste it. Oh, to run up to Mike, slam into his back, and steal that cell phone—what he could learn if he did that!

A few more steps.

Yeah.

He'd learn what would happen after royally pissing off his MI5 supervisor here in New York: bounced out of the Yard, sent off to work foot patrol in a council-housing unit in Birmingham.

Mike stops near an ornate fountain shooting four jets of water that meet in a decorative centerpiece. There are two food stalls, kids running around and yelping, a guy in a mime's costume juggling bowling pins.

Freddie stops, leans against a black wrought-iron fence, yawns like he's incredibly bored. Or tired.

But Mike takes out his phone and makes a call.

An incoming phone call, then an outgoing one.

Something serious is up, and Freddie feels an itch on his ankle—the one where the pistol holster is fastened.

Nadia, now at the park, takes a few strides toward the fountain.

She waits and glances around, trying not to look too conspicuous.

Where is her Mike?

There are men here, and women, and some kids, and some fool performing as a juggler. She ignores the women, looks at the men. Two businessmen in suits are on a bench, talking at each other. Another is staring at a handheld device. A man in blue jeans and a white T-shirt is talking on his phone. Another man, in khakis and a short blue jacket, leans against a fence, yawning. Yet another man, this one with a young boy, enters the park, then stops and watches the fool juggler.

Where is her Mike?

She paces, feeling like an idiot, carrying her metal case and dragging her luggage behind her. On the subway ride to this park, Nadia had fantasized how this important meeting would happen, what Mike would look like, how exciting those first few minutes of finally being with him would be.

But where is he?

She stops moving, takes her phone from her roller bag.

Makes the call.

It rings.

Rings.

A number of shouts break out.

"Freeze it right there!"

"Don't move!"

"Arms up! Arms up!"

Black-clad policemen with helmets, body vests, and machine guns swarm through and around the park, all pointing their weapons at Nadia.

Oh, God, she thinks, holding the cell phone in one hand, her precious case in the other.

Where is her Mike?

CHAPTER 79

WHEN THE police appear, Mike Patel steps back, following the orders of a sweaty Hispanic police officer in standard uniform, holding out her hands, her eyes stern and sharp.

"Move back, move back, folks," she calls out. "We've got a situation developing here. Move back!"

Mike does just that, but still tries to look above the heads of everyone moving with him, just to see what in hell is going on.

More police vehicles roar up and down Broadway and nearby Park Row, lights flashing, horns honking, but no sirens. There are cruisers and squat, lorry-like vehicles that discharge heavily armed men in helmets and full battle uniform. Other police cruisers pull off and stop traffic.

He's pushed back with the other civilians, wondering how the French woman is doing.

Freddie Farrady has always had a high opinion of his NYPD brethren, but even he is impressed at their full rollout. He briefly wonders if they're going after Mike Patel—*wouldn't that be a hell of a thing to tell Portia?*—but no, they seem focused on a scared-looking woman in a black dress, her raised hands holding a cell phone and a metal case, black roll-on luggage nearby.

Kids and parents and businessmen flow out of the park. Freddie overhears a snippet of conversation—

"…Christ, I heard that woman might have a bomb in her luggage…"

—Freddie manages to duck into some park shrubbery, then scrambles up a nearby tree to assess the scene.

The NYPD has set up a perimeter around the fountain, weapons trained on a young woman with eyes wide as saucers. Four of the cops hold rectangular shields held in front of them. Two officers dressed as Michelin men—thick, heavy, dark-green protective gear—gather near a vehicle. It seems the bomb squad has arrived.

A cop emerges from the perimeter, holding out his bare hands, talking to the woman. Freddie can't hear the words but knows he's a negotiator, trying to get her to drop everything on the ground and move away. *That guy has balls made of titanium,* Freddie thinks, to stand a couple of meters from some nut whose metal case is full of C-4 and ball bearings.

Something warm is trickling down her legs. With horror and shame, Nadia realizes she has just soiled herself.

This isn't how it's supposed to be!

No!

Not after the long months of work—the times she came close to contaminating herself, or inhaling the anthrax spores, or after killing poor sweet old Madame Therien. This isn't supposed to happen!

Where is her Mike?

An American police officer is approaching her, speaking soothing words, holding out his hands. Nadia starts to weep, wondering how all this is going to end.

And then she doesn't wonder anymore.

*   *   *

Mike Patel is across Broadway, still close enough to see the park, but no longer close enough to see the woman from France.

More and more police units are arriving, blue wooden barricades are being set up, and he sighs.

One more phone call to make.

He takes out his phone, presses the programmed number.

Freddie hears a voice swear and say, "Get the hell down from there, now!" He swivels his head, sees a sweating and angry white NYPD officer looking up at him.

He says, "Just a sec, mate," wondering if he can convince Portia to check in with her police sources to find out just who in hell that woman is, and if she has a connection to Mike, and maybe—

The flash of light, the billow of smoke, and the heavy *thud* come all at once. There's even a breath of wind as the force of the explosion reaches him.

Freddie blinks his eyes.

The woman is no longer standing by the fountain.

Her luggage is scattered across the bloody pavement.

A cloud of smoke rises above the fountain.

Shouts and yells, and Freddie lowers himself from his perch.

The cop isn't angry with Freddie anymore, but he still looks wound up, his face red and sweating.

"What happened?" the cop demands. "What did you see?"

Freddie says, "Something exploded over there, where the woman was standing."

"Did it kill her?"

Freddie says, "Cut her right in half."

CHAPTER 80

AFTER A brief stop at a sporting-goods store to pick up some sneakers—or *trainers,* as they call them here in this wonderful land—Jeremy drives us through a side gate to RAF Northolt, an air base just a handful of kilometers north of London. It seems to be a relatively small base—only one runway that I can see—and Jeremy says, "If we're lucky and I can spin a good tale, we'll be able to get transportation here to the States. You and I are probably on the local no-fly lists. But I think I can squeeze us onto an RAF flight."

"Local aircraft from the base?"

Jeremy shakes his head. "No, not here. They just have helicopters and short-range transport. We need something faster and bigger."

I say, "We get to the States, we're going to need something actionable."

"You're smoked, I've been Faroe'd," he says, pulling his Lexus into a well-lit parking spot just outside a squat concrete building that looks like it was part of a buy-one-get-one-free deal. "You have an idea?"

"Yes," I say, opening up the door. "A domestic source in the States I can trust."

"You sure?" he asks as we walk up a small pathway leading to the glass doors.

"Absolutely," I say. "He's even seen me naked a few times."

Inside the reception area are two young RAF officers in dark-blue slacks and light-blue shirts, no neckties. Jeremy takes them into a corner by two desks and talks with them in low tones. One leaves through another door, and Jeremy comes back to me and says, "This will be tricky. So please, don't disturb me, no matter what."

I say, "Fair enough. But I need your phone, as insecure as it might be. I want to call my husband."

"Tom? That's . . . oh, I get it. You want to see what he can find out about Rashad."

He pulls out his iPhone, works the screen, and says, "Here. This Word document lists every company and corporation that Rashad is involved with. Hopefully your Tom can find something out."

I take the iPhone. "If Rashad's off to New York, there's got to be some sort of place he can use as a staging area, a meeting place, even an apartment to get a good night's sleep. If it's in New York and Rashad owns it, Tom will find it."

A door on the other side of the small office flies open with a bang, and a very angry and stout RAF officer stands in the doorway. Near the open door, hanging from the ceiling, is a thin TV showing BBC World News.

"Windsor," he says.

"Captain Bloom," Jeremy says. "Thanks for agreeing to see me."

The officer frowns. "That's all I've agreed to do. Come in."

Jeremy walks in, the door slams shut, and the young RAF officer remaining says, "Would you like a cup of tea?"

I hate tea, but he's so damn polite and eager. "I'd love one," I say, plopping my tired butt onto a nearby sofa. My feet are still sore, so I prop them up on a coffee table that holds a couple of copies of

Soldier magazine, *Northolt Approach* magazine, and that day's edition of the *Times*. I start dialing.

It rings.

Rings.

Oh, please...

Click.

"Cornwall."

I sag against the couch in relief, look down at the screen and at the displayed Word document. "Tom, it's Amy."

"Amy!" he cries out. The love and concern—and, yes, even a bit of anger—in his voice reach right into me and squeeze my heart. "How are you? *Where* are you? What's going on?"

I find my voice, "Oh, Tom...I'm okay. Really, I'm okay. And...I'm in an undisclosed location. You know how it is. And what's going on is...Tom, I need your help."

He says, "You got it."

The sweet young RAF officer sets a teacup and saucer down on the coffee table. "First things first," I say. "Ticonderoga. Have you packed? Have you left Manhattan?"

My love says, "Of course. I got the message."

"Where's Denise? Can I talk to her?"

"She's safe," Tom says. "She's out fishing with my Uncle John."

My overworked mind gives up for a moment, and I say, "Who?"

"John Cornwall. Retiree from ConEd. Lives on Staten Island."

I say, "South end, right?"

"Right," he says. "Practically in New Jersey."

I say, "Okay, give her my love, and for God's sake, neither of you leave there, okay?"

"Amy..."

"Tom, I don't have much time."

"I figured as much," he says. "I tried contacting you...and nothing worked. You've been fired?"

"In a manner of speaking, but that can wait," I say, not wanting to get bogged down in a lot of details. "I'm on the trail of someone, and I've come up against a wall, and I need your resources. Please."

"Go," he says. "I'm at my laptop."

"His name is Rashad Hussain," I say, and I spell it out. "Saudi national and businessman. Age thirty. And I've got a list of holding companies and corporations that I'm about to read to you...Tom, I need to know if there's anything belonging to him or associated with him that's in the Manhattan area. And Tom...I'm sorry, please, but you've got to keep this quiet. Nobody else can know."

From thousands of miles away I hear Tom's fingers hitting the keyboard, and that familiar and homey sound almost makes me choke up with emotion.

"This...it's connected to Ticonderoga."

"Yes. But please, don't push me. Not now. It's too important."

Tom says, "I know what you're saying. Nobody else will know. I promise. Okay. Go."

"First up," I say, "is a real estate company, Five Corners Realty..."

And so it goes for another five minutes, husband and wife, devoted lovers, speaking professionally and calmly, trying to stop someone intent on killing thousands.

Shouts are coming from the office into which Jeremy and the RAF officer disappeared. "Okay, Hon," I tell Tom, "that's it."

"When do you need it?"

"Soon," I say, "but you've got some time. I'm going to be out of pocket for six hours."

"Flying home?" he asks.

I laugh. "My dear one, you'll hear all about it, but only after the two of us have a nice home-cooked meal—by you!—and a long shower."

He laughs in return. "Who's taking the shower?"

"The two of us," I say, "but only if you promise to wash my back."

"And the front?"

I feel so much better. "Gotta go. Love you, and Denise."

"Love you, too."

I disconnect and sit back, feeling still better. The shouting goes on behind the closed door, and I know my Tom so well I'm sure he's now working hard, digging, and starting to make phone calls.

Jeremy's phone chimes at me.

I sit up.

It keeps on ringing. The screen says BLOCKED NUMBER.

Jeremy said not to disturb him, but still...this could be important.

I answer the phone. "Jeremy Windsor's phone."

A man's soft voice says, "Is he available?"

"No," I say. "He's not. But he might be free in a few minutes. Can I take a message?"

The man says, "Oh, that's all right. Perhaps I will call later, speak to him face-to-face."

The voice is cultured, civilized, with a slight accent.

I squeeze the iPhone so tight I imagine I might shatter it.

"Rashad," I say, "why don't you give me a number so he can call you back?"

CHAPTER 81

FREDDIE FARRADY is in the midst of breaking another American law—having begun his illegal activities by smuggling a pistol into New York City—and he doesn't really care. He has entered the small brick building on the corner of 30th Street and Newtown Avenue by helping an older woman carry in her shopping bags, and now he is working on the lock for Mike Patel's second-floor flat.

There.

The knob turns open and he puts away the two lockpicks into his pocket, then he quickly enters the apartment and closes the door behind him.

He takes a breath. All right, then.

And something is instantly off.

In all the black-bag jobs like this he's done for Special Branch—no warrants or paperwork—the flats always had a dreary sameness: stench of cooking grease, tobacco, take-away containers or trash on the floor, soiled nappies piled in the loo.

But not this time.

The tiny flat looks clean, ordered. Two windows—sans screens—are open. Before him is a little kitchen area, small table with two chairs. Fridge and two-burner stove.

He steps in farther, begins a quick toss of the place.

Living room with a single couch and one chair. Small TV on a built-in bookcase, the other shelves empty of books.

There's a hint of an odor now, something that tickles his memory.

He goes into the bedroom.

An hour after the bombing at City Hall Park and after numerous attempts, Freddie had managed to contact his MI5 supervisor, Portia Grayson. She had instantly cut him off.

"I don't have time to talk about Patel," she had said. "I've been called to the consulate to work with my French counterparts on finding out who this woman was. All we know is that she came from de Gaulle. Now leave me alone."

Okay, he thinks in Patel's neat bedroom. He's leaving her alone, and he's also working quickly because he knows Patel will be home shortly. But Freddie doesn't believe in coincidences, and it's hard to believe—Portia notwithstanding—that Mike's presence in City Hall Park is not connected to that French tourist blowing herself up.

The bed is made, the place looks clean. Three newspapers on the small nightstand: the *Post*, the *Daily News*, and a four-day-old copy of *Al-Quds Al-Arabi*, published in Britain. The adjoining bathroom has a shower and a toilet. Here, at least, Patel is not perfect: both the stall and the bowl could use a good cleaning.

That little odor seems stronger.

What is it?

It's tickling him like a dream half-remembered during the daylight hours.

What's triggering him?

He opens the closet. A few shirts and slacks dangling from the hanger, two pairs of dirty trainers on the floor.

The smell is even stronger here.

"Oh, shit," he says.

He gets to his knees, pulls the trainers out, feels the floorboards. Loose. He picks up one, then two.

There.

Nestled in crumpled-up newspaper is an American-made M4 automatic rifle.

Gun oil.

That's what he's been smelling.

Gun oil.

He takes out the M4, spies six spare magazines hidden in the packing as well. Thirty rounds each. Meaning two hundred and ten 5.56mm bullets all told, designed to kill and wound and maim in combat, ready to be used . . .

Here, of course.

But where?

And when?

He digs deeper, finds a blue Kevlar bullet-resistant vest under all the wadded-up newspaper.

A shoot-out, then—but Patel isn't going out as a suicide shooter. He's planning on protecting himself.

Freddie thinks for a moment, then takes a couple of minutes to field-strip and examine the M4. When he's done, he reassembles the M4 and replaces it among the crumpled newsprint.

Nestled about the crumpled newspapers is a slip of paper.

He pulls it out, unfolds it, and reads the carefully printed letters and numbers:

LIFT FOUR
6, 6, 8, 9
ACCESS ROOF
9, 8, 6, 6

Freddie memorizes the words and numbers, puts the paper slip back.

Replaces the floorboards.

Gets up, closes the closet door.

Heads out of the bedroom and into the living room—just in time to hear the apartment door being unlocked.

CHAPTER 82

IN A small corner office in the large bonded warehouse in Hoboken owned by one of Rashad's companies, he shakes his head in amusement and says, "Are you sure? Are you certain Jeremy isn't available?"

The American woman on the other end says, "Let's see... yep, both eyes working. He's not here. Can I take a message? Can he call you back?"

Rashad allows himself a laugh and says, "Who is this? His secretary? Girlfriend? Married lover?"

The woman laughs right back. "Sorry, Rashad, I'm his boss. And you've called at a bad time. You see, we're on our way to kill you. How's your day going?"

He stands up from the desk he's been using in this windowless office. On the other side of the door are four of his associates, waiting for one last briefing. He'd been planning to use this call to taunt and upset Jeremy a final time.

Not this.

"Who the hell are you to say such a thing?" Rashad asks.

The woman laughs again. "Amy Cornwall, former U.S. Army, now an intelligence officer for the United States. How's New York been treating you? Getting in the sights? Check out Times Square if you can...not many strip clubs left, but a loser like you could probably find one. I mean, that's the only place you can get up close and personal with a naked woman, am I right?"

He swears at the woman for a long minute and—*damn it*—she laughs at him again!

"Oh, Rashad, come on, is that the best you can do?" she says when he pauses. "Didn't you hear what I said earlier, or do you have desert sand clogging your hairy ears? I served in the United States Army. I heard better swear words from recruits who were so young they couldn't shave. Jeremy and I know all about you, Rashad. We know how your dad hated you. How you've never married. I've even talked to your three half-sisters. They all said the same thing: you cried at night and wet the bed, even when you were a teen boy."

"I did not!" he shouts, ashamed that he's losing his temper.

"Rashad...come on, deep down, you know what's going on, don't you?" her calm voice says. "You hated Daddy growing up, when he had your balls in his back pocket, and you killed him. And with him dead, you thought you could start getting an erection on a regular basis. But even with all your money, you couldn't even do that. Failure, start to finish. Even your precious organization is riddled with informants. Trains, I mean...*trains?* What are you, still ten years old?"

"Failure!" he says, then easing his voice. "You whore, I'm going to stand on top of my wealth and kill thousands of you. Do you hear me? Thousands. And there's nothing you or Jeremy can do. Nothing."

His breathing has quickened. He can't believe how angry this woman has made him.

"Rashad?" she asks. "Still there?"

"I am, you bitch. I am going to find you and kill you and your family and—"

"Hey, Rashad, nice talking to you, but I've got something more important to do: I've got to go change out my tampon . . . and then Jeremy and I are coming after your sorry ass. Later."

The American woman disconnects the call.

Rashad throws the phone on the floor.

Throws open the door.

Stalks right out.

In the dim light, crates and packages stretch into the darkness. Before him, sitting around a round table with paperwork and maps, are his four men: Mike Patel, Marcel Koussa, and two train conductors working for the Hudson Valley Railroad (which he secretly owns): Miguel Marcos, from the Abu Sayyaf group in the Philippines, and Alvi Dudin, from the Special Purpose Islamic Regiment of Chechnya.

All four of them are looking at him with a mixture of respect, fear, and curiosity about what just happened in that small office.

Rashad nods to them, goes over to the table, and removes a 9mm SIG Sauer pistol from his coat pocket. Then he grabs Marcel's hair and tugs his head back.

Marcel starts to talk, but an enraged Rashad sticks the pistol barrel into Marcel's mouth and blows his brains out with one quick snap of his finger.

Marcel's body slumps to the floor.

The three other men stare at him.

Rashad's anger turns inward. Damn that woman! He had planned to take away Marcel and spend long delicious hours with him, finding out how deep his betrayal had gone and how much he had passed along to British intelligence. But his anger took hold instead.

Marcel is dead. A loss, but still, he wasn't a friend. He was just a worker, to be dismissed—or eliminated—when necessary.

Rashad takes a deep breath.

Replaces the pistol in his coat pocket.

It won't do for these three others—who will help him bring down an empire tomorrow—to see him unsettled, unsure, filled with doubt or fear.

He smiles at his brave trio.

"That man was a traitor," Rashad says. "We will not speak of him again. We have much more to discuss about tomorrow's blessed day."

CHAPTER 83

JEREMY WINDSOR leaves Captain Bloom's office feeling worn out and exhausted. *It's one thing to break and humiliate an enemy to gain one's goals,* he thinks, *but another to do it to a fellow service member.* Still, he has to get Amy and himself to New York, even if that means disgusting his own self by telling Captain Bloom what he knows about the captain's tastes when it comes to enjoying some illegal pleasures in Brussels while visiting NATO headquarters.

The ashamed captain had finally broken, but not until after a lot of threats and yelling. At any other time, Jeremy would need a stiff drink and a hot shower to put him right, but there's no time.

In the small exterior office, Amy is on Jeremy's iPhone and he hears something odd as she disconnects and returns the phone to him. He takes the phone and says, "Did I hear you right? Did you tell someone that Jeremy and you were coming after his *ass*?"

"That's right," she says, adjusting her slacks around her waist, the weight of the 9mm Beretta tugging them down. "You've got good hearing."

"Who was it?" he asks, seeing that the two RAF officers—no

doubt having heard the yelling from Bloom's office—have left the building.

"It was Rashad Hussain," she says simply.

Jeremy, putting his iPhone back in his jacket, freezes at what he's just heard.

"Amy, for God's sake, please tell me you're joking."

"I'm not," she says. "I got hold of my husband, Tom; he's busy at work doing research for us, and when our call was completed, a call came in saying it was blocked. I answered it and it was Rashad."

"For God's sake, Amy, why in hell didn't you come get me?"

She says, "You told me not to interrupt your meeting."

"Not if bloody Rashad Hussain called!"

Amy's face hardens. "Sorry, Jeremy, but he was on the phone, and he wanted to talk. I wasn't going to risk putting him on hold or disconnecting him."

"You still should have gotten me."

"Well, I didn't," she says.

Jeremy says, "Amy, for Christ's sake, pulling shit like that almost makes me regret rescuing you back there."

Her eyes glare. "Let's stop rewriting history, Mister Windsor. You didn't rescue me; I rescued me. You offered me a lift, a shower, some food and clean clothes. All greatly appreciated. But don't go medieval on my ass because I didn't go trotting to you when that son of a bitch called."

Jeremy actually grits his teeth. "What did he say?"

Amy's teacup is still on the coffee table. She picks it up, takes a sip, makes a face. "Ugh," she says. "Tastes like dishwater. Rashad? Oh, yeah—he apologized for all he's done and says he's going to surrender to us in front of the Statue of Liberty. He asked that we bring some bagels and cream cheese. Damn it, don't be dense. He barely said a word."

If Amy had been a fellow squaddie from the regiment, Jeremy knows he would have coldcocked her, right here and now. "Stop it," he says. "Tell me what he said."

She takes another swallow, grimaces again, puts the cup down. "Nothing. I wouldn't let him finish. He said he wanted to talk to you. I told him you were busy. Then I told him you and I were on our way to kill him. He didn't take it graciously."

"Anything else?"

"A bit of discussion about his lack of manhood, how he was still desperately seeking Daddy's attention, and I told him I had talked to his three half-sisters, who all said he had nightmares and wet the bed."

"You . . . you haven't talked to his sisters."

"I know that, and you know that, but he doesn't know that," Amy says. "Look, Jeremy, the little shit was calling you to taunt you. I just gave it right back to him. Got him angry. Upset. In a foul mood. That happens, he might do something stupid. Overreact. Be impulsive. All things that can work in our favor."

"That was . . ."

"Not smart?" Amy asks. "Maybe, but what he's going to do otherwise? Plan to kill people twice tomorrow?"

Jeremy shakes his head again. "You . . . enough. I've got transport to the United States—an American Air Force base in New Jersey. Two Typhoon jet fighters will be landing here in less than half an hour. They were designated to fly to Ramstein in Germany, but their orders are now being changed."

"Good job," Amy says.

"No, it was a rotten job," Jeremy says, rubbing his eyes. "You know earlier, when I said that we in the service make steel-like bonds with others, and can rely on them for favors? There's a dark underbelly to that when you find someone's hidden shame, hidden weaknesses, and drag it out into the open to get what you need."

"You had something on the captain, then."

"I did."

"What was it?"

"None of your business, Amy," he says. "It got us two twin-seater Typhoons to America. Leave it at that." He takes a breath. "Come along—we've got to get kitted out if we want to get there before he uses his trains to disperse the weaponized anthrax."

He turns and takes two steps, then realizes Amy isn't following him. He looks at her and sees her head is tilted back, watching a TV broadcasting the BBC World Service.

The news footage shows a park with NYPD personnel gathered around a fountain. There are lumps of something on the pavement, and yellow sheets, and little plastic triangles marking bits of evidence to be collected and recorded.

The slow-moving crawl at the bottom of the screen says:

DEADLY ANTHRAX ATTACK THWARTED IN MANHATTAN WHEN WOULD-BE TERRORIST KILLS HERSELF WITH A SUICIDE BELT...

With near admiration in her voice, Amy says, "That tricky, slippery, son-of-a-bitch eel! First the suitcase nuke, and now this. He spent all this time working with that Frenchwoman, getting her prepared with weaponized anthrax, and at the very last moment sacrificing her to keep his real mission secret. He's very good at setting up red herrings, isn't he?"

Jeremy says, "And MI6 and the CIA will now think Rashad's been stopped."

"Yeah," says Amy, her voice tired. "But we know better, don't we? And we don't have the time or connections to convince our higher-ups otherwise."

Jeremy keeps staring at the scene in Manhattan. Two investigators in large yellow hazmat suits with astronaut-style helmets are waddling toward the lumps on the ground.

"We still don't know what he's going to do," he says.

Amy starts for the door. "Sure we do," she says. "He's planning to kill thousands of my countrymen within the next twenty-four hours. The rest is just details. Come on—we don't want to be late."

CHAPTER 84

FREDDIE FARRADY'S feet and shins ache something fierce, but his growing anger at Portia Grayson from MI5 is helping him ignore the pain.

They are sitting in a Dunkin' Donuts on Rector Street, just blocks away from where he saw the Frenchwoman get blown in half as the NYPD kept her at bay, but Portia refuses to acknowledge the evidence before her thin and disapproving face.

"Portia, don't you see it?" Freddie demands. "A suicide bomber carrying enough weaponized anthrax to kill about ten thousand people...and Mike Patel is in the crowd, watching? You don't think that needs to be investigated?"

They are sitting in a far corner of the coffee shop, on pink chairs. Freddie hates the color pink.

Portia takes a disapproving sip from her late-evening coffee. "There were scores of people near that deranged woman. Did you see Mike talk to her? Or approach her?"

"No, but earlier I saw Mike receive a phone call and make a phone call."

"Do you know if she was contacted by Mike?"

Freddie wants to punch the tired but smug face in front of

him. "Portia, there's something going on with Mike, something big. Look, an hour after the bombing, I got into his apartment and—"

His MI5 supervisor puts her cardboard coffee cup down on the pink tabletop so hard that a little spurt of liquid spouts out from the plastic lid. "You broke into his apartment? Without my permission? Without the necessary documentation?"

"To hell with your permission, and to hell with your documentation," Freddie says. "I found an American M4 automatic rifle with more than two hundred rounds of ammo and a bullet-resistant vest. Portia, he's more than an HVAC tech. You know that."

Portia picks up a brown napkin, gently wipes up the spill, and dabs the top of the coffee cup. "Freddie, you're out," she says, with ice and calm in her voice. "I'll make the necessary arrangements to get a replacement. You've screwed up this job, terribly. Suppose you had been caught in that man's flat?"

As if on cue, Freddie's feet and lower legs throb in painful memory. After hearing Patel unlock the door, he had escaped the only way he could: Freddie thrust himself through one of the two open windows, hung down as far as he could by his fingertips, and then let go, hoping his years-old training in doing a drop-and-roll parachute landing would work.

His feet and legs throb again.

It did work, but it was sloppy. Freddie says, "If I had been caught in the man's flat, then at least something would have happened. We would have brought in the NYPD, figure out what he is doing."

"You would have threatened the investigation."

Freddie keeps his voice low but sharp. "What bloody investigation is that, Portia? All I've done is trail him around Manhattan and New Jersey like some deranged internet stalker. What's the investigation? Why is he being looked into?"

Portia says, "I'm under no obligation to tell you."

Freddie sees his error and tries to walk it back. "Then, please.

My boss back at the Yard will want to know what went wrong, in detail. Help me, then—what is the investigation?"

A pleased look flashes across that severe face. "Immigration."

"What?"

A confident nod. "Immigration. Somehow Mr. Patel quickly got the necessary papers and funds to come here to the States. We believe he's part of an organized ring—located here in New York and Manchester—that is part of a large illegal-immigration organization. And that, Mr. Farrady, is that."

Portia picks up her coffee and leaves the little coffee shop.

Freddie checks his watch.

Fifteen minutes have passed.

His career has just taken a serious hit. You don't screw up an MI5 op like this and not suffer some consequences.

But damn it, he knows he's right!

He takes out his iPhone, starts scrolling through a directory.

"In for a penny, in for a pound," he whispers, as he finds the number he's looking for—745-0200—and waits for it to be picked up.

It doesn't take long.

"British Consulate," a cheery young man answers.

Freddie digs through his memory. Remarkably, he comes up with the name that was passed on to him a long time ago by a retired MI6 field officer giving a lecture on overseas operations and what to do in the event of an unanticipated, serious threat.

"Amanda Trevor," he says. "Agricultural attaché, please."

CHAPTER 85

AT THE Southern Terminal dispatch office for the Hudson Valley Railroad near Hoboken, Orrin Block tries to stifle a yawn as he leafs through that day's manifest for his trip up to Albany. Orrin's been an engineer for Hudson Valley for three years now and hates every minute of it. His father had been a train engineer, his grandfather had been a train engineer, and like a dope, he had agreed to join the family trade.

He takes a deep swallow of his coffee. It's very early morning on May 29 and Orrin doesn't care what the clock says, it's the goddamn middle of the night. The dispatch room is crowded with other engineers, conductors, yard personnel, and there's the smell of coffee, sweat, smoke, and always, always, the stench of diesel fuel, and he hates it so.

But Dad and Granddad had kept on yapping about the joy of being out on the rails, wind in your hair, watching the beauty of the Great Plains, the Rocky Mountains, the Pacific Ocean, the Great Lakes, *blah blah blah.*

The only thing he's seen is the depressing corridor between here and Albany, and with jobs tightening up and most of the railroads consolidating, Orrin's been stuck here—and stuck here as well with his girlfriend, Kimmy.

Another yawn. He had stayed out way too late with Kimmy and her posse of girls—tight clothes, fake nails and boobs, tramp-stamp tattoos—and once again, after a quick lay back at her place, she had gone on about how long they had been seeing each other, and wasn't it time to set a date, and how it isn't fair to lead a girl on like this...

To hell with that.

He looks up from his manifest and checks out his conductor, sitting across from him: Miguel Marcos, quiet guy from the Philippines, with dark-olive skin, brown eyes, and thick black hair, which he combs back in some kind of thick pompadour. Miguel is okay, but he sure is quiet in the cab—all business. Orrin's not sure what kind of experience Miguel had back in Manila, but he's quick on the job and is a good guy to have at your side.

Orrin remembers being at a bar in Weehawken nearly a year ago with some of the other guys from the yard. Some big biker started giving Miguel crap and Miguel tried to ignore it, staying really calm until the biker just started grabbing him and pushing him. Then Miguel snapped and used some Filipino karate shit that left the guy bleeding from his nose and with two broken wrists.

And never again did Miguel say a word about it.

"Hey, Miguel," Orrin says, kicking his conductor's boot with his own under the table. "Ready for another day in paradise?"

Miguel smiles. "Sure am, Orrin."

Orrin says, "I love my job. How about you?"

His smile stays right there. "I sure do."

Orrin laughs, goes back to his manifest. He was lying to Miguel about loving his job, and the funny thing is—Orrin has a pretty good bullshit detector—he's sure Miguel is lying, too.

But why?

*   *   *

At the Northern Terminal dispatch office for the Hudson Valley Railroad in Albany, Brian Lamott sits down near his conductor, Alvi Dudin, with that morning's manifest for their trip south to Hoboken. Brian yawns, still not used to getting up at this ungodly hour, but happy in knowing that he's exactly two months and three days from retirement. And at two months and five days he will take his wife, Elayne, on a long-promised second honeymoon across Canada aboard the TransCanadian Railway, relishing being a passenger on a train and not its engineer.

Elayne has been patient in waiting for this honeymoon, but Elayne being Elayne, she announced last night that their twin granddaughters—Bridget and Lindsay—would be coming along as well. Brian had protested at first, but Elayne set him straight: "The girls hardly know you, and you don't know them. You still can't tell them apart."

"Not true," he had said. "Bridget's the one with the little birthmark on her forehead."

"Wrong," Elayne had said. "That's Lindsay."

Brian goes back to the paperwork for that day's run, smiling to himself, content that Elayne would never know he had secretly wished she would do something exactly like that; the thought of spending a week with his wife and their granddaughters gives him a warm feeling indeed.

"Hey, Alvi," he says.

"Right here, boss," Alvi says, checking his phone.

"Have you seen the manifest?"

"Sure have," he says.

"You see anything out of place?"

Alvi lifts his head from the phone, smiles. "You mean the fact we're hauling more than we should, so Hudson Valley can squeeze more from us?"

"Nah," Brian says. "That's typical. Did you see who the last four flatbeds belong to?"

"Sure," Alvi says. "Department of Energy."

Brian is pleased at his conductor's response. Alvi is a Russian refugee—hardly an accent to his voice—but he has a good work attitude and a sharp eye, and he can memorize practically any document placed before him. Alvi had looked at the manifest more than an hour ago, but the kid could still recall what was listed.

"What do you think the DOE is shipping to Hoboken?" Brian asks.

Alvi shrugs. "Beats me. What do you think?"

Brian makes sure they're not being overheard. Paranoid, sure, but you didn't want a reputation for being a gossiper. Even though Brian is pulling the pin in less than three months, he wants to go out as the pro he's always been.

"I tell you what I think," Brian says. "Department of Energy means more than oil and wind. It's nuclear, too, and think about it: we got two nuclear power plants in the upstate, at Ginna and Nine Mile Point. That nuclear waste's gotta be transported somehow. Why not put it on trains? I've seen it done before on other rail lines."

Alvi says, "Isn't that dangerous?"

Brian shakes his head. "Nah, I don't think so. They're packed in pretty secure casks. But still, you'd think they'd give the train crew a full brief before asking us to haul that dangerous crap a couple of hundred miles, right across from Manhattan."

Alvi smiles. "Yes, you would think."

CHAPTER 86

IN HIS office at One World Trade Center, Tom Cornwall takes a swallow of cold coffee and gets right back to work. It's dark in the other offices, and with the pressure knotting his forehead and the burning feeling in his belly after drinking all that coffee and pulling this all-nighter, he knows he will pay a price later today.

But if he can help his wife, Amy, so what?

He's done a lot of digging online during the past few hours and has gotten a few hits about properties in the Manhattan area owned by this Rashad Hussain. But in his gut, Tom knows there's more. Tricky rich people got rich and stayed rich because of how they gamed the system, how they hid their assets, and at any other time, Tom would spend long hours in front of his keyboards and screens, gently untangling lines of property ownership and offshore accounts. But the tone of Amy's voice earlier tells him he doesn't have the time.

So he's ventured into the dark web, armed with some cryptocurrency accounts that neither Amy nor his boss, Dylan Roper, knows he has. Tom has always been reluctant to wander the dark web—the favorite place for terrorists, drug dealers, and pedophiles to do their business—because he doesn't want any three-letter federal agency to know he's been in that nasty swamp.

But the dark web has other places as well, such as information brokers with the skill sets to get what one needs, and fast.

He yawns, stretches his back, feels a splash of guilt over the lie he had told Amy before.

All right, not a full lie, but a half-lie, because at this moment Denise *is* slumbering peacefully at Uncle John's place in south Staten Island. Yet Tom had told Amy that's where he is, too.

Instead he is here in his office, with the connections, hardware, and software to do what needs to be done.

A soft rap on the side of his open office door makes him nearly leap from his chair.

"Hey, Tom—sorry to scare you like that," says a concerned-looking blond woman wearing tan slacks and a blue sweater. "But what the hell are you doing here so early?"

He wipes at his crusty eyes. "Got a project that needs me, and now."

Stephanie Harris, an exile from the AP who works the night shift, nods and says, "Good luck. And I hope you've got something good. I just ran into Dylan, and he's in one pissy mood."

"That's his usual mood."

Stephanie smiles, steps back from the door. "But this morning it's more usual than ever. Seems a group of investors have called an unscheduled meeting with him, and if it doesn't go a certain way...well, I'll finally have time to write that series of cozy mysteries about tai chi instructors. Hope you got something similar in your back pocket. Take care."

Tom nods, stretches his back again, goes back to the computer screen, checks the time.

Nearly six hours have passed since his last call with Amy.

Where could she be?

CHAPTER 87

AFTER SPENDING just over six hours in the rear cockpit of an RAF Typhoon, I'm walking on the tarmac of McGuire Air Force Base in New Jersey, about sixteen miles south of Trenton. I'm focused on one thing, and one thing only.

Where the hell is the nearest bathroom?

Under my left arm is a pilot's helmet; in my right hand I'm carrying a Costcutter plastic shopping bag holding my civvies, shoes, and a heavy lump in the bottom—the 9mm Beretta. My flight gear feels like a four-layer fat suit: thermal underwear, a woolen "bunny suit," and an immersion suit (to protect my sorry ass if we had ejected over the North Atlantic), all wrapped in a flying suit and G-pants. Various straps and hoses dangle from my person, and I'm wearing borrowed heavy black boots that hurt my feet something awful.

Maverick from *Top Gun* I ain't.

Striding toward me like he was born wearing military clothes is Jeremy. As he gets closer, he calls out, "All right, I contacted an asset in Princeton who's agreed to lend us a car and two cell phones. He's en route."

God, do I need to find a bathroom. There are no bathroom facilities in fighter jets, especially for female pilots, and I wasn't about to wear an adult diaper. And the past six hours over the North Atlantic were long ones indeed.

I say, "You MI6 boys...girls in every port, assets in every city. Glamorous way of doing things."

"Not quite," he says. "I told Captain Bloom back at RAF Northolt that MI6 would reimburse the RAF for the refueling costs over the ocean."

"That's a lie."

"Of course it was a lie," Jeremy says. "Meaning I'll have to pay for it someday...probably by selling my little cottage if MI6 doesn't come up with the funds. And as a hidey-hole, the poor place is now useless."

We walk to a wide-open hangar and I see lines of Air Force aircraft parked on the aprons: KC-10 refuelers, huge C-17 transport aircraft, and smaller, four-engine C-130s. Some Air Force personnel in work fatigues look at us with curiosity as we duck into the hangar and find a desk near the entrance. I dump my plastic bag and flying helmet, hold out my hand.

"Let's see what my local intelligence agency has found out," I say.

Jeremy digs through his flying suit and says, "My guy was Flight Lieutenant Gibbs. Chatted my ear off. How about you?"

"Mine was Jenny Horton, pissed to be missing her son's fifth birthday party. And you're still mispronouncing *lieutenant*."

I use the desk phone to make the call.

It's picked up on the first ring.

"Cornwall."

I briefly close my eyes in relief and delight. My man's voice sounds strong, confident, and oh so close. Being on Staten Island, Tom and my girl are safe—and only an hour away. Sixty minutes!

"Tom, it's Amy."

And I love the pleasure in his voice as he says, "Amy...I guess you're back in the States."

"I am . . . and let me tell you, here for good. No more foreign adventures for your second-best girl."

"Serious?" he asks.

Jeremy is glaring at me and I pull back to reality. "Tom, that's for later. I'm going to put you on speaker—please tell me you've found something out."

"A fair amount," he says. "Got a pen and paper?"

I open the center drawer of the gray metal desk, yank out a pencil stub, and start writing on a McDonald's receipt.

"Go," I say, as Jeremy hovers over me.

"All right," he says. "I won't go into the details of the ownership—it's pretty tangled—but your man Rashad Hussain is linked with three hotels: the Nansen Arms, the Vantage Point, and the Excelsior Suites. There are also two townhouses in Greenwich Village, and two bodegas in Spanish Harlem."

I scribble notes, my mood sinking with every pencil scratch. Good God, today is the day he plans to kill so many innocents, and already we have seven places where he might be hiding.

How in hell can we possibly investigate? With the two of us being smoked by our respective intelligence agencies? Do we dial 911 and say, *Hey, NYPD, not for nothing, but there's a deadly terrorist who might be hiding out in a bodega in Spanish Harlem. Mind stopping by to see if he's there?*

Tom's voice cuts through my dark musings. "Oh, and I saved the best for last."

"What's that?"

Two Air Force officers are coming our way looking pissed, and I have a feeling one of them is the owner of the desk I'm using.

Tom says, "Your man owns a railway in New Jersey."

It feels like the cement floor in this hangar has turned to quicksand.

"Tom, give me more," I say. "It's very, very important."

"It's called the Hudson Valley Railroad," he says. "About four years old. Built up on old right-of-ways and some new track. It runs up and down the valley, has main terminals in Albany and in Hoboken. But here's the funny bit."

"What's that?" I ask.

Tom says, "I managed to get some information on its financials. The railway consistently runs in the red. Almost like your Rashad wants to keep it running."

Jeremy locks eyes with me. "Or *needs* to have it running. Hoboken…"

I nod to him. "Yeah. Right across the Hudson River is lower Manhattan."

The Air Force officers are very near. I feel sorry for the two men, because in about fifteen seconds Jeremy and I are going to blow right by them.

Jeremy says, "Rashad…explosions. There's something he's planning to do with his trains."

"You know it."

"But—"

From the speakerphone I hear some voices, a shout, and Tom says, "Amy, look, I gotta go."

I'm about to say something loving and thankful to him, but he disconnects.

Jeremy says, "How in hell are we going to find out what we need to know about that railway?"

I point to the phone. "You're going to call London—that's how."

CHAPTER 88

TOM CORNWALL hears Amy talking to someone on the other end of the call—a male Brit?—and there's a hard knock on the side of his open door.

His boss, Dylan Roper.

"Tom?" he asks, face red, eyes angry, his usually fine seersucker suit looking like he's slept in it for two nights straight.

"Hey, Dylan," Tom says. "I'm on a call here."

Dylan takes two steps into his office. "I can tell. I've been hearing it for the past couple of minutes."

"You're eavesdropping?"

"Listening," Dylan says. "Looks like you got something big going on there. What is it?"

"Can't tell you," Tom says.

Dylan says, "The hell you can't."

He picks up his phone, says, "Amy, look, I gotta go."

Tom quickly disconnects the call, wishing he had said something more sweet and loving to Amy before doing so. "I don't have a story for you, Dylan."

His boss comes further into his office, and Tom can almost smell the fear and desperation coming off him. Dylan says, "You're bull-shitting me, and I won't stand for it. I heard enough: a Saudi national in Manhattan...his real estate interests...something to do with a local railroad."

Tom keeps his gaze steady toward his angry boss. "Nothing newsworthy there, Dylan."

Dylan uses both hands to lean over Tom's cluttered desk. "That's even more bullshit. I heard your last message. You were saying goodbye to your wife, Amy. Am I right?"

Tom keeps quiet.

Damn.

Dylan nods. "I thought so. What's going on, Tom? You're doing a favor for your wife, an intelligence officer—either CIA or some other agency, I really don't give a shit. But you're passing along something you've learned to your wife. That means you're passing on something to the government."

"Dylan, I was doing a favor for Amy, yes, but I—"

His boss is having none of it. "Stop it, and stop it right now. You listen to me, Tom Cornwall. I have first dibs on whatever it is you've just found out. Whatever you did for your wife, you did it here, in my office, using my equipment, my furniture— hell, even my electricity. That means your work product took place here. And you took that work product and gave it to the government. To hell with that. I have first dibs, Tom. Tell me: what the hell is going on?"

Lots of responses tumble through his mind, but all Tom can think of is what he had earlier said to his wife:

Nobody else will know.

Dylan stands up with a start, and his manner changes. "Tom...please. I just had a brutal meeting with our investors. They're going to shut us down in a month unless we get a turn- around. You've got something going on. I know it, you know it. You write me that story today—take even two days. If it's some- thing that gets the investors' attention, it can save me."

Tom finds it hard to look at the desperate man in front of him. "I'm sorry, Dylan, I can't say a word."

Dylan says, "You . . . all right. I know I'm a pain in the ass. A snob. A prick." He waves his right hand toward Tom's open office door. "But how about the rest of Criterion News? Your coworkers? The people out there who depend on this place for their livelihood, to support themselves, elderly parents, their kids? You know the state of journalism. Do you think it's going to be easy for your friends out there to find a job next month?"

Quietly and with heaviness in his words, Tom says, "No, it won't be easy."

Dylan nods. "Then don't do it for me. Do it for them."

Tom shakes his head. "Dylan . . . I can't. I just can't."

A quick snap of Dylan's jaw. "Fine. You're fired. Get the hell out of here. Now."

He closes his eyes for a moment.

Nobody else will know.

Amy, I promise.

"Fair enough," Tom says. "Give me an hour to gather up my—"

Dylan says, "Jesus, didn't you hear what I just said? *Now.* That means now."

Tom spares a glance around his cluttered office. "Dylan, I've got a lot of files, belongings, other stuff to box up. It'll take me some time. Be reasonable."

"Screw you, and screw being reasonable," he shoots back. "I want to see your Criterion ID and building key card on that desk—right now!—and you out the door. I'll get your crap boxed up and shipped to your home."

"Dylan . . ."

"I'm not in the mood for negotiating, Tom," Dylan says. "Out. Now. Or I'll get building security to escort you out, right past your coworkers. You want that, I can make it happen."

Tom slowly gets up, digs a hand into his left pants pocket, pulls out the key card and drops it on the desk. He takes his Criterion identification card out of his wallet, surrenders that as well.

He closes up his personal laptop and stows it in his bag. As he moves around his desk, he spots the collection of family photos on the wall.

Dylan says, "Hurry your ass up, Tom."

Tom takes down a framed family portrait, his favorite: it shows the three of them at a lake up in Maine last fall, the foliage bright red and yellow, their smiles so happy and wide.

Dylan says, "I believe that frame belongs to Criterion."

Tom doesn't say a word. He goes to the rear of the photo, tries to undo the backing. It's tight. There are four metal tabs that refuse to bend.

He takes the framed photo, smashes it against the corner of his desk. The glass shatters and he digs at the broken frame, freeing the photo. He folds it in half and puts it in his computer bag.

"Deduct it from my last paycheck," he says, walking out past Dylan.

Tom walks through the newsroom with his shoulders straight, not catching anyone's eyes. No time to explain, no time to talk.

He just wants out.

Nearing the elevator bank, he's surprised to see a small crowd of employees and young girls clustered around.

"Man, we've been waiting here for ten minutes already," someone says. "What's the holdup?"

He slings the computer bag over his shoulder, gets out his iPhone, and dials his uncle John, out there on the southern end of Staten Island, safe with Denise.

The phone rings.

Rings.

Twice more and it goes to voicemail. Maybe they're out walking by the marshes, or fishing from Uncle John's skiff, or doing some shopping.

When the phone greeting is over, he says, "Hey Uncle John, Tom here. I'm . . . taking the rest of the day off. I'm coming by to see you and Denise. Lunch is on me. Take care."

He disconnects the call, puts the phone away.

Stands and waits.

Some nearby employees are staring at him.

Why?

He feels something moist on his right hand.

Looks at it.

It's bleeding from where he broke the photo frame.

CHAPTER 89

IN HIS darkened office in Lindsay Hall, Horace Evans of MI6 waits, staring at the silent telephone on his desk. There's a heavy rain outside and he feels that he should switch on more lights, but he's content to stay here in the soft glow from his desk lamp.

Across from him is his assistant, Declan Ainsworth.

Declan is staying quiet. He looks concerned.

Horace says quietly, "There are those who say waiting—for men, women, and plans in motion—is the hardest part of any operation."

Declan remains quiet.

Good.

Horace says, "But I always say it's those few seconds that come at you when the phone finally rings, and you reach to pick it up, and in those few seconds...you're almost dizzy with fatigue and anticipation, knowing it's all been cast in stone, and now it's just the learning what happens next."

Declan says, "The news we have—that Jeremy is in the United States, in New Jersey—that should be a good sign."

"It's a sign," Horace says, not taking his eyes off the telephone. "Nothing else. And we dare not do anything more to interpret it, lest the Americans find out and keep their vows to hurt us."

Declan shifts uncomfortably in his chair. "This may be the wrong time to bring this up, sir, but my actions in this matter ... I mean, I have confidence in you, but ..."

His assistant's voice dribbles off.

Horace sighs. "If you feel as such, you may tender your resignation from the service. Predate it to a week ago, if you're so frightened that things will go awry and you'll be left holding the proverbial bag."

A brief second or two passes, then Declan says, "I'll stay."

"Good," Horace says. "Then stay quiet."

The phone remains silent.

"While we wait," he says.

Aboard a Company-owned Gulfstream C-20, Ernest Hollister looks up as his assistant comes forward and sits down across from him in one of the luxurious leather seats. They are somewhere over the North Atlantic, approximately two hours away from landing at Dulles Airport in Virginia.

Tyler Pope leans forward and says, "We've received signals traffic from the Air Force that two RAF Typhoon fighter jets have made an unscheduled landing at McGuire in New Jersey. Two civilians, a woman and a bearded man—a Brit—left the jets and have departed the base. The RAF aircraft earlier departed from a base about forty minutes away from our site where Amy Cornwall had been held."

Ernest says, "I thought Typhoons were single-seaters."

Tyler says, "These two are from RAF 29 Squadron, used to train pilots. They have seating for two."

Ernest thinks for a moment and says, "Any indication that Horace Evans or MI6 had a hand in their transportation?"

"None, sir."

"How did they grab two Typhoons?"

"I can find out."

Ernest shakes his head. "No. Waste of time. If they are in New Jersey, then they are there illegally. We can't have that. Do we have a squad keeping eyes and ears on her husband?"

"Yes, but so far there's nothing of interest to report. But I'll alert them that Amy is back in the States, so they can grab her if she meets up with her husband."

"Nice start—but there's something else."

Tyler waits patiently. *A good assistant knows when to shut the bleep up,* Ernest thinks.

He says, "The Brit belongs to Hector. Get word to him that he's on our soil, and that he'd better do whatever it takes to run him down. Amy Cornwall belongs to me. She has blood on her hands, she's violated at least a dozen Agency rules and requirements, and most of all..."

Ernest shuts his mouth. He was going to say, *and most of all, she's humiliated me,* but it won't do to say that aloud.

He says, "There's an Army major I know, detached to the NSA over at Fort Meade. Rudolf Meyer. Reach out to him—tell him you're calling on my behalf."

Like magic, a small pad of paper is in Tyler's hands and he's scribbling away. "Yes, sir."

"They have new surveillance-recognition software that they've had success with on a few trial runs," Ernest says. "Called FACE/GRAB. Tell him we're going to need it soonest in an area covering whatever county McGuire Air Force Base is in, and then expanding outward. And then provide him with the best facials we have at Langley of Amy Cornwall."

Pope keeps on scribbling. "What does FACE/GRAB do?"

"It allows the NSA or other duly designated agencies to hijack the stream of any surveillance cameras in an area—ATMs, gas stations, toll booths—and run a facial-recognition software program.

If Amy comes in view of any type of camera in that part of New Jersey, we'll know about it. Better than waiting to see if she hooks up with her husband."

"I see," Tyler says. "And then what?"

Ernest goes back to his paperwork. "Then we'll Gitmo her ass to Cuba before she does any more harm."

CHAPTER 90

LESS THAN an hour after leaving McGuire Air Force Base, I'm with Jeremy on the doorstep of a plain yellow Cape Cod house in a dense neighborhood in Bayonne, New Jersey, that dates to the go-go postwar years of the 1940s. Our borrowed car—a light blue Chevrolet Impala—is parked on the narrow street, and I ring the doorbell again and again.

The sun is rising.

It's a gorgeous day in May, but I feel cold.

Death is coming.

I ring the doorbell again.

Jeremy says, "If nobody answers, then what?"

"Stop with the negative thoughts," I say, then I open the storm door and start hammering at the wooden door.

Just when I'm about to hit the door a third time, it swings open.

A flustered-looking woman in black tights and an oversize New York Giants sweatshirt is before us, hair done up in a blue-gray perm. She scowls and says, "Yes?"

"Ma'am," I say. "We're looking for Gus Carlucci. Is he in?"

She's suspicious, looking at me and Jeremy, me with wrinkled and smelly clothes, my head and feet aching something awful, and Jeremy's getup no better than my own.

"I'm sorry, he's quite busy," she says. "He can't be disturbed."

Jeremy speaks up. "Ma'am, I insist. We need to see him. Please. It's vitally important."

Her frown deepens. She looks to be in her late sixties. "The fool is a retired high-school chemistry teacher. What, are you from the school district? About to finally give him a plaque for his years of service to students who refused to learn?"

"No, ma'am," Jeremy says. "It's much more important than that."

She gives a good look to Jeremy. "You're English, then, are you?"

I let Jeremy take the lead. *Maybe this stubborn woman is an Anglophile?*

"Ma'am, that I am," he says.

She frowns. "Gus loves watching those mystery programs on PBS. Why can't you fellows stop mumbling? It's a pain to follow."

I reach for my Beretta because politeness isn't getting us anywhere, but Jeremy's smile widens and he says, "Ma'am, we're from the Queen Elizabeth II Railroad Society, a sister group of your husband's."

"Well…" she says, stepping away, "this is his quiet time, but I guess I can let you in."

We follow her in past three black-and-white cats sniffing in our direction, across a dull-green carpet to a door by the kitchen, where Jeremy and I go down the carpeted steps into the basement. At the bottom there's an oil furnace; to the right there's a washer/dryer combo, and to the left—

Paradise.

For a train geek, I suppose.

There's a U-shaped desk with two large computer screens, each displaying a graphic rendering of railroad tracks, with little symbols and attached numbers moving along. There is radio communications gear, two scanners, and piles of papers and notebooks.

On the walls are photos of steam locomotives, diesel trains, and logos from railways across the United States.

A pudgy man with a thin mustache is sitting on a swivel chair, eyes blinking at us with distress from behind black-rimmed eyeglasses. He's wearing a pink polo shirt with the logo of the National Railway Historical Society over his left breast—said breast almost as big as mine—and to top it off he's wearing the traditional blue-and-white cap of a train engineer.

Jeremy spots the man's mood as well and says, "Mister Carlucci, so sorry to barge in on you like this, but we've just come from the Queen Elizabeth II Railroad Society."

And just like that, Jeremy and I are in the cult: "Sure—what can I do for you folks?"

Now it's my turn. I step in front of Jeremy, pull my jacket aside to reveal my pistol. Gus spots my pistol and gives it a good look, then glances up at me.

"Gus, I'm from the CIA, and Jeremy is from British intelligence. We need your help. There's a terrorist attack planned for this morning on a local railway, and we're told you're the only man who can help us stop it."

I stare at him with utter seriousness. Then as though his entire sad life has led up to this vital and world-saving event, Gus solemnly nods his head.

"I'm your man," he says.

CHAPTER 91

I STAND to the left of our unlikely savior and Jeremy stands to the right, and I say, "Something is going to happen this morning on the Hudson Valley Railroad."

Gus works a keyboard and mouse; the large screen to the left blinks out and is replaced by a graphic map showing Manhattan, the Hudson River, and the east shore of New Jersey, complete with streets, bridges, tunnels, and the markings for railroads.

"Hudson Valley?" he asks. "For real?"

"For real, yes," Jeremy says.

Gus says, "Doesn't make much sense. You want a real serious attack—something that can cause damage and mass casualties, get lots of headlines—you'd want to rig up a commuter train running into Grand Central Terminal, an iconic landmark. Same with Penn Station. But you ask me, destroying the new Penn Station would be a service to mankind, considering—"

I gently reach over and squeeze his shoulder. "Gus. Please. Hudson Valley. Is it a commuter rail? What's its reach?"

"Nah," he says, working the mouse and keyboard again and zooming into the graphics. "Strictly freight, running from near Hoboken Terminal up to Albany and back again. Funny thing is, it's relatively new. Took a lot of design work and money—replacing old rail lines, installing new ones on rights-of-way that were secured."

Jeremy says quietly, "Like someone with a lot of money was intent on installing a freight railway on this stretch of the Hudson River."

"That's right," he says. "Mostly dual tracks: freight up to Albany, freight down to Hoboken. Day in, day out."

I say, "Gus, can you tell us what trains are running this morning? And what they're carrying?"

"Sure," he says. He works the keyboard until the other large screen springs to new life with numbers, letters, and columns that make no sense to me but seem to mean a lot to Gus.

The door we came through opens up. "Gus! I'm putting the coffee on! Does your company want some?"

He turns his head and shouts out. "Later, Margaret, we're busy down here!"

"Fine, suit yourself."

The door slams shut, and Jeremy rests his hand on Gus's other shoulder. "She doesn't understand, does she?"

He mutters something, and Jeremy says, "I know that's the same for train spotters over in the UK."

Gus's eyes flick back and forth on the lists of numbers and abbreviations, "Oh, we're much more than train spotters," he says. "For one thing, we don't need to go out and get wet and cold. We can use computer programs that, uh...well, we can tap into railway systems and their dispatch centers to see exactly what's going on. Oh, okay, here we go: northbound train number HV412-29, set to depart Hoboken in about fifteen minutes. Carrying...number two fuel oil, lumber, shipping containers, fertilizer, chemicals, and...that's about it."

Jeremy says, "Any other trains?"

"Sure," Gus says. "Southbound number HV414-29, left Albany

about ten minutes ago. Carrying shipping containers, empty flat-cars, chemicals, and...oh. Hoo boy."

"What?" I ask.

Gus says, "That's interesting. The tail end of number HV414-29, hauling four flatcars, is carrying casks from the Department of Energy."

"Nuclear waste," Jeremy says.

"You know it."

Jeremy turns to me and says, "That's it, Amy: nuclear waste. That's what Rashad is doing—he's going to explode those two trains and make the world's biggest dirty bomb, right next to Manhattan. That's it."

I look right at Jeremy and wait for a heavy moment, then say what I hate to say:

"No, that's not it. It has to be something else."

CHAPTER 92

ON THIS day of days, this morning of mornings, Rashad Hussain is running late, due to his PATH train's being delayed from Hoboken to the World Trade Center station on Vesey Street, but he is still in good spirits. On this day he has planned for delays and schedule problems, and his plans are still on track.

Outside the crowded terminal, carrying two heavy black cases, he has luck again, for he is able to hail a cab within just a minute. Allah's will, no doubt, and the driver happily emerges and helps Rashad place his two cases in the trunk. The driver is tall, thin, and angular, and Rashad guesses that he is a Somali immigrant. Taking a chance, he says, "*As-salāmu ʻalaykum*, brother."

The taxi driver grins widely. "And *wa ʻalaykumu as-salām* to you, brother."

Seated in the rear of the cab, Rashad notes the driver's city identification and name—AXMED SAMATAR—and knows his guess was correct. After listening to Rashad's destination—an address near Rockefeller Park on the Hudson River—Samatar instantly starts talking about his family here and back home in Mogadishu, how happy he is to have his green card, the challenges of raising a pious family in New York City, his hope that he and his family will finally make the hajj to Mecca next year, and on and on and on.

On the short trip west, Rashad nods and gives polite one-word answers. Though their circles have never met before and never will again, he is touched by this immigrant's work ethic and piety.

Rashad reaches his destination less than fifteen minutes later. Samatar jumps out, opens the trunk, and unloads Rashad's two bags onto the sidewalk.

Quickly thinking what he should do, Rashad recalls a word the Jews have in their religious writings about doing a good deed—they call it a *mitzvah*—and their saying about *If you save a life, it's as if you save the world.*

"Axmed?" he asks.

"Yes, brother?"

Rashad has nothing personally against Jews. After all, he and they are both descendants of Abraham, and it was simply their misfortune that they decided to settle where they did, rather than in Uganda, which would have prevented so many problems. But they are a wise and industrious people indeed, and in this moment he takes heart in their beliefs.

He reaches into his wallet and pulls out a hundred-dollar bill, then another, and then another. He pushes them into Samatar's trembling hand.

"You are a good man, and you will listen to what I say," Rashad says. "Where does your family live?"

"Queens," he says.

"Good," Rashad says, closing the man's hand over the money. "Then leave Manhattan, leave it now, and pray for me."

Rashad picks up his two cases, which now feel as light as feather pillows.

A *mitzvah*, indeed.

CHAPTER 93

JEREMY IS sharp enough to keep his mouth shut at my contradiction. "You ever see the casks the DOE uses to transport nuclear waste?" I ask him. "Have you? They're friggin' concrete-and-steel vaults. They are designed to withstand the most violent railroad accident, explosions, crashes, burning jet fuel, and anything else you can throw at them. Save for using a tactical nuke to break open those containers, there's no way Rashad is using that waste as a weapon. Jesus, there has to be something else!"

Gus goes back to his screen and again starts reading off what each train is carrying. Then: "That's strange."

"Quick," I say. "What's strange?"

"These freight trains," says Gus. "They have only a crew of two running the engine: engineer and conductor. Cheaper labor costs, but the railways try to balance it out by limiting how many cars they're hauling. With that type of GE diesel and a dual connected to it, you'd figure the northbound and southbound would be hauling about a hundred cars each. But they're both hauling 160. Strange."

As Gus and Jeremy examine each train's manifest, I look at the other monitor—the schematic of the Hudson Valley Railroad and its twin tracks, one going north and the other south.

Dual tracks.

Two tracks.

Binary.

Dual.

Dual-use chemicals.

Holy God.

That's it.

Jeremy and Gus are still talking among themselves, and I'm ignoring them as lots of memories from old training sessions flood my mind. I squeeze Gus's shoulder so hard he yelps. "Jeremy, quick: what's a binary nerve-gas agent?"

"Binary? Uh, well, pretty basic: you have a mortar shell or an artillery shell that has two containers inside. Each container has a chemical. By themselves, relatively harmless. But when you mix the two . . . you make a weapon."

"Gus, go back to the manifests. You said *chemicals* a lot. What kind of chemicals?"

"Standard chemicals," he says. "Nothing unusual, nothing out of place."

"Please," I say, fighting to keep my voice calm. "Define *usual*."

"Well, let's see. On the southbound train from Albany, you've got sodium chloride—lots of sodium chloride. It's a dry chemical, so it'd be stored in regular casks. And northbound . . . *hunh*. Liquid hydrochloric acid—nasty stuff. Kept in pressurized tanker cars."

I hear a sudden intake of breath from Jeremy. "What would happen if there was an accident, or an explosion, on those cars?"

Gus says, "The liquid hydrochloric acid . . . oh, that'd vent out. Again, nasty stuff, but if you were to set up a far enough perimeter, not that dangerous."

Jeremy says, "And the other chemical? The sodium chloride?"

"Even less of a problem," says Gus. "You could just shovel it into a dump truck, haul it away to a landfill or to be reclaimed."

My turn now. Even though I'm asking a question, I already know the catastrophic answer.

"Gus, suppose both of those chemicals, on separate trains, were to explode when they were passing each other, so that there was a massive collision. What then?"

Gus stares at the manifest, whispers, "Oh, sweet Jesus," then frantically digs through his papers. He pulls out an odd and complicated-looking calculator and starts punching its keys. Jeremy is about to say something, but I shake my head. Gus looks up and says, "You . . . you've got to stop it. You've got to stop this, right now!"

"What will happen?" I ask. "Gus, what's going to happen?"

He shakes his head, whispers, "No, no, no," and looks to us both, tears in his eyes.

"That amount of chemicals violently reacting—the dry sodium chloride and the liquid hydrochloric acid mixing like that—you'll create an enormous, hazardous chemical cloud," says Gus, nearly stammering. "As bad as anything used in the trenches in World War I. You'll have clouds of chlorine gas and hydrogen chloride gas, both fatal, and with the prevailing winds . . . and the explosions taking place when both trains are near each other . . ."

Jeremy demands, "How many dead? How many?"

Gus's eyes well up. "A hundred thousand dead. If not more. And hundreds of thousands more coughing their burned lungs out."

"When?" I ask.

He gestures at the two screens. "When the two trains pass each other, in less than an hour, at 11:09 a.m. That's when the dying will start."

CHAPTER 94

AFTER LONG minutes of waiting—during which Tom Cornwall ducked into a men's room for paper towels to sop up the bleeding from his right hand—he finally gets into an elevator, which quickly grows packed. It takes abnormally long to reach the lobby, seemingly stopping at every other floor.

In those long minutes, he's thinking of what just happened and what might happen next. He's been fired. All right—happens to the best in journalism. And Amy, well, her job seems to be gone as well, and the CIA has been heavily subsidizing their Manhattan townhouse.

What now?

Another stop.

Good Christ, what is going on here? Tom thinks.

Well, facing facts—including his bleeding right hand—he and Amy are jobless. Which means leaving Manhattan, taking Denise out of school, a whole host of problems.

What then?

Another stop.

Damn it, this is the slowest descent he's ever been on.

Amy had occasionally talked about moving up to Maine— where she grew up—once they both had enough money socked

355

away. She could get a military consulting gig, and maybe he could purchase a weekly newspaper. Simplify things. Have Denise grow up in a place where the doors are unlocked at night and everyone sleeps safely and—

He looks at the indicator.

Three more floors to go.

Safely.

What is out there—what beast is Amy chasing down?

Ticonderoga.

Something serious, something big, but in the end, maybe—just maybe—a false alarm. In Tom's years of reporting, he's had tips that never panned out, like that dirty bomb supposedly hidden in Lafayette Park that turned out to be a hoax.

Maybe that's the case now.

Maybe.

But when he gets out of here, he'll climb into their Chevy Equinox and haul ass to Staten Island, meet up with Uncle John, and ride out whatever might be coming.

A smile.

Spending quality time with Denise this fine May day—that would be fun. And she so enjoyed going fishing with Uncle John out on Raritan Bay.

The elevator sighs to a stop, the doors slide open, and he walks with everyone else through the bright, shiny, high-ceilinged lobby of One World Trade Center. There's a brief pang of regret that he'll never step into this building again. Dylan is the kind of prick who will keep most angry promises, so Tom expects a few cardboard boxes filled with photos, files, and various memorabilia to arrive at their townhouse in a few days.

He steps out into the warm May morning. Fair enough. It'll probably make sense to keep his stuff in the boxes until he, Amy, and Denise finally move.

And that brings another smile, thinking that Amy's last phone call said she was done with overseas assignments. No more long, secretive trips. No more missed holidays or birthdays.

Time to start what passes for a normal family life.

He picks up his iPhone, meaning to call his uncle John, and sees there's a voicemail message.

From Uncle John.

Standing in the narrow parklike area between One World Trade Center and busy West Street, he checks the message, now fifteen minutes old.

He must have missed it when he was in the elevator.

"Hey, Tom, it's your uncle John. I've been calling and calling, but you haven't picked up. I know this is a surprise, but Denise is insistent I take her into the city today. She says you promised her a tour. Denise is pretty upset, so... I'm on the road now, and let's say I meet you at the Fulton Street entrance to your office at 11 a.m. Thanks. See you soon."

Shit!

He calls Uncle John and it goes straight to voicemail. He knows Uncle John and his devotion to his old flip phone—"I don't need those fancy apps and gadgets"—and lots of times, depending on the weather or even sunspots, you can't reach him.

He's walking up Fulton Street now, seeing a blue-green construction van parked at the corner of Fulton and Greenwich—always, always some construction going on in this place—and he tries again.

No answer.

What promise? What tour?

Then it hits him.

May 29.

Take Your Daughter to Work Day.

He almost laughs. How about Take Your Daughter to the Unemployment Office Day instead?

No matter.

He'll stay here and wait.

He checks his watch.

It's 10:20 a.m.

CHAPTER 95

OUR DONATED Impala is running on fumes. After a quick stop to buy a gallon of gas—"No more than that," I yell at Jeremy as he shoves the nozzle in the tank, "we can't afford to waste time driving"—we're rocketing along the two northbound lanes of NJ-440, heading in the direction of I-78, which I don't plan to take.

"Amy, time," Jeremy says, as I weave in and out of traffic, thinking furiously, running through options, choices, and realizing that as much as I hate to do it, we're going to have to divide our forces.

I say, "I'm goddamn well aware of the goddamn time. We've got two missions ahead of us: stop the trains, and stop Rashad."

Horns blare as we keep speeding north. "We don't know where Rashad is!"

"I know, I know, just...quiet."

Jeremy shuts his mouth. I think of all I've learned about Rashad, about what he wants to do, about his earlier actions, all of them quiet and behind the scenes.

Then he kills his father.

Starts getting bolder. Showing off. Boasting.

Like he's telling the spirit of his father that he's no longer a scared and ignored little boy.

Gotcha, I think.

"He likes to be near the action now, Jeremy," I call out. "Like when he told you about the aircraft going down in Saudi. Being at the nuke-exchange site in France. Rashad wants to see the results of his planning; he *needs* to see the results. He wants to watch the trains explode. He wants to witness the gas clouds form, see people in the distance start to panic and choke to death."

"But where would he be?" he asks.

"His hotels," I say. "When I talked to him back in the UK, he bragged he would stand on top of his wealth and watch us die. His wealth? The three hotels. Get on your phone, find the one nearest the Hudson River. C'mon, pickup truck, move it, move it, *move it!*"

I lay on the horn and sideswipe a delivery van, producing a *crunch/bang* that reminds me of driving in London. I see Jeremy working his borrowed iPhone out of the corner of my eye, and he says, "Gus should be making those 911 calls."

"Of course he is," I say. "And it just might work...*might.* But I'm not going to rely on some poor 911 dispatcher believing Gus telling her what's about to happen...come on Jeremy, what's the goddamn holdup?"

"Here, here," he says. "The Nansen Arms. Right on the water, near Rockefeller Park, and across from Hoboken and the southern part of his railroad."

I punch the steering wheel. "The son of a bitch wants to see it, Jeremy. That's where he'll be."

"And if the bombs on the trains are on timers, he'll want to use a command switch, and detonate them remotely if they're delayed."

"You got it," I say. "And that's your job, Jeremy. I don't know how or where you're going to do it, but you're going to get your Brit ass over to that hotel and stop him."

"And you? The trains? What are you going to do?"

I say, "You tell me right now if there's a park, or a golf course, or some big empty lot nearby, that's your job. And I'll tell you how I'm going to do it, if I can."

Jeremy flips through his donated iPhone and says, "About a half mile to go. Take the exit to Lefante Way. The Bayonne Golf Course is near there."

I check my watch.

It's 10:21 a.m.

"Amy."

"Yeah."

"There's a police cruiser coming up on us," Jeremy says.

CHAPTER 96

IT HAS taken him nearly a month of preparation and permitting, but Mike Patel is sitting in the rear of a perfectly licensed and legitimate service van that has his HVAC company's name and logo on its sides. Mike has taped his parking permit and other necessary paperwork to the windshield so that any passing police or transit officers won't bother him.

He's parked on the corner of Greenwich and Fulton Street, right in the shadow of One World Trade Center, directly across from the memorial site with the walls of falling water and the rows upon rows of inscribed names.

The interior of the van is painted deep black, and a curtain separates the two front seats from where he's sitting, facing the twin rear doors. Both windows are tinted so no one can peer in. If someone succeeded in doing so, however, he or she would see Mike calmly sitting on a raised seat, facing the rear doors. Across his lap is a loaded M4 automatic rifle, with six spare magazines at his elbow.

There's a rope with a pulley system at his left. When the time comes, he will tug the rope and the left-side rear window will lift up. With the dark interior, nothing will be revealed to anyone passing by—especially when he picks up the rifle with the flash- and sound-suppressor, and starts shooting into the crowds.

Mike is wearing a bullet-resistant vest, and the keys to the van are in the ignition. He's a warrior today, but he doesn't plan to be a martyr.

He just wants revenge on those who have called him "Paki, Paki" over the years.

Mike patiently waits.

He doesn't need to know what time it is.

The little surprises he's planted throughout One World Trade Center will let him know when the correct time has arrived.

CHAPTER 97

ABOARD THE GE diesel electric locomotive for his day's trip—said train number being HV412-29, from the Hudson Valley dispatch office—Orrin Block is sitting in the right-side engineer's chair, yawning, watching the gauges flicker and report to him in the green. In front of him are the four control handles that operate this train: a black one to apply the locomotive's brakes, a red handle to apply the brakes for the entire train, an oblong black handle that's the combined throttle and dynamic brake, and a fourth handle to reverse the locomotive.

When he first started, Orrin wondered how he would ever tell the four apart. Now he dreams he's holding them in his hands.

He checks the gauges one more time. Funny thing, the gauges aren't gauges—they're two small computer screens constantly feeding him data on the status of the locomotive and the brake systems leading to the rear of its 160-car load today. But the folks running the railroads are big on nostalgia.

Like where his conductor, Miguel Marcos, is stationed on the other side of the cab, beyond the thick center console that splits the cab in two. Since Orrin is the engineer and sits in the engineer's chair, you'd think that Miguel—being the conductor—would sit in the conductor's chair.

Nope, that chair was called the *fireman's chair,* from the days when a fireman shoveled coal for a steam locomotive.

Tradition.

Screw it.

They're still in the yard near the Hoboken Terminal, and the sun's been up for a while, and Orrin's just sitting, idly watching the other trains and cars in the yard, some of the short-track engines moving lines of freight cars to where they need to be for later runs by other crews. They've both completed their walk-around of the freight cars, ensuring that all is in place and the brake lines are attached.

He says, "You got any plans for when we get to Albany?"

Miguel doesn't hear him. He's staring out the left side windshield.

Orrin is about to say something else when he spots something sticking out of Miguel's heavy jean jacket.

It looks like the butt of a pistol.

What the hell?

Why's Miguel carrying?

What's he up to?

Then Miguel shifts, and Orrin sees that the object is only his cell phone.

Man, he thinks, *why am I being so paranoid?*

This is what he loves. This is what he was born for. Brian Lamott is looking forward to his retirement—now just two months and three days away—but he knows he'll miss this feeling of satisfaction, of leaving a train yard and hauling tons of freight that keeps the country running. There was a time when truckers were supposedly the "cowboys of the highways," the romantic last breed of rugged individuals feeding and fueling America, but Brian knows that's all bullshit.

It's train guys like him and his conductor, Alvi Dudin, who keep this country alive.

The cabin of his GE diesel electric is as familiar to Brian as his kitchen at night. He knows what every switch, lever, and dial does, and a quick glance at the gauges—even though they're really computer screens—shows everything is normal. The main air reservoir in this locomotive is at 135 psi; the hard rubber brake pipes extending all the way back are holding at 90 psi; the speed is an even 55 miles per hour.

Perfect.

Everything on HV414-29 is running as smooth as it could. As they approach a crossing, Brian pushes the square yellow button for the train's horn, giving it a quick four blasts. A couple of kids at the crossing wave at him, and he waves back. A few years ago, a cute young woman was holding hands with her boyfriend at a crossing; as Brian sped by, she let go of her boyfriend's hand and gave him a wave.

Everyone loves trains.

They are south of Albany, passing through Glenmont, when Brian says, "Hey, Alvi."

Alvi turns from his vantage point on the fireman's chair. "What's up?"

Brian says, "We're going to be passing the northbound to Albany at a little past 11 a.m. Wanna moon them as they go by?"

Alvi shakes his head, smiling. "Nah. I don't want to get into trouble."

CHAPTER 98

JEREMY WINDSOR clutches the side of the door as Amy roars the Impala down Lefante Way in Bayonne, New Jersey, passing through what looks like an industrial dumping ground of junk, warehouses, and parked tractor trailers. As they quickly approach a small gatehouse of stone and wood, a man in a security officer's uniform steps out and—

Amy lays on the horn, the man jumps back, and now they're passing through an improved area: the road curves and sways, and up ahead is what looks to be the main building of the golf club— a two-story Victorian-style building with a lighthouse stuck to one end.

The cars parked here are Jaguars, Porsches, and Range Rovers. Amy brakes the Impala hard, shoves it in a parking space near the building, and throws the car into Park as privileged men and women golfers casually stroll by.

"I'm out of here," she says. "You get your Brit ass across the river and try to stop Rashad. I'll take care of the railway."

"How?" Jeremy says, scooting into the driver's seat.

Amy says, "By following your lead: relying on steel-hard friend-ships, always ready to do a mate a favor."

"The time," he says. "Eleven-oh-nine. I puzzled it out. Reverse it. It's nine-eleven. Bastard."

She's out on the pavement, borrowed iPhone in her hand, and leans down. "Get the job done, Jeremy. I don't care what day he's commemorating. We're depending on you."

He says, "On it," but she has already slammed the driver's door shut.

Jeremy is about to back up the Impala when he spots one, then two police cruisers pull up before the clubhouse, lights flashing. Two cops jump out and—

Start running across the nearby practice green.

Like they're chasing Amy.

Not the Impala.

Jeremy calmly reverses, then puts the car in Drive and gets the hell out, glancing at the dashboard clock.

It's 10:27 a.m.

He has a tiny hope that maybe, just maybe, Gus the train enthusiast has raised the alarm.

CHAPTER 99

AT THE dispatch center for the Hoboken Police Department on 106 Hudson Street, Sergeant James Washington is sitting in his chair, left foot aching, looking forward to the end of his shift as a dispatch supervisor.

Not that he minds being here, but he's been in dispatch since surgery to remove a cyst from his foot, and even though it hurts like a son of a bitch this morning, he's determined to tell his doc tomorrow that everything's okay so he can get back on the streets.

Tony Russo—young, heavyset, wearing a civvie dispatch uniform and holding a slip of paper in his hand—pokes his head in and says, "We got another train call a few minutes ago."

"What kind of call?"

Russo glances down at the paper. "Like the previous dozen we've gotten the past two weeks: explosives have been set on the southbound and northbound trains of the Hudson Valley Railroad."

Sergeant Washington groans, picks up his coffee cup. "Not again. Christ, first and second calls, we sent the bomb squad in and there was nothing. Damn hackers. I can't imagine anybody getting their jollies making prank calls like this."

369

"Yeah, but this one's different," Russo says. "The caller didn't use a spoofing program. Made the call legit. Some guy from Bayonne."

"Great," the sergeant replies. "Call Bayonne PD and tell them to pick that guy up. Maybe he can tell us why we've gotten so many goddamn fake warnings about bombs on trains."

CHAPTER 100

I'M RUNNING across the perfectly manicured grass of the Bayonne Golf Club's practice green as the perfect men and perfect women with their golf gear look at me, wondering if I'm some crazed groundskeeper, or perhaps a clubhouse manager gone rogue. Among the thoughts and possibilities racing through my mind, one stands out:

There's a police cruiser coming up on us.

And not just one. Two rolled in and stopped behind Jeremy and me when we got to that ghastly country-club building. And when I started racing across the beautiful greens, two cops bailed out and began running after me.

Why two? Because I was speeding on a New Jersey highway? That's practically the state sport.

No.

The cops are after me.

How?

I plow through some low brush, hit the ground and roll, and—

Yep.

Stupid me.

Gassing up the Impala earlier, I was standing outside, in full view of a surveillance camera, if only for a few seconds.

But those few were plenty for somebody who's very pissed off at me.

Ernest Hollister.

I get up, spare a glance at the gently rolling fairways and little flapping triangular golf flags stretching into the distance.

A number of cops—some in SWAT battle rattle—are stretched out in a line, coming my way.

I take out my borrowed iPhone, start punching in numbers.

It's 10:31 a.m.

CHAPTER 101

IT'S A beautiful May morning and Lisa Bailey is madly, deeply in love. She's in the right-hand pilot's seat of a Bell 429 helicopter, call sign Aviation 19, and with her copilot and fellow New York Police Department officer Joe Woods, she's flying near the southern end of Manhattan, with the best view in the world.

At six thousand feet in this crisp weather, it's CAVU—ceiling and visibility unrestricted—and Lisa's love affair is with this gorgeous flying machine. Its latest police surveillance and tracking equipment includes radiation-monitoring devices, a TrakkaBeam searchlight, and the MX10 EO/IR camera system, which can zoom in and read the numbers on a license plate or the logo on some perp's baseball cap, day or night.

Through the helicopter's intercom, Joe says, "Stop smiling so much, Lisa—you'll ruin your resting bitch face."

Lisa laughs, her left hand on the collective lever and her right on the cyclic stick, both booted feet on the control pedals. "Can't help it. This beauty beats that flying Greyhound bus I'm used to."

That "bus" is the heavy-lift Chinook CH-47 helicopter, old and clunky, prone to leaking hydraulic fluid but otherwise a solid workhorse that Lisa flew many times when she was active duty U.S. Army, performing missions in Iraq and Afghanistan: most of the time delivering troops and supplies through the Chinook's rear ramp, sometimes getting shot at, a couple of times seeing the smoky trail of an RPG wavering up to her.

"Center to Aviation 19," comes a message from dispatch, audible through her heavy crash helmet.

She toggles a switch. "Aviation 19, go."

"Hold one," the woman's voice says.

As Lisa takes in this gorgeous view of south Manhattan—the tall firm buildings, the water of New York Harbor and nearby Governors Island—she thinks of the desert, jagged empty mountain peaks, the small villages of huts and poverty and—

"Aviation 19, Center," the voice goes on. "Switch to Channel 99. We have an incoming telephone message for you."

She looks over at Joe, who shrugs beneath his heavy flight jacket. Channel 99 is encrypted, meaning scanner snoopers can't overhear sensitive traffic. It feeds in only to the pilot's communications system.

"Roger that," says Lisa. She goes to the cluttered dashboard and makes the necessary adjustment, then says, "This is Officer Bailey, NYPD Aviation. Go ahead, caller."

And a voice from the past and the harsh desert slips right into her ears.

"Hey, Fly Girl, this is Captain Cornwall, so glad I caught you."

"Amy!" she answers. "Captain? Heard you went over to the dark side—that agency beginning with the letter *C*."

Lisa's happy and surprised to hear from Captain Cornwall, and she's expecting a hearty laugh and an explanation for why Amy's calling her at this time and place. So her hands tingle with apprehension at what she hears next.

"Lisa, I need your help," Amy says, voice low and firm. "There's an emerging terrorist threat coming from a railway on the other side of the Hudson, south of the Hoboken Terminal. Bombs have been set on two trains that will cause a cloud of poison gas. I don't have time to go through channels. I...I've got less than half an hour. In thirty minutes, there's going to be a terrorist attack that will kill tens of thousands. I need you, Lisa. I need you bad."

She keeps quiet. Talk about the goddamn bolt from the blue.

Amy says, "You're the best I knew back in the 'stan. Anywhere and anyplace you'd fly, no matter the mission. Lisa...this is irregular, I'm putting you in a world of hurt, but please...trust me. I need you."

Lisa looks over at south Manhattan, sees the shining spire of One World Trade Center, remembers her now-dead uncle—also a helicopter pilot in the Aviation Unit. Whenever he got drunk at family get-togethers, he would sit in a corner and quietly weep, recalling the desperate people leaning out of the shattered and smoking windows of WTC One and Two, waving at him, beseeching him to help.

"You got it," she says. "Where are you?"

Amy says, "Bayonne Golf Course...near the eighth hole. In a line of trees."

Lisa says, "There's a helipad on the river's edge."

Amy says, "Great idea, but I got some police on my ass. I can't make it there without being arrested, and I can't be arrested."

Holy shit, Lisa thinks. *What am I getting myself into?*

And the weeping of her uncle comes to her.

"Be there in less than five. Aviation 19 off."

She switches the communication system so that her copilot can hear her. Then she takes a breath and gently banks the Bell helicopter to the left.

"Joe?"

"Right here, Lisa."

She talks slowly and plainly. "That was a CIA officer I served with in Afghanistan, when she was in Army Intelligence. I trusted her with my life then and I trust her now. This…is outside channels, but she needs me to pick her up to prevent a terrorist attack in less than thirty minutes."

The deep thrumming of the two Pratt & Whitney engines is the only thing Lisa hears.

"She's hiding out at the Bayonne Golf Course. We've got no authority, no orders. If this goes south, we'll probably both lose our shields—if we're lucky. So…you can get out in New Jersey when I pick her up."

A second passes.

"Lisa?"

"Yeah, Joe."

"Fly the goddamn bird," he says. "I'm not going anywhere."

CHAPTER 102

JEREMY WINDSOR walks briskly along the floating docks of the Freedom View Marina—*don't run; running always raises attention and suspicion*—until he sees what he's looking for: a lovely 48-foot bright-red speedboat that he knows can reach 80 miles per hour with its twin 500-horsepower Mercury outboard engines.

The trip here after he dropped off Amy took about five minutes, and he feels the weight of time and pressure on his shoulders as he leaps into the boat.

Work, he thinks. *Work fast.*

He pulls apart a section of the dashboard next to the boat's steering wheel, reaches in, and yes . . .

The ignition wires.

He pulls the red and yellow ones out, thinking how fortunate he is that most boats still depend on 1960s ignition technology—nothing like the latest models of cars and trucks. In a few seconds of flicking the raw ends of the wires together, both engines roar into life, throbbing with a noise that instantly relieves him.

Jeremy climbs out of the open interior, unties the stern line and bowline. A man yells, "Hey, hey—who the hell are you?"

He jumps back into the boat, pushes away from the dock. Two men are running down after him, one in khaki shorts and a pink polo shirt, the other in a security guard's uniform. Jeremy waves a hand and says, "Just borrowing it for a few minutes, fellows! I'll do my best not to prang it!"

Jeremy maneuvers the boat through a narrow channel clustered with sailboats and other powerboats of all sizes and shapes—their obscene cost the common denominator—then shoves the twin throttles forward and powers his way out to the Hudson River. It's a gorgeous late-May morning and there's lots of marine traffic out here, from ferries to sailboats.

Jeremy stares ahead. Based on the quick research he did on the new iPhone, there's the Nansen Arms Hotel, rising up near Rockefeller Park, almost directly opposite him. Getting across this stretch of river with the powerboat should take less than five minutes.

But what will be waiting for him when he gets there?

Is there another information source he can tap?

With one hand on the steering wheel, Jeremy keeps the powerboat roaring along on a straight course. With the other he grabs the iPhone and makes a call. After a brief discussion, thankfully, the call goes through.

"Amanda Trevor, agricultural attaché," comes the familiar voice.

"Amanda," he says. "It's Jeremy Windsor. I need your help."

And without a word, she disconnects his call.

CHAPTER 103

I HEAR it before I can see it—my airborne savior and salvation. I break from the narrow stretch of trees and start running.

The noise of the approaching blue-and-white Bell 429 helicopter with the New York Police Department seal on its hull approaches, but even the sound of its engines can't drown out the yells and shouts coming from the police officers who've spotted me running across the greens.

I wave with both arms—my stolen 9mm Beretta bouncing up and down in my waistband—and Lisa Bailey up there must see me, for the NYPD helicopter swerves and then flares out for a descent.

I hear barking.

Glance back.

Dogs—*for real?*

Yeah: two Belgian Malinois have been let off their leashes and are running after me with full strength and righteous fury.

Damn it!

The helicopter is on the ground, the stern rotor facing to my left, the main hull to the right, and a familiar face is peering at me through the side pilot window. Never have I been so happy to see another woman.

The roar of the chopper's engines drowns out the shouts and the barking dogs.

Close.

Closer now.

I duck my head, the prop wash hitting me hard, and skid to a halt as I reach the hull. I grab the door handle and tug it open, imagining sharp teeth about to sink into my calves. Then I toss myself into the rear passenger compartment as Lisa lifts us up.

I roll on the floor, get up, and sit down in a rear-facing padded seat. I fasten the seatbelt, locate a headset with mic, tug it over my head.

Lisa's voice comes to me, sharp and to the point.

"Where to?"

"Railway near the south side of Hoboken Terminal. Freight train heading north. Carrying chemicals. It's been sabotaged. In about—"

I check my watch.

Damn it again.

"Twenty minutes, it'll pass a southbound train on the adjacent tracks. They're timed to explode at the same time, and when the chemicals mix..."

"Got it," Lisa says. "Should be there in less than five. We'll see if we can't stop it."

I settle back in the seat with blessed, sweet relief.

We just might make it—*just might make it.*

Through the helicopter's side windows, I think I catch a glimpse of Staten Island, far away there in the south, and my sense of relief increases.

Thank God my family is safe.

CHAPTER 104

TOM CORNWALL spots a familiar rusty blue Ford F-150 pickup truck coming down Fulton Street. He waves at his uncle John and the truck comes to a halt. John lowers the window and says, "All right if I drop off your cutie and get going? You know how I hate driving here."

"Not a problem," Tom says, and goes around the rear of the truck—with its faded bumper sticker that says LIVE LONGER, EAT MORE FISH—and opens the passenger door, helping Denise out. She's carrying her heavy, multicolored Vera Bradley backpack.

Oh, he's angry at her, but seeing her smile—and her eagerness at being with Daddy—douses his anger. As Uncle John's pickup slides back into the westbound Fulton Street traffic, Tom takes Denise's backpack in one hand and her hand in the other and says, "Hon, you should have stayed home with Uncle John."

"But you promised me!" she says, words angry but face still smiling. "Today is that day everyone is supposed to bring his or her daughter to work...and you promised. I wanted to see where you worked..."

He hugs Denise and thinks, *What am I going to tell her: "Daddy doesn't work here anymore"?*

There are shouts.

Yells.

Even screams.

From the nearby doors, people are running out of the Fulton Street entrance to One World Trade Center.

Denise notices the people running out of Tom's old workplace.

"Daddy," she says, voice suddenly scared. "What's wrong?"

CHAPTER 105

THERE.

Mike Patel smiles with satisfaction, picks up the M4, and pulls back the action, putting a .223 cartridge into the chamber.

The sudden increase in the number of people pouring out of the office building—most of them running—tells him everything he needs to know: in one-third of the floors within One World Trade Center, his carefully placed smoke bombs have gone off. There's no fire, no explosives, nothing save choking clouds of smoke.

Meaning that within minutes, tens of thousands of people are going to be streaming out, jamming the side streets.

Panic, his sponsor Rashad Hussain had told him. *What I want is panic on that day, and crowds of people running to safety toward the Hudson River.*

Mike tugs at the rope at his side and the left-hand rear window slides up, revealing the crowds of people moving and standing on the sidewalk.

Picks up his M4, sights in, wondering which target he will choose first.

Panic, Rashad had told him. *Just shoot into the crowds, move them like the cattle they are, head them to the west.*

There.

That man standing on the sidewalk, hugging a blond-haired girl, colorful backpack at their feet.

"You're first," he whispers.

And squeezes the trigger.

CHAPTER 106

THIS DAY is blessed indeed, for standing at the west side of the roof of his hotel, the Nansen Arms, it's sunny with a steady breeze coming in from the banks of nearby New Jersey, there on the other side of the Hudson River. There are antennas up here, bulky air-conditioning and air-handling units, and he confidently strides over to a huge square apparatus with a splash of orange paint on one corner, hard by the edge of the roof.

He puts down his two cases, kneels on the crushed stone of the roof, and reaches under the square. He drags out a larger, bulkier case, placed here two days ago by his most trusted local associate, Mike Patel.

With all three cases in hand, he opens up the lids and gets to work.

He has practiced this many times before, so it's quick work indeed.

Rashad stands up, examines what is before him: a heavy metal tripod made by Meade, built for binoculars scaled for astronomical viewing. He sets up the tripod, making sure each leg is firmly planted in the crushed stone. A set of what looks like bulky black binoculars comes up next, and is securely screwed into the tripod's mount. The binoculars, however, are a classified Zeiss viewing system built under contract for the German army. Once they've been secured, Rashad toggles a tiny switch that powers up the system.

There.

The little lightbulb comes on red.

Rashad waits, rubbing his hands not from cold or fear but from anticipation. He is not a particularly religious man, but years ago he had stood on this very roof as it neared completion, remembering with cold rage the constant gibes of his father, who had insulted Rashad for going into mercantile work, instead of the honorable profession of being in government service or the oil industry—essentially the same thing—where he might have worked with the Americans and the British to achieve a more equitable world, and those thoughts were on his mind that day when Allah spoke to him.

The little light remains red.

He was at this very spot, ignoring the words of his architects and builders, looking over the Hudson River at the coast of New Jersey, when Allah spoke to him, giving him a vision of a great cloud coming from that coast and sweeping over here, taking down Manhattan and its empire and the dreams and hopes of so many, including his now thankfully dead father.

The light is now green.

There's a small keypad at the rear of the viewing system. After Rashad taps in the appropriate GPS coordinates, the system gently whirs into position.

Rashad double-checks that his 9mm pistol is at his side. If anyone dares to question him in the next few minutes—a maintenance worker or a security guard—Rashad will shoot him dead with no hesitation.

He lowers his face to the twin optics, gazing across the river to an area south of the Hoboken Terminal, where his rail business has its southern terminus. The view is crisp and dramatic, showing cars, fences, pedestrians walking, and a collection of freight cars and trains.

But what is best is that he sees a flashing beacon from on top of a diesel locomotive—an infrared signal visible only to Rashad that tells him the first of his blessed trains is about to depart.

And to change the world.

CHAPTER 107

CLICK.

Mike Patel anticipates the slam of the recoil hitting his right shoulder to go along with the sharp bark of the M4 firing, but...

A click?

Must be a jam.

He lowers the rifle and pulls back the action. A cartridge spins out and hits the metal floor of the van.

He lifts the rifle, pulls the trigger again.

Click.

What in God's name is going on?

Faulty ammunition?

A metallic taste of failure is in his mouth and his hands tremble as he pulls out the rifle's magazine, works the action, and watches another cartridge spin uselessly onto the floor. Mike grabs a fresh magazine, slams it into the M4, works the action one more time.

He aims at the crowds now moving quickly out of the Fulton Street entrance of One World Trade Center, and pulls the trigger to another disappointing *click*. Just then the front passenger door of his van flies open, there's a push through the curtain, and a pistol barrel is shoved into his left ear.

A British-accented voice says, "You amateurs think you're full of jihad and glory, but you stupid gits never check the firing pin's in place before pulling the trigger. Am I right, Mike?"

CHAPTER 108

MY SEATBELT keeps me secure as I swivel around and look at the rapidly approaching New Jersey side of the Hudson. There's the Hoboken Terminal, and a spaghetti mix of rail lines with freight trains of differing lengths scattered across my field of view.

In my earphones I hear Lisa say, "Your freight train is departing Hoboken Terminal?"

"No," I reply. "There's that small train yard, just to the south. That's where it's heading out."

The male copilot says, "Lisa, look over at eleven o'clock. Northbound freight train leaving the yard—must be it."

I turn harder in the seat, and as we close the distance I spot the freight train and its long retinue of freight cars and tankers trundling along.

Dual use, I think. *Gasoline can power your car or burn down your house, depending on how it's handled.*

"Lisa?" I ask.

"Right here," she says.

I look farther up the track and see that the railway cuts through commercial and residential areas, with power lines and pedestrian bridges passing overhead.

The target train is gaining speed.

"We've got to stop that train."

Lisa says, "Yeah, I figured that's the plan."

"But look at all those obstacles down there—the power lines, the abutments, utility poles—"

Lisa swears at me as she increases the speed of the Bell 429. "Shit, Captain, you see any *moojs* down there shooting at me with RPGs or AK-47s? Does it look like the 'stan down there? Is it night or bright daylight? I think I can handle flying into urban New Jersey just fine, thank you very much. So shut up already."

I shut up.

Check my watch.

It's 10:40 a.m.

Just twenty-seven minutes left to go.

God, we just might make it.

CHAPTER 109

AS JEREMY Windsor slows his stolen twin-engine speedboat, he worries how he'll get past the rocky shoreline and onto Manhattan, but bless us all there's a small marina just south of Rockefeller Park, within sprinting distance of Rashad's hotel.

Brilliant.

He slows the twin engines even more and glances back at New Jersey, knowing that if he and Amy don't make it . . . a rising cloud of death will be coming this way in a very few minutes.

Ahead the marina comes into better view. Behind it Jeremy can see ten- or fifteen-story brick buildings, and beyond them the high and shiny skyscrapers of south Manhattan, including that architectural phoenix, One World Trade Center.

The interior of the marina is small, but the luxury yachts moored there are so long and high they could use his stolen boat as a tender.

There.

An open slip.

He steers the boat in, tugs the wires to switch off the engine, and doesn't bother tying her up. A quick glance at his iPhone and the area map tells him where to go, so he starts running—just as two heavyset marina workers come trotting toward him, shouting, faces red, demanding to know who he is, what he's doing here, and why he doesn't have enough goddamn sense to tie off his goddamn boat?

Jeremy points his SIG Sauer at the two men and says, "Not my goddamn boat—but this is my goddamn pistol."

They move out of his way.

He keeps on running.

A minute later his phone rings; he checks it—BLOCKED NUMBER—and says, "Windsor."

"Jeremy, it's Amanda, you bloody idiot," comes an angry woman's voice. "What the hell do you mean by calling me at the consulate after you've been Faroe'd? You're lucky I was able to grab this burner phone to call you back."

Run, run, run. Passing people out enjoying this May morning. The nearby park. Kites in the air. Music being played. Frisbees being tossed.

All of you, he wants to shout, *all of you get out of here!*

"Amanda," he says, slowing his pace just a bit so he can maintain a conversation, "I've got an emerging terrorist threat here that's about to blow in less than twenty minutes."

"Jeremy…"

He dodges a nanny pushing a two-seater stroller. "This is not a joke. This is as real as it gets. Please…Amanda, I need to know if there's anything unusual that MI6 has picked up in the Manhattan area during the last week."

"*Unusual?* Jeremy, please."

"Amanda," he says, raising his voice as he keeps running along North End Avenue, "you know what I mean. Anything that doesn't fit, stands out, sounds strange."

Even against the din of Manhattan traffic, he can make out her sigh. "We got a couple of phone calls from idiots claiming to be Irish separatists, saying they were going to blow up the consulate next year to mark the Easter Uprising. Some Scottish twit accused his roommates of being in league with Satanist pedophiles. A couple of drunken lads called us, joking about wanting to kidnap the Duchess of Cambridge the next time she's in town."

The facade of the Nansen Arms grows larger as he continues to run. Old aches and pains from injuries that Jeremy received in Lebanon and on that deserted runway in France scream at him.

"And here's the latest," she says. "A Special Branch chap called in something he learned about an illegal Pakistani immigrant working at One World Trade Center."

He comes to a halt, breathing hard.

"Go on," he says. "Please make it quick."

"Well, he claims the man was keeping an illegal automatic rifle in his flat," Amanda says. "And I don't blame him, being a Muslim in America nowadays, but the other thing was a code."

"What kind of code?"

"Hold on, I've got my notes here."

He's tries to ease his breathing, tries to keep his focus on what Amanda's telling him.

"Here it is," she says. "This Special Branch fellow says he found these words and numbers on a slip of paper. The words *lift four,* followed by the numerals 6, 6, 8, and 9. Then the words *access roof,* followed by the numerals 9, 8, 6, and 6. That's it."

As she is talking, Jeremy—pen in hand—scribbles the words and numbers on the palm of his hand.

Amanda says, "Do you think this is important?"

Jeremy looks up at the roof of the hotel owned by Rashad Hussain. He knows—sweet Jesus, he *knows*—that the bastard is up there right now, watching everything unfold.

"God, I hope so," he says, then disconnects the call and resumes his race.

One more time check.

The explosions will occur at 11:09 a.m.

It's now 10:43 a.m.

CHAPTER 110

IN HIS seat at the controls of HV412-29, Orrin Block sees clear cruising ahead of him, as they are now north of the Hoboken Terminal. He turns in his padded chair and is about to ask after Miguel's weekend plans again when a dark shadow suddenly dims the interior of the cab, like a passing thundercloud.

Miguel sits up and stares out his side window, and Orrin says, "What the hell was that?" Then comes the roar of engines overhead, and Orrin sits back in fear as a helicopter swoops over them, heading up the track at low altitude....Jesus, it looks like fifty feet, if that!

The chopper turns so Orrin can make out the blue-and-white fuselage, and there's no missing the large white letters on the tail boom:

N Y P D

New York cops?

Here?

"Miguel!" he calls out, as the helicopter refuses to move. "Call Dispatch, see if they know why the cops want us to stop!"

The helicopter moves up the track, then rotates again.

Still at low altitude.

Still blocking their way.

"Miguel!"

He turns and his conductor is standing up, holding something in his hand.

Damn it, he was carrying a pistol after all.

Orrin literally cannot understand what's happening.

"Miguel?" he says, looking down at the pistol and then back to his conductor. "What the hell is going on?"

Miguel cries out something Orrin can't understand, then opens the cab door and runs onto the narrow catwalk at the rear.

The phone receiver to contact Dispatch is right there, but to hell with it.

Gripping the familiar handles in front of him, Orrin throttles back and starts applying the brakes.

He may not know what the hell is going on—either with Miguel or with the NYPD—but Orrin's bringing things to a halt, right now.

Once the train slows enough so he can jump without hurting himself, Miguel Marcos leaps from the catwalk at the rear of the diesel electric locomotive and lands in the crushed stone and gravel between the two sets of railroad tracks.

Tossing the pistol aside, Miguel starts running away from the train. He crosses the other set of tracks and starts climbing up a brush-covered, trash-filled embankment to get away.

The truth is, the Abu Sayyaf terror group had recruited Miguel in error months ago in the Philippines, mistaking him for his cousin Carlos. He's been living in fear ever since, looking for a way to break free but never having the courage to do so.

Until now.

Both of his grandfathers had served as stewards in the U.S. Navy, and Miguel has always loved America, thinking of it as a benevolent if sometimes grumpy grandfather living far, far away. Seeing the New York police helicopter show up, well, now he's found the courage to run away.

He just hopes he can run away far enough before the bombs go off.

CHAPTER 111

"DADDY…"

Instinctively, Tom pulls Denise close to him as more and more people run out of the Fulton Street entrance of One World Trade Center, a faint haze of smoke coming out. A man runs by with his briefcase bouncing against his right leg, screaming, "There are bombs going off in there! Bombs! The whole building is coming down!"

Tom yells, "No, that can't happen," but quickly realizes he's wasting his time. The people running out of the building—crowding Fulton Street, flowing into the nearby memorial park—are no longer stockbrokers or administrative assistants or hedge-fund managers. They are a fearful, crazed mob, and at this moment, with adrenaline flowing through them and only thoughts of running and surviving going through their minds, they won't listen to facts.

Tom knows the facts: OWTC is the safest building in the world. It was built with high-strength concrete. Most metal rebar in buildings is the circumference of one's finger. In this beautiful building, the rebar is as thick as a forearm. No explosives are taking it down.

So what's going on?

Ticonderoga.

"Come on, Hon, let's get out of here," Tom says. The fear that he's too late comes to him as the crowds get harder and harder to move through.

Freddie Farrady of Scotland Yard's Special Branch feels a savage bit of glee when he dives into this van and shoves his pistol in Mike Patel's ear.

"Drop the goddamn rifle or I'll blow your head off," he says.

The rifle falls to the floor.

Patel raises his hands.

"Now, you're going to—"

Patel's left elbow flies back, catching Freddie under the chin. In any other time and place, a blow like that would merely stun him. But he's standing on the edge of the doorframe, and the shock makes him fall out of the van.

Freddie hits the sidewalk hard on his back, his feet tangled up in the passenger-side seat belt. Patel leaps into the front seat, starts up the van's engine, and puts it in Drive with the passenger door still open.

Shit!

Freddie kicks hard and frees his feet from the strap just as the van takes off. His anger at Patel—and his fear of what he's up to—makes him scramble to one knee and fire three shots at the retreating van.

Tom snaps to when he hears the familiar sound of a weapon being fired, and now he's being crushed as more screams erupt. Denise yells, "My backpack, my backpack!" and now the adrenaline surge of being on a battlefield—of being in a place where anything can kill you right at this moment—comes back to him. It's a familiar feeling but God he's so scared, because he's not out on this battlefield alone.

He's on this battlefield with his eleven-year-old daughter.

CHAPTER 112

FOR THE first time in a long time I taste the sweetness of good news: the northbound train starts slowing down.

"Hold tight," I yell at Lisa. "I want to make sure that train stays put!"

She gives me a thumbs-up and I tear off the headset, unbuckle the seat belt, get the door open, and leap to the ground.

Oof.

It's stone, gravel, edges of wooden railroad ties, and I lower my head from the constant thrumming of the helicopter blades overhead, pebbles whipped up by the turbulence hitting my back like a sideways hailstorm. I start running as best I can toward the diesel electric behemoth approaching me, its big lit headlight looking like some evil cyclops traveling here to cause death and destruction. The colors are red and green, with HUDSON VALLEY written in a happy-looking white font on the side, and it's slowing, it's slowing, thank God it's slowing down.

Someone pops out from the right side and jumps to the ground, and seconds later I see him running across the other set of tracks.

I'm close enough that the rumbling of the diesel is louder than the helicopter behind me, and I bring up my pistol, wave it back and forth, back and forth, along with my other hand.

I know there are usually two people running a train, and yes, another one comes out on the left catwalk, looks down at me. He cups his hands around his mouth and yells down, "What's wrong?"

I take three more steps.

God, I think we're going to make it.

I yell back, "Contact the local police, your train supervisors! There are bombs on that train, set to go off at eleven-oh-nine! Do it!"

I turn and start running back to the helicopter, my forearm across my face to shield my eyes from the debris churned up by the helicopter. Lisa's copilot sees me approaching and gives me a wave. Up on the far embankment, curious local residents gape at us over their sagging wooden or chain-link fences.

Quick glance at my watch.

It's 10:55 a.m.—fourteen minutes left.

Knowing the speed of the helicopter and Lisa's skill as a pilot, it won't take us long at all to get to the other train.

We're going to make it, I think.

We're going to make it.

CHAPTER 113

EVEN AT this height and distance—and with the winds from the west getting stronger—Rashad Hussain can make out the faint sweet sounds of sirens coming this way from One World Trade Center.

Lovely.

He stoops to look through the twin eyepieces and yes, the blinking flare of the infrared signal from his northbound train is moving right along.

Rashad stands up, hears the *thump-thump* of helicopters in the distance. With the smoke bombs going off and Patel shooting in the streets, he can imagine what's going on.

Panic.

Pure, lovely panic.

If the point of terrorism is to terrorize, such is the point of panic.

There are tens of thousands of people now around that part of Manhattan, scared out of their wits as to what's happening. The smoke, the gunshots, the resulting crush of people, the stampedes, the car accidents, the fights, even the looters or other criminals taking advantage of the situation...they are all possessed by fear.

And others are feeding upon that fear, responding to that fear.

At this moment hundreds of phone calls are being made:

I hear there's an attack on One World Trade Center...

Repeat, repeat, repeat.

Now the major cable news networks have broken in with the news, and now millions of people are watching the confusion in southern Manhattan.

The police, the fire department, the EMTs are all bravely responding, crowding the situation even more. News reporters and photographers are racing there. Friends and relatives of those working at One World Trade Center are also rushing to the scene. And there will be the hundreds upon hundreds of sightseers and curious folks moving there as well, wanting to witness history.

He checks his watch. Almost 11 a.m.

And with that area choked with people, with millions upon millions watching live as to what's going on, then—oh yes, then—a cloud of toxic gas like nothing else made in this world will drift over the tens of thousands clustered there.

Rashad goes back to the eyepieces.

But not over him, of course. One of those *thump-thump*s out there is a helicopter carrying highly paid and dedicated Serbian mercenaries, ready to pluck him off this hotel rooftop and fly him to safety at the right time, no matter what.

Wait.

He stands up, then looks again through the eyepieces.

The northbound train . . .

It's stopped.

It's not moving.

Rashad stands up, spine straight with concern and fury.

What has just happened?

Jeremy Windsor thinks of a phrase he picked up while deployed with a squad of American Special Forces in Pakistan: *maximum effort,* or getting the mission done even when you're exhausted and bleeding, and bullets are zipping over your head.

He runs into the wide and modern-looking lobby of the Nansen Arms Hotel, across the tile floor, and past the small fountain with its circular settees and chairs. People are lined up with suitcases at their feet, patiently waiting to go to one of three stations at the check-in counter. Jeremy pushes his way through them and demands of the nearest clerk, "Quick! Where's lift four?"

The Asian woman looks at him in confusion. "The what?"

"Lift four, where is—"

Bugger, he thinks.

"The fourth elevator bank, please—where is it?"

There are disgruntled murmurs behind him, but the woman points to his left and says, "Right down that foyer and to the left, sir."

He breaks away.

Resumes running.

Past a news shop and a small café.

There.

To the left.

A small side corridor.

Elevator bank at the end.

With the blessed number 4 in bronze overhead.

A knot of people and a hotel employee with a luggage cart are expectantly waiting, and Jeremy looks up at the indicator light.

The red numeral says 14.

A second later.

It still says 14.

One of the hotel guests mutters, "Jesus, will that frigging thing ever get down here?"

Jeremy checks his watch.

It's 11 a.m. on the dot.

CHAPTER 114

BRIAN LAMOTT checks the time and finds they are right on schedule—just south of Fort Lee, New Jersey—so he says to Alvi, "Hey, get ready to drop drawers in a few minutes! We'll be passing the northbound fellows pretty soon."

Alvi grins from his fireman's seat and says something, but Brian can't make out a single word for the roar of engines passing close overhead. Then a giant shadow, and sweet Jesus, look at that!

A blue-and-white helicopter is flying right in front of them. When it spins to one side, Brian makes out the badge and logo of the New York Police Department.

"NYPD?" he calls out. "Sure as hell are out of their jurisdiction. Maybe they're helping the New Jersey State Police find someone."

Brian holds on to that thought for only a few seconds before the helicopter lifts up and accelerates, heading down their line of track between Fort Lee's pleasant, tree-covered suburban neighborhoods.

The helicopter stops, blocking their way, slowly rotating back and forth.

Brian looks over to Alvi, who's staring at the hovering police helicopter.

"Shit, Alvi," he says. "I think they want us to stop. I'm gonna check with Dispatch."

He's leaning over to the center console to pick up the phone connecting them to Hudson Valley Dispatch when Alvi calls out, "No! Brian, don't pick up that phone."

Brian says, "For Christ's sake, are you nuts?"

The helicopter skips again down the track and pauses once more, rotating even more than before, back and forth, back and forth, demanding that attention be paid.

Brian's hand is on the phone, but Alvi says, "Brian, you pick up that phone, I'm going to shoot you."

He looks with disbelief at his conductor, who is standing away from his fireman's seat and pointing a pistol at him.

Brian swallows hard.

"Alvi... what's going on?"

His conductor, his coworker—his friend!—seems upset, and his Russian accent comes out as he quickly speaks. "Brian, I don't want to hurt you. But you're not calling Dispatch."

Brian says, "Alvi, please..."

He motions with the pistol. "I don't have time for explanations, or to tell you why, or how. You're going to get up from your chair and step outside on the catwalk. There... you will have a chance if you jump. And start running away."

Brian stares and says, "I'm stopping the train. Something's going on. And I know you won't shoot me."

His hands go to the control handles before him and there are two loud explosions. Then a tearing, hammering pain in his chest, and Brian falls back.

Before the blackness comes over him, he hears Alvi saying, "Stupid old man, I warned you..."

CHAPTER 115

LISA BAILEY of NYPD Aviation 19's hands are getting tired from gripping the collective lever and cyclic stick, and a sick feeling is growing in her stomach: this train isn't slowing down, isn't stopping, is still roaring its way south. She's pulled in front of it three times now, and unlike its northbound brother, whoever's operating the damn thing isn't responding at all.

"Shit," she mutters, and she heads down the track one more time.

Next to her Joe Woods says, "Lisa, lots of chatter from back home. Something's going on at One World Trade Center. Center wants to know where the hell we are."

"Shut up, Joe," she says. "They'll figure it out soon enough. Amy?"

"Yeah, Lisa," comes her old Army friend's voice through the earphones.

"It's not stopping."

"I see."

"Gonna try something else," Lisa says, staring at the train barreling down on her. "Joe, I'm going south another hundred yards. Then I want you to fire up the TrakkaBeam searchlight. Maybe we can blind the sons of bitches running that train, melt their god-damn eyeballs."

From the rear Amy says, "Then what?"

Lisa says, "Had a cousin once who worked as a train engineer. There's some sort of dead-man switch built into trains, called an *alerter.* If it senses someone isn't actually driving the train, it'll automatically shut 'er down."

Joe says, "Lisa, let's do it."

"Okay."

She turns around her best girl and this time flies her head-on. The searchlight is built on a gyro-enabled gimbal, and Joe says, "Locked on to the front windows."

"Burn 'em," Lisa says. Even at this late-morning hour, Lisa sees the front of the train light up from the 22,500 lumens she's glaring at them—enough power to signal the goddamn space station at night—and she waits.

Waits.

Waits.

Joe says, "Ah, Lisa..."

The train grows larger and larger in view, a storming and threatening colossus of a machine, and she swears and tugs fiercely at the controls, the Bell 429 pulling up, the twin engines whining, roaring, as their craft tilts back.

Thud, thud, as the landing skids scrape the roof of the train speeding beneath them.

"Shit," someone whispers, and she can't tell if it's Joe or Amy.

She gains some altitude, flies south.

Lisa can make out the shapes and spires of Manhattan, quickly growing closer.

"Amy," she says.

"Yeah."

"Out of options," Lisa says.

"I figured as much."

Lisa shakes her head, amazed at how quickly everything has changed from just a few minutes ago. *Then:* safely and quietly and happily flying in civilian airspace. *Now:* thrust back into a war zone, only one hard choice left before her.

She swallows hard. "Joe, Amy, I'm going to jump ahead about half a mile and let you off. Then I'm going to fly back, get as close as I dare, and land on the tracks. I'll jump out right before the train hits. Hopefully we'll derail the son of a bitch."

"Won't work," comes Amy's voice through the earphones. "No. You've got a twenty-ton locomotive hauling about twenty thousand tons of freight behind it. At this speed it'll crush your chopper and just keep on going."

Lisa snaps back, "You got a better idea?"

Amy sighs. "I do. You're going to land on top of that locomotive, let me off, and I'm going to stop the damn thing."

CHAPTER 116

HIS DAUGHTER Denise is crying, and never has Tom Cornwall felt so helpless, so goddamn foolish.

If only he had listened to Amy! Then he and Denise would be safe at Uncle John's home on Staten Island, instead of being swept up and nearly crushed in this surging mob of people crowding Fulton Street.

Tom's been in panic situations before—once in Sudan when a trampling crowd of starving refugees swarmed over an unexpected UN airdrop of food and trampled him, spraining an ankle and breaking a rib—but that was in Africa, not here!

"Daddy!"

"Hold on to me, Hon;—don't let go, *don't let go!*"

If he was alone, he would have options for escaping the madness: to punch and break his way free, even to climb one of the park trees. But no, not with Denise depending on him, huddled up close.

Tom knows he can't fight against the crowd, wasting energy and perhaps being pushed down. So he does his best to move with the jerky, violent flow, holding one arm against his chest to give him breathing room and using his free hand to keep hold of Denise's shirt collar.

They're getting closer to West Street, and he's hoping that—

A woman screams, falls to the ground.

More screams.

Shouts.

The far-off sound of sirens.

A deep *thump,* and another, as a truck or car runs someone over.

"Daddy..."

"Right here, Hon—right here."

An elbow smashes into his left eye, blinding him there. Denise is crying. He won't let go.

He won't let go.

It must open up on West Street—it has to open up.

Just get to West Street.

He moves with the crowd.

"Hey!"

Who was that?

Even with the crowds shoving, pushing, poking, he sees a taller, bulkier man just yards away.

It's one of his watchers.

Tom turns in panic, goes the other way, dragging Denise with him.

Mike Patel is honking the horn, driving slow, the crowds he's caused flowing around him, some banging on the van's sides.

He's breathing hard, the bullet-resistant vest constricting him, overheating him. This isn't the plan—this wasn't supposed to happen!

More sirens.

Who was that Brit back there? How did he know he would be here?

The streaming and running crowds seem thinner on Greenwich Street. He makes a left, surges forward.

Flashing lights.

Up ahead, two NYPD police cruisers are blocking his way forward at the intersection of Greenwich and Vesey Street.

Cops are running this way.

Shit!

Mike shifts the van into Reverse, hits the gas pedal, goes back down Greenwich Street. More pounding and thumping on the sides of his van.

He's got to get out of here.

Got to.

He manages to turn so he's heading back up Fulton Street toward West Street, which is a larger avenue.

There has to be a way out of here.

Has to be.

He hits the accelerator, going faster through the well-dressed men and well-groomed women—the same kind of people who called him *Paki, Paki, Paki* back in Birmingham.

A thump.

The front end of the van bounces over something.

Mike grips the steering wheel tighter, sees a narrow opening in front of him—a man running toward a girl—and mashes the accelerator down as hard as he can.

The crowd surges and moves and—

Tom loses his grip on Denise.

"Denise!"

He hears her screaming and crying, he can't see her, he's lost her, he can't see her.

There she is!

A brief opening in the crowd, like a dark cloud suddenly opening up and a shaft of light blessedly descending.

He runs forward and scoops her up, then hears the racing of an engine, turns, and sees a flash of white.

Pain and black.

* * *

Freddie races up Fulton Street, pushing his way through the pan-icked crowds, chasing Mike Patel in his van—having tracked him through his supposed last day in America. He whispers an ago-nized *Damn, damn, damn* as he sees Freddie mow down a woman, another woman, a man holding a child, and two more men. The crowd moves in front of Freddie and he can't see the van for a few seconds, but then the son of a bitch is on West Street, heading north, and the crowds are thinner.

But even then—

Bam!

Another female pedestrian is struck and seemingly killed by Mike Patel. *Nope, he's getting away,* Freddie thinks. *We're going to lose him.*

Mike runs a red light on West just as a bright-red NYFD truck comes barreling down Vesey Street, lights flashing, sirens scream-ing, horns blaring. The fire truck slams right into the side of the accelerating van.

Bits of metal and glass fly into the air as the van spins in two complete circles and then hits a dark-green utility pole, nearly knocking it over. The fire truck's sirens wail out as the truck skids, bounces, and then recovers, finally coming to a halt, with smoke rising from its wide tires.

Freddie runs up to the van.

The windshield is gone, and the driver's door has popped open.

The steering wheel is right into Mike Patel's chest.

Blood is streaming from his mouth and nose.

He slowly turns his head, looks over at Freddie.

"Help me, please," he gurgles out.

"Sure, I'll do that," Freddie says.

And he takes his illegal Glock 26, puts it against Mike's forehead, and pulls the trigger.

CHAPTER 117

LIKE THE pro she is, my old friend Lisa Bailey knows not to argue or persuade. Seeing the facts on the ground, she knows there's only one thing left to do.

We're maybe a meter or two above the various freight cars and tankers of the southbound train, closing in on the lead diesel electric locomotive, and now Lisa slows the Bell 429's rate of speed. As we near the train's center exhaust, the stench of the burning diesel fuel makes me gag. The locomotive is also tossing heat into the air, causing thermal bumps and uplifts, but expert fly girl Lisa keeps her craft straight and level.

In my earphones I hear her copilot, Joe, calling out their altitude, any obstructions, and anything in the distance—like utility wires or pedestrian bridges—that can knock us from the sky.

He says, "Lisa, you got it."

Lisa says, "Amy, go."

As I brace myself for the downwash from the overhead rotor, Lisa says, "Put 'em in body bags, Amy. I'll try to keep them occupied from up here."

I tear off my earphones, unbuckle my seat belt, push open the door with both hands. And then I jump.

*   *   *

I've jumped from Blackhawk helicopters, C-130s, and C-17s, but this is one short and violent fall. No parachute, just an ungraceful drop where I hit and try to roll. But the roof of the locomotive is slippery with water and diesel fuel, so I fall flat on my back. The noise from the diesel engine is deafening, compounded by the roar of Lisa's twin engines as she flares off and moves ahead of the train.

I reach for my waistband to get my Beretta.

Nothing.

I fumble around in my slacks, poking, prodding, but there's no comforting touch of gunmetal.

The third line from the Ranger's creed comes to mind, memorized as I became one of the first group of women to pass Ranger training:

Never shall I fail my comrades.

Well, failure is staring me in my damn face without a weapon. I scurry and feel something against my lower left leg, sit up, reach down, and there it is.

Fallen through my slacks.

I grab the pistol, flatten low again for a moment. Lisa is up ahead, moving up and down, side to side. Off to my left, buildings on the island of Manhattan are coming into view, filled this morning with millions of innocents — my comrades.

The top of the train has a flat, slippery section in the middle, with the left and right sides of the roof sloping down. Right off a narrow catwalk on either side are doors leading into the cab.

I'm sure both doors are locked. I'm also sure there's at least one terrorist — maybe two or three — inside the train, riding their way to jihad and ultimate paradise.

I crawl forward, blinking my eyes against the breeze cutting into me. My jacket is a distraction, flapping heavily in the breeze, so I tug it off and ball it up.

It comes to me, the motto that kept me going in Ranger training and through my service in the Army.

Rangers lead the way.

I get moving.

CHAPTER 118

ALVI DUDIN takes a moment to drag his old friend and boss Brian Lamott to the other side of the crowded cab. At any other time the locomotive's alerter would be sounding because no one's driving, but Alvi bypassed and disabled the device last night. This diesel engine will not hesitate.

He drops Brian's arms, takes a breath. "Sorry, Brian, but I was never a Russian. I'm a proud Chechnyan—so proud that I vowed to take my revenge against the Christian Russians who invaded my country, raped our women, and leveled our villages. And left me an orphan when I was twelve."

Alvi passes the center console and sits down in Brian's seat, sees that damn police helicopter still dogging him up ahead, expertly lifting itself up and over utility wires and low pedestrian bridges. He rubs at his eyes. Earlier the helicopter had come very, very close, and Alvi saw something rotating under its belly. Thinking it was a missile or some other weapon, he had ducked down behind the console just as the cab's interior lit up with the brightness of a thousand suns.

Bad, tough Americans. If that had been a Russian police helicopter out there, it would have shredded the cab's interior with

417

machine-gun fire. The two front windows, the two side windows—plenty of opportunities.

He checks the computer screen. Speed at 50 miles per hour, air pressure good, all systems fine.

What a day this will be!

Just a few minutes more.

Something black hits the window in front of him, obscuring his view. He sits back, stunned, and then there's gunfire and breaking glass and the sound of a woman screaming at him.

CHAPTER 119

TIME IS running out in all directions, so I hold onto a metal strut, lean over the front of the loud, swaying train, unfurl my jacket and let the wind slap it tight against the operator's window. I then roll, roll, roll, and come off the left edge of the locomotive, lean over, and fire two quick shots into the side window.

It shatters.

I have one move left, and I don't dare let go of my pistol.

So I slide down the roof, using my other hand to slow my progress, hammer my feet and lower legs through the broken window, and use gravity and my legs to scissor myself into the cab.

I fall heavily on my side, face to face with what looks to be a recently shot man, and I roll over again, seeing there's a center console separating me from the engineer's chair.

The train is rumbling along. I've cut my face and hands along the way.

There's a stream of drying blood on the dirty metal floor from the other side of the train, from where this poor guy next to me was shot.

"Hey!" I yell out. "Let's see your hands! Get out from there!"

There's a loud outburst of some sort of Slavic language I don't understand, then a hidden man laughs. "Hey, bitch! I'm nice and comfortable here. Why don't you come over instead?"

I move around, take stock of my surroundings: center console, chair I'm up against, body of man; terrorist well hidden on other side of console, about a meter away—if that.

"You're out of time," I yell. "Come on, let's figure something out. Let's stop this train, talk it over."

More Slavic-type language from the concealed man, while in my mind an English-type language is screaming, *You don't have time!*

"Nothing to talk about, bitch! I like it here."

"How about your name?" I ask. "Mine is Amy. What's yours?"

Laughter again. "Alvi. If that matters."

I could do a blitz attack around the console, but he's probably sitting up, pistol moving, ready to shoot at whatever appears overhead or around the side.

"Sure, Alvi," I say. "Let's talk things through. Let's find out what's going on here. Maybe I can help."

Alvi says, "Oh, so we're negotiating now, are we?"

"Sure," I say. "I'm open to negotiating. Let's see if we can find a way out of here that works for the both of us."

I look around, seeking something I can toss to distract him.

Nothing.

Right now, I'd sacrifice a finger in exchange for an M84 stun grenade.

"Talking...you Yanks, you're very good at talking. So negotiate. What can you give me, hunh? What can *you* give me?"

"Well...let me think for a moment."

Inside the cab there's nothing but metal, metal, and more metal. Okay, then.

"Alvi, you open for negotiations? Are you? Because I'm ready."

"Sure, bitch, give it your best."

I aim my pistol at a sixty-degree angle to the metal roof and pull my trigger finger as fast as possible until I'm sure only two rounds are left in the clip. The explosive sounds of the gunshots and the whistling ricochets make me flinch.

I sprint around the console at a crouch, give a quick peek, and see a shocked young man in blue jeans and a tan barn jacket, holding a hand to his chest, then pulling it away.

Covered with blood.

"You said . . . we were negotiating," he gasps out, bringing up his other hand, the one holding a pistol.

"I lied," I say, and shoot him again.

CHAPTER 120

BENDING OVER the German-made viewing apparatus, Rashad smiles with satisfaction.

The second train—the southbound one—is coming into view, its infrared beacon announcing its arrival.

Allah be praised indeed.

"Rashad!"

He remains still, watching the train get closer and closer.

"Rashad! Get away from that scope or I'll shoot you right here and now!"

He recognizes the voice, of course, and slowly gets up and turns around, hands open, smiling.

Jeremy Windsor approaches him, limping, eyes red-rimmed, beard a mess, clothes wrinkled and stained.

"I say, Jeremy, you do look fairly worse for wear."

Jeremy says, "If you have a weapon, remove it with two fingers of your left hand, Rashad. Your left."

Rashad nods and removes his pistol from his waistband as ordered. In one quick motion, he tosses it over the side. At this point, he won't need it.

He shrugs. "You were never in danger from me, Jeremy. I welcome you here now, as a witness."

"Stop the trains," he says. "Stop them right now."

Jeremy walks closer, his hand holding a small black pistol.

Rashad shakes his head. "I'm afraid that's impossible."

"Then make it possible."

Jeremy is only two meters or so away.

What a lovely, gorgeous, sweet May morning, Rashad thinks. "Nothing can be done," he says. "The trains will meet. The bombs will go off. Death will shortly arrive."

Rashad wonders what Jeremy will say next when Jeremy surprises him by shooting him.

Rashad grunts and falls to the ground. It feels like a red-hot lance has pierced his lower left leg. He moans in pain and then Jeremy is there, looking down at him.

Jeremy says, "No time, Rashad. Tell me how to stop the trains or I'll make it worse."

And then the MI6 man stomps on his bullet wound with his right foot, and Rashad can't help himself: he howls with pain and fury, waiting until the hot waves of pain in his lower leg ease for a moment before laughing and laughing.

Jeremy leans down, showing Rashad the pistol.

"Laugh all you want," he says. "I'll take your prick off with the next shot."

Rashad takes a series of deep breaths and says, "Go ahead. Shoot all you want. I've thought of everything, even talked to an old SOE man who helped me...He told me of plans they never used during the war because it was winding down...some type of proximity fuse, explodes when it reaches a certain point."

Jeremy says, "Five more seconds, and then I eunuch you."

He chokes out a laugh. "Don't you get it? I can't stop the trains. I can't stop the bombs. They're wired so that when they pass alongside their counterpart, that's when they explode. That's when they'll blow up. And there's nothing you can do to stop it, Jeremy. Nothing."

CHAPTER 121

I STAND up, not daring to look at my watch or look outside.

I force myself to examine the switches, dials, handles, and every other control device in view of this speeding locomotive.

How many movies or TV shows have I seen where the unskilled hero or heroine is forced to land a plane, stop a train, or perform an emergency tracheotomy under pressure?

Too many.

I look and ponder and look again, and—

Oh, for God's sake.

Right in the center of the dashboard, or front counter or whatever the hell they call it, is a bright red lever framed by a rectangular white plate, with red letters announcing:

EMERGENCY BRAKE VALVE

I step forward, grab the handle, and shove it up—hard! I'm rewarded with a decrease of engine noise and a squealing and shuddering of brakes. I don't have to look at any gauge to know we're slowing down.

Done.

I've done it.

Time to get the hell out of here.

"Please . . . please help me . . ."

I whirl around, breathing hard, wondering where that voice came from. The form of the other railroad worker—the one I thought was dead—is weakly holding up his right hand. He's a much older guy, with thinning white hair and the well-worn face of someone who's spent a lot of time outdoors. Yet right now his face is graying out before my eyes.

I hurry over to him, kneel down, and look at his bloody chest, and he whispers. "First aid kit, over there."

The kit is clipped to the wall near an instrument bank, and I tear off two fingernails getting it free. My combat-medic training kicks in as a chant starts up in my mind: *Stop the bleeding, stop the bleeding.*

I unzip his thick dungaree jacket, tear open the flannel shirt, spot a white T-shirt soaked through with blood.

"I'm Amy," I say. "What's your name?"

"Brian . . ."

"Brian, just relax, you're going to be all right—we'll get some help here in a bit."

"Alvi."

"Dead," I say, pushing a compress bandage on one chest wound, then a second on another. They both quickly sop through so I place a fresh one on each, then get a roll of light-brown medical wrap and say, "Sorry, this is going to hurt." I lift Brian up, necessarily hugging him, and he softly cries out, like a small child—which cuts through me more than I think. Then I do my best to wrap his upper torso and secure the two compresses.

"Why . . ."

"I shot him," I say. "There are bombs on the train. They're set to go off shortly . . . when we pass another train."

"Emergency brake . . ." comes another faint whisper.

"Already engaged," I say. "We're slowing down . . . tell me, how long does it take to stop a train like this?"

"A mile . . . maybe a mile and a half."

I quickly stand up.

Look through the unobscured window.

Spot the train Lisa and I had stopped earlier, coming closer and closer into view.

A mile and a half!

I go over, throw open the door leading to the narrow catwalk.

Definitely slowing down, but we're still moving.

Yet not too fast for me to go out there, hit the dirt and roll, then start running like hell.

"Please . . ." comes the plaintive voice. "Please don't leave me . . ."

I look out again.

Slowing down even more. The squeal of the brakes doing their job seems louder now. We're passing through an industrial area— warehouses, parking lots, chain-link fences, trash piled up on embankments.

I could jump right now, get a good run in, and seek some sort of shelter before the bombs erupt and the gas cloud starts spreading.

To save me . . . to save my husband's wife . . . and most of all to save my daughter's mother.

"Please don't leave me . . ."

And a third phrase from the Ranger creed comes to mind:

I will never leave a fallen comrade . . .

I go over to Brian and say, "Never thought of it. Hold on—this is *really* going to hurt this time."

I pull him up and leverage him into a fireman's carry, then bump my way through the door. Brian cries out again and then he's quiet, and I think the lucky guy has passed out—which may prove to be a blessing in the next few minutes.

I maneuver to the rear along the narrow catwalk. Then I manage a controlled fall down a ladder, hit the ground, and stumble but stay upright, my patient still on my back, as the train slides by.

"Come on, Brian," I say, "let's go for a little stroll."

No illusions, no dreams now.

I do the very best I can.

I stagger along the rough terrain of the dirt and gravel between the two sets of tracks, and when I glance back I see the train slowing down, slowing down, as—

The southbound locomotive passes the stopped one and continues moving along, slowing at a glacial pace.

I keep moving as best I can.

Poor Brian.

He seems to be getting heavier with each step.

Boom, boom, boom.

The charges go off.

I've failed. Not Jeremy, not MI6, not even the CIA.

All mine.

I keep moving, Brian getting heavier, and a sharp, dark temptation comes to me, *of dumping the dying guy here and still making a run for it.* I pull up short, awaiting the first whiff of toxic chemicals, imagining the burning in my nostrils and lungs, the drowning in my own fluids here on dry land.

Thump, thump, thump.

There's a heavy roar as the familiar-looking NYPD helicopter comes down for a landing. The copilot's door opens, and Joe Woods—crash helmet, flight jacket, flight suit, and all—races to help me with the wounded train engineer. We move back to the helicopter, each of us ducking our heads as we pass beneath the rotor.

Joe opens the rear passenger door and we fairly toss Brian in. Then, with Lisa screaming, "Move, move, move!" we both clamber aboard.

The door is barely shut and I'm on the floor of the helicopter as it lifts up and roars away. I get on my knees and gaze back at the two trains, watching the clouds start to form.

I failed.

CHAPTER 122

THE HELICOPTER races back toward Manhattan, and with tired hands I put on the earphones and mic, then go back to poor Brian. Joe is working on him, putting an oxygen feed on his face and then using his mic to call ahead to the New York–Presbyterian/Lower Manhattan Hospital, reading out Brian's vitals.

Joe puts his hand over the mic and says to me, "We've lucked out! That's a new helipad, first in the city!"

Luck.

I just nod and sit against the door, not bothering to get in the passenger seat, knees up to my chest, arms wrapped around them.

Some luck.

Only a few minutes pass before I hear the change in the Bell's engine sound. Lisa cleanly and quickly lands us on a large helipad bounded with a chain-link fence and with a circled orange *H* in the center. Joe gets up and I help him with the door, and a squad of doctors and nurses run out of a nearby cubelike structure, pushing a crash cart and a gurney. Joe yells the latest stats into the ear of a physician, her light-blue scrubs fluttering in the wash from the rotor, and in seconds the wounded Brian is placed on the gurney.

Standing on the hospital roof, I watch Joe slam the passenger door shut, race around the front of the helicopter, and resume his position as copilot. After he fastens himself in and closes his door, Lisa guns the Bell's engine and off she goes, returning to duty without a look back at me.

Good for her—though I don't envy what the rest of her day will be like.

I'm with the nurses and doctors as an IV drip is put into Brian's arm, a fresh oxygen hose is draped through his nostrils, and there's a big push as they run back through the entrance door, just yards away. I follow them into an open elevator. When the door shuts, I see Brian's left hand drop free from the gurney.

I hold his cold hand in mine, squeeze it.

A male nurse, cutting off Brian's clothes with a long pair of surgical scissors, says, "What's his name?"

"Brian," I answer, holding his hand tight as the elevator swiftly descends into the hospital. "I don't know his last name. He's a train engineer."

"And you?"

"Amy," I say.

"Do you know him?"

"No."

"Why are you with him?"

I say, "I killed the man who shot him."

When the elevator reaches its destination, the door slides open, the scrum of doctors and nurses push Brian out into a nearby open area, and I realize we must be in the emergency room at New York–Presbyterian/Lower Manhattan Hospital. Another crash cart comes out and Brian really gets attention; curtains are quickly drawn around him.

I'm alone.

I hear other nurses and doctors working, see scrub-garbed medical personnel trotting up and down the wide, shiny corridors. As personnel cluster around a nurse's station, I find a chair and sit down, utterly exhausted and drained.

I wait.

Alone.

How soon, I think, *before more victims come in, coughing, choking, sputtering, their mouths and lungs burned beyond repair? How long before the men, the women, the children, are stacked up here in the emergency-room corridors? How long before they are lined up out in the parking lot, crowding the streets, the dying and choking, all seeking comfort and aid?*

How long?

I close my eyes.

Wait.

A voice.

"Amy."

I open my eyes.

Jeremy Windsor, looking as tired as I feel, stands there.

"How did you find me?" I ask.

"A security officer told me an NYPD helicopter dropped off a wounded train engineer, with a woman accompanying him. Could only be you."

I wipe at my face with my right hand, feeling the moisture there. "Ah, shit, Jeremy, we didn't make it. We failed. So many..."

I can't finish my sentence.

Jeremy sits down next to me, takes my hand. Ordinarily I'd have a sarcastic retort for such a familiar gesture, but not this time.

"Amy," he says. "I did, but you didn't."

CHAPTER 123

AMY'S HAIR is matted and twisted, her face is smeared with diesel soot, there's dried blood on her hands and cheeks, and her clothes are a mess as well, with large splotches of dried blood on her formerly white blouse.

Jeremy gives her hand another squeeze, trying to ignore the bustle around them. "When you stopped the first train, the engineer got word back to his dispatch, and they contacted every police and fire agency along that rail corridor. Evacuations started, roads were blocked."

"But...I saw the bombs go off. I saw the gas clouds."

"You saw *some* of the bombs go off," Jeremy says, not quite believing it himself. "Something went wrong with the devices. Only a few bombs detonated. The others...they were duds, or they were miswired."

"But I saw the gas vapors forming, lifting up."

"You saw some clouds, but nothing like what we thought would happen," Jeremy says. "There were some injuries and some deaths, I'm sorry to say, but it could have been much, much worse. There's an elementary school near where the trains met. They were able to close windows, doors, shut down the A/C, and shelter in place. All because of you."

Jeremy sees Amy's eyes slowly widen in realization of what happened, how close it had been, and he wishes he could shut his mouth right here and now.

"You . . . why are you here?"

Jeremy says, "I got to the hotel roof, found Rashad. I hoped he could stop the trains in time . . . I even shot him in his left leg, trying to make him talk. But it wasn't going to work. The damn explosives were set on proximity fuses so they would explode when they passed each other . . . we were just so damn lucky, Amy."

Amy suddenly laughs. "Rashad . . . did you toss him over the roof after you shot him?"

Jeremy smiles. "I thought as much. But no, I bandaged him up some, called the NYPD, and brought him here. We had a lovely and interesting chat while we waited."

Amy laughs again, and Jeremy—hating himself for what he now has to do—says, "Amy . . . I need to tell you something."

"What?" she says. "What is it?"

"Your . . . Tom and Denise. They're here."

Amy shakes her head. "No, they're on Staten Island."

He gently squeezes her hand again. "No," he says. "They were in a crowd near One World Trade Center. Smoke bombs were set off. It was . . . chaotic. I'm sorry, Amy, they were struck by a vehicle. They're here in the ER."

Amy stands up, pulling her hand free. "Where?"

Jeremy says, "I'll show you."

Amy says again, "No, they're on Staten Island."

"Amy, they're here. And it's not good."

CHAPTER 124

I FEEL like screaming *They're on Staten Island* again, but I walk briskly with Jeremy, letting him set the pace, wanting to grab him by the shoulder and tell him to move faster, please, move faster.

"How...why do you think they're here?"

Jeremy's voice is sad.

God, please don't be sad.

"I went past one of the nurse's stations," he says. "Somebody mentioned *Cornwall*. A father and daughter were admitted...and I checked it out."

Cornwall.

A common name, right?

Must be a mistake.

That's all.

They're on Staten Island.

Tom promised me.

"Amy..."

He tries to put an arm around my shoulders but I push him away, passing through curtains into another ER-patient space.

Two hospital beds, sharing a single area. A heavyset Hispanic nurse, looking up at an electronic display overhead.

Debris on the floor: crumpled papers, bloody bandages, latex gloves, lengths of tubing.

On one bed is my Tom.

On the other is my Denise.

I raise my hands to my face.

Denise is sitting up, smiling, sipping from a juice box. "Mommy!"

Tom is sitting up as well. Grinning with some shame and embarrassment, he says, "Honey, I can explain—honest."

CHAPTER 125

I SLOWLY lower my hands.

Seeing what's *really* there:

The nurse, quietly going through her paces.

My Denise, on the bed, lying still.

Tom on his bed, also lying still.

My beloveds are dead.

I walk forward, feeling like a shell, not feeling human, simply not feeling.

I just know it's not right.

There are scratches on Denise's left cheek. Her perfect blond hair is tangled. A light-blue bedsheet and blanket are drawn up to her neck.

Her chest doesn't rise or fall.

The color of her flawless skin is gray.

And my Tom...

His eyes are closed as well.

A deep bloody abrasion on his chin.

My beloveds.

I failed.

*   *   *

I step around and the nurse finally spots me. "I'm sorry, you can't be here."

"Yes, yes, I can," I say, going to Denise's bed, stroking her hair, my fingers touching her cold cheek. "This is my family."

"Oh," the nurse says. "I'm so sorry."

There's a wide gap between the two beds.

My Tom and Denise are separated.

No, that's not going to happen.

I push against the bed.

It doesn't move.

I push the bed and the nurse says, "What are you doing?"

"They belong together," I say. "Help me push the beds together."

"No," she says, "that's not allowed."

I don't remember pulling it, but my Beretta is out, pointing right at her.

"Help me move these goddamn beds or I'll drop you right here," I say, my voice dim, like it's being spoken a hundred miles away. "Then I'll drop the next person who comes in and doesn't help until I'm out of bullets or I'm dead. Your choice."

The nurse bites her lower lip and Jeremy steps in. "Here, let me help. Amy, please—put the pistol away."

With the nurse releasing the brakes on the wheels and Jeremy pushing, my daughter's deathbed is pushed against her father's. I sit on the edge of Denise's bed, roll up my legs, take my dead daughter in my arms, and then stroke the cold forehead of my dead husband. The nurse leaves.

And I start whispering, and I start weeping.

"Oh, Denise...I wanted so much for you...a life with love and laughs...oh, Denise...my girl...my sweet girl...I'm so sorry... oh, so sorry."

I stroke her hair, knowing that somewhere in the ER I have to find a hairbrush and comb out the tangles. And somewhere back at our townhouse—where I will never spend another night, even if by some miracle my smoke order gets lifted—I will need to find the right clean clothes to . . . to dress her for the last time.

What will I pick? How will I choose?

A deep rending sob comes out. "And I never said goodbye to you . . . never talked to you these last few days . . . and now I never will . . . oh, Hon . . ."

I reach over, touch Tom's forehead, his lips, his cool cheeks.

He has only two suits. Why would a reporter need more than that? Should I buy him a new one?

"My sweet man," I say, weeping again. "I'm sorry for the times I barked at you, gave you the cold shoulder . . . oh, Tom . . . we could have gotten old together, seen our daughter get married . . . spoil her children . . . Tom . . . oh, Tom . . ."

Jeremy sits in the corner, not moving, not saying a word.

And so a good portion of the day slides by, my body feeling like an empty husk, not wanting anything, not thirsty, not hungry, not being.

Time passes.

The curtain opens.

A deeply tanned man comes in, wearing a fine gray suit, white shirt, blue necktie.

His face is troubled, and he spots Jeremy, sees me, and then my dead family.

This man is why I joined the CIA after my service in the Army.

Jeremy stands up and says, "Amy. I need to leave. Please forgive me."

He slips out through the curtains, out to where there's life.

"Amy," the man says. "I'm so deeply, deeply sorry."

I can't speak, can't think of anything, but then words come to me.

"You promised," I say, hating how my voice is wavering. "You promised. You said when I was overseas, you'd have a squad watching Tom and Denise, secretly protecting them 24/7…you promised."

He looks at me without flinching.

"I did," he says. "And I failed."

I touch Tom's hair, then Denise's.

"No," I say. "I failed, most of all."

The tanned man says, "At some point, we'll need to talk."

I touch my dead husband and daughter once again.

"Not now," I say.

"Agreed," he says.

"And if you ask me again, I will hurt you."

CHAPTER 126

IN HIS private hospital room, Rashad Hussain makes himself as comfortable as possible, dressed in ridiculous hospital clothing of loose slacks and a pajama top. His lower left leg feels numb, like it's been replaced with a length of mahogany. With some difficulty he is sipping from a plastic glass of apple juice, because his arms are fastened by chains and handcuffs to the bed, just like his lower legs.

There are sensors taped to his chest and abdomen, and an IV running into his left hand. The television suspended from the ceiling has been switched off at his request.

His company is two New York police officers, sitting in chairs on both sides of the bed. They ignore him, which is fine, since he ignores them in return. The one on the left is an African American woman with funny braided hair; Rashad still can't believe a woman dressed like that could be a police officer.

The other officer is a slumping young male who sits staring at a handheld device, thumbs flying. Earlier the woman police officer had said, "Put that thing away—you want trouble?" and the other cop had just shrugged: "Trouble? From you or from him?"

Rashad tries to bring the cup closer to his mouth, but the straw moves back and forth, back and forth. Disappointed, he puts the cup back down on the bed's movable tray.

He won't be disappointed much longer.

From outside there are shouts, screams, the crashing sound of something falling, and a deep, coughing sound. The two police officers start to stand up just as a bulky, bearded man dressed in black fatigues and body armor, carrying a small automatic weapon with a sound suppressor at the end of the barrel, puts a round in each officer's forehead.

Their bodies slump to the floor.

The man comes over, shouts something, and another man comes in, bearing bolt cutters.

Four hard snaps later, Rashad's restraints are gone.

"Thank you," Rashad says, pulling off the sensors, wincing some as he tugs the IV from his left hand.

"Sorry we are late," the shooter says in heavily accented English.

He turns once more and yells out, *"Požuri! Donesite mi stolicu za točak, odmah!"*

Two armed men enter the room, one pushing a wheelchair, and in seconds Rashad is seated in the chair. "Where now?" he asks.

"To the roof," the leader says. "A chopper waits."

"You've earned yourself a bonus," Rashad says.

"No need," comes the reply. "You pay for job, we do job."

CHAPTER 127

AT LINDSAY Hall in Britain, Horace Evans of MI6 enters his office after a long meeting at Vauxhall Cross in London, surprised to find his assistant, Declan Ainsworth, seated behind his desk.

Declan is usually discreet and differential, but on this late afternoon he sits at Horace's station like he belongs there. Horace can't be too upset with the lad, though: Jeremy Windsor is standing behind Declan, holding a combat knife to his throat.

Horace gently puts his briefcase on the floor. "Jeremy," he says. "It's been a while. Good to see you."

"The same," Jeremy says. His MI6 operative looks worn, tired, like he's not had a good sleep in ages, and Horace recognizes that appearance.

"I take it we're going to have a talk?"

Declan's eyes are very wide and Jeremy has a firm grasp on his hair, tugging his head back just enough to reveal his exposed throat.

Jeremy says, "Seems like that's all I've been doing lately—talking. It started with a long conversation with Rashad Hussain after I shot him in New York last week. He tried to keep quiet, but it's easy to get information from a fellow after you've shot him in the leg. All you need to do is stomp on the open wound a few times."

A slight moan from Declan. Jeremy says, "I knew this op wasn't sanctioned. But I never realized how out of bounds you were, Horace."

"I would have told you," Horace says. "Eventually."

Jeremy says, "Rashad told me of the support he was getting from MI6. Little news tips, hints, information that allowed him to stay one step ahead of me for many, many months. Even recommending a Polish supplier of explosives and computerized proximity fuses. Were you directing him in his activities?"

Horace shakes his head. "More like guidance."

Jeremy says, "Rashad told me he didn't know who was doing the work for him. Just a contact that was handsomely paid. After a frank and candid exchange of views—along with a little nudge here and there—Declan told me he had been Rashad's source. Even showed me his overseas bank accounts. Under your authority. True?"

Horace says, "All of it."

"Why?"

Horace says, "Why do you think? We're at war. Hard decisions must be made. Sacrifices must be offered. And above all, we need to get the Americans back in the game."

"Go on," Jeremy says, voice tight and hard.

"It's been more than two decades since their 9/11," Horace says. "An entirely new generation has grown up knowing that day only as history. And their president and their Congress have turned inward. They no longer care about us…about Europe…about treaties. We needed to break them out of their isolation, and Rashad was our tool. His assistant Marcel was ours as well, making sure our tool did the job we wanted him to. And yes, on my own, I was determined to use him. There was no way this type of operation would be sanctioned. We couldn't repeat the mistakes of their 9/11: heads in the sand, ignoring the real world and wishing for the best."

"The explosives that didn't work…your Polish supplier sabotaged them?"

"That they did," Horace says. "I knew there would be casualties, but nothing as much as Rashad wished for or planned."

"That's pretty damn coldhearted."

Horace sighs. "Don't you see what we face, Jeremy? Rashad represents the new wave of danger. Not East versus West, capitalism versus communism, Islam against what's left of Christianity. No, what we're up against is anarchy versus civilization.

"Rashad was an anarchist, wanting to destroy for destruction's sake. And he was able to recruit discontents whose only religion was revenge against those who had done them harm. Last century, these people…ignored, misfits, fools. Now? With the internet and a connected world? They can be brought together, and using the tools of civilization, they can destroy it. We were lucky this time, driving Rashad where we wanted him to go."

"Innocents died," Jeremy says. "Including the husband and daughter of Amy Cornwall."

Horace sighs. "That was unpleasant. I truly am sorry."

"Others died as well. Namely Ollie."

"Who?"

Jeremy's eyes narrow, his lips purse in anger. "Oliver Davies. SAS trooper, detached here, one of the finest men I've ever served with. And because of Rashad, he died on his knees, in the dirt of some forgotten village in Lebanon, decapitated because of you."

Horace waits. Declan swallows hard, his eyes pleading with his boss.

"What now?" Horace asks.

"I want the Faroe order canceled," Jeremy says. "I want back in . . . but in another section, not yours."

"That's impossible."

"Make it possible," Jeremy says, "or your rogue operation will be made known."

Horace says, "Do you really think you can leave here and do that?"

Jeremy twists Declan's hair, making the man squeal for a second. "I got in, didn't I?"

Horace looks into the determined eyes of Jeremy and the frightened eyes of Declan, then nods. "All right."

Jeremy says, "But a price must be paid."

Reluctantly, Horace says, "Agreed."

With one quick slash, Jeremy drops his hand and Declan cries out, raising his fingers to the blood on his throat. Jeremy strides out of Horace's office. Horace approaches Declan, who is sobbing, then slaps his hand away and examines his throat.

"Stop your blubbering," Horace says. "The wound's not deep. Go put a sticking plaster on it and then come back here."

Declan stands up, and Horace gazes at his prized photos hanging on the wall: Churchill and the young Queen.

"We still have much work to do," Horace says.

CHAPTER 128

ERNEST HOLLISTER of the CIA enters his small tidy home in a deluxe enclave of suburban Arlington, Virginia, and sees Amy Cornwall sitting at his round oak dining-room table just off the entryway, a pistol set before her. Her hair is cut short. She is wearing a black jacket, a white turtleneck, and black slacks. On her lapel is a small American-flag pin.

How patriotic.

He says, "Good job getting past the alarms, especially the one that contacts a security force to respond to a break-in at my house. I suppose I should email the Technical Services Division folks tomorrow to file a complaint."

Amy picks up the pistol, a 9mm Beretta. "If you're alive tomorrow, that might be a good idea."

Ernest says, "May I sit?"

"You may not," she says. Amy looks like she's aged twenty years since he last saw her, back in Britain.

"All right," he says. "What are you looking for?"

"A few answers," she says. "Speak quickly and truthfully, and if I like what I hear, Technical Services just might hear from you tomorrow. *Might*."

"Go ahead," he says. "Make it quick. I need to make my dinner."

Amy says, voice trembling, "*Make your dinner?* You know I have no one left to make dinner for."

He pauses, sees the anger and imminent violence in her eyes, softens his tone. "My condolences, Amy. We've had our differences—obviously—but I wouldn't wish that kind of pain on you. I truly am sorry."

"To hell with your condolences," she says. "Why was I smoked? And don't say, *You know why.* I want to hear it fresh from your twisted mouth."

Ernest says, "You went rogue. You disobeyed orders."

"That's what we do in Special Activities."

He says, "No, that's what our men do in Special Activities. Having women in the field is a huge mistake. Women don't have the upper-body strength, the stamina, the inner hardness to do what must be done. You were the first in Special Activities. I was going to make sure you were the last."

"That's all 1950s chauvinistic bullshit," she snaps.

"No, that's current wishful social-justice thinking," Ernest replies. "Amy...you did your job. You're an outlier, someone who could be in Special Activities. You were a trailblazer...but we couldn't afford to have other women follow your trail. Corners will eventually be cut, requirements lowered, our people killed. I saw that firsthand on the ground in Iraq. Just because there were a handful of women who could do the dirty, nasty job of killing others doesn't mean they all can do it."

"But smoking me...leaving me in the field with no support? Thousands could have died in Manhattan."

"But thousands didn't," he says. "Just a few homeless folks and pedestrians got their lungs scorched."

"But my husband...and child. Others were killed in Manhattan."

"Those were traffic accidents, Amy," he says. "Truly unfortunate, but the luck of the draw."

"Next time," Amy says, "we might not be that lucky."

"And if we keep on using women in the field," says Ernest, "tens of thousands will eventually die. I wasn't going to let that happen. No matter what the social scientists say, women can't handle the strain, the pressure, of being out in the field. Congratulations, Amy: you made history by being the first in Special Activities. And now that history is coming to an end. I won't allow it."

"Even if smoking me was against orders and regulations?" Amy asks, the pistol still firm in her hand.

Ernest says, "I decide what orders are made, which ones are erased. That's my job."

"And my stay at your black site in the UK? That choice?"

Ernest smiles, sensing he's winning this one. "What stay? What black site? There's no evidence you were there—and there never will be. The security contractors you shot died in a training accident. Their families will get a nice insurance settlement. That cute cottage has been burned and plowed under. That's the truth, as much as you might hate it."

He waits, sees her eyes moisten, her hand start wavering.

This is going better than he expects.

Now, then.

"Go on, get out of here," he says, gentling his voice. "You made your point and your questions have been answered. And since you're in mourning, Amy, I'll give you a half-hour lead before I call the State Police and our law-enforcement liaison at Langley."

And like that, she gets up and nearly runs out of his home. Hearing the door slam behind her, Ernest smiles in satisfaction.

Amy Cornwall proves his point.

CHAPTER 129

THE WEATHER should be raining, or sleeting, or doing something foul to match my mood, but it's actually a pleasant early evening in this luxurious development in Virginia, and I walk away from Ernest's home staring at my feet, the heavy weight of the unfired Beretta in my jacket pocket.

There are voices about me: children playing, mothers talking, husbands laughing with their neighbors. God, the voices are still within me, softly whispering, always reminding me of what I've lost.

Mommy, when are you coming home?

Amy, I got your back. Whatever you need.

I pass a storm sewer and I'm tempted to toss the Beretta in. But no, you never know when you might need a weapon.

I keep on walking.

Bear right at a corner.

Walking.

Head down, still not wanting to see the families around me.

Up ahead is a black Cadillac Escalade with Maryland plates.

I open the rear door, slide in.

The tanned man is sitting there. Up front are a driver and an armed female escort. The rear of the Escalade is torn out and replaced with communications gear, like the van I rode in back in London a hundred years ago—an intense slim man is working a keyboard.

I say, "You get it?"

"Got it all," the tanned man says.

"Good," I say, removing the flag pin with the built-in video camera and listening device. "What now?"

"Ernest Hollister is gone, this time tomorrow," he says.

"Where?"

"I hear Cuba is nice this time of the year," he says. "And you?"

I stare ahead at the dark upholstery of the seat-back before me.

"I want my smoke order lifted."

"Done," the tanned man says. "What else?"

"I don't know who they are, or where they are," I say. "But there are people out there who aided Rashad Hussain, or gave him money, or helped him do what he did—actions that ended up killing Tom and Denise."

"I'm sure," he says, then pauses. Clears his throat. "I'm working on some information that may be of use to you. Did you know that in the time leading up to the attack, your husband was corresponding with a news reporter called Yuri?"

"No," I say. "Who is he?"

"He's not a news reporter," the man says. "We're not sure who he is, but once we find out, we'll let you know. In the meantime, what do you have planned?"

"While you're chasing down Yuri, I'm going to do my own work," I say, still staring at the blackness in front of me. "And then I'm going to track those people down, and kill them all."

"How much time do you need?" the tanned man asks.

"Six months," I say.

"Three," he replies.

"Deal," I say.

CHAPTER 130

AT THE Mulia Resort on Bali, Rashad Hussain is relaxing at one of the 108 luxurious villas that sprawl across its private 75 acres, savoring his view of the Nusa Dua beach and its accompanying warm waters. He's waiting for his evening meal to be delivered by one of the many submissive and polite Balinese women who serve so expertly here.

He feels utterly safe and secure here. On the grounds of his villa, four members of a private security firm keep close watch on his surroundings, led by a slim, muscular Russian named Gregor; a former Spetsnaz NCO, he was released last year for excessive cruelty, which certainly takes some effort.

The air is pleasant and fragrant, and Rashad sighs with pleasure, knowing he will rest here for another week—as Roland Abboud, international businessman—while he considers his next move.

He sips from a pineapple-juice drink.

That operation in New York . . . too big, too complex, he now realizes. And whatever he did has been swept under the proverbial rug. The American news media have reported an amazing coincidence: a train accident happened at the same time some electrical fuses blew at One World Trade Center, causing a panicked evacuation that resulted in a few dozen deaths and injuries.

He sips again from his drink.

All right, it didn't go as expected, but that doesn't mean it was a failure. It was a learning experience—and Rashad learned a lot.

Next time it will be simpler, more direct.

Like that suitcase-nuke ploy he tried back in France. It was fake, but surely there are real devices like it out there in the world.

All it will take to find them is money and time.

And Rashad Hussain has plenty of money, and all the time in the world.

A soft rap on the door of his thatched villa.

"A moment," he calls out. He puts his drink down, walks back into the villa and up to its main entrance—even his leg has healed well—and opens the door.

No one is there.

"Hello?"

Something catches his attention. To the left is a small stone patio with a comfortable lawn chair where he has read and napped during his days here. In the soft light from the villa windows, he sees that Gregor is resting there, looking at the front door.

"Gregor?"

No reply.

He walks over, his hands and feet growing chilled.

Gregor is dead.

Blood is dripping from his body onto the stone patio.

Closer now, and he sees the former Russian commando's throat has been cut.

Pinned to Gregor's yellow polo shirt is a note with large lettering: RASHAD, YOU SHOULD HAVE STAYED HOME. REGARDS FROM OLLIE DAVIES.

He turns and runs back into the villa, slams and locks the door behind him, then runs to where the phone is located, near the dining room, intending to call for help.

And one by one, the lights inside the villa begin to wink out.

ACKNOWLEDGMENTS

Brendan DuBois thanks the following for their assistance: Ali Karim, industrial chemistry consultant; Chris Dort, locomotive engineer; Michael J. DuBois, firearms expert; and Michael R. Davidson, former officer, Central Intelligence Agency.

ABOUT THE AUTHORS

James Patterson is the world's bestselling author. Among his creations are Alex Cross, the Women's Murder Club, Michael Bennett, and Maximum Ride. His #1 bestselling nonfiction includes *Walk in My Combat Boots, Filthy Rich,* and his autobiography, *James Patterson by James Patterson.* He has collaborated on novels with Bill Clinton and Dolly Parton and has won an Edgar Award, nine Emmy Awards, and the National Humanities Medal.

Brendan DuBois is the award-winning author of twenty-four novels and more than one hundred eighty short stories, garnering him three Shamus Awards from the Private Eye Writers of America. He is also a *Jeopardy!* game-show champion.

For a complete list of books by
JAMES PATTERSON

VISIT
JamesPatterson.com

Follow James Patterson on Facebook
@JamesPatterson

Follow James Patterson on Twitter
@JP_Books

Follow James Patterson on Instagram
@jamespattersonbooks